Freddy's Letters

Judith A. Frenda

NATIONAL
LIBRARY
OF AUSTRALIA

A catalogue record for this
book is available from the
National Library of Australia

Linellen Press
265 Boomerang Road
Oldbury, Western Australia
www.linellenpress.com.au

Dedication

In remembrance of Frank, Mary May,
Winifred Edith and Lily Louisa

Acknowledgements

Many thanks to Laurel Dumbrell, author and one-time leader and 'facilitator' of the Sutherland Shire Writing Group who persuaded me that with developing confidence, I could write.

To Ingrid M Smith, novelist, who once heard my mother's story, appreciation of her wonderful encouragement to get it down on paper – and finish it.

And to Val Murphy who read my first draft, thank you for eagerly awaiting each new chapter and affirming the story.

Allyson Brown, my second cousin, deserves recognition for her extraordinary ability to ferret out facts concerning family history. Without her input, this book would be less than it is.

Many thanks also to Kate Frenda, English teacher, whose helpful editing has improved the text.

Lastly, I acknowledge Helen Iles of Linellen Press for her impressive book and cover design.

Contents

Foreword

During the 1990s, I became interested in researching family history. I knew about my father's background but little about my mother's. She'd hardly spoken about her childhood in London and, as a youngster, I was not particularly interested. Her history belonged to the past, and England was a long way away. However, when older, I became curious about her story, which was somewhat enigmatic. There was only one photo of her as a child in London when she looked about four years old. This was during the Edwardian period. She was seated next to an older sister among a group of small children in a kindergarten. Missing from the group was an older brother and a younger sister. Another photo of my mother, taken when she was nine, was among a different group, all girls this time, and in another place.

With rising curiosity, I commenced the time-consuming process of family research. Gradually, I collected birth, death and marriage certificates and started talking to some cousins who knew a bit more than I did.

Then one day an older cousin handed me a large wad of letters, written from London from the year 1911 onward. I put the letters aside for some time until I arranged them in chronological order, and read them. Graphic images emerged of life lived in overcrowded London, when a part of society's attitudes was directed unkindly to the poor. Good luck and good health were key issues for the head of a working-class family.

My research and the information in the letters answered many questions I had about my English grandparents and their children's lives. Here, I was acquainted with a poignant account of people experiencing life with its mixture of joy and sadness.

I've only needed to connect the letters with fact and fiction between them, in writing this story. I have changed the names of key people (except for Aunty Esther and Mrs Winsor) as I can only portray a degree of peoples' natures and personalities. My mother and aunts though, were all different with certain traits evident as I came to know them. Their brother Freddy's letters will graphically describe his strengths and weaknesses. I personally esteem this young man, my uncle, who lived a life where he mostly tried to do his best.

Freddy's Letters

Oh, Men, with Sisters dear!
Oh, Men, with Mothers and Wives!
It is not linen you're wearing out,
But human creatures' lives!
Stitch – stitch – stitch,
In poverty, hunger and dirt,
Sewing at once, with a double thread
A shroud as well as a shirt.

Extract from 'Song of the Shirt.'
By Thomas Hood (1799 – 1845)

Prologue

Wentworthville, NSW, Australia
September 1939

The oval mahogany frame was perfect for the portrait and suited the style of those days, so long ago. The photograph had been taken when the woman was relatively young, sometime during the 1890s. She would have been in her twenties then. The face was small, neat, not classically pretty but far from plain. The sepia photo had been tinted by a colourist and blue eyes gazed wistfully past the camera. Masses of light brown hair had been piled on top of her head in a bun, shorter frizzy bits framing her forehead.

The customer paid the shop assistant. He placed the newly-framed portrait in a flat cardboard box and handed it over. The woman put the package into her shopping bag and walked to the bus stop near Parramatta railway station.

On the way home, she wondered why she'd waited so long to have this photo framed. But in reality, she knew. A combination of rearing her girls and a shortage of money was the answer. And nothing but the best frame would have done. Expensive! When she arrived home, she decided where the portrait should hang. Just above the mantelpiece in the dining room. A focal point. She called out to her husband, who was repairing the fence down the back.

"Hey, can you come up here and give me a hand? I've got the photo."

He ambled up the back steps and joined his wife in the dining room. She showed him the framed portrait and asked him to bang a nail into the wall straightaway so the photo could be in place before the girls got home from school. Then she marked a spot on the wall with a pencilled cross while her husband fetched his hammer and a nail, and returned to do his little job.

"At last," she said, as though she were addressing a real person whose image now hung on the wall. "You're where you're meant to be, Mummy, watching over us, as you promised you always would."

She made a cup of tea and took down the biscuit tin. She'd have to tell her sister who lived a few streets away that she'd finally had the photo framed. And she'd write a letter to her other sister and let her know too. She lived up north in Armidale in the New England district.

Sometime later, the girls arrived home and crowded around their mother with news or complaints about their day. Then they were led to the dining room and shown the newly hung portrait on the wall above the mantelpiece.

"Who's that lady?" asked the youngest daughter, still in kindergarten. Of course, the child had forgotten. She'd only seen the unframed photo once, a few years ago.

"She's your English grandmother," her mother explained, addressing all four of her daughters, "and she'll be watching over you all. Remember that, so be good girls and always try to do your best."

England

St Pancras in London, 1899

Frederick

When the alarm clock went off at 5.45 a.m., Fred pushed the button down quickly to stop the confounded din. His parents slept in the next room and Fred would occasionally hear William, his Pa, cursing, as the noise from the clock would also rouse him an hour before he was due to rise. But Sunday was tomorrow, thankfully, and the alarm would not be set and Fred and his parents could relish a few more hours sleep. He decided to allow himself another five minutes in bed before getting up, but he unintentionally fell asleep, waking up with a jolt twenty minutes later.

Leaping out of bed and swearing under his breath, he rushed down to the communal privy in the courtyard, one floor below. Then he had to wait for another man to finish using the lavatory before he could. Afterwards, he rinsed his hands in the water from a nearby tap.

"My God, it's cold today," he thought, noting the thick white fog which he knew would soon turn into a classic 'pea-souper'. The poisonous and penetrating smoke from coal fires in people's grates swirled and billowed from the myriad of chimney pots from the homes of rich and poor alike. Fred mounted the flight of steps back to his room in a hurry, knowing the fog would slow him down as he made his way to work. He entered his room, envious of his father next door, still in bed. His Dad's shift as a furniture removalist started at 8.00 a.m., one hour later than Fred's starting time at the shop. He quickly dressed in front of the remnants of last night's fire, a few weak embers giving out a hint of warmth. His shaving mug, brush and soap rested on the end of a small bench, and a towel hung on a hook close by. Under the table was a bucket of water carried up the evening before from the communal laundry below. This was enough for his early morning wash and for cooking his breakfast oatmeal.

Fred knew he could never neglect to shave. One time when he had, Mr Dobson had threatened to sack him if he turned up like that again, saying it reflected on his business, that people didn't want to see a ruffian behind the counter.

"We can't afford yer losin' yer job," said Fred's mother, Mary, forcefully, after he'd told his parents about Mr Dobson's threat. "Wivvout you workin' we wouldn't be eatin' like we do now."

When Fred had shaved, washed his face and hands, and dressed, he reached into the larder and took out a small loaf of bread, a covered dish of butter and a block of cheese. He knew there was no time to light a fire and get the stove going to make porridge, fry a piece of bacon and make a cup of tea this morning, so he hacked off a few slices of bread, buttered them and cut off a hunk from the cheese, then wrapped up his lunch in greaseproof paper and popped the food into a brown paper bag. Old 'Dobbo' would let him make a cup of tea once he got to the shop. He grabbed his overcoat from his bed which served as an extra blanket on chilly nights; pulled on the coat, buttoned it up and took a handkerchief from a drawer in a small chest near his bed. The hankie was to tie around his face to cover his nose and mouth. The *Daily Telegraph* had advised people to use face masks in thick fogs, as the young and elderly, and those with weak chests, were at risk of dying from the effects of the polluted air. Not that he should worry. He was still relatively young at twenty-nine and had an excellent pair of lungs, in his opinion. During his teenage years, he'd attended Whitefields Tabernacle in Tottenham Court Road and had joined the choir. The breathing exercises imposed upon the singers by Mr Walker, the choirmaster, had strengthened his lungs, he was sure.

When Fred opened the door to exit the building, the fog had thickened and taken on a yellowish-grey tinge. He placed the handkerchief around his face, knotting it at the back of his head. Barely able to see ten feet ahead, he slowly made his way, avoiding people who suddenly materialised in front of him going in the opposite direction. Funny little dances occurred with people nearly colliding and sidestepping each other to left and right in unison, begging each other's pardons and chuckling at the same time. Fred had a few of these encounters as he walked the half-mile to work. He knew his route in the fog. He knew every street and alley in the St Pancras district of London – this was his territory – where he grew up and where he went to work. He counted the street lights as he progressed, noting how a faint yellow blur in the distance would gradually come into focus as a clearly defined lamp as he passed it. Similarly, the fuzzy signage above a shop on a corner, *Dobson's Ironmongery* eventually became clearer as he approached, and Fred had reached his destination at 7.10 a.m.

"You're ten minutes late," admonished Ernie Dobson as Fred removed his overcoat. Then he softened and further remarked, "Well, I suppose I can blame that blasted pea-souper you had to wallow through, eh?"

"You're right there, Mr Dobson," Fred replied, relieved at Ernie's understanding. "I'll get going and get the things outside but I wonder if I could make a quick cuppa first because I didn't have time to get my breakfast this morning."

Ada, Ernie's wife, overheard Fred's request and volunteered to brew a pot for him. Shortly after, she carried out a tray with a small teapot, mug, sugar bowl and milk and a thickly buttered scone topped with plum jam.

"Here you are, Luvvie. You can have a scone as well. You can't work on an empty tum," she said, handing the tray to Fred.

"Thanks a lot, Mrs Dobson. Very kind of you," answered Fred, and he gratefully quaffed down the tea and ate the scone, at the same time being anxious to set up the shop for the day's trading. His strength returned after the tea and scone, and he set to, gathering a few cooking vessels, a kettle, a kerosene lantern, a tin washing up bowl, a bucket, a large tin bath and a laundry basket. These display items were secured on hooks above the shop façade. Inside were wheelbarrows, ladders, tools, gardening things, paints, homewares, chamber pots and other assorted paraphernalia.

The morning sales were slow, few people venturing out in such unfriendly weather. The hours dragged on while Fred busied himself unpacking deliveries to replenish shelves and fixing items with price tags. Goods for delivery such as kindling and coal held in tubs and other assorted things were carried out to the adjoining yard and placed onto the cart which Bessie, the draught horse, would haul along the streets to each stopping-off delivery point. Fred noticed a stiff breeze had sprung up and the fog was starting to lift. A couple of hours later the air was clear, the sun was shining and the number of customers increased.

During those afternoons when Ernie carried out his deliveries with the help of a casual boy worker, Ada would descend the stairs from the living quarters above the shop and join Fred to help out. The work was arduous and, as closing time drew near, Fred would battle the inevitable fatigue and aching legs. Usually, by 6.30 p.m. Ernie had returned from his rounds, set Bessie back in her stall and fed and watered her. Fred would retrieve the goods on display outside and call it a day at last, at 7.00 p.m. The next day was his precious Sunday and a welcome sleep-in.

"Wot 'ya doing tomorrow, Fred?" asked Ernie. "Going up to 'Appy Amstead'?" Hampstead Heath was a few miles north of Fred's place in Warren Street.

"Dunno yet," Fred answered. "Maybe, or I might go to the Regent." Regent's Park was much closer to where Fred lived. Only a short walk away.

He grabbed his overcoat, said his goodbyes and made his way out of the shop. The weather had turned cold and blustery, and Fred felt gnawing hunger pangs as he made his way home.

Never them again, he thought, remembering a period in his childhood when he was seven years old, his sister Matilda twelve. The family was getting by when his mother, Mary, fell ill with the 'flu. She'd been so unwell she'd had to give up the laundering job she'd had at the nearby hotel and was off work for three months. Pa could barely afford the roof over their heads with her wage missing. The rent alone took nearly half his earnings. It was bread and dripping for breakfast, with sometimes a kipper or a piece of bacon, bread and cheese for lunch and a thin soup followed by bread and jam for tea. A good stew only once a week. Pa had lowered his pride and asked for some out-relief from the Guardians from the Poor Laws Board. They had refused, while emphasising that he was lucky to have a job as many were worse off, particularly in the Spitalfields area. That was true.

Mary had eventually resumed her laundering job at the hotel after that hard time and life had become better again for the family. And when Fred turned nine, he'd helped out too. He'd become a shoe-shine boy, sitting outside the hotel for clientele. When he grew bigger, he'd had a job cleaning windows there and later on he'd run errands for the Post Office delivering telegrams and parcels. He was nineteen when he'd secured the shop assistant position at Dobsons Ironmongery – he'd been there now for nearly eleven years.

Fred rounded a corner and heard the sing-song voice of a Barrowman tempting people with his pastries and cakes. He stopped by and eyed the hot muffins hungrily, pointing toward them.

"How much?" he asked.

"A penny each and you won't get none any better anywhere," the man said in a persuading tone.

Fred paid three-pence for three, grabbed the muffins and continued on his way, eating one of the cakes to relieve his hunger. Nearly home and dusk was falling. He passed a side alley and noticed an elderly man dressed in tattered clothing sitting in the gutter in the lane with his head bowed.

"Poor old blighter," thought Fred, "I hope he doesn't end up going to the workhouse." From what he'd heard, desperate men seeking a night's refuge in that place might have been better off in the street except for the cold. Crowded into a room with thin straw mattresses on the floor and a moth-eaten blanket, sleep was almost impossible, with some of the drunks arguing and cursing. Others were lucky, falling asleep in the small hours while many were kept awake by loud snoring. At least there was shelter from the cold and rain, and some sort of breakfast before they were turned out of the place in the morning.

Fred knew he could do nothing to help that man, so he turned his thoughts homeward. He was nearly there with only a small stretch to go. He finally reached the tenement building at 27 Warren Street; where he mounted the steps to the landing, and wearily continued up another flight to the first floor where he and his parents shared the two rooms they rented together.

"Come and ge' warm, laddie," said his mother as Fred opened the door and entered. "I've made a good po' of pea and 'am soup. Pa and me 'ave 'ad ours already."

Fred needed no invitation. He cut off a slice of bread, pronged it with a fork and toasted it by the fire in the grate. After his dinner he fetched the muffins and put them onto a plate, surprising his mother.

"There's one for you and Pa. I ate mine on the way home. I was a bit hungry."

"Oo ay!" said Mary, a smile on her face, "they'll be luvvely. Make a cuppa now, Will, for us to 'ave wiv' 'em."

They were all in the room where Fred slept, his bed in a corner, the dining table and chairs in the middle of the room. A small coal-fired stove stood near the fireplace where the fire in the evenings warmed the room when it was cold. He felt lucky. His parents had to retire to the other room, to their unheated bed, but they never complained, always saying they were glad they had a roof over their heads.

When the meal was over, the family sat around the fire and talked about their day. Mary told Fred that his sister Mattie had called in that afternoon and was coming over for lunch tomorrow. Mattie had a good live-in job as a domestic housemaid with a wealthy family who lived in Kensington.

William, Fred's Pa, told about his day.

"You know the Simpsons? Them that lives a few doors down at No. 35? Well, I 'ad to move 'em out. 'Ee got sick and 'ad to give up 'is job, poor blighter, and they've only got 'er wage now. They've gone into a single room in Euston Road. That's wot keeps me in a job. People always 'avin' to move into cheaper rent."

"Oh! The poor souls," said Mary, a concerned frown on her face, "and 'er gettin' old and 'avin' to keep up bein' a charwoman for vem toffs in vat big place round the corner."

The subject was dropped. It was every man for himself these days.

A short while later, Mary resumed her enquiries.

"And you, Fred, 'ow did your day go?"

"Much the same as ever," replied Fred resignedly. "It was pretty slow in the morning because of the fog. I hate it then. The time drags and the day's so damn long."

Mary replied. "Well, keep yer pecker up, lad. I know it can be 'ard sometimes but yer go' a good job an' there's some as don't 'ave one. Yer keepin' yerself. Yer don't owe anybody anyfin' and vat's somefin' to be proud of."

Then she excitedly announced, "Bernie Ellis is at the pub tonigh'. I found ou' today. Why don't we 'ave a look-in? I know you two are knackered but it'll do us all a lo' of good. Tomorrow's Sunday. We can sleep in. Come on, let's pop in fer a coupla hours, eh?"

William and Fred reluctantly agreed, hoping to please Mary who always loved a good old sing-a-long around the piano.

Bernie Ellis, a roving entertainer, gained short stints at various hotels around the country. Dressed in a black suit, red cravat and bowler hat, he would thump out all the popular music hall songs on pub pianos. People would crowd around and sing their hearts out. The dining area would be cleared of tables and chairs, making space for energetic ones to dance.

The family put on their overcoats and left, walking the quarter-mile to *The Squire's Rest*, and arriving at eight-thirty.

"Blimey! It's noisy in 'ere," said William as they entered the crowded room. A cacophony of voices belted out *Allo! Allo! Who's yer Lady Friend?* Mary quickly joined in, her shrill soprano helping to keep the melody, which tone-deaf people were murdering.

That number finished, Bernie stood up and announced: "And now ladies and gentlemen, we're going to sing, *There was I, waiting at the church, waiting at the church, waiting at the church, And then I found, he'd left me in the lurch, Lo, how it did upset me* … I'm sure you all know the rest of the words, so come on, let's raise the roof with this one."

Everyone cheered and clapped and the song got underway.

William joined Fred near the bar and they both ordered a beer.

"Eh! let's go into vat uvver room where it's a bi' quieter," suggested William, "we might ge' in a game o' darts."

A few others were playing and William and Fred had to wait their turn. Fred sat on a stool, watching the game in progress while William found a chair on the other side of the room. He grabbed a newspaper lying on a small table nearby. After half an hour or so, the dartboard became free so Fred and William began their game. This is what William loved, a good game of darts, which he was good at due to a lot of practice. Each Wednesday evening after his dinner, he would meet up with his chums in the pub and they would enjoy a few beers and a game of darts.

"You've gotta have something to look forward to," an old codger had remarked a few weeks ago.

There was a lull in the noise from the other room while Bernie had a coffee and a short break. William and Fred had finished their game, and agreed to go and see how Mary was doing. At that moment, Bernie stood up and made an announcement.

"Now ladies and gents, you've 'eard about Lottie Collins, she who's so popular at the music 'alls these days. Well, she's a bit naughty and some folks might be a bit offended. She does some 'igh kicking in her acts and shows a bit of leg when she sings Ta-Ra-Ra-Boom de-ay, but I think it's 'armless fun anyroad. Now some fella wrote a song about 'er singing *Ta-Ra-Ra-Boom–de-ay*. I'm gunna sing the verses and you can all join in the chorus and if you want to do some 'igh kicking of yer own, get onto the floor. Go on! Try ter kick as 'igh as Lottie. Right oh? Well, let's go.

"*Lottie Collins lost her drawers, Will you kindly lend her yours, Cause she's going far away, To sing Ta-Ta-Ra-Boom-de-ay'.*

"Now come on everyone, *Ta-Ra-Ra-Boom-de-ay*, and see 'ow 'igh you can kick!"

The crowd enthusiastically joined in the chorus, those on the floor kicking up a leg at each BOOM-de-ay.

William and Fred elbowed their way through the crowd; made their way over to Mary, who was sitting on a chair, shrieking with laughter.

"Cor Lumme!" she exploded. Then she calmed down a bit and explained: "See that great big woman over there?" she pointed. "Well, she just give this skinny bloke wot lives round the corner from us, you know, Charlie wot's 'is name, a wallopin' big kick up his Khyber Pass and it sent 'im flyin' over to that small table where Essie Lawson was 'avin' a lovely cup o' tea. 'Ee crashed into the table, over it went and with Essie's cuppa too. They're cleanin' up the mess now. See?"

William and Fred couldn't help laughing along with Mary and, when they had settled down, they all agreed they'd stay for one more song and then go home.

Daisy, Daisy, give me your answer do, I'm half crazy over my love for you. It won't be a stylish marriage. We can't afford a carriage. But you'll look sweet upon the seat, of a bicycle built for two.

Toward the end of the song, William, Mary and Fred stood up and made their way out the door. Mary reviewed the evening's entertainment.

"Well, we may not 'ave much but we do know 'ow to enjoy ourselves."

William agreed.

"I'm knackered," said Fred. "Saturday is always hard, being the end of the week, you know. I can't wait to get into bed."

"Fred," said William, a note of encouragement in his voice, "I was lookin' through the newspaper tonight when you were watchin' them on the dartboard an' I read somefin' very interestin'. Looks like the Shop Assistants Union are goin' for a 'alf day off in a week for you people."

"Well I hope it's sooner rather than later," said Fred with a sigh.

They were almost home, and the cold was starting to penetrate their clothing.

"Ere we are. 'ome at last!" announced William, glad the evening was over even though he'd enjoyed himself.

The family mounted the stairway to their small flat and let themselves into Fred's room with the fireplace. They gathered around it, holding their hands close to the residual warmth.

"Watcha doin' termorrer afternoon, Fred?" asked Mary. "Goin' to the Regent after lunch ter stretch yer legs?"

"Dunno yet. I'll have m' sleep-in and then decide," he answered.

William and Mary said their 'goodnights' and retired to their bedroom, leaving Fred sitting near the remains of the fire. He could hear murmurs from his parent's room as they made ready for bed and smiled as he thought of his Mum's enjoyment at the pub. She was a simple soul, with a great sense of fun. She was unable to read and write yet was schooled in wisdom and experience. But his Dad, as a boy, had been lucky enough to attend a Sunday school that also taught pupils the basics in reading, writing and arithmetic, as well as religion. Fred knew his father had wanted a better life for him than what he'd had, and Fred had achieved more than his Dad and was grateful. He'd had a better education and become a semi-skilled worker. A year after he was born, the London School Board was established, and in 1870 the Elementary Education Act ensured that all children in England and Wales, between the ages of five and thirteen, would be provided with an education. Fred thought of his parent's personal sacrifice for him and Mattie. They'd scraped out a meagre living so they could provide school expenses, shoes, decent clothing and enough food for their children. Fred had been a bright boy, having reached Standard 6, but he'd been forced to leave school at thirteen years, even though he'd wanted to continue on to higher education. His family, however, had needed him to earn some money to ease their situation. This was despite the headmaster taking a special interest in him; refining the way he spoke; 'not dropping his aitches' and 'finishing words correctly'; pronouncing his vowels and consonants properly, and not talking like an uneducated Cockney. But Fred still loved the rhyming slang of the Cockney talk which he joined in with his family and friends on many occasions.

He felt restless as he often did. He had food, clothing and shelter, family and friends and a good job, taxing as it was. There were exciting football matches to go to. He could get a 'bus up to 'appy amstead' with friends and have a picnic now and then. And occasionally he could pop into a pub for a beer or two and meet up with a lot of friendly people. But was all this enough? He knew there was more to life than just basic needs and entertainment. He knew what he was missing. He needed warmth, companionship, sharing and intimacy with someone special. So far, a serious relationship had eluded him. Over the years he'd had a couple of flirtations, one girl in particular at Whitefields Tabernacle who'd stolen his heart. He'd been twenty-one. He remembered walking with her all the way to St Paul's Cathedral, laughing and joking, and once inside that great church, gazing in awe at its vastness and the exquisite works of art.

Then, brushing together, their hands touching, he'd taken her hand in his, and a pleasurable tingle had run up his arm, and he knew she was the one. They'd returned home still holding hands, talking and giggling. Fred had delivered her to her address and lingered with her on the pavement. Then impulsively, he'd put his arm around her and they'd kissed. For the next few days he could think of nothing but her, but he soon came to learn that her father had disallowed any further entanglement of his seventeen-year-old daughter with the likes of him, an ironmonger's assistant. After all, they were well off and what could Fred offer her? So he'd locked that memory away in his heart, treasuring it.

All this reminiscing was not getting him into bed. Tomorrow was Sunday and a sleep-in. And his sister Mattie was coming for lunch. He had one day to gather his strength and prepare himself for the next working week and so changed into his nightshirt, threw his overcoat over the blankets and climbed into bed.

St Andrews, near Bristol, 1899

Johannah

This was the last day Johanna would walk along the well-trodden paths of St Andrews Park. She was sorry in one way because she'd enjoyed watching its development over the years since the Grand Opening in 1895. It had been such a festive occasion, she remembered, with hundreds of people turning out and the surrounding streets decorated with colourful flags. The newly constructed bandstand just managed to fit in Bristol's Community Orchestra which robustly played the National Anthem after the initial speeches. Later, the crowd had been treated to renditions of traditional songs, such as *My Lady Greensleeves*, *Land of Hope and Glory*, and even a few bouncy Music Hall numbers to lighten the atmosphere. People had then been invited to walk along the winding paths to inspect the newly planted trees and flower beds which were blooming in time for the occasion. There were dahlias, geraniums, snowdrops and asters among other bushy flowering shrubs. Some children, breaking away from their parent's control, had rushed over the lawn to the duck pond, returning to beg crusts from picnic sandwiches to feed the ducks.

So many memories of this place that had become a sanctuary for Anna, if only for short moments – Anna the name most people called her. Yet she was not sorry to leave Bristol as she would be escaping her engagement with the Fergusons whose palatial home stood across the road from the park. Strangely enough, Mr Ferguson had become quite chatty when he'd given her a month's notice. She remembered the conversation.

"I'm sorry to have to tell you, Miss Telford, that I have just sold my business and your services will no longer be needed. There are far too many bootmakers in this town today, and the competition with Fergusons Boots has become too big for me to attract enough clients to make a profit. So you and Connie will have to go. I'm giving you a reference because you've done good work for us over these years, and young Alice has become fond of you. I'll be joining my brother in Bath. He's got apple orchards and makes cider and has expanded his business. And I'll be glad to get away from the smell of tanning."

Just then Anna noticed Connie walking towards her. She shifted to the end of the park bench, making room for the woman who'd been scullery maid and cook for the Fergusons for fifteen years. Both women eagerly looked forward to their half-hour break at four o'clock each afternoon and mostly spent that time together in the park.

"Oh! Connie," said Anna as her friend sat down, "our last day. I'll miss you when I'm back in London, and I'll miss Alice and the friends I've made at church, and I'll miss this beautiful park. The gardener told me last week that the lime trees he planted on each side of that path across there will grow so tall that one day they'll reach over to each other and form a shady arcade."

"Well, I won't be around to see that," replied Connie flatly. "They'll take years and years to reach that height and I'm nearly sixty now."

"Did Mr Ferguson give you a reference, Connie?" asked Anna, changing the subject.

"Yes, he did and lucky enough for me. I've heard along the way that some folk in service aren't given one when they leave and that makes it harder for them to find another job."

"Well thankfully, I got one too," joined in Anna, "and I'd have been very angry if he and his Missus hadn't given us one. I've worked my heart and soul out for that pair. It's been 'Yes, sir. No sir, three bags full sir'. And how often I've had to bite back my words for fear of being called insolent by *her* when I only wanted to express a different opinion. I did it once and I learnt my lesson."

Connie agreed and remarked that her experience had been the same. She added, "Being both a housemaid and nursery maid has been hard work for you, Anna …" She put her arm comfortingly around

Anna's shoulders. "… and you've done a wonderful job. Look how little Alice cried when she was told you'd be going away."

"Yes. I'm going to miss that little girl. I've looked after her since she was a baby and now she's six. She's always loved coming to the park with me and playing on the swings and looking at the pretty flowers."

Connie noticed Anna's eyes moisten, and changed the subject.

"So, you'll be on the train tomorrow for London, my girl. I imagine you're all packed up and ready to go?"

"Yes, I am. Everything's in my suitcase except for my nightgown and toiletries. You know I was very surprised when Mrs Ferguson gave me a brand-new pair of boots which a client had failed to pick up over six months. She thought they might have been my size and they were. So she's sent me off on a pleasant note."

"I'm pleased for you," said Connie. "That'll save you a bit of money in the future. Good boots are so expensive. Now I want your address, and I'll give you mine. I'd like to hear how you get on in London Town."

"And I'd like to hear how things work out for you too," answered Anna.

"I think it'll be easier for you than me. You're quite young and have a prettier face," said Connie wryly. "I'm going to stay with my sister here in Bristol for a short while until I get another position."

The women chatted for a further fifteen minutes until Anna glanced at her watch and mentioned it was half-past four.

"Goodness me!" said Connie, surprised. "How quickly that half-hour has flown by."

The two women agreed they'd better get back to the house across the road.

"I've got to get their tea ready," mentioned Connie. "I've made a hearty mutton soup with vegetables, and after that, they can have fresh bread and raspberry jam which Alice loves."

"And it's Saturday night. I've got to run her a bath and get her into her nightgown," added Anna, "so we'd better get going."

They crossed the road; walked up the path to the imposing front door of the large, prestigious home Mr Ferguson – of *Ferguson's Boots – They Always Fit!* – had had built twenty years previously. The women entered the capacious entry hall, Connie turning left into the kitchen to prepare the meal, Anna mounting the staircase to the first floor, where she entered Alice's bedroom. An antique chest of drawers stood by the window. Anna pulled out the second drawer and selected a flower sprigged little nightie, smelling sweetly of lavender from the sachets spread throughout the drawers. Then she lifted a small pink dressing gown from a hook on the wall and picked up a pair of slippers from near the bed.

The living room was on the same floor, and Anna knew Alice was probably there with her mother, idling the time until her bath and teatime. The child loved having her bath and eagerly ran over to Anna when she entered the room.

"Look!" said Anna, "I've got a clean nightie for you tonight. It's your favourite one that you always look so pretty in."

"Well, get on with it," said Mrs Ferguson a little brusquely. "I want you to wash her hair, and that will take extra time before tea."

"Yes, ma'am," replied Anna, accustomed to the lady's mercurial temperament. "I'll do my best."

After her bath, when Alice was dressed in her nightclothes, the child would often put her arms around Anna, and the two would enjoy a covert little hug, after first making sure Mrs Ferguson was not around. They were to have their last embrace after this evening's bath.

Dressed in her nightie and gown, Alice was delivered to her mother in the living room. From there, they would move into the dining room after Connie and Anna had carried up the family's evening meal.

Anna descended the staircase to the kitchen and joined Connie.

"We'll take things up now," said Connie, handing Anna a tray and lifting up the other.

When the women returned to the kitchen, they ate their meal of leftover soup, toast, and bread and jam. Anna would then help Connie do the dishes and clean up the kitchen.

"So!" said Anna, "nothing more for me to do around this place. I'm all finished. I have to be up early so I'm going to bed pretty soon and I'll see you in the morning. Goodnight, dear Connie."

"Sleep well, my dear," answered Connie, and the two embraced.

Anna retired to her attic room and packed her new boots into her suitcase, along with her clothes, two maid's uniforms and other odds and ends. After her ablutions, she changed into her nightgown, settled into bed and fell asleep almost immediately.

She was up early the next morning and donned her travelling clothes. After breakfast with Connie, they bade each other farewell. Then Anna waited on the back porch for Mr Ferguson who'd offered to take her in his dray to Bristol Temple Meads railway station. To Anna's surprise, he turned up with Alice who had pleaded to go to the station to say goodbye to Miss Anna and to see a big steam train which she hadn't seen close up before.

Outside, on a gravel yard, the horse and dray were ready. Mr Ferguson lifted the luggage onto the dray and Anna and Alice climbed up three rungs to the front seat of the dray. Mr Ferguson took the reins, and they were off, waving to the mistress of the house and Connie as they left.

"We have over an hour before your train goes, Anna," announced Mr Ferguson. "We'll be there in forty minutes, so don't worry, you'll have plenty of time to buy your ticket."

Alice sat in the middle, her left hand clutching Anna's right one, all the way to the station.

The railway station was a grand building, with a clock tower in the centre and two small spires each side of it. Anna walked to the ticket office, bought her ticket and asked from which of the seven platforms she should board the train for Paddington. She found her way there with Alice and her father following behind.

She had been allocated the first second-class carriage, and the three made their way down the platform until they reached the cream-and-chocolate-painted coach. By now, the huge green locomotive was firing up, hissing loudly and blowing out steam not far from them. A terrified Alice clung to her father until he reassured her she was safe. They waited patiently for permission for Anna to board the train. In a few minutes, the guard walked along the platform with a whistle, informing the passengers to now board their carriage as the train would soon depart.

Anna climbed the step to her compartment and was pleased to claim the window seat. From there, she looked out and waved to Alice, whose little face looked sad. The little girl raised her arm and waved feebly. Anna blew her a kiss then the whistle blasted, and the train slowly pulled out of the station.

Anna settled back on the comfortable seat and decided to enjoy her trip to London, which would take nearly two hours. Her thoughts returned to Alice. Would she ever see that child again? She knew it was unlikely. Would she ever have children of her own? Maybe, but her husband would have to be earning an adequate wage. She sighed at the thought. Money! It all relied on money, didn't it?

Over the nine years she'd worked for the Fergusons', she'd managed to put some money aside, but not much. She'd saved up for one other trip back to London to see her parents, a few years ago. Her position with the Fergusons had included her accommodation, food and her maid's outfits. Her wage was roughly £25 a year, allowing for small pleasures only, no luxuries. Even so, she felt a grudging appreciation for the demanding job she'd had. There'd been a comfortable bed, good food, and she was no burden to anyone. Also, Connie had been a wonderful work companion, warm-hearted and always pleasant. Anna had made other friends too, meeting them at church and sometimes at the local tea shop for a cream tea when she'd had some time off. Now and again, a picnic or a walk to the river. No! At twenty-six years of age, there were people a lot worse off.

Anna watched little streams, green hills and valleys pass by, noting the varying shades of autumn leaves adorning the deciduous trees. Sheep and cows grazed in meadows. Cultivated fields attached to small farms were growing healthy-looking crops – such rustic and peaceful scenery. Larger towns and occasional small hamlets with church spires streaked by. After passing through a few short tunnels, the train slowed down; the township of Bath was not far off. One day, she thought, she may be lucky enough to visit this place she'd heard so much about with its Roman baths, beautiful abbey and historic buildings. She loved the sound of the chuffing engine, its whistle, and the screeching sound of the brakes as the locomotive pulled into Bath Spa station, and was enjoying the trip to London.

Three people left her compartment at Bath and were replaced by two others. She smiled at the new travellers as they settled into their seats. After a few minutes, the train was on its way again, and her thoughts turned to Paddington Station, where her father would be waiting. She'd written to her parents as soon as she'd been given her month's-notice, telling them of the date and time of her arrival. They'd answered immediately. She could sleep on the sofa and stay with them until she found another position, although they warned her that it may be hard to find something in London. The city had become overcrowded with people moving into it from the country to find work in the new industrial areas. But Anna felt confident – she had a reference, even though it only stated that her service had been 'satisfactory'. She'd wondered if Mrs Ferguson had been responsible for that paltry report. She knew she had deserved more.

"Next stop, Swindon," announced a portly man sitting opposite her. He'd boarded the train with his wife at Bath. Anna had been falling asleep but was jolted awake again at the man's loud, penetrating voice. She looked out the window and noticed a high green hill rising up from behind the approaching township. Closing sleepy eyes, she attempted to doze off again, but the noisy man had started up a conversation with his wife. The train pulled into Swindon. No-one left the compartment and Anna resigned herself to continuing her journey in a less than restful atmosphere. In no time at all, the train had covered the short distance to Didcot Parkway as the important man again announced this next stop.

"Didcot Parkway, and after this, it's Reading."

His wife nodded.

Taking this as a sign of approval, the man decided to conduct a running commentary on the journey to Paddington.

"From here, we enter the Thames Valley and we'll cross the river three times before we get to London."

Anna, fully awake now, became interested and began to follow the self-appointed tour guide as he pointed out important landmarks. After a while the train pulled into Reading.

"Now, here we are at Reading, a very big and important centre in Berkshire. Only one more station before we get to Paddington. On the way, we'll go over Maidenhead Bridge. You can get a good look at the Thames then."

Anna didn't want to miss the river, so she remained attentive to the man's narrative. Soon they passed over the bridge and below the beautiful Thames flowed between small houses and grasslands on each bank.

It goes all the way to London, she thought, *and I'll soon be there.*

The man with all the knowledge asked his wife for the timetable as he'd forgotten the name of the next railway station they were approaching.

"It's Sluff," said the lady, pointing to *Slough* printed on the station sign.

"Don't be silly. It rhymes with COW. It's Slough," he growled, glaring at his wife.

Anna didn't like the man's tone or the way he'd emphasised 'cow'.

"Well, who would know?" she asked her husband timidly. "It's an 'o-u-g-h' word. It could just as easily rhyme with tough."

The pair were quiet for a while, until the man announced, "We are now pulling into Slough, which rhymes with cow. Not long to London. Watch out for the Wherncliffe viaduct on the way. We'll soon be going over it."

Shortly after this latest information, Anna noticed the ground fall away and assumed the train was on the viaduct. She glanced down and saw a river underneath.

"We're on the viaduct," announced the man importantly, "and

that's the river Brent we're going over."

I'll be glad when I get to London, thought Anna. *I'm getting tired of listening to this old geezer.*

It wasn't long before the train pulled into Paddington London railway station. Anna gathered her luggage, climbed down the step onto the platform and walked the long distance to the ticket barrier, resting a few times due to her heavy suitcase. She handed in her ticket then, struggling on with her luggage, looked around for her father. *I hope he's not late*, she thought, making her way to the station exit. Then she spotted him, not far off near a refreshment kiosk.

"Dad!" she sang out, walking towards him, dragging her suitcase. Samuel Telford looked up and quickly strode to his daughter, eager to relieve her of her burden.

"Well, my girl," he said as he gave her a kiss and took hold of her luggage, "how was the trip?"

"It was lovely until the last part," answered Anna, "but one old fella was very loud and annoying."

"There's always someone like that on trains," remarked her father. "Well, come along, my girl, I hope we won't have to wait too long for a bus."

They made their way through the large, crowded station to the street outside where horse-drawn omnibuses were waiting. Sam walked along the line-up to read their destinations and was about to climb into one when Anna laughingly told him he was getting onto the wrong bus.

"Oh! so I am," he replied apologetically. "What made me do that?"

Anna decided to ask a driver on the pavement, how long they needed to wait for their bus and was told 'about fifteen minutes'.

"I've got a reference," she informed her father, "so I hope I can find work quickly. The reference could have been better though – Mrs Ferguson's little girl, Alice, was an only child and I think the woman resented the affection she had for me so paid me back with a pretty ordinary reference."

"Well," replied Sam comfortingly, "you're a nice-looking lass and have a lot of experience. Someone will want you."

After further conversation, with Anna enquiring after her mother and brothers and any special news, their bus drew up.

"We'll give the horses a bit of a rest before we go, but you can get on board now," announced one of the drivers.

Six other passengers climbed up the back steps into the coach, Anna and her father declining to climb to the top deck, preferring to be near their luggage. One of the drivers came around with a leather pouch attached to his belt and collected the fares. When the horses had finished drinking and munching a little hay, the drivers climbed up to their positions and took up the reins. Then they were off!

There was plenty of traffic on the road at midday, and the going was slow. Pedestrians were often a problem as they crossed the road, dodging between horse-drawn vehicles and deposits of manure. A good half hour passed.

"We're getting off next stop," Sam warned Anna as he made his way to the back of the bus to collect Anna's suitcase. The horses pulled up at a stop near a corner, and Anna and her father stepped down to the footpath, Sam thanking the drivers for a good trip.

"Only about a hundred yards to go now," he said as they started out.

They reached the steps leading to the front entrance of 27 Warren Street, where Anna's parents lived in a two-roomed flat on the top floor.

Anna went on ahead, eager to see her mother after their years apart. She mounted the steps to the foyer then hurried up the stairway to the front door of her parent's apartment in the back of the building. Sam followed behind, struggling with the suitcase.

"Welcome back, my darling," said Martha as she hugged her daughter. "Now you sit back and rest after your trip and I'll get us a sandwich and a cuppa."

Sam excused himself after their lunch and went to the other room to have an afternoon nap.

"I'm worried about him, Anna," confided Martha. "I hope I'm

wrong, but he's getting very vague. He forgets people's names, and he often goes out to get something and then forgets what it was. To be honest, I didn't want him to go and collect you at Paddington, but he insisted."

"Well, he wasn't where we'd agreed to meet just outside the barrier. I had to go looking for him," replied Anna, "and I had to lead him to the right bus for here. He wanted us to get on another one."

"Oh dear, is it that bad?" said Martha, with a frown, "Well, at least he's still got his labouring job for the time being."

A Sunday Roast Dinner

Mary knocked on Fred's door and tentatively entered.

"Get up, me luvvie. It's just after ten o'clock and I've go' to fire up the stove and git the roast goin'. Mattie'll be here before we know it."

Fred had been awake for about fifteen minutes, awaiting his mother's call. He'd been making the most of his Sunday morning sleep-in and hadn't wanted to rise a minute too soon. He'd decided to go to Russell Square in the afternoon after lunch to get his bit of fresh air.

"Eh! What a grand time we 'ad last night, Fred," said Mary. She started humming *Daisy, Daisy, give me your answer do*, as she bustled about fetching coal and kindling from two wooden boxes in a corner.

"Yeah! It was a good night," answered Fred, pleased his mother had enjoyed herself so much.

At that moment, William entered the room. Fred knew this was the signal for him to get out of bed. He had a good stretch before he sat up and put his feet on the wooden floor. He walked to a corner to some shelving and gathered some clothing, then opened the door to his parent's room to get dressed, but not before the usual dash in his nightgown to the privy in the courtyard below.

William was getting breakfast things ready and would make a pot of tea when the fire was going. Soon it was alight and crackling. He fetched a canister from a small dresser and spooned some oatmeal into a saucepan then mixed some condensed milk with water in a jug and placed it on the table with a bowl of sugar. The breadboard was hanging from a bit of string hooked over a nail in the wall. He grabbed it and a loaf of bread from the larder, a small block of butter and a jar of jam. This was this family's standard breakfast most days, and although it was simple, it would be eagerly looked forward to. Occasionally, bacon and eggs, or kippers were enjoyed as a special treat.

Fred returned and pulled out the plates and cutlery and set them on the table. By now, the oatmeal was starting to cook, which didn't take long as it was finely ground; the kettle was then placed onto the stove and they tucked into their food, enjoying every mouthful. In no time the kettle whistled and William made the tea.

"Ooh! I do enjoy me cuppa each mornin'," said Mary, as William placed the pot onto a trivet. "It gets me up and goin'."

After breakfast, Fred went out to buy the Sunday paper from a shop a bit further along Warren Street. This was a luxury. Each Sunday morning William and Fred would read it from front to back, sharing the news with Mary who was unable to read. When Fred returned with the paper, William eagerly scanned the current news.

"Looks like that Millicent Fawcett 'as been 'olding some more meetin's," said William. "She's been takin' petitions to Parliament about women 'avin' the vote. Well, she can do that if she likes, but my point is, would the average woman be able to understand 'ow the Parliament works?"

Mary flung down the potato she was peeling and, with eyes blazing, took on William.

"Well, I never 'ad the chance to learn to read and write bu' I can understand everyfin' like anyone else 'oo can read and write. Now, you stop puttin' down women and insultin' their brains. Some women are runnin' businesses these days and hirin' people and payin' taxes. If they're good enough to do that, then they're good enough to vote. An' you watch out Willie Nash. You keep talkin' like that and you'll soon see ME joinin' vem girls and goin' to vem meetin's too."

William was surprised when Fred agreed with his mother, who was still bristling.

"Calm down, Mum, I'm on your side. The vote for women WILL come one day. You'll see."

Mary, placated a little, and pleased to have her son's support, resumed her preparations for their Sunday roast. She walked to the cooler and took out the rolled beef she'd bought the afternoon before.

"'Ere," she said to Fred, handing him a bag full of peas, "shell 'em for me, luv. There's a lo', so do 'em straigh' away."

Fred settled down to his task, sneakily eating a few juicy younger peas now and then. William had resumed reading the paper focusing on the sports section.

By now the roast was in the pan with the dripping, and the oven was considered hot enough.

"It'll take nearly two hours," said Mary as she put the meat in the oven. "The spuds can go in later wiv the Yorkshire puddin'. Everyfin's comin' along well."

She took down a canister from a shelf and measured out six ounces of self-raising flour into a mixing bowl and grated three ounces of beef suet into it. Then she added a pinch of salt, a dessertspoon of sugar and a precious egg. These items she combined with enough water to make a dough.

"I'm makin' a jam roly-poly pud for afters," she announced. "Git me the rollin' pin, Fred."

Fred handed it to her and Mary in a practised manner, rolled out a near-perfect rectangle.

"Git me the strawberry jam, Fred." He duly obliged and Mary spread the jam liberally over the dough, and then rolled it into a log shape. "When the meat comes out, this'll go in, and I'll make the custard in a while."

Fred had finished shelling the peas, so he helped Mary tidy up the cooking things, placing them into a large, tin washing-up bowl for later. He then set the table in preparation for Mattie's visit and their monthly roast dinner.

A knock sounded on the door.

"Gracious me! She's early," said Mary as she took off her apron while bustling to the door to open it.

"Come on in, me luvvie," she welcomed with arms outstretched, and gave Mattie a giant hug.

"Something smells good, Mum," said Mattie, wrinkling up her nose to emphasise the point.

"It'll be a good while ye' but let's all 'ave a cuppa and we can catch up wiv our news. Now come on, Will, git the kettle on."

William's job had always been chief tea-maker. He rose from his chair, gave his daughter a hug and fetched the kettle.

While the family enjoyed morning tea, Mary told Mattie about their evening out at the pub with Bernie Ellis at the piano, and chuckled as she described the high-kicking antics on the dance floor.

"I bet Charlie's go' a sore bum today," she added.

Everyone had a good laugh.

William told about items of news he'd read in the paper, avoiding the one about Millicent Fawcett and the women's vote as he didn't want another outburst from Mary.

"And what's been happening in your world, Fred?" asked Mattie.

"Nothing much different," Fred replied. "Yesterday I slept in and was ten minutes late for work. Lucky I've got a good boss. He knew I'd had to battle through that blasted pea-souper."

"Now, Mattie," said Mary in a concerned voice, "you make sure yer keep inside and out of vem fogs. They always make yer asthma much worse."

"You can be sure I will, Mum," reassured Mattie.

"Well, I've go' a surprise," announced Mary. "You know the Telfords wot live upstairs in that flat at the back? I bumped into Marfa at the grocers last week, and she told me tha' their daughter Jo'anna is comin' back for a while 'til she finds work somewhere 'ere in London. I know she's 'ad a job out near Bristol wiv a bootmaker as a 'ousemaid and nursemaid and Marfa said 'ee's closin' down 'is business. She was worried because there aint much work 'ere in London jus' now for 'ousemaids. I seen their girl once before when she come back to visit some years ago. She only stayed a few days then, but I thought she was a pre"y li"le thing. She 'ad this lovely brown 'air all the way down 'er back. I wonder if she's already 'ere?"

"Well, I hope it all works out for her," said Mattie sympathetically. "I'm so lucky to have such a good job."

Mary had been attending to the dinner throughout all the chatter, turning the meat, putting in the potatoes and Yorkshire pudding, boiling up the peas and carrots and making some gravy and the custard. Now the roast was ready to be served. She popped the jam roly-poly pudding into the oven and set aside the custard she'd already made during the family's conversations. The four of them sat around the table while William carved the meat. Dinner served, they all tucked in, appreciating Mary's efforts.

"No-one can make a roast dinner like my Mum," said Fred as he scraped up the last of the gravy.

After they'd finished eating, Mary and Mattie cleared the table while the men compared the results of their rival football teams. William favoured Fulham; Fred supported West Ham. Occasionally, when they could afford it, William and Fred would attend a match, always making sure they made it to the Grand Final.

It was getting a bit cool and Mary decided to keep the fire in the stove going for a bit. In the comfort of the room, Mattie stayed for another hour then took her leave, promising to see her family again before too long.

Fred went down below to carry up another bucket of water to heat up for the washing up. When the water was ready and poured into the large tin vessel, the wire mesh soap-saver was agitated in the water to infuse the soap. William washed the dishes and utensils while Fred did the drying up.

A Bit of Fresh Air

That's it! thought Fred after he'd dried the dishes. *I'll put on a jumper and go out for a while.* He needed to escape from the confines of the flat, which was cramped at the best of times with three people living in two rooms. While he'd enjoyed catching up with his sister, any extra people in a congested area always brought on mild claustrophobia. Today he decided to go down to Russell Square and, after telling William and Mary where he was going, he set out.

The air was fresh and crisp with winter on the way. For the last few days, the nights had been unseasonably cold with that awful fog closing in like yesterday morning. But on this afternoon, the air was clear, the sun shining, and Fred relished its warmth on his face as he made his way down Tottenham Court Road. Along the way, he passed the almost completed new chapel where the original Whitefields Tabernacle had once stood. That huge, majestic edifice had once housed nearly three thousand people and Fred had once been a choirboy there. He knew the history of that church … built in 1756 for George Whitefield, the eighteenth-century evangelist – a great pioneer of Christian revival in England and Wales. Fred had witnessed the demolition of the tabernacle in 1890 after its foundations had been declared unsafe. On the site, a temporary iron building had housed many worshippers, who were now looking forward to moving into the new church. It was due for completion in about a month.

In another fifteen minutes, Fred reached Russell Square and the park. He always enjoyed going to parks in his area; he could find space for himself and a sense of freedom for a while. Here; there were no walls confining him, like in his home or workplace. Here, he could recharge and prepare for the week's work ahead of him. Ahead was an empty bench on the central pathway leading to the fountain, and he sat and watched grey squirrels scampering around on the opposite lawn; smiled as they scattered a carpet of autumn leaves under a large lime tree. A young family ambled along the pathway, their leashed collie dog led by their little boy. When the dog noticed the squirrels, it bounded forward to chase them, dragging at its leash and pulling the boy onto his backside. He let go. The squirrels raced up the tree trunk to safety. Fred laughed aloud at this; smiled widely as the family passed by and the dog returned to them. After some time, he stood and wandered along the pathways enjoying the fresh air and exercise and the seasonal plantings in the garden beds. Bumping into a regular customer from Dobson's Ironmongery, he remembered it was time to get back home and prepare for work the next day, but not before he diverted to inspect the impressive marble pillars and stairway in the foyer of the newly built Hotel Russell.

He crossed the road, gazing in awe at the magnificent eight-storeyed building, its colouring an unusual terra cotta. He mounted the steps from the footpath to the foyer entrance and went inside. He whistled low on seeing the grand glittering chandelier over the staircase; committed it all to memory so he could give his mother a good description of the place. She had asked him to do this, as she'd felt not quite able to go there herself. Fred had reminded her forcefully that she could hold her head up high in any company or in any place.

He left the hotel and set out for home, returning along the same route as he'd walked earlier. This afternoon had been a much shorter outing than usual due to Mattie's visit, but he nevertheless felt refreshed and ready for the week ahead. Maybe next Sunday, he would go to Regents Park, only a stone's throw from Warren Street where he lived.

The cold had set in when Fred returned home and he was glad his father had lit the fire.

"We're 'avin' toast and bloater spread for tea tonigh' ", announced Mary, "an' if yer still 'ungry, there's some roly-poly left over. Yer can fill up on tha'."

"Sounds good to me," answered Fred, "and Mum, I've decided I'm not going to tell you about the staircase in The Russell. I want you to see it for yourself. So one day, as soon as you're ready, put on your best frock and we'll all go down there. I'm going to walk you up that staircase, and you can see it all, including the chandelier. Then I'm going to buy you and Dad a drink at the bar before we come back."

"Cor lumme!" exclaimed Mary, "that would be too grand for the likes o' me. Bu' I wonder ... do you think it could really 'appen? What an occasion!"

"It certainly *will* happen!" said Fred decidedly. William nodded in agreement. "I'll make it a BIG occasion."

The two men busied themselves, Fred cutting slices of bread and William making a pot of tea.

A Week Later at Warren Street

It was Sunday again, and Fred had volunteered to go and buy the newspaper. As he started down the staircase, the young woman ahead of him reached the landing. Her wavy brown hair hung almost to her waist, and he remembered his mother's description of a young woman with hair like that. *So, this must be Johannah Telford who's just come back from Bristol to stay with her parents.*

He hurried his steps and caught up with her.

"Hello, I'm Fred Nash. Frederick if you want to be formal. I live in this building, and if I'm not mistaken, you must be Johannah Telford. My Mum bumped into your mother the other week, and she said you'd be coming back here from Bristol for a while."

"Yes, I'm Johannah, but most people call me Anna. I'm looking for work in London, but so far I've had no luck … but I've only been here for a week."

"Something'll turn up soon, I'm sure," said Fred reassuringly.

They fell in step with each other until Fred announced, "I'm only going down the street for a bit to get a paper. Where are you off to?"

"I'm going where you're going, I think," replied Anna. "My Dad loves to keep up with what's going on in the world."

"Well! We have that in common then," said Fred glancing at her. "My Pa really looks forward to his newspaper every Sunday."

They reached the shop, bought their papers and stepped out of the shop to return home. On the way back, Fred told Anna about his job at the ironmonger's shop; he also mentioned how he loved to get out each Sunday for the fresh air – if the fogs had lifted – and to explore the local parklands.

"Well!" replied Anna, "I can understand that. There was a beautiful park just opposite where I worked near Bristol and my workmate Connie and I just loved going there every day in our little break. And sometimes, if I had the whole day off, I'd meet up with friends and we'd go down to the river and have a picnic. I feel I'm a bit of a country girl at heart."

Fred felt encouraged by Anna's willingness to keep the conversation going.

"Do you know that my grandparents were agricultural labourers in Somerset and I think some of that has rubbed off on me," said Fred. "It may sound a bit sissy, but I enjoy looking at the flower plantings and trees in the parks and watching how the seasons can change everything."

Anna smiled at him, and Fred noted how her blue eyes crinkled up at the corners. He suddenly felt emboldened. They'd reached the tenement building where they lived.

He impulsively asked her: "Look, I'm going to Regents Park this afternoon. Would you like to keep me company? There's a lot to explore, and there's a lovely lake with ducks and everything. I could bring some bread along, and we could feed them."

Fred felt his invitation had been a bit clumsy, almost as though he had invited a child 'to feed the ducks'. He hoped Anna would not take offence.

"I'm not sure," she replied slowly, "I'll have to see if my mother needs any help this afternoon. When would you want to set out?"

"What time would suit you?" asked Fred.

"Oh! about half-past one, after we've had our lunch. If I decide to come, I'll knock on your door at that time, and we could spend a couple of hours in the park and be back by three-thirty."

"Well, I hope you *will* be able to come, Anna. I'll be eagerly waiting for your knock."

They ascended the stairs until they reached Fred's door. He gave Anna a little wave before he entered the flat and Anna climbed a further floor to her parent's place.

"Here's your paper, Dad," she said as she entered the flat.

Her mother looked at her enquiringly and asked, "You were a long time getting the newspaper, Anna. What kept you?"

"Oh! I bumped into that fellow who lives downstairs. You know, Fred someone, and we got talking. He loves getting out and walking around all the parks every Sunday, and he's invited me to go to Regents Park this afternoon to keep him company."

"And are you going?" asked Martha cautiously.

"I'm not sure," replied Anna. "I thought you might need me to help you with the darning."

"Well, I don't, and I think you should go," Martha urged persuasively. "You need to make new friends now you're here in London, and he's a nice boy."

"He's not a boy Mum; he's a man."

"Well, anyway, the walk and the fresh air will do you good. I'll make some sandwiches …

"Oh! stop fussing, Mum. We'll be going after lunch and can buy a lemonade there if we get thirsty."

Anna's father, pretending to read the paper, also hoped Anna would be joining young Fred on his walk.

The conversation was dropped. Sam resumed reading the paper. Martha pulled out the darning wools and socks, and Anna went down to the laundry to do some washing.

While she was downstairs, she decided she *would* join Fred on his walk to Regents Park. She hadn't been there since she was seventeen, and besides that, her mother had become rather controlling since she'd returned from Bristol, and she'd grown used to being her own boss while away. Getting out would give her a break. She returned from the laundry and helped get lunch.

Fred, meanwhile, watched the clock while he read his portion of the newspaper.

"I bought a nice bi' of cheese at the grocers yesterday," Mary announced as she set the table. "We can 'ave it on bread wiv pickles and afterwards a currant bun I got cheap we can share. Now, William, stop readin' that bloomin' paper and make the tea, will yer?"

William obliged and commenced his usual task. Fred sat down while noticing it was already ten past one. He quickly prepared his sandwich and cut off a piece of bun to have with his cup of tea.

"So, you're off to the Regent this afternoon, Fred, eh?" inquired William.

"Yes," answered Fred. "I should be back by about four or so."

"Why the 'urry to go? Stop scoffin' down yer lunch like that, Fred. You'll ge' indigestion," said Mary.

Fred finished his lunch and sat on a chair staring into space while he waited for a knock on the door. He was starting to lose hope when it happened at twenty minutes to two.

"I'll get it," said Fred as he bumped into Mary, muttering, "Oo, could that be?" as she also made for the door. But Fred got there first and opened it to partly reveal Anna outside.

"Goodbye," said Fred in a dismissive tone as he left and closed the door. He and Anna walked down the staircase and out into the fresh air.

"Well, I never!" exclaimed Mary to William, "it was that Jo'anna from upstairs. I seen 'er outside the door. I didn't know ee'd met 'er yet."

"Well, she only lives one floor up for goodness sakes, Mary. He probably met her on the stairs comin' and goin'," replied William, exasperated.

"Well, I 'ope they 'ave a lovely time in the park," said Mary, and she turned her face away from William to hide the sneaky little grin on her face.

Regents Park

Fred and Anna stepped out onto the pavement and agreed it was a lovely afternoon for a walk.

"Well, let's be off then," said Fred, resisting the urge to take Anna's arm as it occurred to him that they hardly knew each other and she may be offended.

They walked along Warren Street until they arrived at the entrance to the park.

"How wonderful for you to have this place so close to your home," said Anna.

"It is, and it's such a large area with so much to explore. I never get tired of coming here, and with the Zoo at the top end, it's a great place for Londoners to visit and have a good time."

"Where's the duck pond? Did you bring the bread?" asked Anna.

"Oh! I'm so sorry, I forgot," lied Fred. He had not given the bread a single thought after thinking he may have previously offended Anna by treating her like a child. "Anyhow, we can always come again and feed them next time."

"Well, if I get a live-in job, there may not be a next time," said Anna practically.

Fred experienced a small sinking feeling, which he covered up by saying, "Well, I'm sure something will turn up for you soon and hopefully it'll be close by so you can come again."

Anna looked at Fred and smiled, her eyes crinkling up. "Yes, I'd come again, Fred. This is a great place to go for a walk."

They'd entered the boardwalk and joined a straggle of people coming and going to different features in the park. There were people on benches, people sitting on the grass, some reading books, nursemaids wheeling perambulators, families with noisy children on swings and a see-saw, and groups of young people enjoying their day off.

"Looks like the roses are nearly finished, but look at that gorgeous yellow one," said Anna. She walked over to inspect the flower more closely. "And the perfume! I think yellow roses are my favourite."

"You should see the rose beds in spring and summer," joined in Fred. "All colours they are."

They continued walking toward the lake where ducks and swans and other waterbirds gathered around a couple of small islands, Fred telling Anna about his night out at *The Squire's Rest* with his parents and the *Ta-ra-ra-boom-de-ay* episode. Anna laughed aloud and, reciprocating, told him about the annoying man in the train from Bristol and how his wife had called the township of Slough, Sluff. "Remember, Fred, it rhymes with cow, not tough."

They reached the lake and sat on a bench to rest their legs for a while; watched row boats and the antics of birdlife. After about half an hour, Fred suggested they walk to a small, gabled cottage where ginger beer, lemonade or fruit punch was sold.

"I don't know about you, Anna, but I've worked up a bit of a thirst. Let me buy you a drink."

Anna declined, insisting she pay for herself as she could well afford to. When they reached the cottage, Fred bought a ginger beer, Anna a fruit punch. Refreshed, they continued walking to the northern area of the park. Anna flinched when she heard a distant roaring sound.

"That would be a lion at the zoo," explained Fred. "I'd love to go there one day."

"Well, I wouldn't!" insisted Anna. "I think it's cruel to keep animals in cages and out of their natural habitats."

"Well, you may be right, after all," said Fred, not wanting any disagreement to spoil this idyllic afternoon.

It was now half-past three, and they both agreed it was time to head back home.

Anna said she'd read in her father's newspaper there were a few positions she wanted to apply for in the coming week, and Fred said he had things to get ready for work. They retraced their passage back to their Warren Street address.

"Did yer 'ave a nice time in the park?" inquired Mary as Fred walked through the door,

"Not bad," answered Fred. "The weather was beautiful."

"Was that all?" persisted Mary.

"Oh! shut up," said William in a rather loud voice, "and mind yer own business."

Another Week Goes By

Fred turned up for work the next day thinking how long the week would drag on before he could go out with Anna again. He hoped quite selfishly that Anna's job would not turn up for another week or so, and when it did, it would be close enough for them to continue a friendship. He thought of her a lot; found himself numbering all the things he liked about her. He decided he would knock on her door during the week to find out how her job searching was going. That would be an excuse to see her again if only for a short time. And if it was alright for another walk in a park, which one would he suggest this time? Maybe they could go down to Russell Square where he went a fortnight ago. He always enjoyed watching the squirrels darting about. Would she like that too?

"What's the matter with you today?" growled Mr Dobson. "I've just had a customer complain to me that you short-changed him. And another earlier said you'd given him a pot of emerald green paint when he'd asked for mint green. Keep ya mind on what yer doing, Fred, and remember, there's plenty of good fellas looking for work just now."

Gasping inwardly, Fred realised he'd not been concentrating on his job. "Sorry, Mr Dobson. I hope you agree it's not the way I usually attend to customers. I admit I did have my mind on other things, but I'll put them aside for now."

Ada joined in. "Fred, we've always been pleased with you over the ten years you've been with us. Is anything troubling you?

"Not really, Mrs Dobson. I've just been thinking of some lovely walks in the parks I've gone on lately."

Ada looked at Ernie and made a face, and decided to tell him later what a daft reply she thought Fred had made. Almost like he'd gone bonkers. She knew Fred often got some fresh air on Sundays but to suddenly dwell on those walks to the extent that he neglected the customers was not like him. Then her imagination sparked, and she wondered if Fred had found someone to go walking with … like a lady friend? She looked at him afresh, thinking, *You're a nice-looking young man and decent, and you're a very good employee. And it's about time you got married, my lad.* Then she pulled herself up realising she may be going too far. If it was meant to happen one day, then it would.

Fred applied himself diligently to his work and managed to put Anna out of his mind, for the time being. He'd been warned by Ernie and knew that unemployment was pretty bad these days and many were desperate for work. He realised how lucky he was to have such a good job which had sustained him for so many years.

Two more days passed. Fred returned home on Wednesday evening.

"I go' a bi' of scrag end from the butchers today, Fred, to make a stew. 'Ave some toast wiv i' and it'll warm yer up." Mary served up the family's dinner, which Fred ate with a good appetite.

He felt nervous at the thought of going upstairs to speak to Anna. He was a bit tired and splashed his face with water to freshen up, then combed his hair. He did this when Mary went into the other room so she didn't ask questions. He mounted the stairway and knocked on the Telford's door. Anna answered.

"Hello, Fred, how's work been going? As far as I'm concerned, I've had no luck so far. One job turned out to be for a charwoman which I couldn't abide. Too much scrubbing! I'm a housemaid and a nursemaid and have more qualifications than that. And the other job had already been taken, so I'll have to look again."

"Well!" answered Fred, secretly pleased, "that means you can come walking with me on Sunday, doesn't it? Or I hope it does."

"I think so. I enjoyed it last Sunday. So, where to next? You told me you like to vary your outings."

"Either to Tavistock Square or Russell Square. I think Russell might be better. Opposite the park, they've built this enormous hotel. It's very grand, and I'd like you to see the marble staircase inside."

"That sounds good. I'll knock on your door again next Sunday at half-past one," Anna said with a smile.

It was a bit awkward continuing the conversation, standing there in the doorway with Sam and Martha close by, so Fred said, "Goodbye for now," and surprised himself by giving Anna a little wink before he left.

Anna was surprised too but enjoyed the conspiratorial note of that wink. She looked forward to Sunday and Fred's company.

During the week, Mary and Martha bumped into each other on the staircase landing down the bottom, one going out and the other coming back.

"I fink it was lovely, vem goin' out togevver for that walk on Sunday," ventured Mary. "I wouldn't 'ave known 'e'ed asked 'er, except that I seen 'er outside the door. I fink they make a luvverly couple."

"Don't jump to conclusions, Mary. Anna has told me they're just good friends. I'm pleased Anna's getting out a bit but don't forget, she could be in service in a week or two, and that could be the end of any walks."

Martha secretly thought Fred was a very nice fellow and liked Anna befriending him, but knew Sam had reservations about a permanent relationship because of Fred's low wage. He hoped Anna would one day meet someone who could wholly support her.

"Well, yer right, I suppose," agreed Mary, "but I wonder, are they goin' out again next Sunday?"

"Whatever will be will be, Mary," said Martha philosophically. "But in the end, it will be all up to them."

The two women went about their business, and the week progressed to Sunday.

Some Family History

The morning passed in the usual way, but this time Mary and William had been told Anna would be knocking on the door, Fred having realised everyone already knew he and Anna had become friendly. What he wanted to conceal was his growing fascination with his upstairs neighbour. One-thirty arrived, but this time Anna did not keep him waiting, and Mary did not attempt to open the door.

"I wanted to ask 'er in, ter ge' a good look at 'er," said Mary to William after the two had left. "So far I've only 'ad a glimpse of 'er. I've been 'opin' I'd cross 'er on the stairs, but no!"

Fred and Anna walked along Warren Street until they reached the intersection of Tottenham Court Road which they turned into. Anna stumbled on a rut in the footpath and Fred quickly grabbed her arm and steadied her. He lessened his grip but did not release his hold. It seemed natural that they ended up walking arm in arm down the road and Fred was pleased Anna had not objected to this.

When they reached the park, Fred led Anna to the same bench he'd sat on a fortnight before. Sure enough, the scampering squirrels were there under the lime tree. Fred told the story of the little boy and his dog, and Anna laughed and said she was glad the squirrels had escaped.

"Were you born around here?" asked Anna.

"Yes. I've always been a Londoner. I was born in St Giles, Finsbury, not far from here, so I know this area pretty well."

"What about your parents?" Are they Londoners too?"

"Yes, they are today, but my father was born in Bristol," replied

Fred. "He came to London when quite young and picked up the Cockney accent, but his forebears, and mine, of course, came from Somerset. Do you want to hear a bit of my family history? I know it by heart. It's a legend. I hope I won't bore you."

"Yes, I'm interested," said Anna. "Go ahead."

"Well, back in 1793, my great grandparents, George and Mary Nash, had their two children, Thomas and Lucy, baptised in the Church of the Holy Ghost in Crowcombe in Somerset. He was an agricultural labourer working on dairy farms and cattle farms. It was a hard life, I'm told, made worse when smaller farms were enclosed to make larger holdings. They struggled but managed to survive, and when Thomas, my grandfather, grew up, he continued working on the land like his father George.

"In 1825, Thomas married Sarah from Chew Magna. They had a boy, Thomas, in 1825 in Chew Magna, who died when he was tiny, then a daughter called Eliza who was born in 1827. Things got worse in Crowcombe for the family because farm machinery came onto the fields, and many manual workers lost their jobs, so Thomas and Sarah decided to move to Bristol. They packed up all their belongings in a hand cart and with baby Eliza, set out on foot for Bristol about forty miles away to find better-paid work."

"How brave of them," remarked Anna, "and how desperate they must have been to do that."

Fred nodded and continued.

"The roads and pathways were rutted and the going was slow, about four miles an hour with their load and a small child. They slept rough at night and had only enough food and water they could carry. I think on the way some people might have helped with a few handouts. Anyway, they finally got there and settled in some rooms at Clifton just outside of Bristol. Thomas got some labouring work there. In 1830 they had another boy, also called Thomas, like their first boy who'd died, and then my father William came along in 1835."

"I've heard of Clifton near Bristol," said Anna. "A lovely town."

"They stayed there for some years," continued Fred. "My

grandmother Sarah took in work as a laundress, and in 1841, when Eliza was fourteen, she took up dressmaking at home. Now there were three incomes in the household, and life was easier. Thomas was eleven and my Pa, William, was only about five."

"When did they come to London?" asked Anna.

"Well, they'd been moving around a bit from place to place in Bristol. Living conditions were not the best, crowded, and not very clean, so round about the mid-1850's they decided life might be better for them in London, so they moved. A heap of other people thought the same. They weren't to know how crowded London had become. Grandfather got a job as a porter on the railways. My grandmother got a job as a charwoman – very hard work scrubbing floors and cleaning fireplaces. And do you know, she had to work every day with only one day off in a month."

"That was nothing but slavery. How cruel!" interrupted Anna.

"My Dad met Mary, my mum, in 1859. They got married and moved to St Pancras. She was born in 1835, the same year as Dad. My Dad had a job as a car-man then. Today he is a furniture removalist, and my mother works as a part-time laundress at the local hotel."

"Are you an only child?" asked Anna. "Do you have brothers, sisters?"

"There's only me and Matilda, or Mattie as we call her, out of five children born. I came along in 1869. Mum often says how lucky we are to be alive and how lucky she is to have us."

"She sounds lovely."

"She is," replied Fred rather softly. "My mother hasn't had much education, but she has wisdom, a sense of humour and a warm heart."

"What's more important than that?" remarked Anna.

Fred wondered if he hadn't told Anna too much about his family and how poor they'd all been and still were. Maybe all that information would turn her off him.

Anna looked at Fred and noticed how quiet he'd become. Suddenly she understood the reason.

"Never be ashamed of your family, Fred, but be proud of them.

You've told me about decent, hardworking and courageous people who've overcome a lot of odds stacked against them. When I think of your grandparents trudging all that way to Bristol pulling a cart and with a little baby to care for as well, I can only feel a deep admiration for them. And don't forget that my parents too have had a struggle and also live in a tenement dwelling. My father has had to earn his living as a labourer, but he is an intelligent man. They are here today in Warren Street because it's cheaper than where they were."

"Well, somehow we've all managed to get through," said Fred with a grin. He felt he was now on equal ground with Anna.

"Yes, survival it has been," added Anna with a wry smile.

"Do you know much about your ancestors, Anna?" asked Fred. "Where did they all come from?"

"Well, to begin with, I'm a Telford, and my father was born in Wellingborough, Northampton. My mother, Martha Sanderfield, was born at Doddington, Cambridge. I don't know how my parents met but they were married in 1868 at Holy Trinity Church in Clapham, Surrey. I was born there in 1873, their first child. Oh! Goodness, now you know how old I am."

"Why the secret, Anna?" asked Fred. "You're twenty-five, which makes me four years older than you, as I was born in 1869. Any brothers, sisters?"

"Yes, after me came four boys, but only George and Stephen lived."

Anna continued.

"I know I have French blood on my mother's side, the Sanderfields. One fellow, William, married a French girl, Mary Dournelle in 1740. We've come down from persecuted Protestants from somewhere in France. They were called Huguenots. These people fled to other parts of Europe, and my ancestors finally settled in Cambridge here in England. This is our family legend passed down by my grandfather. He told me that our people were named 'Vennin' and they left France way back in 1595. And he said these refugees were clever people who brought a lot of industries to England which were not here then. Over time, some settled in the Wandsworth area in Surrey, where I was born."

"What a history you've got, Anna. French, eh? Let me see … do you look French?" said Fred, studying her face.

"You be the judge, Fred. But seriously, I don't think the French look too different from the English, do you?" replied Anna.

"Well, their girls are pretty," said Fred, feeling he was making a little headway.

Anna turned her head away, not wanting to encourage Fred in passing compliments about her looks. She knew hers were above ordinary, but could not be classified as beautiful.

A sudden breeze sprang up swirling the autumn leaves in the park and blowing around a few newspapers that had been left lying on benches. People quickened their steps to exit the park, and a passing woman took an umbrella out of a large carry bag. Fred looked up and noticed a dense bank of threatening black clouds overhead.

"Blimey, Anna, we'd better get going," he said urgently. "There's a storm on the way. I didn't expect this, and I don't have a brolly. We'll have to run for it."

He grabbed Anna's hand, and together they set out for home in a rush.

A Heavy Thunderstorm

The rain hadn't started yet as they turned into Tottenham Court Road, but as they neared the almost completed Whitefields church, the rain came down in splotches. Then it settled into a heavy downpour and Fred, pulling Anna along, dashed into the building for shelter. They were both laughing and took off their coats to shake off the water. Then they hung them on hooks on the wall.

"Listen to that thunder out there," said Anna, her eyes wide open. "Glad we could come in here." She took out a handkerchief from her handbag to dry her face then patted Fred's face too.

At that moment, a middle-aged woman approached and cried out in surprise, "Well, I never! It's young Frederick Nash I do believe. Where have you been all these years, Fred? We've missed you. Come on in with your friend and have a cup of tea with us downstairs in the hall. Our ladies have made some cakes for afternoon tea. And who's your lady friend?"

Fred nearly laughed, remembering his family's night out at *The Squire's Rest* when Bernie Ellis had the people singing *'Allo, 'allo, Who's yer Lady Friend*, but he suppressed the urge. "This is Anna Telford; she's just returned to London after working at Bristol for a while. Anna, meet Sister Hester Howell – she is a deaconess and social worker here at the church. We all call her Aunty Esther."

"And you can still call me that now," said Sister Hester with a smile. She led Fred and Anna downstairs and into a smaller room off the main hall where a long trestle table was laid out with cups and saucers, plates and tea-making things. Several people were gathered in groups talking. Hester introduced Fred and Anna to a few then invited them to take their places at the table. She then busied herself brewing the tea. When she had finished, she returned to the table and sat down.

"And Fred," she questioned, "how's it going with your job at the ironmongers? Mervyn Lowe and Donny Henson shop there and tell me now and again that you're still there. I'm glad to hear you have a good job."

"Yes, it's a good job, Aunty Esther, but rather tiring. The hours are a bit too long, but there's talk of a half day off being given to shop assistants soon," answered Fred, pouring out the information in a sort of flood. Aunty Esther had always been a good listener in the past and ready to help during peoples' ups and downs. Fred could remember her rummaging around in donated goods to fit out needy people with food, clothing, boots or other commodities.

"I hope that half-day comes soon for you, Fred, then," said Sister Hester. "I remember you had a very good singing voice when you were a lad in the choir in the old church. We still sing the same hymns today that we did then. Charles and John Wesley hymns they are. Do you remember your favourite one?"

"It was some time ago," said Fred, his brow furrowing, "but one comes to mind now, and we would sing it in harmony. It was called *Oh! For a Thousand Tongues to Sing.*"

"Yes, that's a popular one, Fred. You know, we'd love you to come back and join in again. In a few weeks, our new church here will be dedicated, and it's to be called Whitefields Central Mission."

Sister Hester poured three cups of tea and invited Fred and Anna to help themselves to the cakes. Fred chose a buttered rock cake and Anna reached for a scone, some whipped cream and strawberry jam while Sister Hester cut off a slice of Madeira cake.

Rain still drummed on the roof, making conversation difficult. An elderly man decided to fill in the time by giving an impromptu concert on the piano, his recital ending when the sound of the rain ceased. Fred looked outside to see whether he and Anna could make it home without getting drenched, and they walked up the stairs to the entry porch. It appeared that the storm had passed, so they took their coats from the wall hooks and put them on.

"Don't forget to pop in again, my dears," Sister Hester said as she gave Fred a little hug, "and remember, the evening service starts at 6p.m. with a light meal before, at 5p.m."

"I'll keep it in mind, Aunty Esther," said Fred, smiling as he and Anna walked out the door into a cold, blustery wind. They hurried their steps, knowing their parents would have a fire going.

"That was an interesting interlude, Anna," said Fred, "and I sure enjoyed our unexpected treats. I haven't had a rock cake in years."

"But I sometimes enjoyed a cream tea in Bristol when I was there," replied Anna. "I would meet friends from church and we would go to some tea rooms."

"Did you go to church often?" asked Fred.

"Nearly every week," replied Anna. "It added another dimension to the life I was leading, which was repetitive and often tiresome. I must say I found comfort there in the message too."

"Well, I might go back again one day," said Fred. Then he changed the subject. "I didn't get to show you the staircase at the Russell Hotel, Anna. It's magnificent! I told Mum about it, and she said that people like her didn't get to walk up staircases like those, but I told her that one day I'd take her there and make sure she went up it. And I will!"

"Oh! Fred, she has every right to walk up that staircase like anyone else. I'll come with you when you take her."

They'd reached their address and said their goodbyes as they went up the stairs.

"Hopefully, same time, same place next week," said Fred with a grin, stopping at his doorway, "but let me know how the jobs are going for you."

"I will. I'm going to knock on doors this week around this area. I'll even take on cleaning, or better still, there may be a nanny's job."

"Good luck!" said Fred as he watched Anna climb the steps to her parents' flat.

"Cor lumme, me lad. Were you and Anna out in that wretched storm?" asked Mary as Fred came through the door.

Fred told Mary and William about their escape into the new church and how he'd reconnected with Aunty Esther.

"I'm pleased about tha'. She's a luvverly lady and helped us out a lo' when we was down and ou' a few times. An' yer should go back there, Fred, and join the choir again and use that singin' voice yer go'. Now sit down and 'ave yer tea. It's 'aricot bean stew wiv taters and bits o' 'ogget through it."

Fred had his tea then sat near the fire to get warm. He hoped Anna was getting warm too and then wondered why he related everything in his life now, to her. He decided to knock on her door again on Wednesday night to see if she'd found a job yet.

Finding Work in London

The following morning Anna was up early and dressed carefully in her Sunday best, knowing she would be calling on local hotels and grandiose houses in the district, seeking employment. She'd abandoned the idea of looking for work in the provinces or too far away from London. There was so much to explore here … lovely parks and … Fred? She surprised herself at the thought; reasoned that he was a very nice friend to have found, and right here on her doorstep. *And good friends are treasures, aren't they, these days? So many people don't give a toss about you anyway.*

After breakfast, she washed her hands and face, cleaned her teeth, put her hair up in a bun and grabbed her handbag, making sure the reference from Fergusons was in there.

Setting out on her quest, feeling half hopeful and nervous at the same time, she approached the door of an imposing, three-storey home around the corner. Sculptured lions rested on pedestals each side of the staircase leading to the front landing. She took a deep breath, went up the steps and knocked on the door. A woman in a maid's uniform answered and told Anna that Madam had all the staff she needed.

"Well, that's the first one," muttered Anna as she walked back down the steps. Then she thought, *I'll try for a cleaning job at The Squire's Rest where Fred went.* She was unlucky there too.

During the day, she covered a couple of footsore miles knocking on doors of hotels and office buildings and offering her services, but to no avail. Disappointed, she returned home.

"Have a rest tomorrow and try again on Wednesday," said her father that evening on noticing her tired, crestfallen face. "I'm sure something will turn up soon."

On Wednesday, Anna went in a different direction; turned her steps towards St Pancras railway station.

I might as well try here, she thought, as she gazed in wonder at the enormous Midland Grand Hotel adjoining the station.

"Isn't it a gorgeous building?" remarked a woman who suddenly stood near Anna and who'd felt a compulsion to share her impression with someone. "I've heard it said it's the most beautiful hotel in the world and it's right here in our London."

"Yes, it's very impressive indeed," said Anna with a smile and then she leaned a little closer and confided to the stranger. "Please wish me luck, I'm going in there to see if they have any jobs going. I'm desperate for work in London."

"Good luck, my dear," replied the woman. Then she added. "You're a nice-looking girl, and that's a lovely outfit you're wearing. Be confident. I do hope you'll be lucky."

'Thank you so much. You're very kind," said Anna.

Encouraged by the lady's flattery, she crossed the road, walked through the revolving door and into the entrance foyer. She stood still for a moment, entranced by the exquisite decor in the place, the vibrant colours, the wallpaper and the majestic staircase covered in brilliant red patterned carpet. Then she noticed the reception desk and summoned her courage. A serious-looking man in horn-rimmed glasses looked up expectantly as she approached.

"Are you here to make a booking, madam?" the concierge asked pleasantly.

"No, sir," replied Anna, drawing up her shoulders. "I'm actually looking for a position in service as a housemaid or kitchen maid. I have just returned from Bristol where I had a job for eight years with a bootmaker there. I have a reference from them and … …"

"Not so fast, lady – don't get ahead of yourself. I'll have to telephone the management. If there is a vacancy, you can tell all that to someone else."

The man dialled a number and waited for a reply.

Meanwhile, Anna's heart thumped and she uttered a quick, silent prayer, *Please, dear God, let there be something for me.*

The short telephone conversation ended with the man saying, "Yes, Wilfred, I'll send her up." He turned to Anna. "You may be in luck. Go up the staircase to the first floor, turn left and you'll see a door marked 'Personnel'. Knock on that. The interviewing officer is Mr Wilfred Armstrong. Good luck, miss."

The interview seemed like a blur when Anna reflected on it as she made her way down the stairway and into the street. She'd been nervous but had managed to present herself in her best possible way, choosing her words carefully as she outlined her experience, and smiling when appropriate. She'd filled out a form after Mr Armstrong had said, "Well, Miss Telford, you've turned up at the right time. One of our older women gave in her resignation two days ago due to ill health. You'll clean up rooms after guests have left and prepare them for the next people. Your hours will be from ten in the morning until four in the afternoon with a half-hour break in the afternoon from one till one-thirty, and you'll have Sunday off. Your salary will be about twenty-six pounds in a year, but we'll settle that next week. I expect you to turn up for duty next Monday at nine-thirty to collect your uniforms. That will be all for now. Goodbye."

Anna felt like dancing all the way home; she could hardly believe she now had a job and in such a wonderful place. And how quickly it had all happened. *How pleased Mum and Dad will be*, she thought, and planned to tell them the news when they returned home from their jobs. *And I can't wait to tell Fred.* She decided to visit Fred that night after he'd had his tea, around eight o'clock. She also wanted to meet his parents whom she'd heard a lot about, particularly his mother.

On returning home, she filled the day cleaning the flat to surprise her mother, and doing personal washing, and later on taking up a supper cloth she was embroidering. The day passed according to her expectations. Her parents were thrilled at her news, especially her father, and after her tea, she descended the steps and knocked on Fred's door.

Mary opened the door and exclaimed, "Oh! me goodness, if it aint

Jo'anna from upstairs. Come in, luvvie and git warm by the fire. 'Ere, William, make a fresh po 'o' tea, will ya? And git that packet o' biscuits out. I luv ya 'air done up in a bun like that, Anna. Fred calls yer that, doesn't ee?"

Anna sat on the chair Fred pulled up for her, close to the fireplace. "Lovely to meet you both," she greeted Will and Mary, "and guess what? I've got good news. I'm starting as a room servicer at the Midland Grand Hotel next Monday. It was just luck. You should see the place. Talk about a posh place to work! I can't wait."

There were congratulations all round as they settled down to their cups of tea.

Later on, Fred ushered Anna to the door; went out onto the landing with her, closing the door behind him.

"Anna, let's go and celebrate at *The Squire's Rest* next Saturday night, eh? How about we get some fish and chips on the way and then go and have a couple of beers at the pub. I'll pick you up at eight?"

"Sounds good," replied Anna. "Let's do it!"

Before he knew it, Fred had his arms around her. "You deserve a hug after your good work today, Anna."

"Thanks, Fred," said Anna and she responded by closing her arms around him, "and you deserve a hug for being such a good friend."

They lingered in their embrace until hearing a noise like something being dropped on the other side of the door. They sprang apart, then laughed on realising the thin door could be opened at any moment.

"See you on Saturday night at eight o'clock," said Anna as she climbed back up to her parent's small apartment.

Fish and Chips and a Beer

Fred found it hard to sleep that night. He was getting to know Anna better and knew he wanted to get to know her more. *What if?* he thought. *We've both got jobs.* He tossed and turned, thinking of possibilities, abandoning them as surely he couldn't be that lucky; thinking of possibilities again, until he finally dropped off to sleep.

The next three days dragged on, and Fred counted the hours before he could see Anna again. At the same time, he was careful to apply himself diligently to his job as it seemed extra precious to him now.

After he'd had his tea on Saturday night, he freshened up and changed into his best clothes. *Now!* he thought, *up the steps to collect her.*

Anna was ready and somehow sensing Fred would be better dressed, she'd put on her favourite floral blouse, navy skirt and woollen jacket and grabbed a thick muffler to keep out the chill. She was ready to answer the door when Fred knocked, even though he was five minutes early.

He greeted her parents when the door opened, and Sam said, "Look after her, Fred, and don't get her home too late, will you? As you know, she's starting a new job on Monday and needs to rest before then."

Anna responded to this with annoyance. "Dad, I'm not a child, you know. And I know how to look after myself by now."

Fred nodded to Sam, and Anna moved to the door, waving to her parents as she left.

They walked to *The Squire's Rest* in hurried steps due to a cold wind that had suddenly sprung up. On the way, they both complained about their lack of complete independence due to their living arrangements with parents.

"Nothing annoys me more than being treated like a child," said Anna. "… and even though I was in service in Bristol, those people did not interfere in my private life."

Fred agreed. "I know how you feel. My Mum and Pa are good to me, but sometimes I feel like a caged animal. I long for my own space, and actually, my own place."

They rounded a corner and called into the local fish and chip shop. A large vat of boiling fat was kept going by a coal fire underneath. After ten minutes they picked up their order, paid ninepence each and sat at a table to eat their meal straight out of the newspaper it was wrapped in, with the bread and butter and a cup of tea that was included.

"My, that was good, but rather greasy," said Anna as she wiped her mouth with a handkerchief then offered it to Fred. He did the same then they continued on their way to the pub. As expected, it was rather noisy. Fred persuaded Anna to try her hand at a game of darts, but she was hopeless and gave up after the first game, so they sat at a long table near the windows overlooking the street. Fred went to the bar and bought two light lagers. Anna had never tasted beer before and pulled a face at the first mouthful.

"It's bitter, isn't it? Do you really like it, Fred?"

"It's an acquired taste, Anna. I often have a drink with Pa, but no more than three or four a week as I can't afford more than that."

They were joined at the table by a group of young people who were also drinking. Fred recognised Dennis Freeman, an old school chum from way back and felt pleased he had Anna by his side, thinking Dennis might suppose they were a twosome. But a note of wisdom entered his thinking and warned him not to act as if this were so, as it may turn Anna away from him. There was much laughter at the table as jokes and funny stories were shared, and Fred was able to tell about Bernie Ellis at *The Squire's Rest* and the high-kicking antics. An hour passed before Anna mentioned to Fred that she was getting a bit tired and maybe they should go home. Fred agreed because he wanted to have Anna all to himself once more. They said goodbye to everyone and left the pub.

Outside they linked arms and walked the short distance back to their homes. When they reached the lower landing in the building, Fred looked to see if anyone was around. No-one was, so he took the initiative and put his arms around Anna outside his parent's flat, as he'd done on Wednesday evening. But this time, instead of responding to him, Anna drew back, saying she really must go because it was getting late and she wanted to be fresh for Monday and her new job. Fred was taken aback and disappointed.

"Anna!" he asked softly as she started to go up the stairs, "will I be seeing you tomorrow for our Sunday walk? I thought we might go somewhere different this time."

Anna hesitated, smiled at Fred and replied, "I'll let you know tomorrow after lunch, Fred. It's nearly Christmas, and I want to make some new paper chains to hang up. The old decorations are faded, and parts are torn. We've had them for ages."

Fred looked at her, waved, and let her go. He went into his place and was relieved that his parents had gone to bed and that his mother would not be asking any questions.

Anna greeted her parents when she went into their apartment and immediately started to make up the sofa into the bed she slept in. This was taken as a hint by her father who said to Martha, "Let's turn in too, Love. We could do with a good sleep too."

Anna could not sleep. All sorts of thoughts tumbled around her head. *This is all happening too quickly. Fred seems to be getting serious about me. It's getting out of hand. I've only been back from Bristol for five weeks or so. I've landed a good job now, working in a beautiful place. I've been living alone before and supporting myself quite well. Do I really want to get involved with him? Do I want to have to struggle like my Mum and Dad have all their lives? The problem is, I like him. I like him a lot. He's such a charmer, and I liked it when he held me the way he did. Oh! dear! Should I go with him tomorrow or should I hold back a bit? I'll think about it in the morning.* Anna turned over and finally dropped off to sleep.

Fred could not sleep. Thoughts of long ago plagued his mind. Thoughts of the seventeen-year-old and the feeling of rejection and disappointment he'd suffered when that romance had been snuffed out. Would he have to suffer those feelings all over again? What was he doing wrong with Anna? He'd really felt she was getting interested in him. She'd lingered in his embrace outside the door on Wednesday. They'd laughed a lot together and so enjoyed their outings. Maybe he'd been pushing her too much to get involved. He'd wanted to kiss her this evening, and he'd felt her pulling back. He was asking himself why this was happening when he finally dropped off to sleep.

Christmas Decorations

Anna rose early from the sofa in the morning, pleased it was Sunday – it would give her a whole day to prepare herself for her new job on the Monday. She decided not to go walking with Fred in the afternoon; expected him to call on her after lunch, and she knew he would be disappointed, but her mind was made up. She also thought the short break would do them both good; they would have time to sit back and look at their situations realistically. Fred was supporting himself quite well from all accounts, and this new job of hers paid three pounds a year more than the Fergusons had paid her.

"Are you going out this afternoon?" asked Martha after breakfast, (really meaning, "Are you meeting Fred?") She'd been counting the times Anna and Fred had gone out together and was no less curious about a possible outcome of their friendship than Mary one floor below.

"No," answered Anna, a little curtly. "I've got a lot to do today to get ready for tomorrow. I must wash my hair, and where do you keep the boot polish? I'm not wearing my new boots. I haven't broken them in yet. I'll polish up my old ones again. After lunch, I'm making new paper chains for Dad to hang up. I bought the crepe paper through the week, red and green. Christmas colours."

"Good on you, Anna. Something I've been meaning to do for years," said Martha.

"And I'm also going to write a letter to Connie in Bristol to let her know about my new job," Anna added.

The morning passed, and Anna completed all her tasks with a little time to spare before her lunch. She relaxed for a while before her mother served up a ham sandwich and a cup of tea. Then she fetched the crepe paper, a pair of scissors and a pot of glue and laid these on the table.

A knock came on the door. Anna prepared herself to disappoint Fred, which she felt uncomfortable about. He stood with a hopeful look on his face when Anna opened the door.

"Anna," he said with forced joviality and a wide smile, "I hope you've decided to come. I thought we might go down to the new Hotel Russell so I could show you that marble staircase I was telling you about."

"Another time, Fred," answered Anna a little too firmly. "I'm making new Christmas decorations just now, and I'll be walking up another staircase tomorrow morning when I turn up for my new job."

Anna immediately regretted her insensitive reply when she noticed Fred's face fall, then she added more gently, hoping to soothe his offended feelings, "Don't worry, I'm really looking forward to walking your mother up that Russell staircase one day with you but at the moment I do have my mind on other things."

"Well, I'll let you get on with it then," said Fred with a hint of resignation in his voice, "and all the best for your new job. Let me know how it goes."

Anna thanked him and let him out the door with a smile; watched him for a little while as he started down the steps. When he reached his own place, he decided to go for a walk anyway and grabbed his overcoat and set out for the Tavistock Hotel, where he hoped to meet a friend and have a drink. On the way, he began to have misgivings about Anna's new job. While he was glad she'd found a position, he was sorry it was in such a grand place, where the well-off gathered and splashed around their money. *Anna's a lovely girl*, he thought, *and very attractive, bordering on beautiful. What if some wealthy young critter pays her attention and catches her interest?*

As he entered the Tavistock, he shrugged, knowing he could do nothing to change anything if that was meant to happen. He ordered an ale and settled on a lounge chair, hoping someone he knew would turn up. No-one did, so he stayed for another quarter-hour then returned home to prepare for the week's work ahead.

Anna settled down to the job at hand, cutting the coloured paper rolls into half-inch strips then into five-inch lengths. Martha joined in to help with the gluing and linking of alternate red and green pieces, and after a few hours, the Christmas decorations were ready for Sam to hang.

The Midland Grand Hotel

The following morning Anna rose early to prepare for her first day of work. She had her breakfast, dressed, put her hair up in a bun and grabbed her overcoat and handbag. Allowing a good half an hour to walk to work, knowing she would arrive at the hotel at least fifteen minutes early, she farewelled her parents and set out.

December was just around the corner and the air was chilly. She was glad there was no fog to delay her progress. She'd tested out her route two days before and was confident she would not be late, which could possibly mean instant dismissal if she was. She walked through the revolving door at the entrance to the Midland Grand Hotel at around a quarter past nine, and waited in the foyer for ten minutes before walking up the stairway to the Personnel office to see Mr Armstrong. He was expecting her when she knocked and entered the room. He asked her to sit and sign an employment contract. After this, he handed her a set of rules and regulations governing the behaviour and demeanour expected from the hotel's employees. Then he phoned for the lady in charge of room service staff. Mrs Reeves soon turned up and took charge of Anna, leading her to a room where she was provided with two uniforms. She was then led to a lift which surprised her. She had never been in one before and had thought the only access between the hotel's floors were steps. They ascended to the third floor. Mrs Reeves allocated Anna six rooms to be responsible for and outlined her duties.

There would be fireplaces to clean in the winter months, floors to be swept with a sweeper, dusting of furniture, beds to be made with clean sheets and pillowcases. Resting on an ornate table was a crystal water jug and two tumblers and a large porcelain bowl for hand and face washing. Water must be provided, and items kept clean. Fresh towels must be laid out. Directions for the two bathrooms on this level must be displayed on a smaller table where a vase with flowers sat. Fresh flowers must be renewed. And lastly, a chamber pot must be placed under the bed after emptying and cleaning the used one.

"You'll have to work hard, Miss Telford," said Mrs Reeves, "especially in winter with the fireplaces. Six rooms is a lot, you know."

"I'm sure I'll manage, Mrs Reeves," said Anna with a smile. "I've been a housemaid before, but I will have to watch the time with six rooms to do."

Mrs Reeves led Anna to another room where all the equipment needed for room servicing was kept and, after showing her the bathrooms, she gave Anna the room numbers and told her where to pick up the keys.

Anna set to work, keeping her eye on the time as she prepared the rooms for the guests who would check-in at 4 p.m. She was pleased to have finished her chores on time, although it had been a frantic rush. She went to the change room, redressed into her day clothes, dropped off the room keys and signed off for the day.

On the way home, she realised her job was an arduous one. She'd had to work like a beaver to get it all done in time. *I'll be glad to get home and put my feet up,* she thought.

The week passed, every day like the day before, a race against time to prepare the rooms for guests. She did not call in to see Fred through the week and give him a report as he'd asked her to do – she was just too tired. Nor did he knock on her door to enquire.

"Every new job takes a bit of getting used to," advised Martha. "In no time at all, you'll find it a lot easier, my dear. You'll see."

On Saturday evening, Fred decided not to call in and see Anna even though he wanted to. He'd felt hurt that she hadn't chosen to let him know about her job through the week.

Maybe the glamour of the place and the people she's meeting are more exciting than plain old Frederick Nash, eh? he told himself.

The following morning Fred slept in and rose at nine o'clock wondering whether he should go up to Anna's place and enquire how she was. He'd been doing a bit of thinking and realised he'd been acting like a jealous lover even though they were not lovers. He'd decided to give her the benefit of the doubt even if she was giving him the brush off for another reason. After all, they were neighbours, and his mother had always taught him to be pleasant to neighbours and get on with them. With this in mind, he decided he'd knock on her door after lunch to see how she was.

Ablutions

Anna had slept in even though her parents were clattering breakfast things around in the room. Her father woke her up when he brought her breakfast on a tray.

"I know you want a bath this morning, Anna. I'll get it ready for you after your breakfast and Mum and I will go out and call on Ivy and Doug down the street. We'll be back about eleven o'clock."

Anna ate her oatmeal and toast and sipped her tea while she thanked her father for the breakfast, and the bath he was to organise.

Sam brought out the hip bath from his and Martha's room and started to heat up two buckets full of water in separate vessels on the stove and fireplace. Anna fetched a towel, a washcloth and a cake of soap. A third bucket of cold water was at hand to add some to the hot water, and they all waited until the bath was ready. Sam and Martha put on their coats and left.

Anna washed her hair first with shampoo she'd bought at a chemist shop nearby, and then her body. She had to be quick as the water would usually get cold after a short time. A bath was a necessity rather than a pleasure, and Anna was pleased her father had placed the hip bath in front of the fire. She felt refreshed after she'd dried and dressed herself. Her father would bail out the bathwater when he returned and carry the buckets down to the laundry to empty them. The sofa looked inviting, and Anna read bits of the Sunday paper and relaxed until her parents returned. Sure enough, they were back by ten past eleven with news of their friends' comings and goings.

Anna wondered if Fred would call in to ask about her job. She felt a bit mean for having turned him down last Sunday and decided she'd go out with him after lunch if he wanted to. She helped her mother tidy up the room and get lunch ready. About two o'clock a knock came on the door and she opened it to see Fred standing with his overcoat, a striped muffler around his neck.

"Hallo," he greeted, in a forced casual manner. "I'm going out for my Sunday constitutional. I was wondering if you'd like to join me?"

'Yes, I'll come," answered Anna decidedly. "It looks like it's cold outside. I'll just grab my coat and scarf."

They said their goodbyes to Sam and Martha and walked down the steps to the pavement below.

"Where to?" asked Fred. "Got any ideas?"

"No, actually," replied Anna, "but this time, not too far. This job of mine is exhausting, and I was very tired today."

A Misunderstanding

"Sorry to hear your job's so tiring, Anna. I had the feeling this was a dream job for you in that place with all that splendour around you."

"You are so insensitive, Fred. I've hardly had the time to look at it, and besides, the décor of the place makes no difference to the amount of work I have to do." Anna looked away.

Fred realised he'd made his hidden fears influence his last comment and apologised, agreeing with her that he'd been unfair.

"You'd be the last person on earth I'd ever wish to offend, Anna, and if anyone understands hard work, it's me, so I should have known better. Let's go down to the Russell Hotel and I'll buy you a drink, and you can see the marble staircase."

"Alright," said Anna, placated, but she didn't link her arm in Fred's as he would have liked.

"Only three weeks to go before Christmas," said Fred, "and I'm going to bring Mum down to the hotel on Boxing Day and walk her up the stairs."

When they entered the hotel, and Anna viewed the marble, pillared staircase, she agreed with Fred that Mary should go up that staircase and she would love to be there to watch her do it.

They lingered in the hotel for a while after their drinks then crossed the road to walk in the park for a short time before going home. Fred felt disappointed at the way the afternoon had gone. He'd wanted to reconnect with Anna and enjoy the closeness they'd shared before, but it hadn't happened. They walked briskly up Tottenham Court Road as it was getting cold, and soon arrived at their address.

Fred touched Anna's shoulder and said, "I really hope the job gets easier for you this week, Anna. I'll be thinking of you when I'm working and I hope you'll be thinking of me."

Anna smiled wryly. "I guess we are just two workhorses, Fred. Maybe one day it will be better."

They walked up the steps and went into their apartments to prepare for the following week.

On Monday, Anna signed in at the Midland Grand Hotel, caught the lift to the third floor and went to the change room. She knew all the procedures by now and collected the keys to her allocated rooms. In the hallway to the first room, she bumped into Mrs Reeves, who was seeking her out. She told Anna she only needed to do four rooms as two would be vacant until Wednesday and Anna had already cleaned them on Saturday.

"So you'll hardly ever have to do six rooms in one day, Anna. If no guests book a room for certain days, then it's good luck for you. It was a test last week to see how you went, and you passed with flying colours. Some girls don't make the grade."

Anna could have kissed her! The thought of having to do all those rooms in one day had made her feel depressed; had sapped the life out of her. She thought of Fred and how distant she'd felt towards him yesterday as a result of her mood. Life was manageable now.

A Presumptive Guest

Anna collected all the cleaning things and took them to the first room, which she finished in record time. Then she went into the next room – the 'posh' one, she called it. It was a plush room with more expensive furnishings and exquisite wallpaper. Anna knew that important people, probably the wealthy, would be given this room. She cleaned the carpet with the sweeper and dusted the furniture before stripping the double bed. There was a knock on the door, and Anna opened it. A middle-aged man with greying hair, dressed in a well-tailored suit pushed passed her and entered the room.

"I've come back to get my umbrella. I always forget the blasted thing, and it's raining," he said curtly, striding over to the wardrobe.

Anna stood back to make way for him, and he retrieved his umbrella. On the way out, he looked at Anna and paused.

"Well! You're a bit of awright, aren't you, dearie? I see you're making the bed. How about I give you a hand, eh?" The man winked, "Then afterwards … eh?"

Anna noticed his expression turn into a lecherous grin and interrupted him. "I do not need your help, sir, and I'd like you to leave immediately."

"Well, who's the hoity-toity one, eh? Do you know who I am? I could buy and sell you over and over. I own a pretty big concern up north, and there's many that tip their hat to me when I pass."

"Well, I'm not one of them," retorted Anna quickly. "Now please go, or I'll report you to the management."

"And do you think that would do you any good?" the man asked roughly. "It'd be your word against mine. I've known a few sluts before, and no-one takes any notice of 'em."

"Now, just get out, you disgusting person …" Anna glared and raised her voice as she strode to the door and opened it wide, "… and if you don't go, I'm going to start screaming, I promise you."

The man walked slowly to the door, leering back at her. "You say one more word like 'disgusting' about me and I'll make it hard for you, Miss. I'll tell the people downstairs that you came onto me and were insolent as well. That might cost you your job, eh?"

The man left, and Anna watched him as he walked down the hallway to the lift. Then she burst into tears. It had all been too much: the hard week before – hurting Fred – and now the insults from this ghastly man. Her thoughts were in turmoil as she feared he might carry out his threat and tell lies about her. Just when Mrs Reeves had assured her that her workload would be easier and she'd felt better about things. Now this!

She walked over to a chair and sat down, trying to pull herself together and get her work done, come what may, when Mrs Reeves entered the room; she asked what had been going on as she'd heard loud, angry voices. Anna described the whole episode amid little sobs and expressed her worry that her job may be lost.

Mrs Reeves put her hand on Anna's shoulder and said, comfortingly, "I should have warned you, Anna. We've had a few types like him from all classes over the years – they treat the staff like dirt under their feet. But now we know about his offensive behaviour, I'll report this incident. This man's name will have a cross against it, and he will never be given a room here again. That's all we can do. If you get someone like that, leave the room at once and come and see me. Now you go down to the tea room and have a cup of tea, my dear. Your job is safe."

Anna was so grateful that Mrs Reeves had taken her side. She would know what to expect if that happened again, and she would not be upset in the future. She returned to the room she was cleaning after the cup of tea and resolved to make up for lost time.

She felt tired on the way home, the shock of that episode taking its toll on her; she debated whether or not to tell Fred about it. Perhaps not, but she would resume the friendship as it had been before and not shut him out anymore. He was such a lovely man, always treating her with consideration and respect. Maybe she would call on him through the week and let him know about the recent limitations on her workload. She knew he would be pleased.

A Visit From Anna

Feeling discouraged and disappointed over yesterday's outing to the Russell with Anna, Fred's thoughts tumbled as he made his way home after his day at the ironmonger's shop.

She still seems to be pulling away from me. It must be because she's tired, due to that awful job at the hotel. Maybe she can get something less taxing later on. I'll mention that to her next time I see her.

But when will that be?

Should I go up and see her through the week or will that be flogging a dead horse?

He climbed the steps to his flat, and Mary greeted him in the usual manner.

"'Ow was it today, Luvvie? Git yer dinner in ta yer. It's smoked 'addock, taters and peas ternight. I've been keepin' it warm for yer."

"That'll be good, Mum. Crikey, it's cold out there."

Fred looked at his mother and warmed to her. He was so glad of her constancy and love and the effort she always put in to feed her family. *She's a good old brick*, he thought.

Two more working days passed, and it was Wednesday evening. Anna knocked on Fred's door. Mary opened it and invited her in. She'd become aware that Anna and Fred had not been seeing each other much in the past couple of weeks, but kept her lips buttoned and invited Anna in to have a cup of tea with them. William heard the invitation and immediately put the kettle on the fire.

Fred was relieved when he heard of Anna's reduced workload and moved over to sit closer to her near the fire. There was a lot to say between them, but they were inhibited by William and Mary. Mary tried to be extra jolly, thinking this might help Fred's cause somehow.

But it was none of her business, as William had pointed out on more than one occasion. A half-hour passed, and Anna said she'd better go upstairs and get some sleep before tomorrow. Fred saw her out the door and was surprised when Anna whispered that she'd like to go for their usual walk next Sunday afternoon. She noticed the broad smile break out on Fred's face at her suggestion, but there was no hug as they said their goodbyes and wished each other a good night's sleep.

Mary's Pudding

The next afternoon, Mary put on her apron and made some space on the table. She'd had a hard time at the laundry that morning and felt tired when she arrived home, but that was not going to put her off. The job had to be done straight away. For two months she'd saved every penny she could, kept it in a treacle tin, so the money would be there to pay for Christmas dinner. All the ingredients for the pudding had been bought two days before. The recipe had been handed down to Mary from her mother, and Mary knew by heart how to make the pudding.

Yesterday afternoon, she'd chopped up one pound of raisins and one pound of currants and soaked them in just enough apple cider to soften the fruit overnight. She pulled out the mixing bowl with the fruit and started. Firstly, she fetched her set of scales then grated a pound of suet and added it to the fruit, then three ounces of sugar and one and a half ounces of grated lemon peel. She grated half a teaspoon of nutmeg and mixed it with one teaspoon of ground ginger and added it to the bowl with a quarter of a pound of flour. After mixing everything thoroughly, she set the bowl aside to wait for William and Fred to get home from work. When they'd both arrived, she set the bowl on the table and beat together six eggs in a separate bowl and added them to the mixture.

"Now, come on you two, yer gotta 'ave yer wish. Ere's the spoon and give i' a good stir. You first, Will. Make sure yer wish for a bi' more money for us next year, won't yer?"

William stirred the pudding clockwise according to tradition and made his wish, which agreed with Mary's suggestion.

"You next, Fred," urged Mary. She watched him as he took the spoon, closed his eyes and made his wish. *I know wot you'd be wishin' for, Fred*, she thought, making sure her face was a blank page.

After that small ceremony, Mary made sure the batter was not too thin, or too stiff, but just firm enough to put into the calico cloth. Then she tie the cloth up in a knot, leaving enough room for the pudding to expand when cooking.

William got busy lighting the fire and boiled up the water in a small cauldron. Then he carefully lowered Mary's pudding into the water. It would take four hours of cooking, and the water would have to be topped up now and then to keep it at the right level. After a couple of hours, William raised it up from the water for Mary to have a look.

"It's comin' on nicely," she noted. "It's swollen up well and the cloth's nice 'an tigh' over it."

William replaced the pudding in the pot, and they settled down to wait another two hours for the cooking to finish. They filled in time by having their tea, cleaning up the mess and then playing a couple of board games. Fred always won at Chinese Checkers, but Mary was a strong opponent. When the pudding was cooked and hung up on a hook to drain and cool, the family retired to bed.

A Positive Answer

The following Sunday, Fred collected Anna at half-past one, and they decided to stay close to home as the weather was freezing and both did not fancy a long walk.

"The Regent sounds nice," suggested Anna. "I'd like to go back to the lake and see if we can find somewhere sheltered to sit and watch the birds."

Fred agreed. "I think we may have a few things to talk about too."

Anna fell silent. She knew Fred had been falling for her since they'd met and she knew she had encouraged him by not physically pulling back on a couple of occasions when they'd hugged. She'd tried to resist him for a while and had worked out reasons why she should not get serious about him, even though she'd felt drawn to his embraces.

They entered the park and walked along the paths to the lake where they found a park bench under a large spreading oak tree.

"It's cold," declared Fred, "and I think we should cuddle up to get warm, don't you?" He looked at Anna as he put his arm around her without waiting for her reply.

"Yes," Anna agreed with a grin and moved closer to him.

Fred took her hand, and they sat for a while in silence while he summoned up his courage. He'd decided that Anna would either accept him or reject him, but he had to know just where he stood, the uncertainty driving him mad. He would rather have her say 'No' than live in false hope.

"To begin with," he said, "I have to admit that I was jealous when you got the job at such a swanky place. I imagined you'd be meeting chaps with a lot more going for them than me. I'm so sorry. And now

I've admitted I was jealous I suppose you know how I feel about you."

Anna gave him a serious look. "Fred, if you knew what I've been through in that place … with this vile fellow trying to seduce me then insulting me when I refused his advances … you might understand that all types book into that place. I was very upset and thank goodness Mrs Reeves came to my aid."

Anna explained the whole incident to Fred, who was mortified to think he'd misjudged the situation and possibly Anna. He was also angry.

"He'd have got a thumping big punch on the nose if I'd been there."

"Well," said Anna, "I'm just a room servicer there anyhow. No-one takes much notice of us."

Anna took up the thread of their previous conversation after Fred had apologised again.

"Well, Fred, if apologies are in order, I think I owe you one too. I've been erratic in the way I've treated you. I've been so mixed up since I came back from Bristol. I had a good job there in service even though I didn't like the lady, but I felt secure, just looking after myself. Now I'm back here in London, I see people struggling. Good, decent families like ours. People might be better off single, you know. Once they get married and have children, that's when the problems start."

Fred nodded. "That's true, but even so, life isn't perfect either way. On the one hand, single people feel secure by just looking after themselves, but they miss out in other ways. Our parents have both had a struggle, but they've made a life for themselves and survived. They've accepted their lot and been happy together, even with an occasional upheaval or disagreement. But I think that's the better choice."

Anna stared into space, considering Fred's comparisons. Then she said, "Your Mum's great at making the most of things, Fred. She's always so enthusiastic about everything, isn't she?"

"Yes, she is, Anna, and she always looks on the bright side."

Fred didn't want to continue talking about his Mum; he wanted to get to the point. "Anna," he said softly, looking into her eyes, "life will never be perfect for the likes of us, but I believe it will be easier and a lot more fun if we go through it together." He stroked a wisp of hair away from her eyes. "Marry me, my darling. I think you know how much I've fallen for you."

Anna's eyes crinkled up as she smiled at him. "Oh, Fred, I must confess, I find it hard to resist you when you give me those hugs. I've been attracted to you from the first time we met when we were going to get the Sunday papers that day, but it's all happened so quickly … almost like a dream."

"Let's keep the dream going," said Fred gently as he drew Anna into his embrace and kissed her. They stayed in each other's arms for a long time. Then Fred drew away and said, "You haven't given me an answer yet, my love. Yes or No?"

"It has to be yes because I can't resist you," Anna replied.

"Anything will be better than sleeping on that sofa, won't it?" asked Fred teasingly.

Anna laughed and agreed.

"And I've felt hemmed in living with Mum and Dad. I'll be glad to get out."

They sat under the oak tree, making plans. Firstly, they agreed to keep their commitment to themselves and surprise everyone on Christmas day. They discussed the money aspect. Fred had some savings in the bank, and Anna also had some money put aside. They would arrange to get married as soon as possible after Christmas. So much to do and organise.

The sky had clouded over and it started to sprinkle.

"Time to get going," said Fred, pulling Anna up from the seat. "We don't want to get drenched like last time."

They linked arms and fell into a little run until they became breathless. Still walking quickly, they arrived at Warren Street slightly damp and ran upstairs to their homes.

Christmas Plans and Carollers

Two weeks ago, Sam had hung up the red and green paper chains. Martha and Mary had agreed that their two families should spend Christmas time together this year, and they had planned the Christmas dinner. Mary had emptied out the treacle tin and bought a leg of pork in the afternoon for tomorrow's feast. Martha had shared in the cost of it. She had made some mince pies a few days ago. Both women had made a pudding. It was decided to have Mary's one and keep Martha's for New Year's Eve. There were to be no presents. Fred had bought a packet of Christmas crackers, and Anna had bought a box of chocolates to share. Also on the table was to be a bowl of stoned fruit and a bowl of mixed nuts, two rare treats. Martha had a bigger room in her flat and a larger table so they were to have Christmas dinner in her place. Mattie was coming, but Anna's brothers, George and Stephen, lived too far away. Anna had sent them two homemade greeting cards from the family.

On Christmas Eve, William, Mary and Fred finished their evening meal and relaxed by the fire with a cup of tea before doing the washing up. Then they heard the carols.

"Let's go down and join 'em," suggested Mary eagerly. "They come 'ere every Christmas Eve."

Fred dashed up the stairs and grabbed Anna. Her parents followed them to the street below where a group of carollers sang in harmony, 'Hark the herald angels sing, Glory to the newborn King.' William and Mary arrived shortly after. A crowd of familiar faces from their building and from other tenements nearby gathered. Everyone joined in, singing with gusto as the piano accordion player introduced different carols. After half an hour the carollers left to go elsewhere, and the crowd dispersed.

"That's what Christmas is all about," said Martha. "It's about love and family and celebrating the birth of Jesus."

Mary suggested they all have an early night because the next day was going to be busy.

Christmas Day 1899

Mary was out of bed early as there was a lot to do. She roused William and urged him to get up and get going. He'd wanted another half hour but she'd insisted, so he slowly crawled out from under the blankets. Earlier, he had visited the privy below and reported to Mary that there was a bit of a blizzard blowing and it was snowing.

"Only light, mind you, but freezin' cold."

They knocked on the door to the other room, entered, and rekindled the fire in the grate. All the noise woke Fred, who turned over to get in another half hour like his father had wanted, but Mary was relentless.

"Now, git up, m'lad, It's all 'ands on deck today. Yer got to carry fings upstairs la'er on, so let's 'ave brekkie and then get busy."

Upstairs the others were bustling about too. After their breakfast, Anna removed the bedding from the sofa and put the cushions back. Sam got the oven going in preparation for Martha to bake the pork. He lit the fire in the fireplace for warmth. Anna got out her mother's best white damask tablecloth and cleared the table of some littered items before spreading the cloth onto it. She arranged a display of artificial holly with red berries in a vase for a centrepiece. Plates and cutlery were laid out in readiness. Mary, downstairs, was to do the vegetables and boil up her pudding for an hour and make the custard. Christmas dinner was planned for noon.

"I do 'ope Mattie's wrapped 'erself up well to walk 'ere," murmured Mary as she peeled the vegetables with Fred's help. William boiled up the water in the small cauldron and the pudding was already heating up. He'd lit the stove for baking the vegetables in the dripping left over from previous cooking.

Mattie arrived at half-past eleven bearing small gifts for everyone.

"It's only lavender water for the Mums and beer mugs for the men," she explained after Mary mildly roused on her for breaking the 'no presents' rule.

Upstairs, the pork was in the oven, and Anna had made some apple sauce. She'd also laid out the Christmas crackers, the bowls of fruit and nuts, and the mince pies.

Fred carried up the four chairs from his flat and with the four chairs in the upper flat, they all had seating for the feast, which was just about ready. William took up the roast vegetables while Sam carved the meat. Martha finished off the gravy.

Everyone agreed it was fitting to say grace on such a day then they all tucked in, their plates piled high, and Mary checking they all had a bit of crackling. After the roast, they rested for a while before the pudding arrived from downstairs, proudly carried up on a platter by Fred. William fetched the custard. A small bottle of brandy, provided by William, was poured liberally over the pudding before lighting it. While it was engulfed in blue flames, they all wished each other "Merry Christmas!" and Mary remarked, "Too much brandy, Will … we'll all git drunk!"

Everyone had a good time in the warm, cosy, festively decorated room. They'd eaten their pudding and agreed it was a delicious one and not soggy. William handed out the crackers, and they pulled hard on the ends, enjoying the little explosions, the corny jokes inside, and the paper hats.

Fred sat near Anna, and gave her a nudge and a wink, and whispered, "Now!"

When there was a lull in the conversation, he took advantage of the silence.

"I have something to tell you all," he said with a slightly nervous smile. He took hold of Anna's hand. "… and I won't waste words. In short, Anna and I have decided to get married."

"Well, I never!" said Mary, her eyes wide open in mock surprise. "Oo'd 'ave thought i'?"

The others crowded around congratulating the couple on their engagement, although there was no engagement ring. It was going to cost enough for just the wedding ring. Mattie asked if they'd set a date for the wedding. Anna replied it would be as soon as they could make arrangements in the new year. Everyone was thrilled by the news and offered to help how ever they could. Anna looked at her mother and noticed she had tears in her eyes. *I'm sure from joy*, she thought.

At four o'clock, Mattie said her goodbyes and left the party to battle through the terrible weather and return to Kensington. William poured brandy for the men, and Martha made a pot of tea for the women. Anna passed around the chocolates.

"It's been a lovely Christmas," said Martha, "and all the nicer because my girl's getting married."

They were all tired after the big day and the feasting. Martha and Mary cleared the table and did the washing up in turns with Fred and Anna drying the dishes. The chairs and Mary's things were carried down to the flat below, and the celebrations came to a close.

"Don't forget we're going to the Hotel Russell tomorrow, Mum," reminded Fred. "It's Boxing Day, and I promised to take you there to see the marble staircase. And you're going to walk up it. Remember? Anna's coming too."

"Oh! my Goodness. I'd forgo' all abou' i'," said Mary a little worried. She moved to the door to her and William's bedroom. Then she came down to earth.

"Come on, Will … come and git some sleep. The day after tomorrer, it's back to work for all of us."

The Marble Staircase

Everyone had slept in on Boxing Day. After a late breakfast, Fred went upstairs to see Anna and set a time for their walk to the Hotel Russell. They decided to leave at two o'clock. When Fred returned, Mary was fussing over the clothes she should wear to such a grand place, saying, "it ain't like I'm jus' goin' to the grocer's shop, is it? An' it's cold today, ain't i'?" She poked around the back of her wardrobe and brought out a black, gored, woollen skirt she'd forgotten about. Then she took out a blue, woollen high-necked blouse with leg o' mutton sleeves. "An' I'll throw tha' grey woollen shawl over i' all, an' I'll put on that li"le blue 'at I go' years ago when we went to that christenin' at Whitefields, remember, Will?"

William nodded as he brought out his only suit of clothes which was becoming slightly frayed at the cuffs.

Fred picked up Anna just after two o'clock and invited her to call in to see Mary in all her finery.

"Will I do, Anna?" asked Mary, looking self-conscious. "I 'aven't worn this skir' for years. Is it still in fashion?"

"You look lovely, Mrs Nash. The skirt is fine, and I just love your hat."

Fred reported, "The snow has melted away from yesterday, and the sun is shining. Let's get going."

They walked along Warren Street and turned into Tottenham Court Road, and soon arrived at The Hotel Russell. Mary composed herself, drew a deep breath and entered the foyer on William's arm. Fred and Anna followed behind. Mary's eyes took in all the glamour and splendour of the place while trying to appear casual as wealthy guests wandered in and sat down on chesterfield couches. Some went up the staircase.

"Jus' look at them marble pillars," muttered Mary to William through semi-closed lips, not wanting to reveal she was impressed. Fred overheard her and reminded her that she'd soon be walking up the staircase herself, along with anyone else going up.

"Cor lumme!" she murmured as an elegant woman in a highly coloured brocaded frock with an expensive fur stole and a beaded handbag swept passed them. The woman sailed up the staircase, paused at the top landing, turned around and observed the foyer with an imperious look before disappearing up the next level.

"Alright, Mum," said Fred, "you're going up now. And you're doing it all on your own. When you get to the landing, wait there, and we'll come up and join you."

"All them toffs goin' up an' me in these clothes?" asked Mary, with a small tremor in her voice.

"Go on, Mum," encouraged Fred, squeezing her arm. "You can do it."

Mary hesitated, then took a few small steps towards the staircase; she took another deep breath and walked slowly across to the first step. She turned, looked at Fred, Anna and William, who all smiled and nodded at her. Mary took the first step up. An elegantly dressed young couple mounted the stairway along with Mary, whose passage was slower than the young ones.

I'm goin' up, she thought with determination. *I can't disappoint 'em.*

She watched the young couple ahead of her proceed up with confidence, then step by hesitant step, Mary mounted the staircase. She reached the landing, relaxed her shoulders and let out a small sigh of relief. She'd done it! With a faint smile, she turned around to look at William, Fred and Mary below and signalled them to join her. When they were on the landing with her, Mary had lost her inhibitions and marvelled over the ornate chandelier over the foyer, the colours, the wallpapers, the carpet.

"I' looks be"er from up 'ere," she said.

After they'd been on the landing for a few minutes, Mary suggested they'd better go back down and start off for home as they all had to get ready for work tomorrow.

"No!" insisted Fred. "We're going into that room over there. It has a bar and I promised you and Dad I'd buy you a drink, remember? That includes you too, Anna."

They walked into the lounge and sat down on beautifully carved chairs at a large oak table. Fred and William went to the bar, ordered a pint of ale each and lemonade for the women and carried them back.

"Well, how was it, Mrs Nash, going up those stairs?" asked Anna, with a curious smile. "You seemed to have managed it quite well."

"I go' up there orright' Anna, and I've been finkin' about i' all, an' I reckon tha' finkin' about sumpfin' is worse than the doin' of it sometimes. An' me legs got me up just as good as that posh li"le couple goin' up before me. So if me legs are just as good as theirs fer goin' up, then I reckon the rest o' me is just as good too."

"You're dead right, Mum," Fred affirmed.

The other three agreed and said they were very proud of her. After another twenty minutes, William mentioned he was feeling tired and thought they should go home now and rest up for work.

"It's been a luvverly couple of days, 'asn't it, but tirin' jus' the same," commented Mary, "an' yer do look knackered Will."

They retraced their route back home, passing the newly built church where the old Whitefields Tabernacle once stood.

"I have the feeling we'll be going there one day, Fred," said Anna. "I heard you sing on Christmas Eve when the carollers called round. You have a lovely voice."

"Asn't ee?" agreed Mary proudly. "An' I've go' a photo of 'im in choir robes when 'ee was about fifteen."

The subject then turned to the upcoming wedding and all the arrangements.

"Anna and I have agreed it's going to be soon, with very little fuss and as cheap as possible," announced Fred pointedly. "Just the family and a few friends."

"An' when yer dress up, Anna, you gotta 'ave somefin' old,

somefin' new, somefin' borrowed and somefin' blue," insisted Mary.

"I'm sure I can arrange that, Mrs Nash. I know it's an old tradition," said Anna with a smile.

"Ere we are at last," said William with a sigh as they reached their building. Even though his home was small, he was always glad to get back from somewhere and enjoy its simple comforts.

"An' there's somefin' we've all forgotten about," he reminded the others before they mounted the steps. "In a week it's New Year's Eve, and not only tha', bu' it's the star' of a brand-new century. The year nineteen 'undred is just around the corner. Imagine that!"

"Yes!" enthused Fred. "We can leave the old behind us and start out on the new, eh?"

They reached the first floor. Fred gave Anna a hug before she went further up, and Mary and William said their goodbyes to her with a wave and a smile.

"Now git busy Will and make us a cuppa. I go' tripe and onions ter cook for dinner," said Mary.

Mr Dobson's Generosity

Next morning, Fred arrived early at the shop, finding it easier to get out of bed now. He credited this to Anna, and a small rush of excitement would surge as he thought of his upcoming marriage. He had a future now with the girl he loved, and his step was lighter, his smile broader.

"There's two ways of thinking about it, Ada," said Ernie Dobson as Fred walked through the door to start work. "Some say the twentieth century doesn't start until the year 1900 has finished, and others say it's starting next week. Good morning, Fred, did ya have a nice Christmas?"

Fred gave Ernie and Ada a good account of his Christmas then told them of his upcoming marriage.

"*Now* I know what's been going on," declared Ada. "There were some days when I could see you had your mind on something, Fred, and I even wondered if it could be a girl. I'm very pleased for you."

"Congratulations, m' lad," said Ernie, beaming, as he shook Fred's hand. "How old are ya? Thirty, I think. It's about time, eh?"

"It certainly is!" agreed Fred.

He was glad it was a short working week like the previous week as New Year's Day was the following Monday, which meant a public holiday. The rest of the week passed quickly as he threw himself into his work in a new frame of mind. He was let off early on Saturday and arrived home at six o'clock. He bounded up the steps to give Anna some good news: old Ernie Dobson had pressed an envelope into his hand as he left the shop, and he'd opened it on the way home. Fred grinned widely – the extremely generous bonus gift would help fund the wedding – and Anna felt gratified when Fred told her of Dobson's generosity.

New Year's Eve

The next day was New Year's Eve, the eve of the New Millennium. London buzzed with excitement. Mary enjoyed a cup of tea with Martha at half-past four while Will and Sam drank in the new year at *The Squire's Rest*. The two women had become closer since their children's engagement on Christmas Day.

"We're goin' to be relations now, Marfa," Mary had said when she'd called on her through the week to borrow a cup of sugar.

Anna had been out for a while, but arrived home when the tea was still hot in the pot, so she poured a cup and told her mother and Mary she and Fred were going out that evening to celebrate. "We're going to buy some food from a street barrow and get a cup of hot cocoa from somewhere."

Soon after she grabbed her overcoat and a muffler, wished the two mothers a happy new year, planted a kiss on their cheeks and left to pick up Fred. They were off to join the celebrations in London.

Mary and Martha continued chatting for some time, excited at the coming wedding and making plans of their own.

"I'm going through everything I have," said Martha. "I've got some extra things I don't need that they could use."

Mary thought hard. "I 'ave too. I'm gunna give Anna this big, gawdy vase me aunt give me when I got married. She said it migh' be a genuine antique. I ain't never used i'. On the uvver 'and, Anna migh' be offended. She migh' think I'm off loadin' it ter get rid of it, bu' maybe she'll like it. I'll 'ave ter think abou' it."

William and Sam arrived home, and the women's chit chat broke up as it was time to get the evening meal going.

"There's a bi' of brandy left after the puddin'," said William. "Enough for all of us ter welcome in the new year a' midnight."

A Walk to St Paul's

Fred and Anna walked hand in hand to *The Squire's Rest*. The place was crowded, standing room only, and they stayed just long enough to awkwardly manage a drink. Then they took a long walk to St Paul's Cathedral to see what was going on there, buying a pork pie, a baked potato and a slice of gingerbread from a Barrowman on the way. Further on, they bought a cup of steaming hot cocoa from another barrow.

"There's a bench over there," said Fred, pointing to a seat just inside a small square. "Let's put our feet up for a bit."

When they'd finished their food and drink, Fred put his arm around Anna; she leaned on his chest, turned her head and they kissed passionately. Few people roamed in the park, most people in the streets walking to venues of celebrations, so Fred and Anna cuddled up against the cold and enjoyed this rare chance for the closeness they both yearned for.

"What about our parents?" asked Anna. "How will they be able to live without our help?"

"Well, your Mum and Dad managed before you came back from Bristol. They both have jobs and a roof over their heads and they haven't starved, have they? And my Mum and Pa have done alright so far with me living with them, and I know Pa has put away most of what I've given them for rent along with their funeral fund. They have that to fall back on. And Mum has always been great with managing the purse. We've had simple food, God knows, but we haven't starved either, except for that time when I was a boy and Mum got sick for a while. We were hungry then. That's the only worry, Anna. Everything's alright until sickness comes and one can't work anymore, but we mustn't worry about our parents. They are battlers; they are survivors. They know how to get by."

"What about us, Fred?" said Anna, a small frown creasing her brow. "What if one of us gets sick?"

"While ever I'm loving you. my darling, I'll never get sick. Your love will keep me alive. And my love for you will keep you going."

They rose and, hand in hand joined the people making their way to St Paul's.

A man bumped into Fred and apologised. Fred grinned at him. "That's alright, old chum," he said. "Not surprising. It's so crowded."

The two men started chatting and the man showed Fred a column in a newspaper he carried. "Can you believe it? This is from the *New York Herald* and this bloke, Alfred E Henschel, reckons in this coming century, 'locomotion in the air will be as common as bicycle riding is now'."

"Go on!" remarked Fred. "I find that hard to believe."

Anna mentioned it couldn't happen because of gravity. "The person who believes that is barmy!"

The conversation continued, the man asking if Fred and Anna had ever ridden in those new-fangled motor cars.

"There'll be more of them on the road soon. They run on gasoline, not on steam like before."

Anna and Fred mentioned that they'd seen quite a few and that wealthy people drove them around.

"They're dangerous, and they frighten the horses," said Anna with concern. "It's a safer world without them."

A great number of people had gathered in front of St Paul's. Fred and Anna finally arrived and joined in the festivities. Excitement and a sense of expectation hung in the air. A band played well-loved melodies and current songs and everyone sang. Stalls sold food and drink. Soon Big Ben would ring in the new century and fireworks would light up the night sky. With all this anticipated, everyone quietened down as midnight drew near. Only five minutes to go, then four, three, two, then one. The countdown began. Suddenly in the distance, yet quite clear, the chimes of Big Ben rang in the New Year and the New Century. At the twelfth chime, a huge roar erupted, and the fireworks began. People embraced and kissed, and the strains of *Auld Lang Syne* broke out. Many gazed up at the glow of the fireworks, the rockets launched from the Embankment not far away.

The Year 1900

Fred and Anna held each other close, unaware of the clamour around them.

"A new beginning, my darling, starts now," said Fred, and he noticed the tears in Anna's eyes. "It's the year 1900 and the year of our wedding, my love. It's already Monday, the first of January! Let's get our heads together and plan everything. The first thing I'm going to do is to find us somewhere to live close to our jobs and …"

"Hold back a bit, Fred," said Anna gently. "It's been a big night, and there's plenty of time tomorrow to talk. I'm excited too, you know, but let's get a good night's sleep first, eh? or what's left of it." Anna linked her arm in Fred's, stretched up a little and gave him a quick kiss on the cheek.

The walk back home from St Paul's seemed longer than it had been in getting there. Quiet had descended on their building when they finally arrived, most everyone had already gone to bed. Far off though, they could still hear people celebrating. They said goodnight, tiptoed up the steps to their homes and flopped into their beds.

In the morning, many people were holding street parties, but Fred and Anna and their families slept in late. There was much cleaning and many chores to do in the two households in preparation for the working week ahead. Later on, the afternoon was free and Fred and Anna linked up and walked to Regent's Park; sat on the same bench where Fred had proposed, and outlined their wedding plans. Fred hoped he could find a place close enough for them to walk to work as public transport would take up much of their earnings.

"I'll be asking customers in the shop if they know of any vacancies around here and I'll also be seeing agents," Fred said eagerly. "Places often become vacant for lots of reasons. As soon as we find somewhere, we'll get married straight away and move in."

"I have the feeling something will turn up soon, Fred," said Anna, placing her hand on his arm. "Let's just be patient and not force things. It'll happen soon."

They walked back home after a short walk to the kiosk for a drink. The next day, it was back to work.

A Place to Live

It was another pea-souper the next day, but Fred arrived at work on time. Ada greeted him with a big smile and asked him to bring Anna into the shop to select a complete dinner and cutlery set from their range of gift items. Ernie joined in.

"Fred, you can go through the shop and take pots and pans and any kitchen things you want to get yourselves set up with. I'm a bit overstocked just now."

Fred was overwhelmed by their generosity and thanked them greatly. Then he started enquiring about housing, asking customers, but to no avail that day. And no luck with local agents either. He felt disappointed and discouraged after a week of no breakthroughs.

When having a drink at *The Squire's Rest* after work, a fellow told him of a place in Regent's Square not far from St Pancras railway station which would soon be available. Friends of his parents lived there and were moving shortly to Chichester, Sussex. Fred took down the address and made his way there in haste, hoping the place had not already been taken.

First floor. That's good. It's not the basement, he thought as he knocked on the door. He wouldn't put Anna in any basement flat. They were usually gloomy, partly unventilated and full of dampness and mould.

He rapped on the door again, and a woman answered his knock.

"Good evening. My name is Frederick Nash. I have been told by Archie Goodwin whose parents you know, that you are moving to Chichester shortly. Is that correct?" Fred asked, hopefully.

"Yes, that's true. We're moving out on the twenty-seventh of this month. Are you interested in renting this place?" the woman answered.

"Yes, I am. It looks ideal. Archie told me it has two rooms, and it's close to where my future wife works," Fred said eagerly.

"I'll give you the landlord's address," said the woman, and she went inside and returned with the address written on a piece of paper. "He'll show you inside. Good Luck!"

Fred thanked her, took his leave and walked down the few steps to the pavement. With a sense of urgency, he hurried to the landlord's address about half a mile away. He was puffed out when he arrived and spent a minute collecting his breath before knocking on the door. He introduced himself to a lean, serious-looking man, and explained how he'd just spoken to a lady in Regent Square who was moving out and how he needed somewhere soon due to his impending marriage. The man invited him in and proceeded to lay down a few rules and regulations before Fred could consider signing a lease.

"To begin with, I will require a character reference from you and your intended wife. Next, a statement of your earnings and thirdly, you are not to occupy the place until you are married. And there will be a bond of course. And you are to understand that any drunken or riotous behaviour will see you evicted without notice. I will show you through the place after I've made arrangements with the present tenants and if you meet the requirements, it's yours, and you can sign the lease."

Fred readily agreed to the conditions, and he and the landlord shook hands, a verbal contract. Fred promised to bring the references the next evening. He couldn't wait to tell Anna he'd found a place.

It was nine o'clock when he reached home.

Hoping Anna and her family were not yet in bed, he quietly knocked on the door. Anna answered. Sam and Martha had retired; Anna had been sitting on the sofa thinking about making it up and going to bed too. Fred flopped on the couch and pulled Anna down to sit near him. He took her in his arms.

"My darling," he quietly explained after he'd kissed her, "I've finally found a place, and it's not too far away from the Midland Grand Hotel in St Pancras."

He went on to tell about the evening's events. "You will need to get your reference from Fergusons and a statement of your present earnings. Then he and Anna said their goodnights and Fred went down to his flat.

Mary poked her head out of her bedroom door when he entered and said in a worrying voice, "Where the dickens 'ave ya been, Fred? Ya 'aven't 'ad ya dinner yet. It's corn beef an' cabbage bu' you'll 'ave ter eat i' cold now. Wot's been goin' on, Fred?"

"I'll tell you tomorrow, Mum. There's nothing to worry about, only good news. Go back to bed."

Mary obeyed, having been woken from her sleep at Fred's homecoming. He ate his cold dinner and also retired.

The next afternoon, the landlord called into Dobson's Ironmongery. He told Fred the tenants had agreed on an inspection for the following Sunday afternoon at three o'clock. They could show him their references and earning statements then.

"I'm excited, Fred," said Anna, with a couple of small jumps on the spot, after he'd told her about inspecting the flat next Sunday. "Now I want us to dress nicely so the fellow can see we are respectable people and not ruffians."

It all happened so quickly when they inspected the flat. It was neat and tidy and importantly, no mildew or mould on walls and ceilings.

"And there's a gas stove," observed Anna, impressed. "That will make life easier."

The landlord read the two references and examined their earning statements and was satisfied. The rental price was discussed and agreed to. It would take about a quarter of the combined earnings of Fred and Anna, but this was the usual proportion for an average working couple. The lease was quickly signed. The key would be dropped in to Fred at the shop on Saturday afternoon, the twenty-seventh of January after the present tenants vacated the day before.

"You can move your stuff in the next day, and when you're a married couple, you can move in," said the landlord in a slightly censorious tone.

"I'm going to make floral curtains for the windows and get some mats for the floor," said Anna excitedly.

"And I'm going to order in a comfortable double bed," said Fred with a wink as he looked at Anna.

"But we're going to have to get married first, Fred, and we're going to have to organise the wedding pretty quickly. Now let me count. Today is the fourteenth of January … we could get married on the first Saturday after the twenty-seventh after they move out." Anna counted on her fingers. "There's only three weeks to go before we can move in. Our wedding day should be the third of February, the day before!"

"I'll ask Dobbo tomorrow if I can take an hour or so off to go to the Registry Office at the Strand and make that date. And we'll have to go somewhere to buy a wedding ring too."

"I just want a basic ceremony, no fuss, and as little expense as possible," insisted Anna.

"I'll make a list of all the things we'll need to set up home," added Fred. "The Dobsons are being so kind. They said you could go to the shop and pick out a dinner set and a cutlery set from the stock."

Anna was overwhelmed. "People have been so kind. Mrs Reeves said I could have a few days off to get married, too."

The interval before their marriage passed quickly as all the hurried particulars were finalised. Ernie Dobson promised Fred that he'd deliver all the things they needed to the flat with old Bessie and the cart.

"We've never had kids, Ernie," said Ada, "and you know, I've always had a soft spot for young Fred. Let's help them all we can to get started."

Ernie readily agreed.

Preparing for the Big Day

Fred had been to the registry office and booked the date for Saturday, February 3rd at twelve noon. He'd paid the £2 fee, which everyone thought was exorbitant. He and Anna had gone to a jewellery shop near St Pancras Railway station and bought a simple gold wedding ring.

Anna had decided on her outfit: a smart white blouse she already had, the sleeves of which were quite full, having superseded the leg o' mutton ones worn in the early nineties. She would buy a new skirt in medium blue and a full-brimmed hat, either blue or white. And she would wear the new boots Mrs Ferguson had given her when she'd left her employment in Bristol.

"Well," said her mother, "now you've got to get something old, something borrowed and something blue. The boots will be the new thing. You can wear my cameo brooch, which is blue with the white lady's profile. You know the one. Would you like that?"

"Yes," replied Anna, "that'll be nice at my throat."

Later on, Mary told Anna she could borrow the white lace gloves she hadn't worn in years. But the old item was a problem until Martha offered an old petticoat of hers, still in good condition.

Fred's grey suit was taken out and dusted down. William and Mary bought him a new shirt and a cravat and a smart waistcoat in dark blue. The local tea room around the corner had been booked for half-past one on February 3rd.

At Dobson's Ironmongery, Ada had been caught up in all the excitement. Then she had an idea.

"Ernie, you know that small cottage your brother Norm has in the backyard of his place on the edge of Hampstead Heath? Go and ask him if they can have that for a couple of nights after they get married, eh? That'd be a lovely little honeymoon for 'em, don't you think? They don't have much, and I think they deserve that, eh?"

Ernie hesitated at first but was won over by Ada's persuading.

A New Home

Fred and Anna had gone to a furniture shop and bought a double bed and mattress, pillows, a cheap wardrobe, two chairs and a small table which was delivered to the ironmongery shop and stored in a shed in the yard. Mrs Reeves had donated some sheets and pillowcases, two blankets and a bedspread from old stock from the hotel.

Things were going to plan. The flat at Regent Square was vacated on Saturday, the twenty-seventh of January. The next morning old Bessie was hitched up to the loaded cart at the shop. Ernie and Ada climbed up to the driver's seat and Bessie got going, arriving at the flat at eleven o'clock. They all worked hard, and in two hours the flat was furnished. Anna fixed the floral curtains at the windows which she'd hand-sewn, and scattered a couple of cheap mats she'd bought at a jumble sale. Ada spread a tablecloth over the table and set out the charming dinner set patterned in yellow roses which Anna had selected from the shop.

"In six days, I'll be a married man with a gorgeous wife," Fred announced, grinning at Anna and raising his eyebrows a couple of times.

"Yes," said Anna happily. "Soon we'll be an old married couple!"

Ernie observed Fred would have a longer walk to work from Regent Square and offered him an old bike he hadn't ridden in years, promising to look at the tyres and get some new inflated ones fitted if needed.

Finally, the flat was prepared for occupancy. Everyone set off for home. Only five working days to go and then the wedding … on the 3rd of February, 1900.

The Wedding

By eleven o'clock Anna was dressed in her wedding clothes. She'd decided to please Fred and not do her hair up in a bun under her new hat, but let her hair ripple down to her waist. Her mother had used a set of heated tongs to emphasise the curl. Fred had surprised her with a bouquet of Lily-of-the-Valley flowers delivered to her door. He had dressed in his suit with his new shirt, waistcoat and cravat. Nervously he hurried his mother as she finished dressing.

Fred, Anna and their parents walked down the stairs to the pavement below. A small group from their building had gathered to wish the young couple good luck and bestow their blessings. The wedding party walked to the bus stop at the end of Warren Street. According to schedule, the horses and carriage arrived in good time to deliver them to the Registry Office stop at the Strand by noon.

They waited in a vestibule while another couple were being married. Then it was their turn. Fred and Anna went through the formalities without a hitch. They signed the register in the presence of two staff witnesses and were declared husband and wife: Mr and Mrs Frederick Nash. Congratulations rang out all around and their parents hugged and kissed them. Anna noticed her mother's tears and hugged her harder. They left the building and made their way to the bus stop to travel back to Warren Street, where they walked to the tea room where Mattie, Anna's brothers, George and Stephen, and a few friends were waiting.

It was not an elaborate affair, just a bowl of soup to start, followed by mixed sandwiches and an assortment of small fancy cakes. Martha had made a wedding cake which the café had permitted her to bring to the table. William had brought along a bottle of sherry to toast the bride and groom, and the party was under way. The usual speeches took place – from the fathers of the bride and groom – and the last one from Fred, who pledged his undying love for Anna. Other patrons in the tearoom joined in with congratulations when Fred and Anna together cut the cake. Cups of tea or coffee were served to finish off the occasion. Sam and Fred settled the bill with a bit of help from William. Everyone left the tearoom joyous.

The wedding party arrived back at Warren Street at three o'clock. Fred and Anna dashed up the stairs to their parents' flats and changed their formal clothes for warm day wear, and grabbed their coats and mufflers. They had packed a light overnight bag each and left their families with hugs and kisses before setting out to catch the omnibus to Hampstead Heath. The bus stop was close to the cottage where they were to stay for two nights.

"Enjoy yerselves, both of youse, 'an 'ave fun," Mary shouted after them enthusiastically.

William shot her a sharp glance, which Mary noticed, and added, "Well, they're goin' up to 'appy 'amstead, ain't they, Will?"

Two Days at the Heath

It was the last month of winter and Fred and Anna linked their arms and walked briskly to the bus stop. In just over an hour, they arrived at their address. Ernie Dobson's sister-in-law had done them proud. There was a plate of mixed cold meats and cheese on the table with butter and bread for their tea, along with griddle scones and a pot of jam. A fireplace sported a good supply of newspaper, kindling, coal and matches. In the other room, a large comfortable bed had been made up with fresh white linen, warm blankets, an eiderdown and comfortable pillows.

Fred lit the fire and dragged two armchairs close by to catch the warmth.

"I can't take it all in, Mrs Nash. Are you really my wife, or am I going to wake up and find this is all a dream?"

"It's real, Fred, and we have two days to get used to it," answered Anna, tousling his hair.

"It won't be a hard job to get used to it," said Fred dreamily. "I tell you what, Anna, I'm knackered after these last few weeks and you must be too. We'll get a pot of tea going to have with our meal and after that, let's have an early night."

Anna agreed. When they had eaten, they went into the bedroom and changed into their nightwear. Martha had bought Anna a white flimsy nightgown which Anna had coyly donned.

Fred held out his arms and Anna walked slowly over to him and they held each other close.

Suddenly they started to giggle.

"Come to bed, Mrs Nash."

So they walked to the bed. Anna climbed in first and waited for Fred to extinguish the two oil lamps. Then he climbed in and took Anna in his arms.

The Next Morning

We won't be seeing much of the Heath today," said Fred as he looked out the window. Rain had fallen all through the night and it was still wet and miserable at ten o'clock.

"It'll probably clear up later on," suggested Anna. "Let's have our breakfast and then see what it's like."

"If it's still pelting down, we could always go back to bed, couldn't we?" said Fred with a grin and a wink.

"It may be one way of keeping warm, eh?" said Anna with a laugh.

"More than that, my girl!"

"Stop it, Fred. You know I want to see the Heath. People have told me it's lovely in winter too, and sometimes it snows up here."

At about eleven o'clock, when the rain stopped, they ventured outside, letting themselves out of a small gate at the back of the allotment. Then they walked along a muddy track through an extensive field.

"It's rougher here than I thought," Anna noted as she viewed the row of trees on a ridge they were approaching.

"We're climbing up there and then walking along to Parliament Hill where I can show you a wonderful view of London," Fred advised.

"Look at the rabbits, Fred. Over there. Oh! they've disappeared. Did you see them?"

"No, but keep looking. You can see foxes and squirrels sometimes, and birds, kingfishers and jackdaws. It's a great place for wildlife, you know."

They walked hand in hand, avoiding low bushes and tracts of muddy sand as they made their way to the hill. Soon they arrived and sat on a park bench to catch their breath.

"It's a bit misty but squint your eyes and you might see St Paul's, Anna," Fred suggested as he drew her close.

"Yes, I can see it, but only just. We'll have to come up here in summer when we can get a better view."

Fred pulled Anna to her feet and suggested they walk back along the ridge to have a look at some of the ponds. To their right and down the slope they came across a stretch of water where Anna noticed some men in the water.

She squealed, "It's winter, Fred – they must be freezing."

"They swim all through the year, Anna, even in London. They break the ice with a hatchet and go into the Serpentine there. Come on, let's find a pub and have a bite of something and a coffee."

They retraced their steps to their cottage, walked past the main house and out into the street where they found a cosy little pub with a fire blazing. They stayed for some time after eating, warming their hands and enjoying the comfort of the place. Then they set out on another walk, this time in a northerly direction.

"It's a bit of a hike but I want you to see an enormous mansion," said Fred. "It was built round about sixteen hundred and something, for some rich blighter."

They wandered through a patch of wooded glades and open fields, up small hills and rough terrain until they arrived at Kenwood House.

"Why, it's huge," exclaimed Anna, her eyes open in wonderment at the sprawling white mansion. "Look at the entrance with those lovely columns, and what an enormous front lawn."

"Yes, it's got quite a history, you know," added Fred.

"Well," said Anna with a laugh, "our mansion of two rooms is not quite so large, but we'll be happy in it, I'm sure, my darling."

"I'd be happy anywhere with you, Anna," Fred said softly as he drew her into his arms, "but let's get going. We've got a long walk and it's getting cold. I'll light the fire when we get back and we can have our dinner in front of it."

So they trudged back to the cottage and flopped into the armchairs to relax after their walk. Fred lit the fire while Anna heated some soup which Ernie's sister in law, Margaret, had left for them, with a date loaf to follow.

"People have been so kind to us," Anna said. "I hope we can repay them in like manner one day."

"No need to, I'm sure." Fred smiled. "Everyone is so happy for us."

After their meal, they washed the dishes and returned to sit by the fire and enjoy its warmth. Fred glanced up at some shelves and noticed a set of Chinese Checkers and some country magazines.

"Let's have a game," he said, taking down the box. "We play this at home sometimes. It's a lot of fun."

"Yes, Connie and I used to play it sometimes. The Fergusons would lend it to us."

After a few games, Fred had to admit Anna was the better player. She won two out of the three games. Suddenly he jumped out of his chair and pulled Anna into a tight embrace.

"I'm sick of these silly Checkers. I can think of something better to do. It's time for bed now, madam."

"Yes, my darling," Anna agreed, impishly. Then coming down to earth with a downward mouth, she reminded Fred, "Tomorrow we have to go back and start living an ordinary life. All this bliss will end."

"It will never end for me as long as I have you," said Fred as he tilted up Anna's chin and looked into her eyes.

She smiled at his words.

Fred stoked the fire to warm the cottage while Anna climbed into bed. Then he extinguished the lamps.

"Hop in, Fred. I need you to warm me up. Let's have a little snuggle."

The next day they tidied the cottage after lunch and left a thank you note for Norm and Margaret before setting out at three o'clock to catch the bus to London and begin their new life together.

It had been snowing through the night which delighted Anna.

"Some parts of this place look like winter scenes on Christmas cards, don't you agree, Fred? That cottage over the road there with the small pine tree in front. All the tree needs is a star on top and some tinsel."

Fred smiled at her fancy as he pointed out deeper drifts of snow in the road's verges.

"I'll bring you up here in summer when the fair is on," he promised. "It's so exciting. There are bands playing, lot of stalls to buy things, food and drink stands everywhere and oh! these big swings, donkey rides, a Dutch organ and kids running everywhere."

"Sounds wonderful," Anna replied, "but look, Fred, here come the horses! We're getting closer to getting home and I can't wait. We'll buy our dinner tonight, eh? Fish and chips, eh?"

The bus trip lasted nearly an hour and Fred and Amy disembarked at the stop closest to the fish and chip shop and placed their order. They sat on a rough bench while they waited until their food was ready.

When they'd eaten, they walked around the corner to their new address at Regent Square and mounted the stairs to their flat. Fred turned the key in the lock, opened the door and with a sweeping hand movement, ushered his wife into their new abode.

"It's a workaday world for you and me tomorrow, my love," said Anna in a practical voice, "so we'd better get ready for it."

"You're right there," Fred agreed, "but one thing I know for sure. Life will be easier now I have you to come home to each evening."

He walked over to her and kissed her lips. Then he lit the fire and made a pot of tea.

"I'm worried about you, my darling, riding that bicycle to work each day," said Anna, frowning. "Please be careful of those dangerous gasoline vehicles on the road. Big buses now too. They're so fast. I've heard they go at about twenty miles an hour. People really are safer travelling on trains or horse drawn carriages, or just simply walking."

"I promise you, my darling, I'll be extremely careful."

They laid out their work clothes for the morrow. Fred organised his shaving equipment and Anna set the table for breakfast which would follow the usual tradition of oatmeal, toast with fish paste or marmalade and a cup of tea.

"Hey!" announced Fred with a wide grin, "don't forget we've got a brand-new bed to try out tonight."

He and Anna raced over and bounced up and down on it, laughing, until Anna said, "It's very comfy, Fred."

"It'll do," answered Fred, with a big smile.

Back at Warren Street

During the afternoon, Mary and William had been discussing their new situation with their son not living with them anymore.

"I wouldn't 'ave i' any uvver way," said Mary, 'but it's goin' ter be 'arder fer us wiv not 'avin' the rent from 'im, but we managed before 'ee was workin' an' we'll manage again. We can cu' down on food a bit. We'll 'ave pancakes fer tea every Saturday nigh'. I know you love 'em with the lemon juice and sugar on em if I fry 'em in bu"er. They'll fill yer up real good, Will"

"They'll do me, Luv," agreed William, "bu' I won't give up me newspaper each Sunday. I jus' 'ave to know what's goin' on in the world."

Mary continued. "Let's 'ope and pray life won't be too 'ard on 'em. There's a lo' 'o luck in it for the likes of us … gettin' married and 'avin' kids."

"Well, they've bofe got jobs, Mary, and that's the key to i' all. As long as they can keep on workin' to keep a roof over their 'eads, they'll be orright. They're goin' to 'ave their ups and downs like we've 'ad but y' get by if y' keep y' pecker up."

"Well, they love each uvver, Will. I seen it from the start. And they like to laugh a lo' and that 'elps."

Upstairs, Martha had prepared a cup of tea to share with Sam who'd arrived home from his job at the factory five minutes earlier. They sat at the table and Martha shared her news.

"There's a letter here for Anna from Bristol. It must be from Connie, the woman she worked with over there at the bootmakers. Anna wrote to her to let her know she'd found a job here. I must take it round to her, maybe tomorrow night."

Sam joined in. "I hope our girl is going to be happy with Fred. I know he's a nice fellow and they seem to get on well, but I was hoping she'd meet someone with a better paid job over there in Bristol, with more money to support her."

"Well, we can't decide our children's future. You know that, Sam. Look at you and me. No-one told us who to marry and they've had that choice too."

"As long as they don't have too many kids. That's when the trouble starts. Two's enough," insisted Sam.

"As long as they keep healthy and strong, they should be alright. It's no good worrying, Sam."

Family

Three months after the wedding, Anna walked to work feeling decidedly unwell; the last few days it had been the same. At first, she thought she'd caught a cold from someone at work but the condition did not improve as each day wore on. Surely, it couldn't be! Although her period was overdue, this was not unusual for her. They'd always been irregular. And she and Fred had tried to be careful. *No! It's just a little infection*, she reasoned, but by the time she'd arrived at the hotel she felt much worse … felt like vomiting. After she'd changed into her uniform, she walked to a bathroom, closed the door, dry retched and threw up, hoping no-one would come near. Then she knew for certain what she had feared.

This is morning sickness, she thought. *I'm pregnant.*

But how to tell Fred. They both wanted children but not yet. They were saving whatever they could for a fund to cover the extra expenses a baby would one day bring. She'd wait a while to make absolutely sure before she'd let on. Perhaps she'd miscarry. Her emotions were mixed: strangely, excitement overshadowed her concern. *A little Alice of my very own?* She hoped it would be a girl.

After the episode in the bathroom, she felt better and was able to get her work done during the day. Tomorrow was Sunday and she could rest.

She slept in the next day, as did Fred, and for once, she refused his advances.

"I'm very tired today, Fred. I just want to sleep a bit longer."

"As you will, dear one. Later on, eh?"

Suddenly Anna rose from the bed and dashed to the privy below.

When she returned, Fred looked anxious.

"What's the matter, Anna? Aren't you well?"

"Well, Fred, it's going to happen again for a while so I might as well tell you. I have morning sickness. I'm pregnant. I'm sorry it's happened so soon."

Fred walked over and put his arms around her as she cried a little.

"Don't cry, Anna. I know it's earlier than we wanted, but it's our child and to be honest, I feel rather pleased about it."

"It's the expense, Fred. We're going to have to buy a lot of things like a perambulator, baby clothes, a cot and covers and a heap of napkins. Oh dear! We haven't saved enough yet."

"We don't have to buy everything new. Anna. Remember Whitefields? That church we dashed into in Tottenham Court Road when we got caught in the thunderstorm? Aunty Esther will help us out. She used to help Mum and Pa when we went to the old church before it was pulled down. People donate all sorts of things to that church. Let's go there next Sunday, eh?"

"Oh, Fred, it sounds like we're just going there to get things."

"Anna, you've already told me you wanted to find a church around here to go to. We couldn't find a better one than Whitefields, and Aunty Esther knows me from way back. I stopped going once I got a permanent job but now, we are a little threesome, almost, I really feel like going back. And I'd like to surprise her anyhow and tell her I'm married to a wonderful girl and I'll soon be a father."

"Not so soon, Fred. I'm just over two months on the way. We'll spill the beans later on."

"It's all going to work out okay. As long as you are going to be alright."

"Fred, this is normal and it usually doesn't last longer than about six weeks from what I've heard. As long as I can hide my condition at the hotel, I can get through this and keep working until the last month or so. I'll tell Mrs Reeves in a few months."

"I'll get breakfast, Anna. You rest, and I'm going to help you all I can. Mum used to say, 'a burden bared is a burden shared'."

They spent the rest of the day indoors, Fred doing all the chores and cooking dinner in the evening. Anna spent some time answering Connie's letter.

"How amazed she'll be. Not only a new job, but a husband and a baby on the way too."

Everything went well through the week and Anna successfully hid her morning sickness from the staff at the hotel.

After a month, the sickness had gone and Fred and Anna decided to tell their parents their news.

Martha and Sam were delighted at the thought of a grandchild on the way, promising to babysit and help in any way they could.

"Cor lumme!" shrieked Mary when she heard the news. "I jus' knew you'd be 'avin' one soon. I'll be there to give youse a 'and when yer need one, me luvvies, and wha' a Christmas presen' the li"le one'll be for yer both."

A month later, a parcel arrived from Bristol from Connie. Inside was a letter congratulating Anna on her wonderful news with a promise to knit the baby some bootees. And she'd finally found a new position as a cook with a wealthy family in Bath. Also enclosed was a book entitled, *Mrs Beaton's Household Management and Cookery*. This was a wedding gift.

"She always used this book in Bristol and got a lot of recipes from it," explained Anna to Fred. "I'll have to write her another letter and thank her for her wonderful gift."

When they went to church at the six o'clock service at Whitefields a few weeks later, Aunty Esther welcomed them with her usual warmth. And when she found out that Fred and Anna were married and expecting, she rallied round with offers of help.

"We often get prams and cots donated and baby clothes. I'll keep an eye open and keep these things specially for you," she promised.

As the weeks passed, Anna's maid's uniform was becoming tight around her middle. She was worried she would be dismissed once her secret was out. She realised her condition would eventually be revealed in spite of herself, so she decided to speak to Mrs Reeves and hope and pray she would be allowed to work almost up to her confinement. With lips trembling and tears gathering in her eyes, she owned up.

"This has happened much sooner than my husband and I wanted, Mrs Reeves. I'm feeling quite healthy and strong and I hope I can work here for a while yet. We need the money for the baby, you know"

"I've known about your secret for some time, Anna. A few months ago, I heard you being sick in one of the bathrooms after you'd arrived, and I put two and two together, particularly as you weren't looking well in those weeks, but you kept on working, to your credit. Don't worry, my dear, your job here is safe. If you're up to it, you can keep going for a while yet. I can hire some temporary staff to cover the time you'll be away when you're having the baby. Now come along and I'll fit you with a bigger uniform."

Anna felt like hugging Mrs Reeves as she followed her into the fitting room. That was an anxiety removed. She'd even been promised work after the baby! When she'd finished her shift, she hurried home to tell a relieved Fred the news about her job. She finally felt total calm at the prospect of motherhood after her initial apprehension.

During the last fortnight, Aunty Esther had collected a cot and mattress, a small cupboard for baby clothes and necessities, and was keeping her eye out for a 'pram. Martha was knitting a layette and Mary was hand sewing two little nightgowns and two flannel pilchers to go over the nappies.

Unexpected

On Friday, November 23rd, William woke and said, "I ain't goin' in today, Mary. Dunno wot's wrong with me bu' I've been damn tired lately. I could 'ardly lif' the stuff onto the van and unload i' so I'm takin' i' easy today. Nearly fainted a few times too. 'Ow about you make the cuppas and bring me brekkie 'ere in bed, eh?"

Indeed, the last four days had been hard for William.

"I could see ya ain't been yerself lately, Will, and today yer look worn out. Stay in bed and rest up, m' dear. I'll leave yer some lunch before I go ter the wash 'ouse."

William slowly ate his oatmeal and toast and a piece of bacon. Then he sipped the tea. Mary stoked the fire and suggested he move into the warm room and get into Fred's old bed.

"You'll be fine, Will. Yer jus' need a good rest. We're gittin' old, ain't we? Yer been gaddin' about too much, goin' to the pub, rushin' around fittin' out Fred's place wiv them shelves."

William lay back and closed his eyes; slept for about an hour. Mary went into the other room to make their bed and tidy up. When she returned, William was sitting on the edge of the bed. Mary noticed the ghastly grey colour of his skin and he seemed to be staring into space. He stood up, swayed; took a few faltering steps before he pitched forward and fell on his face. Horrified, Mary rushed to him and, with much effort, managed to roll him onto his back. Slowly, his mouth opened, and his jaw dropped.

"Will, Will," she begged, as she put her hands on his shoulders and shook him, "please don't leave me, me darlin'. Will, come back ter me. Will, can yer 'ear me? I love yer, Will. Yer can't go now, not NOW, Will."

She stayed by his side, sitting on the floor until she realised her beloved husband had gone from her … so quickly. She placed her ear on his chest to listen for a heartbeat. There was none.

The shock was tremendous. This sudden departure of the man she loved! With tears flowing, she kissed his face and put a pillow under his head. "It'll make yer more comfortable, me Luvvie," she said aloud, "an' I'll pu' a blanket over yer too."

After she'd done these things and wept for a bit longer, the practical side of her moved in. She knew she had to contact the doctor who lived two streets away. How she walked there she would never know, as she explained to Fred later on.

Doctor Sommers called in almost immediately and confirmed that William had died, probably from a massive stroke or heart attack. "But I'm ordering an autopsy to find out the cause of death," he informed Mary, "and I'll arrange for transport straight away to remove him to the morgue."

When the doctor left, Mary walked up the stairs to Martha's and Sam's flat and knocked on the door. Martha answered, and Mary burst into tears, telling Martha the news between sobs. The two women held each other closely until Martha led Mary to the sofa and made her a cup of tea.

"Jus' when 'ee was goin' to be a grandpa, too. Ain't life cruel, Martha?

Martha agreed it could be most unfair to some, while others got all the breaks.

"The doctor tol' me 'ee'd get a message ter Fred at the shop," said Mary, "an' we'll 'ave ter let Mattie know too."

"Mary, I want you to stay here with me until Will's been moved out. You've been through enough today. It won't help you to see him like he is just now."

"Marfa, I'm goin' down to 'im. Yer never know wot 'ee still knows. Ee's go' a spirit. It migh' be waitin' fer me there."

So Mary went down and stayed by William. Fred arrived about an hour later, completely shocked at the sudden news. Ernie Dobson had said, "Stay with your mother and come back after the funeral, Fred. Ada and my casual boy can help until then."

After William had been taken away, Fred stayed with Mary and left at six o'clock to go home and tell Anna. Martha and Sam promised to keep an eye on her.

The autopsy revealed William had been suffering from a disease of the heart and lungs, resulting in his sudden death.

"'Ee worked till 'ee dropped," said Mary later, controlling her tears at the funeral.

Martha added, "It's the blasted smog around here. Coating everything in soot. The air's not fit to breathe. That's why his lungs were in a bad way."

"A lot of people are dying lately of consumption. It may sound cruel, but he went in a much kinder way than they do," observed a neighbour.

Family, friends, Aunty Esther and neighbours made their way home and wondered what Mary was going to do now she was a widow. How would she manage?

Christmas Eve

As Anna grew larger, she began to feel that time was standing still.

"Will the day ever come, Fred? I feel as though I've been pregnant all my life."

And the day did come: on Christmas Eve, at around five o'clock.

"I've got a backache, Fred. I'd better lie down. I wonder if this means the baby's on the way? I'm past nine months now. … Oh! that was a funny achy pain. Didn't last long!"

Five minutes later, another pain hit Anna, slightly stronger. Fred reacted.

"I'm getting on the bike and getting our mothers and the midwife over. Keep calm, my darling. I'll ask Florrie Clark from upstairs to come and sit with you. I should be back in under an hour. Keep calm, keep calm."

Anna smiled as she watched Fred get ready to go.

He's got the jitters, and he keeps telling me to keep calm, she thought. *I'm the calm one, not him!*

Fred called into Florrie's place upstairs, and she eagerly agreed to go and sit with Anna.

"I have experience with this business, Fred. Now calm down. Everything will turn out well, you'll see."

She thought Fred looked like a nervous wreck, and Anna's labour had barely started.

Fred fast pedalled to the midwife a few blocks away then to Warren Street to summon Mary and Martha.

Florrie arrived on the scene to find Anna standing up and mopping the floor.

"My waters broke when I stood up, Florrie, and I'm going to get into a nightie."

"Yes, get into your nightie and onto the bed, my girl. You're on the way. I'll clean up the floor, no trouble. You'll probably have your baby by tomorrow. Christmas day, eh? The best gift ever!"

Anna drew in her breath and told Florrie she just felt a sharp pain.

Fred arrived at Warren Street and quickly announced that Anna was having the baby.

Then he rode back to be with her. Sam decided to accompany Martha and Mary on their walk to Regent Square. When they arrived, Sam cautioned Fred to keep well away from the birthing process as it was purely women's business.

"I won't be hanging around here, Fred, and you shouldn't either. We'll just wish her good luck, and then we'll be off. We'll hear the news in good enough time."

But Fred declined.

"I won't be in the *room*. I'm going outside on the landing. I just feel I can't be too far away from her."

So Sam joined Fred on the landing and tried to talk sense into him.

Six minutes later, Anna doubled up with another pain.

"Oh! it's all coming back to me," muttered Martha, who was shushed by Mary.

"She'll find ou' soon enough without you tellin' 'er," she cautioned.

Mary took a bed sheet and tied it around a bedpost at the foot of the bed and twisted it into a rope.

"The pains are goin' ter ge' closer an' a bi' worse, me Luvvly. When they ge' 'ard, jus' pull on this sheet. It'll 'elp."

There was a knock on the door and Mary bustled over and opened it.

Fred and Sam stood there, wanting to wish Anna good luck.

"Now, git the 'ell out of 'ere, you men," she said fiercely. "Anna already knows yer wishin' 'er luck. There's nothin' yer can do, just standin' there like dummies. Go 'OME."

"I'll be around the place, out in the street, or somewhere," said

Fred meekly. "Give her a kiss from me, will you?"

"There won't be no kissin' tonight," muttered Mary under her breath. "Tha' sor' o' thing is wo' causes all the trouble."

Sam decided to go home, but Fred opted to stick around somewhere, as the baby might be here soon.

The midwife arrived as another pain hit Anna. She placed her bag of equipment on the table and pulled out a waterproof sheet which she placed under Anna. Then she gave her a good antiseptic swab.

"You've still got a long way to go, my dear," she announced after an examination, "but everything looks fine. If the pain gets worse, I've got something to help with it."

"Will it get much worse?" Anna asked anxiously as she'd pulled on the sheet and gritted her teeth.

At this point, Florrie decided to leave, feeling a bit faint, and knowing she was no longer needed.

Martha went over to her daughter to comfort her, saying, "I'm sure it won't be much longer, darling. We've all been through it. Once it's over, you'll forget all about it. I promise you."

But the hours dragged on. The contractions came at shorter intervals, stronger and more painful.

"Mum, I don't know how I'm going to keep on with this. The pain is worse than I ever imagined."

Anna suppressed a scream as another contraction hit two minutes later, and the midwife administered the laudanum. It dulled the pain somewhat and induced a dream-like state in Anna.

At one o'clock in the morning, Fred decided to return to Warren Street and join his father-in-law to wait things out. There was nothing he could do to help by pacing the streets and worrying. Apart from that, it was freezing cold, and he had started to shiver. Several times he had ventured up the stairs to his apartment door and had heard low moans coming from within which had distressed him.

He arrived at Warren Street and wearily walked up the stairway to Sam's flat.

"I've been expecting you, Fred," said Sam as he opened the door.

"You've done right to come back here until it happens. Now get onto the sofa there with a blanket and get warm. We'll go back in the morning and see if you're already a dad."

Fred took Sam's advice and in no time was fast asleep.

All through the night, the contractions continued until they suddenly stopped for about half an hour.

"This is called the transition, and shortly Anna will start to push the baby out," the midwife explained to Martha and Mary.

"Thank the good Lord for that," said Martha with a weary sigh. "It's been dreadful watching her suffer."

Mary put her arm around Martha and said, "Those damn men don't know wot we women go frough. If they 'ad to do i', there'd be no kids born ever, would there?"

Anna began to heave and push, then rested for a while, then pushed again and again.

'The baby's coming … the head is appearing. You've got the boiling water ready so I can sterilise the scissors and clamps, and is the bath ready too?" asked the midwife urgently.

"Everyfing's ready an' I've go' the clean towels out," assured Mary.

Accompanied by a loud groan, Fred's and Anna's little son was born. There was no immediate cry from the baby and after a short while, the midwife gave the child a sound smack on his bottom. He uttered a loud wail and took his first breath. The cord was cut and clamped, and the baby was carried over to the warm bath to clean him up. He was then swaddled in a towel and carried over to his mother.

"He's just *gorgeous*," said Anna with a broad smile as she looked at the perfect little face. Then she lay back, exhausted and sleepy after her ordeal. The baby was taken from her and placed into the cot from Whitefields and covered with the sheet and little blankets.

Christmas Day 1900.

"It's five o'clock, and it's Christmas Day. What a wonderful day for a birthday," said Martha. "A little boy, but she had really hoped for a girl."

"Do you know somefin'?" said Mary in a quiet voice. "It don't matter wha' i' turns ou' to be, when yer look at the baby you've just borned, it's love a' first sight."

"Anna told me if it was going to be a girl, she would be called Amy and if a boy, he would be christened Frederick after his father but they would call him Freddy to not mix him up with his dad."

The midwife congratulated Anna, packed her bag and left – her task had been completed and the birth scene cleaned up. She would call in the next day to check on Anna. She left her bill on the table. It was cheaper than a doctor's would have been.

Anna fell asleep, and the two grandmothers tiptoed over to the cot and gazed with pride at their grandchild.

"Freddy, little Freddy," said Mary softly, "'Ee's perfick." Then she started to cry when she remembered William's joy at the thought of becoming a grandpa. "'Ee got the short straw, 'ee did."

At seven o'clock, Fred woke with a jolt and told Sam he was going back to see how Anna was getting on, if his mother would let him. Sam went with him. When they arrived and knocked on the door, they didn't hear a sound so they waited a while then knocked again.

"Shush," whispered Martha as she opened the door. "They're all asleep, including Mary. Tiptoe over to the cot, Fred, and say hello to your little son."

When Fred looked at his tiny boy, he thought he would burst with pride and joy. He then turned his thoughts to Anna.

"She came through it quite well," Martha said quietly, "considering it is her first, but she has to stay in bed for ten days. We can take shifts looking after her."

At that moment, Mary woke up and sprang out of her chair, throwing off her blanket.

"Cor lumme!, it's my Fred. You've seen y' boy already? Don't wake 'im up now, will yer, Fred?"

But the baby had woken at Mary's sudden leap; he uttered a wail and became more insistent, waking Anna also.

"The midwife said to give him a feed as soon as he wakes," Martha advised, but Anna hadn't heard her. Fred was hugging her and telling her how proud he was of her.

Mary broke in. "'Ees 'ungry. I'm bringin' 'im over now Anna an' yer can give 'im a feed." She lifted Freddy tenderly and took him to Anna, who put him to her breast. The child quietened immediately after clumsily locating the nipple. Then he took his first tiny meal.

"Today we should all rest," Martha suggested brightly. "It's been quite a night. You and I should go home, Grandad," she said to Sam, who couldn't stop looking at little Freddy. "I'm tired and need a bit of sleep."

"Christmas Day! This is one I'll never forget," said Fred as he sat on the bed near Anna and his son.

"I'm gettin' us all a good brekkie," announced Mary, taking down a tin of oatmeal and putting out bread, butter and kippers. "Now you, Fred, git the kettle goin' and make us a good pot o' tea, will yer?"

"We'll celebrate Christmas quietly tomorrow," suggested Martha, "with cold meats, Mary's pudding and my cake … and we'll bring it all here." Everyone agreed.

After breakfast, Martha and Sam left to go back home. Martha felt worn out and needed some sleep. Mary made up the sofa and prepared to move in for a week to look after Anna after the birth.

Important News

A month later, Anna returned to her job at the hotel. Florrie Clark had agreed to look after baby Freddy during Anna's working hours, for a third of her wage.

At the shop, Fred eagerly awaited closing time as he always had, but lately, he would dash home quickly on his bike to be with Anna and the baby. He and Anna were both tired as Freddy would wake through the night to have his feeds and he often suffered from colic. As the child was now only bottle-fed, Fred would alternate the feeding with Anna.

It was tiring work at the hotel, but Anna threw herself into achieving her quota each day, knowing that not all married women and particularly one with a baby were privileged to have a job. Most women, after marriage, were obliged to give up work and rely on their husband's wage to support the family. This ruling would often cause great privation if the husband's wage could not cover unexpected expenses or if too many children came along. But Fred and Anna were doing well so far, and Freddy was gaining weight and starting to smile.

On the evening of the 23rd January, 1901, when Fred arrived home from work, he informed Anna that Queen Victoria had died.

"I was going to tell *you*, Fred," said Anna, "I found out about it too. She died at about half-past six last night, and that is why we heard bells tolling and paperboys yelling out something before we went to bed. Remember? We wondered what was going on."

"It's all in the papers today," said Fred and he told Anna what he had read. "She was eighty-one years old and living on the Isle of Wight, and she died of a stroke. She'd been Queen for almost sixty-four years, and no other monarch would ever reign longer than she has, according to this paper."

"I've heard she never got over her husband's death and was in mourning for forty years," added Anna.

"Well, in spite of that, a lot of good things happened during her reign. Britain has become a mighty power."

"There's going to be a lot of pomp going on with the burial," said Anna, "and later the crowning of the new king. I'd like to go along and see the processions."

"I read a proclamation – it said that the Day of Mourning would be on Saturday, the second of February. It will be a military-style funeral because she was a soldier's daughter, and it's what she wanted. Her coffin will be brought to London, and everyone will be able to see the procession. And do you know," added Fred, "that everything is going to be filmed as it happens? Not just still photographs, but moving pictures. Imagine that!"

"Goodness knows what the future holds. Maybe we'll be able to go and watch stories told in moving pictures one day. Wouldn't that be wonderful?" said Anna.

Another nine days passed before Fred and Anna walked into the heart of London to watch the funeral procession. It was a freezing day with light snow falling. Mary had decided not to go because she didn't want to be in the midst of such sadness.

"It's too soon after me darlin' Will has gone," she explained. "Leave little Freddy with me. It's too cold to take 'im anyway. You two go and enjoy yerselves."

An enormous crowd had gathered on each side of the funeral route jostling to get the best view of the proceedings. During the procession, everyone became silent as eight white horses pulled the gun carriage and coffin, which was covered in white satin. Behind, walked the new King of England, Edward the Seventh, followed by members of the Royal family and five reigning monarchs from other countries. Different regiments of the military and the fleet marched by, a solemn drum beat matching their steps.

"I love to see the grenadier guards marching," Anna whispered to Fred, "and did you see the crown and other royal things on top of the coffin?"

"Yes, I did," whispered back Fred, "but I like the horses as much as anything else … and all the regalia."

"After this, she's going by train to Windsor Castle, and she'll be buried next to her beloved husband," Anna added.

The crowd began to break up as the last of the procession approached, people looking forward to going to back to their warm homes after standing for more than an hour in the cold.

Fred and Anna linked arms and waited in a queue at a nearby barrow to buy a cup of hot chocolate.

"Well, we're not Victorians any more, Fred. We're Edwardians now. I wonder what's going to happen in Edward's reign? Moving pictures for everyone? And those motor cars going even faster?"

Fred nodded and changed the subject.

"I'm glad the landlord's finally got another person to rent the other room in Warren Street," said Fred, relieved, "Mum was having a devil of a time making up the money. She had to dip into her funeral fund. All this stress on top of Dad's death is not doing her any good."

"Well, she's got the better deal. She'll be in your old bed and warmer with the fire in the room. I hope the new tenant is a nice lady and they'll get on. It's a bit of a risk, isn't it?"

"Yes, it is," replied Fred, "but Mum told me the woman is in the same boat as herself. She's got a job as a charwoman somewhere close by, and Mum said she seems nice enough."

"I think it's good she'll have some company. They can look out for each other," said Anna reassuringly. "She's moving in next week, isn't she?"

Fred nodded.

Sipping their cocoa, they slowly made their way back to Warren Street to pick up Freddy. Mary wanted to know all the details of the funeral procession, and Anna gave her a good description of the event as Mary nursed her grandson on her lap.

"It's 'istory! Freddy'll be able ter watch everythin' wot'll 'appen in King Edward's reign as 'ee grows up. But there's one fing I 'ope for 'im. This parliament's got ter lower the rents we poor people 'ave ter pay them money grubbin' landlords wot charge us nearly 'alf the wage we earn each week fer livin' in mouldy 'ovels. I've been waitin' for months ter 'ave the window in the other room fixed up an' in the end, I 'ad ter git a neighbour to nail a bi' o' cardboard over the glass wot's broke. They're quick ter take yer money, ain't they, but they're slow ter give somethin' back."

"I'll speak to Ernie Dobson about it. He knows a glazier he supplies with putty, and I'll make sure that bit of glass is soon replaced before the new lady moves in," promised Fred.

After little Freddy had been given his bottle and changed, and placed into his pram, Fred and Anna hugged Mary and said their goodbyes.

"I found it hard to call her Mum at first after our wedding," said Anna as they walked home, "but she's such a dear and so lovely with Freddy. It's easy now."

At home, Fred quickly got the fire going while Anna lit the gas stove to prepare dinner. After the baby had settled and dinner was over, Fred made a cup of tea.

The Best Place for Sam

In June 1901, Samuel was placed into care.

"It's the best thing that could have happened, my sweet," said Fred, putting his arm around Anna as she cried. "He couldn't have kept going the way he was after that stroke. Now we won't have the worry anymore. They'll know how to look after him. Think of your mother, Anna. It's been hell for her these last few months, particularly with the senility getting worse."

"I know, Fred. But Grove Hall Lunatic Asylum! What a place for Dad to end up in. People are so horrible – they'll call him names."

"It's the only place for him now, Anna. He hardly knows who we are. You know that."

"Oh! Fred, I know it sounds awful, but I think your father went in a kinder way. Dad could linger on for years in that place."

"Anna, do you know what the life expectancy is for people like us? The deserving poor we're called, who live in crowded tenements, often run-down, working our backsides off to put bread on the table with long hours and poor pay. Working-class men in London are lucky if they reach the age of sixty. They're mostly in their forties and fifties when they go. Now Pa was sixty-eight when he went, and your Dad is sixty-four, so they've had a good run compared to a lot of others. Don't cry. He's been a happy man and made the best of things. We'll visit him and get your Mum to move down to Clapham to be closer to him."

"It doesn't matter how much you're expecting it, Fred, it always comes as a shock. Your father is gone and now my father is in that awful place. All this in just over a year. Poor little Freddy. Not a single grandpa to look up to."

"Your Dad hasn't gone yet, Anna."

"Well he might as well have. That's no life for anyone."

Laid to Rest

"Four months he lasted in that place, Fred," said Anna with a little sob, "but he went peacefully, and I'm grateful for that."

"Your Dad was such a lovely man, right to the end," answered Fred as he endeavoured to comfort Anna. "Even in that place, smiling at everyone and so co-operative. I reckon he enjoyed being there these last few months."

Anna shrugged. "I hope so, Fred. Anyhow, another funeral to arrange," she said with a sigh. "Funny, it was bronchitis on his death certificate. I suppose he was so weakened with his heart condition and what was it again, vascular and cerebral disease, that everything just gave out in the end."

"Your Mum would blame the London air for his lung condition," added Fred, "and I'm sure she's right."

It was a simple funeral. The minister, family and friends gathered around the grave plot as Sam was buried. Martha was inconsolable. Only little Freddy made a difference when he was handed to her when she sat on a nearby bench. The child started to bounce up and down on her lap, kick with his legs and smile at his grandmother. In no time at all, Martha's tears dried up as she responded to the little boy.

After a while, Anna suggested they all go home as there was not much point in lingering around the grave any longer. She took Freddy from Martha and put him in his stroller.

"If I know Sam," said Mary gently, "E'ed want us to git on with our lives. E'ed want us ter be 'appy. That doesn't mean we'll ever ferget 'im, does it? It'll take time, Marfa, but yer've got yer memries and they'll comfort yer like mine do when I think of me darlin' Will.

Time 'elps, yer know."

They made their way to Martha's new place in Clapham and had a cup of tea and some fruit cake before leaving to catch the 'bus home. On the way, Freddy grew hungry and wailed lustily for part of the way, which jangled Anna's nerves. Mary made her way to Warren Street from the 'bus stop when they arrived, and Fred and Anna continued on to their place. They were worn out when they reached home, particularly Anna, who'd fought to control her tears during the funeral. She heated up a pot of pre-made stew after Freddy had been changed and fed and put into his cot. Soon he was asleep.

"It's just occurred to me, Fred," she said as she walked over to him and leant against him. "You're the only man left in the family now, except for my brothers who I hardly ever see."

"Well, I'm not really the only man, you know, Anna. You do have your Uncle John in Northampton apart from your brothers. But I see your point, but you know I'll always be there for you and Freddy."

They embraced, and Anna let her tears flow.

"He was a good Dad even though I hardly saw him when I was away in Bristol for all those years. I'll miss him, Fred."

They ate their dinner, washed and changed into their nightclothes. Freddy was still asleep in the other room, and they tiptoed over to their bed.

"Thank goodness, tomorrow's Sunday," murmured Anna as she cuddled into Fred. And even though they were weary, they made love.

Anna's Secret

There were only ten days to go before Freddy's first birthday, which would fall on Christmas day. A dual celebration. Anna had organised everything for the two occasions although there would be no presents for the adults as usual. Only for Freddy. Mary had sewn him a stuffed rabbit made of odd scraps of colourful rags, and Martha had picked up a rattle from a local jumble sale. At Whitefields, some wealthy people had donated brand new toys, and Fred had brought home a teddy bear.

Anna's joy was clouded as she made her way home after her stint at the hotel.

After Christmas, I'll wait until after Christmas, she thought as she congratulated herself on having kept her secret for so long. When she'd first found out, she was angry and blamed Fred for having been careless. But as time went on, she realised this was unfair. It was both their faults. She was lucky this time. There'd been little morning sickness, and Mrs Reeves hadn't noticed a thing. But how to tell Fred? It had all happened too soon. There'd be not quite eighteen months between Freddy and the new one. How would they manage now with two children so young? But in time she'd become accustomed to the fact that she would be a mother once again and was starting to look forward to the new baby. A brother or sister for Freddy. She hoped it may be a girl this time. Her own little Alice at last? She'd tell Fred on Boxing Day.

Christmas Day 1901

Fred and Anna awoke early on Christmas Day to the insistent demands of Freddy wanting his bottle and the thin oatmeal he had lately been introduced to. After everyone had eaten, Freddy was dressed in a brand-new romper suit and given his teddy bear.

"Did you see how his eyes shone when he saw it and clutched it to him?" asked Fred.

"Yes, I did," joined in Anna, laughing. "It'll be interesting to see how he takes to that rabbit Mum's made, and the other things later on."

"Well," said Fred, "it's off to Whitefields for the service and the carols and the Nativity Play the children are putting on. I think Freddy is up to enjoying things there now."

"He'll love the Christmas tree anyway," said Anna.

Aunty Esther dashed over to them when they arrived and wished Freddy a happy first birthday. "The same day as Jesus, little one," she enthused. "You're in good company."

Mary had arrived on foot and presented the rabbit to Freddy, which he looked at and flung onto the floor.

"Oh! Freddy, that's mean. Granny made that especially for you," said Anna, embarrassed.

"It's alrigh', me Luvvie. I fink it's because it's go' a weak neck and its 'ead won't stay up. I'll take it 'ome and put more stuffin' in it. Me feelin's aint 'urt. E'es only a baby and meant no 'arm."

After church, they walked to Fred's and Anna's place and found Mattie waiting for them on the steps.

The three women prepared a simple Christmas dinner and

afterwards brought out a birthday cake with a single candle for Freddy. Mattie gave him a squeaking, yellow rubber duck for his bath.

"A shame Mum hasn't been able to be here for this," said Anna, explaining to Mattie. "It's too far for her to walk up here at her age and the cost of the 'bus fare is beyond her now, but Fred and I are taking the baby down to see her tomorrow."

"Yes," answered Mattie, "our numbers are down, aren't they with our two dads gone and Martha not here."

Mattie left at four o'clock to return to Kensington and Fred walked his mother home to Warren Street. When he returned, Freddy was having his bottle and then a small portion of mashed vegetables. Fred changed his nappy and put him to bed as Anna was resting in an armchair.

"I'm so tired, Fred. It's been a big day today, hasn't it? And we have that trip down to Clapham tomorrow with Freddy." Anna paused, looked at Fred and said in a small voice, "Tomorrow, it's Boxing Day."

Fred couldn't understand why but he thought Anna looked strained.

She was thinking, *I'll have to tell him tomorrow.*

Boxing Day

It rained. Fred grabbed two umbrellas while Anna packed some leftover goodies from the day before and the baby's things. When they reached the landing below, Fred put the baby into his stroller and covered it with a macintosh. Then they made their way to the bus stop where they waited for ten minutes under a shop awning.

The trip to Clapham took fifteen minutes. Martha now lived in a single room in a fairly run-down tenement building. When they arrived, she held out her arms and embraced them, especially Freddy.

"I haven't seen him since the funeral, and I can see a big change. Happy birthday, little fella."

Martha presented him with a rattle in the shape of a puppy which Freddy eyed with curiosity.

"It's humble, but it's home, and I'm comfortable here, but how I miss your Dad," said Martha, tears forming in her eyes.

Anna comforted her mother. Then she brought out the food and a box of chocolates which she set on the table. Freddy whinged for his bottle, which he was now able to hold himself. When he'd had enough, he crawled over to a chair and drew himself up, holding on.

"He's been doing that for a couple of weeks now," said Fred. At the sound of his voice, Freddy looked at his father and slowly released his grip on the chair. He took five wobbly steps toward Fred before landing on his bottom. Everyone praised Freddy and clapped.

"His first steps and they happened right here," said Martha, beaming. "That's the best present I could have had … to see him start to walk."

After lunch, the Nashs left for home, arriving at about two-thirty.

The baby was tired and grizzly and was put to bed. He quickly fell asleep.

This is it! thought Anna. *I'll have to tell him now.*

She took a deep breath. "Fred, there's something I must tell you. I haven't wanted it to be so soon, but it's happened," she almost stammered. "There's another baby on the way, Fred." She looked down.

Fred stared at her, open-eyed, then quietly asked, "How far along are you?"

"I'm nearly two and a half months."

'And you've waited all this time to let me know!" Fred exploded. "I'm not angry because you're pregnant, but why have you kept me in the dark all this time. I'm the kid's father, for goodness sake."

Anna started to cry and then blurted out, "I didn't know how you'd take the news. It's too soon. Oh! Fred, I'm all mixed up. At first, I didn't want the baby and hoped I might miscarry, so I didn't say anything. Then later I got interested, and I regretted feeling the way I had. You know, about wanting to lose the baby. Then I thought I'd wait until Christmas was over and then tell you. It'll be only eighteen months between the two, and I know we wanted three years so we could get more money saved, but now, Fred, I really want this child, and I know it'll be so hard for us but … but, I'm hoping for a girl."

Fred walked over to her and put his arm around her. "It's sooner than we wanted, Anna, but we're in this together. You should have trusted me more. Stop crying now."

"We've been careless, Fred. It's so easy for people who can afford those birth control things, but we can't."

"Well," said Fred with a twinkle in his eye, "we should be alright for the next few months, eh?"

Anna laughed and finally relaxed.

"Speaking of secrets, I hope Mrs Reeves doesn't notice. It's too soon yet, but in a few months, I'll have to tell her. I'll ask her to keep me on until I have the baby."

About Mattie

Four weeks passed. On a Sunday afternoon, Fred and Anna busily tidied their home, preparing for the next week's work when an insistent knock came on the door. Anna opened it and Mary burst into the room, almost shouting.

"It's about Mattie. She's gettin' married. Never thought I'd see the day. She met 'im where she works. A 'andyman 'ee is. Walter 'Arrison. 'Ee's a widow an' nearly sixty. Been married before. Too old fer 'er, I reckon but Mattie's thir'y-eight and beggars can't be choosers. An' she's no oil paintin' either, poor Mattie, but a luvverly girl which is be"er than bein' jus' pre"y because they can be shaller, yer know."

"Sit down, Mum. You're like a waterfall," said Fred, laughing. "This is really good news. My big sister, finally getting married. When's it to be?"

"In April sometime. They gotta make arrangements, but they're doin' that soon."

"I wonder if they'll ever have a child," mused Anna. "I think thirty-eight may be a bit late for Mattie."

Mary was emphatic. "No i' aint! She'll 'ave one, I bet. Women can 'ave 'em in their for'ies. Look at me! I 'ad Mattie when I was for'y an' Fred when I was for'y-six"

Mary changed the subject and pulled the restuffed rabbit out of her bag.

"'Ere you are, Freddy. 'Ee looks be"er now, don't ee? Can look yer full in the face with 'is 'ead 'eld 'igh. Make sure li"le laddie, you do the same. 'Old yer 'ead up 'igh an' look people full in the face."

Anna served up afternoon tea. Fred looked at Anna and nodded.

"It's time to tell you *our* news, Mum. We're having another baby in June. Roughly six months to go."

"Blimey, so soon?" Mary grinned. "Yer mus' be fertile, youse two, that's all I can say. 'An 'ow about a sister fer Freddie? That'd be nice, eh? Yer know, it's gunna be 'ard for youse. Two li"le ones and one man's wage, but I'll 'elp ou' as much as I can with baby si"in' or somefin'."

"I'm hoping I can work until the baby's born and if I can arrange childminding, then I may be able to work afterwards," said Anna hopefully.

"Yer dreamin' Anna, but git the baby out first and then see what 'appens."

Mary left to go back to Warren Street, pleased with her children's news. A wedding and a new baby!

Anna remarked when Mary had gone, that the rabbit still had one ear longer than the other and had lopsided eyes.

Mrs Reeve's Decision

Anna arrived at the hotel wearing a full-length coat which she held together to hide her swollen stomach. She was now five and a half months pregnant. She made her way to the change room and hoped her apron would cover the gaping buttons of her uniform underneath. She'd decided she could get away with things for another week and then she'd tell Mrs Reeves about the baby. After she'd prepared one room for occupancy, she retreated to the kitchen area to get a glass of water. She bumped into Mrs Reeves there, who was boiling up a kettle to make a pot of tea.

"How far along are you this time, Anna?"

"Oh! Mrs Reeves," stammered Anna in a shocked voice. She was completely taken aback. "I was going to tell you next week about the baby and have a discussion about me staying on here until it's born and …"

"You didn't need to wait until next week," interrupted Mrs Reeves, with a faint smile. "It's been quite obvious for the past three weeks that you're expecting. And about you staying on until the child is born, well that's not going to happen. The management here has been quite lenient with you up till now. Usually, married women are never employed. It's their husband's duty to look after the family. In your case though, an exception was made as you only had one child and your work was very well done. But now, it's different. How would you manage with two children to look after? I know you have a lady looking after Freddy, but to look after two would take most of your wages. I can give you another four weeks here only and then you'll have to go. Here, sit down and have a cup of tea. I'm sure everything will work out for you in the end. You can get work to do at home like laundry or mending."

Anna sat down and sipped her tea, feeling weak.

"Fred's only a shop assistant, Mrs Reeves. It's going to be hard. I'm very healthy. Maybe one day, somehow, I can come back here."

"Not likely, Anna. Your place is in the home now looking after your family."

Anna finished her day's work and headed home. She picked up Freddy at Florrie's flat above, and told her the news, feeling relieved for the lady that she had only four more weeks to care for such an energetic and demanding little boy. Anna had previously helped Florrie put everything out of reach of small investigating fingers. She carried Freddy and his toys down to their flat.

Now to tell Fred she would be leaving her job in four weeks.

Fred was reassuring. "Look at our parents, Anna. They've battled through and brought up a family. So can we. And Mum has struggled all her life, having borne five children with only two surviving and apart from those times of grief, she's come through smiling. I remember she once said to me, 'When are you going to realise, Fred, that worrying about something doesn't make a damn difference.' And she believed in the power of prayer too. I heard her say once that poor people like us either drink or go to church. I'm grateful today that we all chose going to church, and still go, and still pray."

"You know I've never heard your mother complain, Fred," added Anna, "but I do wonder how we are going to live on just your wage with two children."

"I'll ask Ernie Dobson if he can give me a small rise. We can cut down on food a bit, and there's always Whitefields for clothing, boots and things. And Anna, we can go to church earlier on Sundays before the evening service and tuck into the sandwiches and cakes for our tea," Fred suggested, grinning and raising his eyebrows cheekily.

"That sounds awful, Fred, as though we're taking advantage."

"A lot of people go there, Anna. And Aunty Esther would be the first to understand our situation. She stood by us when I was growing up, and she's looking out for you and me now. Think of Freddy's high chair a couple of months ago – she kept just for us when it came in."

"Yes, I know. Perhaps I can do something to help in the church after the baby's born."

It was ten o'clock, and Freddy had finished his bottle. Anna changed him and settled him down in his cot. Then she and Fred went to bed. Tomorrow was another working day.

The weeks passed quickly for Anna until her retirement day. To her surprise, Mrs Reeves arranged an afternoon tea, allowing the servicing staff half an hour to see Anna off. A couple of short speeches were made, and everyone wished her well. Then a crystal vase was brought out and a crocheted baby blanket for the new little one. Anna was overcome. With tears in her eyes, she promised to visit and show off her new baby, as people had asked her to.

Mattie's Wedding

Mattie's wedding day in April 1902 soon arrived.

"Look at Mattie, will yer?" Mary whispered to Anna, "with 'er 'air all curled up and that pink lipstick, she looks quite pre"y. My girl, eh! Gettin' married at last."

"Shush," cautioned Anna as she heard Mary's voice rise in excitement above her whisper, "you're louder than the official."

It was a quick ceremony at the Registry in the Strand, the same venue Fred and Anna had been married in.

"I now pronounce you husband and wife, Mr and Mrs Walter Harrison," announced the Registrar.

The reception was held at a restaurant around the corner. Everyone agreed Mattie looked delighted. The newlyweds later left for their honeymoon, travelling by train to Sussex.

"Ee's goin' to show 'er the white cliffs of Dover while they're down there, she tol' me last week," said Mary on the way home. "'Ee can afford it, to go down there and give 'er a good time."

Fred walked his mother to Warren Street while Anna made her way to their place when she would pick up Freddy from Florrie's flat above.

Soon Fred arrived back looking tired.

"There's always something going on lately," he said as he sank into an armchair. "I've just realised it's only about two months before the baby arrives. I've got to get a little bed for Freddy. He'll have to move out of the cot."

"I wonder if Aunty Esther could keep an eye open," suggested Anna. "She might find something."

"And another thing, Anna. I'm looking around for a cheaper place to move into, hopefully before the baby comes. We could save some money that way. Funny, isn't it? Pa was always moving people into cheaper rent. Now it's happening to me. Anywhere but the east end. That'd be awful."

"When we move, Fred, ask Mr Dobson if he could help us out with Bessie and the cart. He did it last time for nothing, Maybe …"

"I hate asking people for help, Anna," said Fred, exasperated, "except Aunty Esther. Apart from her, I've always stood on my own two feet, but I suppose there's no choice now is there?"

"I know how you feel, Fred. I was always independent too, but now we are a family, and there's only one wage coming in. Anyhow, we'll have to muddle along and do the best we can. See what you can do with getting us a cheaper place. It would help."

Ernie Dobson agreed to give Fred a rise in wages, but only a small one as his business only yielded a modest return for him and Ada to live on but he readily agreed to help out with the moving.

Another Place and Another One

Fred knew he had to act quickly to find another place. After a few false leads and disappointments, a two-roomed apartment turned up at 106 Sandwich Street, in St Pancras.

"I'm glad it's got gas," said Anna gratefully. "It makes life far easier."

Four weeks later, the family moved into Sandwich Street. Anna had a sense of urgency to get things ship-shape in time for her confinement.

"Stop doing so much," urged Fred. "You need to rest more. You know what's ahead of you."

"The place needs a good clean. I can't let us live in this dirt, especially with Freddy and a new baby coming. I'm nearly done. I can rest up next week."

A few days later, in the early morning of the sixth of June, Anna felt her first contractions.

"This baby has decided to come a bit early, Fred. The pains are only mild at the moment. Please go and fetch your Mum and come back here with her. Then get on your bike and tell the midwife that I'm in early labour. Then you'd better ride over to Ernie and tell him you won't be in today, then come back and take Freddy to Warren Street and spend the day there with him. I wouldn't want him here while I'm having the baby."

Fred nodded at each of Anna's directions, feeling her sense of urgency. She was in charge now. He quickly dressed and cooked breakfast for the three of them. When they'd eaten, he cleared up the dishes, then walked over to Anna and wrapped his arms around her.

"Good luck, my sweet girl," he quietly said as he kissed her on her forehead.

"Oh! Fred, just *go*! I don't want to be here alone. Go and get your Mum, and be quick."

Fred was not in as bad a panic this time. As he cycled to Warren Street, he kept assuring himself Anna would be alright during this birth. Freddy's arrival, according to the midwife, had been completely normal. But he was still worried about the pain she would suffer.

"Goodness gracious me!" gasped Mary when he told his mother about Anna. "It ain't due fer another week or two. I'll pack me bag and git me coat and 'andbag, Fred, 'an I'll git over to 'er. I can walk there meself. I'll call in at the laundry and let them know I won't be in for a week or so. They can always git someone else. Now you git on that bike and git the midwife. 'Urry up now, she could be 'avin it."

Fred looked horrified and quickly departed.

Don't take risks, old boy, he warned himself as he dodged in and out of the busy London traffic on his bike. *Your children are going to need a father.*

The midwife said she would check on Anna in the next half hour and Ernie Dobson heartily agreed that Fred should have the day off. Ada came down the steps and told Fred not to worry.

"I'll help out today, Luvvie," she said.

Fred thought: *she called me Luvvie and I'm a grown man.* He felt like crying and couldn't understand why.

When he arrived back at his place, Anna's labour was progressing slowly.

"It's not bad yet, Fred. I've packed Freddy's things. Just get the stroller, and you'd better be going."

"I'll get you a cuppa first, Anna," he offered as Mary burst through the door.

"Yer'd better git goin', Fred," she said with a menacing look, "I told yer last time, this ain't no place fer a man. Grab Freddy and off yer go."

Fred did as he was told, and made his way down the stairs, with

Freddy under one arm and the stroller holding the bag under the other.

"Ta ta's, Dadda?" asked Freddy when they reached the pavement outside. Fred plodded on hoping the midwife would soon be there with Anna. When he reached his former Warren Street address, he let himself in the flat with a spare key and settled Freddy down on his old bed, now slept in by his mother.

"I'll get you some bread and butter, Freddy, then you can have a sleep, and after that, we'll go to the park, eh? We'll go and feed the ducks, eh?"

"Duckies, Dadda," the child agreed. "Fweddy feed duckies."

Back at Sandwich Street, the midwife had arrived. She prepared Anna for the birth and inspected her progress.

"You've been two hours in labour, you say, Mrs Nash?"

"About that," answered Anna, as Mary attached the twisted sheet to the bed end for her to pull on.

"Only that long, eh? Well, you're coming along nicely, my girl. It's quick this time. Baby should be here by this afternoon."

"Well, I 'ope yer won't take that laudanum stuff this time, Anna. It's my opinion it don't do the bubba much good. That's why Freddy was knocked out when 'ee come along 'an 'ad ter 'ave 'is botty smacked ter git 'im 'goin'. I never 'ad nothin' like that when I 'ad mine and they was all alert when they come out. Jus' grit yer teeth, me darlin'. Yer doin' well. It'll all be over soon."

Anna bravely took Mary's advice and continued on, refusing the drug during her labour which came to an end a few hours later when the baby was born.

Fred tried to heed his mother's advice about 'not worrying because it doesn't change anything', but he failed miserably. He wheeled Freddy around Regents Park to the swings then to the lake to feed the ducks. He'd taken their lunch and a drink for Freddy. Then he made a quick decision to walk to Sandwich Street to see if the new baby had been born.

When he arrived, he left Freddy in his stroller on the landing below and tiptoed up the steps to listen. This time, instead of silence, he heard the whimper of a newborn and the voices of the women.

"I've cleaned 'er up, Anna. 'Ere, take yer li"le girl, Luvvie. She's a beauty. Fair 'air an' blue eyes like 'er bruvver. Fred'll be tickled pink when ee sees 'er."

Fred dashed down to the landing, grabbed Freddy and the stroller and took them up to the door where he'd eavesdropped.

It's all over, he thought, *and I think I heard Mum say I have a daughter.*

He opened the door, gave Mary Freddy and walked over to Anna with a huge grin on his face. Anna was holding the baby.

"Let me introduce your daughter Amy to you, Fred. Your timing's great. She was only born about an hour ago. The midwife's just left, and the bed's been changed. Oh! Fred, remember I told you some time ago that I would love to have a little girl like the one I looked after in Bristol? Alice was her name. Well now I have my own little Alice."

Mary cut in quickly. "Well, she ain't Alice, Anna. She's Amy! And yer not ter compare 'er to any other girl. Ever!"

"Of course, Mum," Anna replied, chastened. "I know that. Amy is absolutely beautiful and unique, and I wouldn't change her for any other."

Fred took Freddy by the hand and drew him over to see his new little sister. Freddy took his sister's hand and inspected it closely and then traced his fingers over her face.

"Bubba, my Bubba."

"I'm gittin' us somethin' to eat, now it's all over," announced Mary. "Now you, Fred, git the kettle on will yer and we'll all 'ave a cup o' tea."

Fred obliged while Mary prepared lunch and milk for Freddy.

"Tomorrow's Saturday," said Fred, "and the day after is Sunday. I can't wait to get to know my little princess. Doesn't she have the perfect little face, Anna?"

Anna smiled and put Amy to her breast as the midwife had advised she should as soon as possible.

After lunch, Mary made up the sofa in the kitchen room for her to sleep on. She was to stay with the family and look after everything until Anna was back on her feet. But Anna insisted she felt much better this time and could see herself getting up far sooner than the recommended ten days.

Freddy had a new bed with a bigger pillow and two tartan blankets and a quilt. Over the months Fred had managed to save up enough to buy the bed and mattress, but the sheets, blankets and pillow had been donated by Whitefields.

After seven days, the visiting midwife declared Anna fully recovered from the birth. Anna insisted on taking over the household again, and Mary went back home to Warren Street, reminding Anna that she'd be available for baby minding whenever needed, after her work hours.

"She never left a stone unturned, Fred, and was lovely with Freddy, but I'm looking forward to getting out my cookery book and trying out some more of Mrs Beaton's recipes," said Anna.

"Mum can make a wonderful roast dinner," answered Fred, a little defensively.

So Busy

Anna was busier than she'd ever been. She thanked the Lord that Amy was a good sleeper and a more placid child than her brother, but life was a challenge just the same.

Each morning she would prepare the traditional oatmeal breakfast and cut Fred's lunch, knowing his long hours of work were beginning to tell on him. She'd noticed his hair starting to grey at the temples, *and he's only thirty-three*, she reminded herself. After the children were fed and changed, she would take them down to the vestibule where the perambulator was kept. It was large enough for the two children at this stage and Anna would take them to the parks in the surrounding area for fresh air and a play on the swings for Freddy. Then she'd go to the grocery store to get the day's supplies before returning home.

It's a bit of a hand to mouth existence, she'd sometimes think, puckering her brow, *but our parents got by, and so shall we!*

Sundays were easier. Fred was there to help, and often Mary would walk over to their place and take Freddy off their hands for a few hours. In the afternoon, the family would walk over to Whitefields and join others for a meal before the evening service. To Anna's shame, as she once admitted to Fred, they would stuff themselves with food which would cut out the expense of one meal in the week.

Fred had laughed and advised Anna to keep eating and enjoying the food, "They are happy to help out."

Aunty Esther took a particular interest in the Nash family. She'd asked Anna to join a young mothers' group which gathered each Wednesday afternoon when childminding rosters were kept for the crèche.

She needs some company apart from babies, she thought, *and I think I'll suggest she takes on some light cleaning here through the week to help them out.*

Anna eagerly agreed to the idea of a small part-time job at Whitefields. After a discussion with Fred, they wondered if Mary would be willing to look after the babies from four o'clock till six o'clock two afternoons in the week.

"I'll ask her next Sunday," promised Fred.

The next day when Fred returned home from work, he announced that the coronation of King Edward and Queen Alexandra had been postponed because the King needed an urgent operation due to a stomach complaint. The coronation would no longer happen on the twenty-sixth of June, but on the ninth of August.

Little Amy was doing well and putting on weight. Freddy was asking more and more questions and asserting his independence.

Two is enough, thought Anna, tired out but pleased with her children. *A boy and a girl, but we're going to have to be careful in the future. Any more will be too hard.*

About Mattie Again

At four o'clock the following afternoon Mary knocked on the door at Sandwich Street. When Anna opened it, Mary burst in, announcing in a loud, enthusiastic voice, "Yer won't believe wot I'm gunna tell yer, Anna. She's on the way. Mattie, on the way already. She tol' me yesterday, bless 'er 'eart. 'Er, nearly thir'y-nine an' all. I'm so pleased for 'er, Anna. Yours'll be gittin' a cousin, think o' tha'."

"Hold on a bit, Mum," said Anna, laughing, "I'm not all that surprised. You talk as if Mattie's over the hill. She's only thirty-eight and you had Fred in your forties, remember? I'm so pleased for her and I reckon she'll make a great mum. Now sit down on the sofa and I'll get us a cup of tea."

Mary stayed until Fred returned from work to tell him the news about Mattie. Meanwhile, she busied herself with some cleaning and nappy washing downstairs. At ten minutes past seven, Fred returned home and wearily sat down but not before his mother bombarded him with her news.

"Yer gunna be an uncle, Fred. Mattie's 'avin' a baby. Think o' tha'! 'Er nearly thir'y-nine an' 'im around sixty an' all. But the good Lord's meant it ter 'appen, I reckon. Don't you?"

Fred grinned. "I'm very happy for both of them, Mum, especially for Mattie. All I hope is that Walter lives long enough to see the child grow up."

"'Ee's 'ealthy, Fred. 'Ee mus' be, seein' Mattie's 'avin' a kid. Anyroad, ain't it wonderful? I'm jus' so 'appy fer 'em bofe."

Mary stayed on for dinner and helped Anna settle the children before she left for home.

"Family is everything for her," said Anna. "As long as everyone's happy, then she is too."

"The babies have been a great help after Pa's death. They take her mind off her loss," said Fred.

Five weeks later Fred returned from his job and reminded Anna of the impending coronation of the new king and queen in the Abbey.

"It's just around the corner, Anna, next Saturday on the ninth of August. But because poor Edward hasn't fully recovered from the operation he had, the procession in London for the people has been postponed until the 25th October."

"I'd almost forgotten," said Anna, pulling a face. "I'm so busy. That's something to look forward to Fred. Amy's too young to take much notice, but Freddy will love the horses.

The Procession

Martha Telford travelled up from Clapham the day before the procession. She slept on the sofa at Fred's and Anna's that night, accepting the discomfort of the makeshift bed, and not complaining.

"It's been worth dipping into my funeral fund for the fare up here, my dears," she remarked the following morning. "These events don't happen very often in a lifetime, and I wouldn't miss it for the world."

"Well, I'm excited too, Mum, and particularly for Freddy. He's old enough now to enjoy it all."

They'd been busy after breakfast, getting the children ready and packing drinks and biscuits.

"It's good we're leaving early. We should get a good spot to see everything," said Fred as they spilled out from the tenement building onto the footpath.

"I hope your Mum's ready," said Anna a little anxiously as they made their way to Warren Street to pick up Mary.

"She will be," Fred replied confidently. "She missed the funeral of Queen Victoria to look after Freddy. It was just after Pa's death, remember? But wild horses couldn't stop her from coming today."

They reached Warren Street, where Mary stood on the pavement below her flat, wearing her best hat and carrying the shawl she'd worn to the Hotel Russell when she'd walked up the staircase.

The route through London had been carefully planned for the benefit of the London public, and the family walked to the nearest vantage point, taking up their places in the second row of spectators. They'd managed to squeeze in the stroller carrying Amy. Throngs of people gathered in the next half hour.

"Look at all them decorations and Union Jacks up there on the buildin's," Mary pointed out to Freddy.

The child was becoming fractious due to the long wait, but soon distant music hushed the crowd and heightened expectation.

Fred lifted Freddy higher so he could see the approaching mounted guards. As they passed by, the child extended his arm, pointed and shouted, "Look at all the horsies, Daddy!"

The procession continued, delighting the crowd as they eagerly awaited the coach bearing the recently crowned King and Queen and other visiting Royals and dignitaries walking behind.

"They're nearly here," announced Martha rather loudly, and everyone in the crowd craned their necks to get a better view of the magnificent coach as it approached. Loud applause and cheering broke out as King Edward and Queen Alexandra passed by.

"I think I seen Queen Alexandra, but I'm not sure. Someone's 'ead go' in the way," whispered Mary to Martha and Anna.

"They went by so quickly," joined in Fred who'd overheard his mother's observation, "but look, here come the Grenadier Guards, Anna."

Amy began to wail, the cheering of the crowd waking her. Anna picked her up and tried to comfort her, but the crying continued.

"It's nearly over anyway," said Martha. "Why don't we make our way to this park behind us and give Amy her bottle?"

Everyone agreed. They'd seen most of the procession, and it was time to leave; they struggled through the crowd and finally reached the edge of the park.

"Over there," pointed Anna, indicating a spare park bench. "You old girls can rest your legs. We others can sit on the grass."

Martha nursed the baby and gave her the bottle. "Nearly five months old now. I don't see enough of her and Freddy."

"We'll have to remedy that somehow," said Fred, "but it's the cost of the fares, isn't it?"

Anna opened her carry-bag and pulled out a packet of fancy

biscuits, a bottle of lemonade and some tumblers.

"You know what?" said Mary between sips of her drink. "While I was waitin' in tha' crowd, I looked across and seen a posh lookin' lady in a big 'at with all these fancy fevvers on it. She give me a lovely smile and waved an' I smiled at 'er and waved back, an' I said ter meself, we're all the same terday, rich an' poor, it don't ma"er. All of us, standin' 'ere togevver and united like a big 'appy family because of the way we love our royals. 'An I bet' in a 'undred years, people'll still be doin' the same as us terday, standin' in the streets, wavin' an' cheerin' 'em on."

Christmas Day 1902

Fred gazed at his assembled family after their Christmas lunch at Sandwich Street. It had been a rewarding year overall, and Freddy was now two years old and talking in short sentences. Little Amy was now over six months old. And what about dear old Mattie, her belly already swelling as her pregnancy advanced?

Baby Hilary

Six months later, in April, 1903, after a prolonged, difficult labour, Mattie gave birth to a healthy baby girl. Mary was on duty again, helping out her daughter until she was strong enough to look after little Hilary.

"I'm so glad she 'ad a girl," Mary confided to Anna when calling on her a month later. "Amy and 'Ilary will always 'ave a friend now to play wiv while they're growin' up."

Anna agreed as she gathered garments Amy had grown out of for the new baby girl.

"I won't need these any more, Mum. You can give them to Mattie. I don't think there'll be any more baby girls coming along. My family's complete with Freddy and Amy."

"Yes," agreed Mary quickly, "two's enough. Yer got yer quota, youse two. You'd be barmy ter 'ave any more."

Anna got down the biscuit tin and made a cup of tea. Mary had been busying herself with the children, firstly helping Freddy make something out of his building blocks then nursing Amy and giving her a bottle. The conversation turned to housekeeping.

Housekeeping

"Yer run off yer feet, ain't yer, Luvvie? I take me 'at off to yer. Yer keepin' the place 'ere lookin' lovely too".

"I have to," replied Anna, "but it's a battle to keep it clean. You know what it's like Mum. The dust from stoves and chimneys coat the windows and blacken the curtains if a window's open. And when a wind blows up, it all comes in onto the furniture and gets into our clothes and beds. I worry about living here in London. I wish we could move to the country with fresh air, but that's just a pipe dream, isn't it?"

"It's the same fer everybody 'ere, Anna. There ain't nuffin' we can do abou' i'. I'm jus' grateful Fred and Walter bofe 'ave a job ter go to. I dunno 'ow some manage wivout a man's wage comin' in or wivout sharin' wiv someone."

Anna reflected silently on her situation. She'd recently seen some semi-starving children in rags a few streets away as she'd walked to Whitefields. They'd been left to their own devices while their mother, probably deserted, scrounged around the district for some sort of work in order to put bread on the table. Anna had come home distressed about the children. She'd felt fortunate that her family was thriving.

"I'm so thankful, Mum, that I have that little cleaning job at Whitefields. It's not much, but it helps me get household things we need and treats for the children. It makes a difference. Do you know that Fred has been saving up for some time now because he wants to take us to Hampstead Heath on Bank Holiday – I'm so looking forward to it."

"Yer should 'ave a bloomin' good time, me Luvvie, bu' it'll be crowded, mind, on Bank 'Oliday."

"The last time we were there we were on our honeymoon and Fred promised we'd go back in summertime when it wasn't snowing. I didn't realise then we'd have two children before we could get there again."

"That'll make i' more fun, Luvvie. Freddy'll love vem big swings an' the Punch and Judy show. But I'd better git goin'. I got some washin' ter do."

Mary made her way back to Warren Street but felt troubled on the way, as she remembered the struggle she and William had had bringing up Fred and Mattie. *I 'ope life'll be kinder to vem two.*

But how to help them, apart from child minding? Then she almost stopped in her tracks as an idea occurred.

An Ugly Vase

"There's that vase, vat ugly big fing me aunt give me when I got married. No wonder she wanted to git rid of i', all covered in grape vines and lumpy fruit bits stickin' out. 'Orrible colours too! Murky greens and browns an' purples. She said it could be werf a bi' o' money, but she weren't sure. Next week, I'll take it to vat place in town where they tell yer 'ow much fings is werf 'an auction vem antiques."

Mary lightened her steps as she thought of the possibilities of helping Fred and Anna along the way a little. She mounted the steps to her home, opened the door and went straight to a cupboard and took out the vase, covered in dust.

I'll give i' a wash and take it to vat place, she thought as she eyed it critically. *Maybe I'll ge' a few shillin's.*

The next morning Mary wrapped the vase in layers of newspaper and took it to the laundry with her. She put it in a safe place in a corner away from people's feet. When her shift finished, she placed the vase in her carry-bag and headed to the auction house, arriving just before closing time. Drawing in a breath, she approached an assistant.

"I go' a lovely vase ter show yer. I 'ate partin' wiv it because it's been in va family fer years and years yer know, ever since I got married. I know it ain't cheap so I want yer to 'ave a look a' i' and give me wo' it's werf. Someone'll want i' I'm sure, if yer pu' it in the winder and … …"

"We'll have to have a look at it first," interrupted the distinguished-looking man behind the counter; he waited expectantly as Mary unwrapped the vase from its layers of newspaper.

"Ere i' is," Mary said hopefully as she wiped off a small area of grime near a handle with her finger. "Ain't i' beautiful?"

"I'll have to consult with my colleague about this," the man said as he lifted the vase and eyed it closely. He disappeared into a back room and shut the door behind him. Placing the vase on a table, he summoned another man.

"Look at this, Harold. I'm sure this is the missing mate to that one in the cupboard over there. Let's see the mark on the base. Well, I'm blowed! After all these years. To think that old girl out there has been hiding it all this time. No wonder no-one answered our advertisements. She probably never reads a newspaper."

He lowered his voice. "That pair of vases is in demand, you know, circa 1720 or near enough. Very rare! We'll advertise the two and put them up for auction in a month or so. Hopefully we should get close to forty pounds for them. How much should we offer the lady?"

"Oh!" answered Harold pondering, "I think she'll be happy with a couple of pounds by the looks of her. Let's offer her that and see what she thinks."

The two men made their way out to the counter and offered the money to Mary. Her face beamed as she accepted the offer and made her way out of the place, remarking as she left that she hoped someone would buy the vase as, although it was lovely, it wasn't really to her liking.

Mary was elated as she made her way home. *Two bloomin' pounds*, she enthused, *'an I would 'ave been 'appy wiv a few bob. Can't wait ter give it ter Fred fer Bank 'oliday up at the 'Eath.*

Mary presented the money to Fred and Anna the next day, refusing their offer to keep half for herself. "You jus' go 'an 'ave a good time up at 'Appy 'Amstead, me Luvvies, and spend the lot!"

August 3rd, Bank Holiday

Time to get up, my darling Fred," Anna urged excitedly. "It's past eight o'clock and breakfast is ready. The children have had theirs and we're only waiting for you now."

Fred rolled over and rubbed his eyes; stretched before sitting up and grinning at Anna.

"Thanks for doing all the work, my dear, I really appreciate the sleep in you let me have. Now I'll get busy after brekkie and help you get the picnic things ready."

"There's nothing to get ready, Fred. I'm just taking a bottle for Amy, a few plates and some biscuits and a drink for Freddy. Oh! and that check blanket from our bed to sit on. We're going to buy all our food up there and ice creams too. Remember, your mother said we had to spend up big at the fair and I intend to."

Fred agreed and said they both needed a break and no stress about spending money up there.

Anna had been worried about Fred's energy levels lately, which was why she'd let him sleep in.

He sprang out of bed, dashed to the privy and quickly dressed when he returned. Anna had set out some kippers for her and Fred to have with bread after their oatmeal. Fred ate quickly as he didn't want to hold Anna up who'd finished first.

She dashed into their bedroom and fetched her straw boater hat with the black ribbons and gathered the blanket from the bed. She pirouetted before Fred when she returned to the kitchen as she knew he loved to see her in that hat with her hair tumbling down from under it.

As Anna expected, a compliment followed. An air of excitement and expectation filled the room.

"Quick, Fred, make us a cuppa and then we'll get going. Freddy and Amy are getting restless."

After hurried cups of tea, Fred rinsed the crockery and dried it.

"Come on, let's go," he announced as he gathered up Anna's large bag and the picnic blanket. Taking hold of Freddy's hand, he led him downstairs while Anna carried Amy down and placed her in the stroller in the vestibule. They walked to the bus stop, and joined a large assembly on the footpath that was also going to the Heath.

"I've never seen so much traffic," Anna observed as the first omnibus pulled in and was quickly filled by most of the waiting throng.

"They've put on extra buses for today," answered Fred, "but we should be able to get on the next one."

They waited for about five minutes until the horses drew in, and Fred, Anna and the children were able to board the carriage.

"Horsies, Daddy, horsies," piped up Freddy, excitedly, "on the bus with horsies."

A group of young people in the back seats struck up a rousing chorus – *Now if yer want a 'igh old time, just take a tip from me, Why 'Amstead, 'appy 'Amstead, Is the place to 'ave a spree. (Albert Chevalier, 1893).*

"They look like they have jobs in service," Anna whispered to Fred. "The girls are wearing their aprons. I hope they have a wonderful day off. They deserve it."

It was a noisy trip to the fairground with lots of laughter and good humour. The journey was quick as the bus, once filled to capacity, made no more stops.

Everyone spilled out of the vehicle; made their way through the entrance between the East Heath Road and the Vale of Health. The Nash family walked along an extensive row of hawkers' stalls and wagons, the owners shouting out and inviting people to inspect their wares.

"I'm not buying anything just now, Fred. Let's go first to the merry-go-round and give the children a ride on that."

They followed the sound of the music which was pumped out by a steam organ. The fairground spread out before them – booths, swing boats, coconut shies, hoop-las, peep shows, freaks, boxing booths, waxworks, shooting galleries and acrobats.

"There's more along here," Fred said ushering Anna and the children along a short side lane that led to a paddock with ponies.

"It's only a penny a ride," urged Fred, knowing of Freddy's fascination with horses.

"We'll fit that in later for Freddy but first let's get some ice creams," Anna suggested. "It'll be something new for the children."

After the treats, they walked back to the merry-go-round and waited their turn to mount the colourful horses. They managed to grab three, Anna and Freddy riding on one each and Fred nursing Amy on another.

"Again, again," implored Freddy after the ride, and was promised another turn later in the day.

"I'm going over to have a skip, Fred," announced Anna, as she dashed away to where two men were turning a rope rapidly. Young girls were lining up to pay their penny to have a go. Anna felt a bit sheepish but decided she was not too old to join in.

"I'm not as good at it as I was," she remarked as she returned to the others after her turn.

"The main thing is you had a go," said Fred encouragingly. Then he added, "Now it's my turn, Anna. I'm going to the shooting gallery. I've never held a gun in my life. Maybe I can win us something."

While he was away, Anna took the children to a stall selling children's toys. She opened her purse and took out some of Mary's vase money and bought Amy a colourful rag doll, and Freddy a toy locomotive painted green.

"I rode in a train once, pulled by an engine just like this one, Freddy. When you're bigger, maybe you'll go on a real train too."

Freddy smiled and put the engine down and pulled it along by a string.

"Fweddy's twain," he proclaimed, his eyes shining.

Fred returned, saying with a wry face that shooting wasn't his forte as he could only hit one target out of six.

"Leave shooting to the gangsters, Fred. You have other talents," Anna consoled. "I'll win us something. See the hoop-la? I'm having a go on that."

After two bouts, Anna came back, triumphantly carrying a box of chocolates.

They made their way to a row of tall structures supporting ropes that carried boat-shaped, open carriages. Squeals from girls and loud whoops of joy from boys pierced the air as the swings rushed to and fro at great speed.

"I'm not going on those swing boats with Amy," declared Anna. "They'd frighten the life out of her."

Fred pondered. "Should he take a small boy on one of them?"

"Daddy, I want to go on the big swing," begged Freddy, who'd sensed his father's hesitation.

"Alright, I'll hold on tight to you," agreed Fred.

After the exhilaration of the ride, Freddy pleaded to have another ride, but Anna intervened, saying it was lunchtime and they must all be hungry by now. Fred agreed and told Anna he knew of a quiet spot where they could spread the picnic blanket.

They bought some small meat pies, sandwiches and jam tarts from a nearby stall and then called in to a ginger beer and lemonade kiosk where they sat on a wooden seat and had a drink, including Amy, who pulled a face after a sip of lemonade. She started to grizzle and Anna increased their pace, knowing that Amy needed her bottle and a good sleep.

They rounded a corner and mounted a small bank where there were a number of large spreading oaks on a flat expanse of parkland. Several people were picnicking, but another short walk brought Anna and Fred and the children to a suitable spot.

"Here!" said Fred, as he pulled the blanket out of Amy's bag and spread it on the grass. Anna had packed a few plates and some serviettes in her bag and they all tucked into the food.

"She's eaten a bit of sandwich, Fred," said Anna as she settled Amy onto her lap and offered her her bottle, "I've brought a small pillow so she can have a sleep on the rug."

"The little fellow could do with a bit of a nap too, by the looks of him," added Fred. "Would you like to lay down with Daddy, my boy?" he invited Freddy.

Freddy's eyes were half closed so Anna lay him down on the blanket and to her surprise, Fred lay down also and in no time, was gently snoring.

Amy finished her bottle and Anna settled her also on the blanket to have a nap.

At that moment four young laughing girls walked by. "I was one of those once," thought Anna as she noted their uniforms and aprons, "but I wouldn't want to be Johannah Telford again. I'm glad I met Fred even though times are often hard, but I can't imagine life without him and the children."

While Fred and the children slept, Anna passed the time watching people pass by including a highly decorated pearly king and queen. She began to feel rather tired herself and decided they'd all spent enough time on the heath and should go home when the others woke up.

Fred roused first and agreed with Anna. "The children have had enough but we promised Freddy a ride on a pony, remember?"

After Freddy had had his ride, they walked to the bus stop outside the complex.

When they got home and the children were settled, Fred made a welcome pot of tea.

"That's what I've been missing all day," said Anna with a relieved grin. "I think I'm an addict."

"Me too," agreed, Fred. "I was brought up on it."

"This has been a lovely summer, Fred, and the Fair was such fun today, but next month is the start of Autumn and the Heath will look different with all the colours of the trees. We should go up there again soon."

"Why not?" Fred replied, but he leaned back on his chair looking tired and strained.

"Let's hope that half day off they promised you shop people will be along soon," ventured Anna, observing Fred's fatigue.

"They take their time in getting these things through the Parliament. The Union should become more insistent I believe," said Fred with a sigh, "but I shouldn't complain. At least I have a job."

"But those hours are so long and you're mostly on your feet all day and just Sunday off to catch up and do other things you need to," joined in Anna sympathetically.

Fred felt pleased to have Anna's understanding. He'd made it a point to never complain in front of her as he'd remembered his mother's advice that worries and complaints were not able to alter anything.

"It's alright, my love. So far, so good. I think we're doing well and the children are thriving."

Christmas Day 1903

Freddy turned three on Christmas Day. The whole family had gathered at Warren Street for the dual celebrations. New Year's Eve came and went and after some time, Anna remarked how quickly the year was passing.

"Tomorrow is February Fred. I'm looking forward to next month when it starts to get warmer."

By the time March had arrived Anna could no longer put aside her growing fear. She'd even attempted to ignore it but the time came when she could no longer deny the truth. But how to tell Fred again? Last time he'd been so angry because she'd delayed telling him straightaway, so she'd better get it over with as soon as possible. Then she felt angry. Why did she need to feel guilty because she was having another baby? As though she'd done something wrong by conceiving. She thought of past comments some people had made about family sizes – 'two's enough Anna', 'don't have any more,' 'think of the cost of their support,' 'there's only one wage coming in you know, and even two is a struggle sometimes.' Comments even made by her mother and Mary!

"It's alright for some," Anna thought, feeling resentful. "They can have as many as they like and even get compliments each time they're expecting."

It was a Saturday and Anna decided she'd tell Fred tomorrow after he'd had a sleep in.

After lunch the next day Anna braced herself and told Fred her news.

In a face with little expression, Fred reacted.

"Anna, I've only got to look at you and you get pregnant. Another one on the way, eh?"

"How *dare* you!" replied Anna hotly, as she broke into sobs. "You behave as though it's all my fault. From now on you can keep away from me. We'll run the household and bring up the children and live as brother and sister. That'll suit me," she bellowed.

Still sobbing, she moved over to the couch and bent over, her head in her hands.

Fred joined her on the couch but she wriggled away from him.

"I can't promise you Anna, that I'll always be like a brother to you. I'll try, but the fact is, I'm your husband and I love you and I may be mistaken but I think you love me too. That relationship will make it hard for us but I'll try. And I'm sorry I was so insensitive just then and upset you so much. Your news came as a shock rather than a surprise but I'm sure we can fit in another little one. We have a cot and Amy can sleep with Freddy in his bed. It's big enough."

At that moment, Fred and Anna became aware that both children were crying and upset at the row between them.

"Mummy crying," said Freddy as he walked over to Anna. She sat him on her knee and gave him a cuddle.

"We've all been crying, little fella, but everything's alright now and Daddy and I are good friends again."

Fred had picked up Amy and calmed her down as well. He decided to make a cup of tea before they got ready to go to Whitefields.

"You know what?" announced Fred, "I'm sure everything's going to be alright. You and I are tough. We've proved that, haven't we? And we'll have help from the church again, you'll see."

"Fred," answered Anna, "do you realise how many people are in need today in London? We are not the only ones. We can't always expect Whitefields to come to our rescue every time we have a crisis. There are many in the church who are just as badly off as we are."

"I know," said Fred, looking serious, "but Aunty Esther has always helped us out. In a way, she's like one of the family."

Anna gathered herself together, pleased that she'd spilt the beans about the baby and that peace had been restored to the household but she felt drained after all the upset.

"Well, we'd better get ready for church Fred. I don't want to be late. I'm rostered on to help get the tea tonight."

Moral Support

The family set out on their walk and soon arrived at the church. Trestle tables had been carried into the middle of the room and chairs placed around them. Anna and a group of other helpers brought out donated foodstuffs and drinks from an adjoining room and laid out the spread on the tables. Grace was said and people tucked in. There was plenty to go around. After the meal, Anna led Freddy into the children's room for activities and Fred took Amy to the crèche.

Tables were quickly taken away and chairs rearranged into rows, ready for the evening's worship service. Fred had rediscovered his love of singing. It was 'peoples' choice' this afternoon whereby favourite hymns could be nominated. Some were those composed by the Wesley brothers, Charles and John. Fred called out the title of one of his favourites, 'Jesus, Lover of my Soul'.

When the service was over, Aunty Esther sat down next to Anna and commented on how well the children looked.

"And how are you, my dear?" she enquired.

Anna looked at Aunty Esther and found herself sharing her news in spite of herself.

"I'm afraid I'm expecting again. I'm not over happy about it. Another mouth to feed you know. It'll be harder on Fred. He works so hard and gets very tired."

"You'll manage, my dear," replied Aunty Esther reassuringly, noting Anna's downcast expression, "I remember last time you were expecting Amy, you told me it was too early to have her, but look how you've coped with things and you even have a little job to do here. You're a very good mother Anna. I know you're not sorry you had that beautiful little girl and I know you won't be sorry to have this next child. Each one is a gift from God and brings its own unique contribution to the family. Take heart Anna. I'm sure things will work out. You're all healthy, aren't you?"

"Yes, we are, but as I said before, I worry a bit about Fred. His job is too demanding but we need every penny he earns. It's not like he should get something easier because that would bring in less."

"I understand Anna and I agree with you. The hours are too long but I'll tell you something. I've known Fred since he was a small boy when the family first came to Whitefields. I've watched him grow up into a lovely man but through the years he often seemed sad and I just knew he needed someone like you in his life. When you came along, he suddenly had a spring in his step and a readier smile and after he married you? Well! we've all seen the difference here. He is just so proud of you and the children and I know that even though his job is hard, he wouldn't change his life for anything else, even if it was easier."

"Thank you, Aunt Esther. I feel better now. I know how much he loves me and the children and do you know what? I love him too."

The evening drew to a close and the family made their way to their home in Sandwich Street. After the children had been put to bed, Fred lit the fire and made a cup of tea. He sat at the table near Anna and looked at her with narrowed eyes and a slight grin.

"Let's forget about that business today, my dearest. We have two beautiful children and are about to have a third one. We'll make do as we always have done. Bye the way, when is the little one expected?"

"I'm not quite sure. Probably around the end of August or thereabouts. I'll get some remnants and make some new clothes for the baby. I gave Amy's clothes to Mattie for Hilary."

Fred said he was having an early night as tomorrow it was business as usual. Anna hopped in beside him and in no time, they were both asleep.

A Worrying Letter

When Fred arrived home from work, Anna handed him a letter which had been delivered in the afternoon.

"I'll look at it after I've had dinner," he said, placing it on the table.

After the family had eaten, Fred picked up the letter.

"Now, let's see what's in this," he said as he tore open the envelope.

Anna watched as Fred read the letter and noticed a furrow gather on his brow. He then placed the letter on the table with a deep sigh.

"What is it Fred? What's in that letter?"

"That wretched landlord has put up the rent. He said the rising costs of repairs to his properties has forced him to do it."

Anna exploded. "How dare he do that to us! He's getting nearly half your wage as it is Fred. Does he expect people to starve or what? And what's he done to improve this place anyhow? A leaking tap and mould on the walls. How can we manage now? We're only just getting by as it is. And another one on the way. Oh! Fred, what are we to do?"

"The same as we did when we moved out of Regent Square to here when we were having Amy," said Fred with a resigned expression. "I'll have to look around and find a cheaper place."

"Well, I'm six months now so there isn't much time to organise a move. Oh! my Lord! We've only been here two years. All that bloomin' packing again and me getting bigger. You'll have to get going Fred and find something quickly. Do you think Ernie Dobson could help us out with the move again?"

"He didn't mind last time. If only Pa was still alive. The place he worked for would've lent us a van. I remember he said once that people moving into cheaper rent kept furniture removalists in a job. I never thought he was talking about us. Anyhow, I'll start looking tomorrow. You never know, I might find a nicer place than this, Anna." He gave her a hopeful look.

"I hope so, Fred. I'll get some cartons from the grocers tomorrow and start packing."

"Don't panic. I first have to find something and then give notice here. We'll have time after that and we'll always have Mum to help."

"Thank Goodness we've still got some of that vase money from her."

"That'll pay for the midwife in the next few months. Lucky we've got it."

Fred told Anna there was an agent not far from the ironmonger's shop and he'd call in tomorrow and have a chat with him.

"We should get a good reference from our landlord here, my sweet. You've looked after the place well."

Three weeks later, Fred arrived home from work and gave Anna the news.

"There's a place at No.4 Burton Street, cheaper than here. I had a look at it in my lunch time. The second room's rather small but the kids should fit in it alright. I told the agent we'd be taking it. Sorry you haven't seen it, but we have to grab it before someone else does. At least it's not in the East End, Anna."

Anna looked relieved.

"Burton Street, Fred? That's just a couple of streets away from here. I'm willing to go anywhere after all this stress, not knowing what's to become of us."

The following afternoon Anna walked to Warren Street and told Mary about their new place in Burton Street.

"Glad yer found somefin' Luvvie. I'll 'elp yer with the packin'. You'll need it. Yer getting' big ain't yer? And I'll 'elp yer with the cleanin' when yer move in. Some people leave a place lousy when they go."

At Burton Street

After the move to Burton Street, Anna had decided not to complain about the apartment to Fred. She knew it wouldn't be fair after all his efforts to find somewhere for them to live.

"At least it's a roof over our heads and maybe later something better will turn up," she thought.

There was a month to go before the baby arrived and she knew she had to rest up and gain strength after the move which had exhausted her. In the evenings she passed the time sewing little garments for the new arrival. Whitefields had donated a dozen new nappies and a couple of hand knitted matinee jackets, some bootees and bonnets.

August passed quickly and Anna was hoping the baby would soon arrive.

"I'm enormous Fred. The longer you're overdue, the bigger the baby. Oh! I do hope it's soon."

On September the second, at four o'clock in the morning, Anna woke up with an insistent backache. She nudged Fred awake and suggested he take the day off.

"I'll make a cup of tea and we'll wait till six and see what happens," he replied hastily.

Then he outlined his plans.

"If you get your pains by then, I'll take the kids to Mum's first to let her know and then I'll drop them off at Florrie's place at Regent Square, then I'll bring Mum back here."

An hour later, Anna got her first pain and Fred swung into action. He quickly got breakfast, insisting Anna not help. He knew the ropes and seemed calmer than he'd been during the previous times. Anna packed the children's necessities into two bags while Fred rode to the shop to let Ernie and Ada know he wouldn't be in, then hastened to the midwife and then to Florrie's place who agreed to mind the children. After nearly an hour he was back at Burton Street, thankful that his calling points had been fairly close to each other. He then embraced Anna, wished her luck, gathered up the children and set out for Warren Street. He walked quickly, wheeling Amy in the stroller and with Freddy sitting astride his shoulders.

Mary welcomed the news of Anna's labour and Fred's arrangements with Florrie.

"Come ter Granny 'an we'll 'ave a cuddle," she invited Freddy with outstretched arms. "Then yer goin' to Auntie Florrie's place. She'll look after youse today. She's got toys and lollies and later on, Mummy's goin' ter give youse a new little baby. Won't that be luvverly?"

The children look bewildered and Amy started to cry.

"Don't cry little one," said Fred comfortingly as he picked up the child. "No need to worry."

Mary quickly packed a bag and they got going, making their way down the stairs. On the way to Florrie's, Fred spoke firmly to the children.

"Be good for Auntie Florrie today, and you, Freddy, look after your little sister. Granny and I will have to go back to Mummy because she needs us."

Fred, Mary and the children continued on. Florrie warmly welcomed them all and then led Freddy and Amy to a box of toys. Fred and Mary hastily made their way down the staircase and continued on to Burton Street with a sense of urgency.

"This one's going to be quick, I think," said Anna, doubling over as Fred and Mary entered the flat.

Shortly afterwards the midwife arrived and Mary told Fred to clear out of the place.

"I'll be happy to," he replied thankfully as he gave Anna a kiss and wished her good luck. He decided to ride to Warren Street on his bike and stay there for a couple of hours. When he arrived, he lay down on his old familiar bed and quickly fell asleep.

One hour later, at Burton Street, Anna gave a final push and the baby was born.

Fred woke up after a fitful dream in which Anna had produced twins.

"Heaven forbid," he thought, "I'm sure it's only one, but I'd better go and check."

He had a sense of deja vu as he rode to Burton Street. "I've done this before."

He crept up the steps to the flat and listened at the door. He could hear Mary's voice. He tentatively knocked and she let him in.

"Look a' 'er, Fred. She's different, ain't she? She's got brown 'air and bluey green eyes, not like the uvvers. 'An 'er skin's a ligh' olive colour. It must be the French in 'er, don't yer fink, from Anna's side?"

"Who knows, Mum?" said Anna with a grin. "Some English people have colouring like that. We're not all blue eyed with fair hair. Do you like her name? It's Edith."

"Well, this one, Ediff, is goin' ter be a beau'y, I can tell. An' do yer know somefin'? I git feelin's about fings sometimes and Amy an' 'er are always goin' ter stick togevver no ma"er wha' 'appens to 'em in life. They'll always be there fer each uvver."

Fred walked over to the bed and sat on the edge. Anna was cradling the baby in her arms. He leant over and gave Anna and his new daughter a kiss.

"That was quick. All over and done with, eh?"

He took hold of the baby's tiny hand and gazed at the child for a while. Then he said, "Welcome to the world, little one, welcome, my little Edith."

"It's goin' ter be a bi' crowded fer a while wiv six of us 'ere," said Mary, "but I'll be gone in a week 'an that'll 'elp.

Anna was falling asleep and Mary and Fred decided that Freddy and Amy should not be fetched home until the afternoon.

Later on, when Fred arrived at Florrie's place at Regent Square, she looked relieved as the children ran over to their father.

"They've been good and behaved themselves. They had a sleep earlier on and they've had lunch and we've been out for a walk."

"And we played with blocks and Aunty Florrie read stories," announced Freddy importantly.

"Well, little ones, home to Mummy now and you can say hello to your new sister. Say thank you to Aunty Florrie and we'd better get going."

When they left, Florrie murmured to herself,

"Another mouth to feed, that'll be hard on 'em."

After they arrived home, Amy inspected her sister intently and was told she was called Edith.

"Edie, new bubba Edie" said Amy softly as she touched the baby's face.

"Edie! Well I expect that's what she'll be from now on," remarked Fred with a grin.

"Except when she's naughty," added Anna. "Then she'll be Edith."

Mary made up the sofa for herself and then gathered some vegetables from the larder and some ham bones to make a soup for dinner. Then she made up the cot for the baby and tucked her into it. Fred fell asleep in the easy chair. Anna took Freddy and Amy into bed with her and read them some nursery rhymes.

"Well, they all fi' in 'ere some'ow," thought Mary, "they should be orright, but no more babies, Anna please."

The next day Fred brought home a newspaper from the shop and read out an article.

"Listen to this Anna, Mum. It says here that poverty is rising dramatically and there's one hundred and twenty-two thousand people in London on poor relief and two hundred and fifty thousand in England in workhouses."

"I can't imagine anything worse that going into a workhouse," replied Anna, pulling a face. "From what I've heard, I think I'd rather die."

"Well, we're alright. We're managing here, my love. No need to worry."

Christmas Day 1904

The Nash family had travelled down to Clapham to Martha's place and had pooled their resources for Christmas dinner. Mattie and Walter and little Hilary had joined in and Martha was ecstatic. It wasn't often she was able to see Freddy, Amy, Hilary and baby Edith all together. Somehow, the adults had managed to buy a few cheap toys for the children from a popular department store called Marks and Spencer.

"You're four now Freddy an' gettin' ter be a big boy, ain't yer? Daddy'll 'ave ter take yer down to a lake somewhere ter sail yer new boat," announced Mary, when she observed the boy's happy face as he hugged his present to his chest, "'an I'll make the girls a new dress each fer their dolls. The baby's too young fer presents yet."

Anna had turned aside and secretly grimaced at the idea of Mary's sewing attempts. The rabbit she'd once made for Freddy had lost an arm and an eye, but strangely, Amy had adopted him and wouldn't part with him at bedtime. At the sudden thought of this, Anna had felt mean and realised her daughter had appreciated the value and love behind the gift, more than she had.

New Year's Eve was soon upon them and Fred and Anna had celebrated quietly at home.

"We'll drink in the new year with some apple cider," announced Fred, as he removed the cork from a small bottle. "Happy 1905, my dear one. We'd better make some new year resolutions, don't you think?"

"We already have, Fred. Don't you remember? Just after Edie's birth we pledged to live only as brother and sister from then on? So far it's worked alright and I for one intend to keep it going."

"It'll be hard, Anna, as I've said before, and we'll try our best, but I'm looking forward to the time when we can remove that vow."

Anna moved away from Fred and sat down on the sofa.

Let him dream, she thought, *but I know the reality of things for the likes of us.*

Making Do

Anna still had her two afternoon cleaning jobs at Whitefields. Each week she would inspect the donations to the clothing pool. She needed underwear for Amy but no little bloomers appeared. Then she remembered a neighbour down the street had told her once that grocery shops would often hand out empty calico flour bags to make undies out of. She had consequently collected four bags from the owner in the corner shop and had patiently hand sewn some bloomers for Amy.

Sunday for Fred was anything but restful and a welcome sleep in was now out of the question with a crying baby and two other children pestering him for attention after six days near absence, while he was at work.

"For Goodness sake, take Freddy to a lake somewhere to try out his boat, Fred," suggested Anna crossly, one Sunday. "It's not fair he hasn't been able to sail it."

Fred saw the point and set out with Freddy to walk to Regents Park to a pond. On the way back home he realised he'd enjoyed the small excursion and decided to go somewhere each Sunday morning with his son.

"I'll take him down to the Thames to watch the boats and another time we'll go to St Pancras station to see a steam train and there's the new double decker buses on the road now running on gasolene."

When they got home, Anna supported Fred's ideas about entertaining young Freddy each week. He suddenly remembered his escapes to the parks each Sunday when he was single and living with his parents in Warren Street.

It's just the same, he thought with a small sense of guilt. *It's that old feeling of being shut in and having no space of my own.* Then he looked at Anna and his guilt increased.

Look at her! he thought. *Run off her feet with everyone's needs, her only escape each week going to Whitefields to a mother's club or to clean the place. It isn't fair.*

"Anna," he said softly, "I think you need a little escape from this place and the children now and again. I could get Mum to stay over one evening each week and we could go to some place on our own, eh?"

"We couldn't afford it Fred and you know it," replied Anna quickly. "I sometimes dream of going to a moving picture show or even a magic lantern evening, but it all costs money and I'm struggling to feed us properly as it is. We'll just have to keep going as we are until Freddy is old enough to help out. Like you did with your family back then."

"I guess so," answered Fred with a grimace, "but he's not even five yet, quite a way to go until then."

"Anyway, we're going to church at Whitefields tonight," answered Anna, changing the subject. "We can stuff ourselves there with the food. I've stopped feeling guilty about that. There's always enough to go round."

"You're right there, Anna. And Jesus urged the rich to share with the poor. Remember?

Fred and Anna were struggling through the year feeling pleased that the children were healthy and happy. Freddy was due to start school after Christmas, Amy had turned three in June and baby Edie had turned one in September and was now walking.

"Somehow, we're getting by, even though it's a grind," remarked Fred with a reassuring grin, as the family sat down to their breakfast oatmeal on the morning of October 25th.

"It's taking its toll, though," answered Anna with a weary sigh. "How long is it going to take Fred before you get that half day off they promised? Have you heard any more about that?"

"Nothing at all. It was about six years ago when Pa told me about that proposal in parliament."

"Well, I hope they get a move on. It's unfair to expect people to keep hours like you do."

Anna did not continue the discussion, knowing it would not help Fred in his situation. She admired the way he carried on and never complained even though his fatigue was obvious and his hair was greying.

They set about their business after breakfast. Fred kissed them all goodbye when he left for work and Anna cleaned up the kitchen area and attended to the children's needs. The day passed as usual until Mary called in to mind the children while Anna cleaned the premises at Whitefields Central Mission. When she returned home, Mary had prepared the evening meal and Fred had also returned. After they'd all eaten and the two girls put to bed, Mary exploded with her news.

Suffragettes

"Do youse know wo' I 'eard today at the laundry? It 'appened up in Manchester last Friday. They call 'em suffragettes now and two of 'em, one called Annie Kenny and anuvver one went to this meetin' wiv all the big wigs and caused a big 'ullabaloo. Annie yelled out and asked this bloke Winston Churchill when the women were goin' ter git the vote. Well, 'e didn't bovver to answer 'em so Annie and vat Pankhurst lady started shoutin' out. A policeman frew 'em ou' of the meetin' an' one of them girls spat in 'is face and started hittin' someone else. They were fined some money but vey said they'd go ter gaol instead. Now this is wot 'appens when people are not taken seriously. They git frustrated. Now that carryin' on won't 'elp 'em yer know, but I can understand 'ow they feel. I'm angry too. Do you remember, Fred, that Millicent Fawcett years ago? She just 'ad quiet marches wiv banners an' be'aved 'erself. Yer know somefin'? I felt like joinin' 'em back then."

"It's silly isn't it?" affirmed Anna. "Women in mansions who employ men like gardeners and servants aren't allowed to vote, but those men are. It just doesn't make sense."

"It'll come one day," said Fred, who was feeling ganged up on. "You'll see."

"It'd be"er be sooner than la'er," answered Mary grimly. "Vem girls are ge"in' angrier and angrier. Lord knows wot could 'appen."

Fred decided at that point to put on the kettle and make a pot of tea, hoping the subject would change. Mary obliged.

"Tha'll be nice Fred, just wot I need before I git goin'. It'll warm the cockles of me 'eart. It's gittin' cold now, ain't it? Don't the years go quick? It'll soon be Christmas again an' anuvver year comin' up and Freddy goin' off ter school. Cor lumme! I can't believe it!"

After the cuppa, Mary grabbed her coat, scarf and handbag and hugged everyone before leaving to go home.

"Speaking of Freddy going off to school," said Anna, reminding Fred, "we'll have to get him new clothes, new shoes and a satchel."

"Yes," said Fred, trying to hide his concern, "I'll put aside whatever I can for those things."

"One of the mothers at Whitefields told me there's a good secondhand shop in Tottenham Court Road and they have cheaper clothes there," said Anna, "I'll have a look soon. I don't want him to look shabby."

"Aunty Esther can look out for a pair of shoes for him too," added Fred. "That'll save a bit. Bye the way, I've got some good news. Someone told me today that The Education Board is getting a grant for free lunches for schoolchildren this coming year."

"That'll be a help," said Anna with a grateful smile.

Christmas Day 1905

Freddy turned five on Christmas day, and the year 1906 was looming up. The child was excited about becoming a schoolboy. When the big day finally arrived, Anna dressed him in his new clothes and shoes which she'd bought at a rummage sale. Whitefields had provided a pair of braces for his knickerbockers, and a jumper a size too big, but he could grow into it as Aunty Esther had remarked. A neighbour in their tenement building had volunteered to look after Amy and Edie while Anna was away with Freddy during the enrolment.

They made their way to the local school at Cromer Street and joined a queue waiting for registration. After the formalities, Freddy was led by a serious-looking matron to a classroom with stools and small desks. He was sat down near another new boy and Anna was waved away by the woman and ushered to the door.

Oh! she thought, *I couldn't even say goodbye to him.*

She looked back at her son and waved, and Freddy waved back, a pleased look on his face, but Anna felt like crying as she knew another phase in Freddy's life was beginning. She was to pick him up at three o'clock in the afternoon and was looking forward to hearing how he'd passed the day.

He was silent about school on the way home with Anna, but in the evening after dinner, he opened up and emphatically announced that he wasn't going to go anymore. Fred had the job of telling him how he'd get used to it and would get to like it as he learned to do clever things. Over many days, the child accepted his schooling and was no longer reluctant to walk to school in the mornings.

Life Goes On

Anna was busier than ever. Amy was over three years old and little Edie was nearly eighteen months. Keeping them amused was a challenge and often interrupted the house cleaning which was so important in sooty London. Anna often felt she couldn't cope with all the demands made upon her and would sometimes shed a secret tear. One night in bed she started to cry, believing Fred was asleep but he wasn't. He reached over the separating pillow between them, so they wouldn't touch each other, and stroked her upper arm.

"It's hard, isn't it, my dear? Life's a grind for us. Let's go to Regent's Park next Sunday for a break instead of church. We can take some sandwiches and cordial and relax a bit. How about it,eh?"

"Fred, going to church each week helps me, you know. I always feel refreshed and ready to face the week again."

"I know," answered Fred, agreeing. "He restores our souls as it says in the Twenty Third Psalm. You know Amy, God never promised that life was going to be perfect for anyone in this broken world whether rich or poor and we should remember that He is with us in the bad times as well as in the good times, to strengthen us."

"That's true Fred," Amy replied, softly. "Well, let's get off to sleep now. Tomorrow's another day and we need our rest."

The next morning on the way to work Fred was feeling frustrated. He entertained the thought of finding another job which would pay him more but he quickly abandoned the idea when he weighed up the pros and cons. Apart from odd jobs, his only real experience was as an ironmonger's assistant. Other stores were too distant and he'd have to take an unpaid day off which he couldn't afford, to attend a possible interview. No! Better to stick it out where he was. He knew he was lucky to have a job and the Dobsons had become friends, often helping out in small ways which he knew other people wouldn't.

During the morning, Ada descended the stairs in order to mark some gift items with prices. Fred was unpacking deliveries.

"How's it going these days Fred? And how's Anna? She must be a busy little bee now you have three children. Is she still cleaning at Whitefields?"

"Yes, she is," answered Fred as he felt himself weakening. Should he let Ada know how hard life was for them both, or button up and pretend that everything was fine?

At that moment Ada glanced at Fred and noted a familiar expression of late on his face, the mouth drawn downward, a furrow on his brow.

"Do you get out much together Fred, like having time just for you and Anna? Everyone needs a break now and again, laddie. Ernie and I often go out somewhere each Sunday to ease the burden of running this shop, you know."

"We go to church each Sunday and that helps," answered Fred.

"Yes, I'm sure it does, but I mean somewhere else too. Just for you and Anna alone Fred. Like an outing somewhere?"

"Can't really afford it, Mrs Dobson. Children are expensive you know and now Freddy's started school …"

Ada cut in, "Fred, it's about time you called me Ada. No more Mrs Dobson from you. You've become more like a friend to us than an employee. I really wish we could pay you more but if there's any other way we can help?"

"We're getting by," replied Fred with a smile. "So far everyone's eating and we have clothes on our backs and a roof over our heads. Anna and I just get tired, that's all."

An Offer From Ada

Ada was becoming increasingly concerned about Fred each day and kept dwelling on his wan expression. That evening she had a talk to Ernie.

"I feel for that little family. Such a struggle Ernie, and Fred and his wife never having any fun on their own. You know that marvellous show we saw last week, 'Hale's Tours of the World' in Oxford Street? Wouldn't they both love to see that? The fare to go in is only sixpence each and we could afford that, don't you think? Put some money in an envelope with an extra five bob so they can buy themselves a dinner somewhere afterwards, eh? Come on Ernie, be a sport."

"Well, I've never had any worries with him over the years in the shop. Alright, let's do it."

The following day, Ernie handed Fred the envelope which also included an illustrated pamphlet advertising the show.

"Oh! Mr Dobson!" exclaimed Fred, overwhelmed, but before he could continue, Ada spoke.

"It's Ernie and Ada now Fred, remember? No more Mr and Mrs Dobson. Alright?"

"I can't thank you both enough for this. I know Anna will be thrilled. Moving pictures, eh?"

"Go there soon, Fred, it's already June and I don't know how much longer it'll be on."

"I can't wait to tell Anna," replied Fred happily. "She's always wanted to see a moving picture."

After work, Fred's steps were lighter as he made his way home, the envelope with the money safe in his pocket. He greeted Anna with a big grin as he pulled the envelope out and waved it in her face.

"Guess what Anna? We're off to see Hale's Moving Picture Show in Oxford Street. Ernie and Ada are giving us a treat. Not only that, they're paying for us to have dinner afterwards."

"Oh! how kind of them Fred," said Anna, her face shining. "I can't believe how good they are to us. Every Sunday when I get out my yellow rose china set, I'm grateful. Aren't we lucky?"

"One day after work next week, we'll go, eh? I'll ask Mum to sleep overnight and look after the children. I don't think she likes the sofa much with that broken spring but she'll do it just for us, I know."

The following Wednesday night was chosen for the big night out. Mary came early to cook the evening meal for herself and the children. Anna arrived home after her job at Whitefields and was eagerly awaiting Fred's return from the shop. When he arrived, they changed into their Sunday clothes and set out.

"It'll take about half an hour to walk there," explained Fred as he linked arms with Anna.

When they arrived at the venue, Fred told Anna what to expect.

"I've read the pamphlet and this is what happens. We'll join the queue there and go up to that platform and when the current session ends, people will come out and others will go in, about fifty at a time. Ernie told me the show lasts for about twenty-five minutes and it's amazing what we are going to see. Ya sit down in what feels like a train carriage, like you're going on a journey and all these moving pictures of people and scenery from all around the world come onto a screen in the front, and ya feel like you're really there."

"I can't wait Fred," said Anna excitedly as she squeezed his arm.

When they reached the platform, a conductor collected their fares and they walked into the mock carriage and selected a wooden bench to sit on. An assistant took his place at the back, ready to give a running commentary as the show progressed. There were a few muffled squeals and gasps as the carriage began to rock and vibrate as it felt like it was turning a corner to match the passage of the journey of a hurtling steam train or some other type of vehicle on the screen.

The sound effects also, were startling. The rumbling of wheels, a clanging bell to clear any traffic if travelling in a motor vehicle. Now and again a sharp whistle from a locomotive.

When the show ended, Fred and Anna emerged from a side exit and looked at each other amazed.

"I've seen so many places that I didn't even know existed, Fred. And I feel excited about the future of moving pictures. Already they're making films with real actors and actresses in them, acting out stories. Someone told me that one day there'll be sound as well."

"Yeah," agreed Fred. "Our children are going to see some incredible things in the future. There'll be big machines with wings that'll fly to destinations through the air. Imagine that!"

"I'd never go on one," said Anna with a shudder. "If something went wrong it'd be a long way to fall, but Fred, I'm getting hungry. Let's find a place to eat. See that place over the street? Let's go there."

They entered a small pub which specialised in roast dinners. They both ordered lamb and mint sauce and bread and butter pudding for dessert.

"And we have enough for coffee too. A change from the usual cuppa, eh?" said Fred happily.

"A rare treat for us Fred but I still enjoy our cuppas."

After their dinner they left the café to walk home and Fred put his arm around Anna as they slowly walked along Oxford Street while admiring the wares in shop windows. Then they held hands.

They were both enjoying the closeness and touching which they'd denied themselves since Edie's birth but they almost sprang apart as they climbed the steps to their apartment. Fred looked at Anna with a wry smile then quietly laughed. Anna joined in, then said, "One day, Fred, my love, one day."

Mary was asleep on the sofa, quietly snoring when they entered but she woke up in spite of their tiptoeing and quietly asked them about their outing.

"Make a cup o' tea Fred and tell me all abou' it."

But Fred declined, promising to tell her about it in the morning.

"We're tired Mum, it's work for me tomorrow. Let's all go to bed."

The next morning on the way to work, Fred nearly ran his bike into a bus which veered suddenly in front of him to pull up at a stop.

Be careful, you fool, he castigated himself. *Keep your mind on what you're doing. What if I get killed? How would Anna manage without me, eh?*

He knew he'd been thinking about last night's outing and more specifically about their walk home together.

It's just like before we were married, when I was so much in love. Dear God in heaven, how long must I wait for her again?

He steadied his mind and decided to walk his bike along the footpath, rather than ride, not trusting himself to forsake his thoughts of yearning for the closeness which he knew they both wanted.

Ada greeted him at the door of the shop when he arrived and eagerly asked him about their outing.

"We had a wonderful time Ada, and Anna was surprised at everything she saw on the screen. And we had a lovely dinner afterwards, a really nice roast. Thank you so much for giving us this treat."

"I wish I could do more Fred. But seriously, you and Anna must get out more together in future. It strengthens your marriage."

Fred grinned at her and nodded, thinking, *Yes! I know all about it, Ada.*

An Outing for the Children

Fred's working days passed uneventfully after Ada's treat to the picture show. A week later he made his way home, pausing to buy a small bag of sweets for the children from a barrowman. When the family had finished their dinner, Anna joined Fred on the sofa for a while before they started to do the washing up.

"I'm looking forward to Bank Holiday when we can go up to Hampstead Heath again and see what's going on there, Fred. We don't have money to spend like last time but there'll be some free things to see like a Punch and Judy show. Freddy and Amy and even Edie would love that."

"Yes," agreed Fred. "It's about six weeks away. Let's do it!"

Their plans for the visit to the Heath were changed when Aunty Esther chatted to them during their attendance at Whitefields on the following Sunday.

"There's a group of wealthy ladies who work in with Whitefields and the Salvation Army around here, who help fund outings and holidays for poorer children. There's a trip planned to take some kiddies down to Brighton on Bank Holiday. I thought you might let young Freddy and Amy go along. It's not often struggling families like yours are able to afford the train fares which are very expensive. This is a great opportunity for children to see the ocean, Anna. The pier is fairly new and I'm sure the funds will allow them to have a couple of rides and an ice cream. Edie's a little young for the excursion. You could drop her off here for the day to spend in the crèche. And you two could have a day out together alone without the children for once. What do you think?"

Anna answered quickly with a look of appreciation.

"Oh! Aunty Esther, they'd love that I'm sure. Freddy in particular. He loves going down to the Thames with Fred to see the boats there. I'm excited for him and also for Amy."

"Well, that's settled," replied Aunty Esther with a smile. "I'll put their names down."

"We won't tell them about it until a week before. Six weeks is a long time for a child to wait for something like that. It would seem never ending," remarked Fred.

Anna felt buoyed up at the thought of the impending experience for the children, as she explained to Fred the next day.

"I've seen the ocean a few times Fred. When I was in Bristol, I'd save up and some friends and I would travel down to the Bristol Channel and see the ocean there."

"Maybe one day you and I will be able to travel to Brighton and see the new pier for ourselves, eh?" suggested Fred, "but in the meantime we should make plans for Bank Holiday for ourselves. The Heath? Regent's Park? Maybe a walk to St Paul's or Buckingham Palace to see the changing of the guard. And I'll save up for a cream tea somewhere. Any other ideas?" asked Fred.

Anna shook her head. "Just to have a day off and put our feet up will be enough for me."

Away for the Day

Monday, 6th August soon arrived and Freddy was jumping up and down with excitement. He and Amy had been told about their outing a few days previously. Anna had packed a little bag for each of the children to carry with a cardigan, a hankie and a few oatmeal biscuits in case their lunch was inadequate.

"No need for that Anna. I'm sure they'll have plenty to eat," said Fred reassuringly.

At eight o'clock Fred walked the children to Whitefields and dropped them off, reminding Freddy and Amy to behave themselves during the day. Edie dropped her bottom lip and looked ready to cry when taken to the crèche but settled down when given a lolly and a doll and a hug from one of the carers she knew.

Fred returned home and made a pot of tea.

"It'll be a long day for them and I'm looking forward to hearing how they went," said Anna.

"There'll be lots of stories I'm sure, but they'll both be pretty tired, I'll bet," remarked Fred.

"By the way, when should you pick them up at Whitefields?" enquired Anna.

"Half past four," replied Fred, then he added. "That was an early morning Anna, with Freddy waking up at five o'clock and pestering us to get him ready to go on the steam train. He didn't like going back to bed for a while did he?"

"No, he didn't. Amy was far easier to handle. I had to wake her up. Anyway, Fred, we still haven't decided what to do today. As for me, I feel like having a bit of a rest after all the fuss this morning. I'm just going to lie down for a bit."

"Me too," answered Fred. "You know me, I could always do with more sleep."

Anna went over to the sofa and stretched out after collecting the dividing pillow from the double bed she and Fred slept on. Fred covered her with a blanket and then settled down on the bigger bed for his rest. They quickly fell asleep. After half an hour, Anna woke up, uncomfortable on the sofa with the broken spring.

"How on earth Mum sleeps on this when she visits, I don't know," she muttered to herself, half awake. "I'm getting back onto our bed. My back aches."

She tiptoed over to the bed and quietly lay down, careful not to disturb Fred who was quietly snoring. In her weariness she'd forgotten to pick up the dividing pillow.

Fred woke up some time later and was surprised to see Anna lying beside him on her side, asleep. Her arm was lying across his middle. A quick gasp from Fred woke up Anna and she quickly withdrew her arm.

"I was asleep when that happened Fred and I only came here because I couldn't sleep on that wretched couch over there."

"You don't have to apologise, dear one. I didn't mind, you know."

"Well Fred, we mustn't do anything. I'm getting the pillow."

She made a move and attempted to sit up but Fred pulled her down and wrapped his arms around her.

"We won't do anything if you don't want to my darling, but Anna, I have so often longed for you. Would it matter, just once?"

"It might Fred," replied Anna, pulling away. Then she fell back, an anguished look on her face. "It's not fair, having to live the lives we do because we can't afford the risk of adding to the family?"

"I'll be careful Anna, I promise."

She moved closer to him and wrapped her arms around him and they kissed, ushering in the start of intimacy.

"You said just once, Fred. Remember?" giggled Anna, a few hours later.

"We've had some catching up to do, my darling."

"I hope there won't be another one Fred. What if?"

"We have three and we've struggled through. We'd have to move though. That small room next door couldn't take another one."

"Maybe we shouldn't have Fred," said Anna with a small frown.

"Maybe we should have," answered Fred. "After all, we ARE married or have you forgotten?"

"The children are all different, aren't they Fred," said Anna. "Look at Freddy. Such a steady little boy and set in his ways and if they aren't fighting, he's so protective of his sisters, have you noticed? The real big brother. And Amy, well she's a home girl. Quiet and placid and a little mother to Edie. Family will always be important to her, no matter what. And Edie, an absolute tearaway. She's into everything. So hard for me to handle. Anyway, it's three o'clock and we'd better have something to eat. I'm starving. We have to pick them up at four thirty, remember?"

Fred nodded. He and Anna rose from the bed, freshened up and got dressed. Then they had something to eat. Fred cut some slices of bread and they opened a tin of sardines. He then made a cup of tea and Anna got out the biscuit tin and allocated two oatmeal biscuits each.

"Before we go Fred, the pillow's going back on the bed between us," Anna stated firmly. "Hopefully nothing happened today but we can't risk it in the future."

Fred reluctantly agreed, nodding and with a resigned look.

"We'd better get going," Anna said at a quarter past four. "They'll be tired after their day and we shouldn't keep them waiting."

Aunty Esther greeted them when they arrived at Whitefields and asked Anna how they'd spent their day.

"Oh!" stuttered Anna, blushing, as she tried to quickly invent a phantom venue they'd visited. Fred came to the rescue and said they'd rested up as they were both very tired.

"Yes, I'm sure you both must be," agreed Aunty Esther, "and I know a quiet day at home can be most enjoyable too."

Edie rushed over when she saw her parents in the doorway of the crèche and clung to her father. Freddy and Amy soon appeared. The family made its way back home, Edie in the stroller and the two other children dragging behind.

"They're worn out," Anna observed as they waited for Freddy and Amy to catch up.

As soon as the family arrived home, Anna took control.

"Heat up some water Fred and get the basin out. I'll wash their hands and faces and get them into their pyjamas. And you can heat up that soup I made yesterday for tea. Then they can go to bed."

Freddy was sitting on the sofa with Fred and was telling him about the trip to Brighton.

"Mr Turner told me the ocean goes all the way over to a country called France and I saw a big ship on the water. I want to go on a ship like that one day, Daddy when I'm big, and we were up high on the pier and I saw some boys playing in the waves and some people were on the beach."

Amy joined in. "We had a ride on the merry go round and ice cream and Mrs Wilson bought Brighton rock and we had some."

"Water ready yet?" asked Anna, smiling, as she listened to her children's chatter. She got out a face washer and some soap.

After the children had been washed, fed and put to bed, they quickly fell asleep.

"I'm a bit worried about today Fred," confided Anna. "We've never had any trouble conceiving and I just can't imagine how I'd manage with another one."

"I'm sure nothing happened, but come what may, we'd get through it together, my sweet."

"Do you realise Fred, that in just under a month on the 2nd of September Edie will be two. And in another three years she'll be off to school. Life will get easier for me then and hopefully that half day for shop workers will be granted and things will be easier for you too."

"We can only hope, Anna," said Fred, gazing down at the table.

A month went by and Anna was relieved that she had not

conceived.

Edie's second birthday was celebrated on a Sunday with the arrival of autumn. After she'd blown out the candles on her cake and been given her presents Anna mentioned how quickly time was flying by.

"Heaven's above! It'll be Christmas before we know it, and another birthday" mentioned Anna. "I can't believe our Freddy will soon be six."

Christmas Day 1906.

All the family gathered at Mary's place at Warren Street.

"We're gittin' crowded now, ain't we?" said Mary as she looked at her assembled family of ten which included Martha, Mattie, Walter and little Hilary. "First, we'll feed the kiddies a' the table and then they can si' on my bed while we grown-ups 'ave ours. An' later on, we can 'ave the birfday cake, eh, Freddy?"

"I never knew that room was so small," said Fred as his family walked home after the celebrations. "But strangely we didn't have too bad a time, and Mum's pudding, as usual, was pretty good. The old girls together gave us a nice lunch, didn't they?"

"I brought some things along too, remember?" Anna responded petulantly.

"You did too. The salads and mince tarts were delicious. But now we've got to look forward to New Year's Eve. Perhaps we can walk the children down for the fireworks at the Embankment."

"Too late for them, Fred. We'll probably put them to bed and just stay home as usual."

"Six days to go till New Year's Eve. Then I'm having a week off. Can't wait!"

Anna had bought special treats for New Year's Eve: jam tarts from the local grocer to have after dinner, and a small bottle of cheap red wine for her and Fred to toast in the year 1907.

The children were allowed to stay up later than usual on the night. Freddy joined a group in the street below who were letting off fireworks at eight o'clock. When he came back, Anna decided it was bedtime for the kids, and an hour later they had all settled down.

"Oh! peace at last. I'll stoke up the fire. It's freezing in here," said Fred as he drew his cardigan about him and moved to the fireplace. "I'll make a cuppa and we can sit near the fire, Anna."

"You know what, Fred? I'm going to bed soon. Straight after my cuppa. That's the best way to get warm, I reckon."

"Good idea. I'm joining you. How about I bring the bottle of wine and a couple of glasses and we can have a drink to the new year in bed, eh?"

"Well, we've never done that before, but we'd better make our new year resolutions first, Fred."

"They don't always work, my darling. Remember Bank Holiday? I certainly do."

"But the pillow's back, Fred, and that's where it's going to stay."

Fred nodded wearily as he and Anna changed into their nightclothes. They climbed into bed and started to warm up the freezing sheets. In time they dropped off to sleep but were awakened at eleven o'clock by some revellers in the street below. Edie also woke up and Anna settled her with a small glass of milk and a cuddle. She soon dropped off to sleep.

"They're all asleep, Fred. Out like lights," whispered Anna as she climbed back into bed.

A Bottle of Red

"I'm opening that bottle of wine you bought, Anna," Fred announced. "It's time for our own little celebration. Let's hope 1907 will bring some nice surprises. Perhaps Dobson's will do better, and I'll get a pay rise or something, eh?"

"I don't know, Fred. As long as the children are doing well, that's all I want."

By this time the bottle was uncorked and Fred had poured the wine into the two glasses.

"It's a claret, Fred, and was going cheap. I've never had red wine before. Just a little for me. When I saw it in the shop, I thought you might like it. I thought it might help you to relax."

"I've fancied a good ale in the past, Anna, but let's give this a go. Happy New Year, my love."

Anna took a few tentative sips, then a couple of mouthfuls.

"It's lovely, Fred, and it's giving me a warm glow. How's yours?"

Fred raised his eyebrows and agreed it was pretty good.

"Come on," he urged as he sipped a few mouthfuls. "Drink up, my girl. It's New Year's Eve, remember? We'd better drink a toast to it. May all our dreams come true."

They clinked their glasses together and leaned over for a celebratory kiss. Then they drank some more. After that, Anna quietly giggled and said her head was going round and round.

"It's having a funny effect on me. I'm not used to it, Fred. No more of this stuff for me."

Fred had finished his glass and told Anna the wine had certainly relaxed him as she'd wanted it to. They placed their glasses on a bedside table then lay back, pulling the blankets up over them.

"I can't get warm, Fred. Sitting up and drinking, I got cold," said Anna, slurring her words.

"There's one way to get warm that I can think of, dear one," Fred whispered in Anna's ear as he leaned over closer to her, "but this stupid pillow's in the way."

"Then get *rid* of it," answered Anna as she flung it onto the floor.

They made love only once that night and slept through until six o'clock in the morning of New Year's Day. Anna had a slight headache and resolved never to touch red wine again as she attended to little Edie and the others when they woke. But she let Fred sleep in, knowing he needed to.

There was hardly any money to spare after the expenses of the festive season, so the family caught up with what was going on in the parks. Fred enjoyed his week off with the children but also made sure he got extra rest, knowing of the demanding year ahead.

January came to an end, and Anna knew. She had accepted her condition with resignation, realising that worrying about the inevitable wouldn't change a situation, a philosophy drummed into her and Fred by Mary. But she would give Fred a little longer to be free of the worry of another mouth to feed. She would tell him after the march on Saturday, the 9th February, which had been organised by Millicent Fawcett and Lady Strachy to campaign for the women's right to vote.

The Mud March

Anna had decided to go down to the Strand and watch the march; she'd heard it was going to be a big turnout.

She remembered Mary's words: "Millicent is a lady, Anna. Not like vem uvvers, the Pankhursts, with their hittin' people and spittin' at 'em. They don't act respectable. Now this march is goin' ter be quiet an' law abidin' with 'igh-born ladies walkin' along with Millicent in the front. I reckon they've got courage to do vat, don't you?"

Anna had agreed with Mary, mentioning that the marchers risked their reputations, their employment, and could invite ridicule as well.

On the day of the march, Anna noticed heavy clouds gathering. She wondered momentarily whether she should venture out in bad weather with the children to see the march but decided to risk it. The Suffragists had her strong support, so she gathered rainwear for everyone and Fred's large umbrella and set out, aiming to arrive at Exeter hall in The Strand at the finishing point of the march. To her surprise, huge crowds lined the streets, most people sheltering under umbrellas. She eventually found a good place near the finishing point. She settled the children down with lollies just as she heard the march advancing. Fortunately, she'd found an elevated position up a few steps outside a building and had a good view. And there was Millicent proudly walking and leading the march with a group of wealthy, aristocratic women surrounding her.

The rain pelted down but did not disrupt the resolute walkers who numbered about three thousand women from all walks of life and strangely, a small number of men. Anna was amazed at the size of the turnout and felt pleased she'd made the effort despite the difficulty she'd had by bringing the children. There were placards, flags and women calling out for recognition as the crowd kept coming.

They all look so dignified and proud, Anna thought as she watched the tail end of the procession draw near. Then she nearly gasped aloud. There was Mary, sopping wet and holding up a large placard with the words - WOMEN AREN'T STUPID – GIVE US THE VOTE.

"Mum!" Anna yelled out, waving. "It's me. Good on ya. I'm proud of you, Mum." But Mary didn't hear due to the musicians behind her and a contingent of carriages and motor cars following.

I wonder why she didn't tell me she was going in the walk, mused Anna as she gathered up the children to go back home.

"Well," Mary explained a few days later, "once I wouldn' 'ave been able to do tha' because I wouldn't 'ave wanted ter make a display of meself, if yer know wo' I mean, but after I walked up tha' staircase at the Russell 'otel, I knew that even though I wasn't 'igh-born, I 'ad the same right as anyone else to go up there, an' it gave me courage ter be meself because it 'adn't scared me after all, but I didn't know if you and Fred would approve."

"Mum, I felt proud of you. Of course, we approve of the fight that's going on for us to vote. Who made that placard you were carrying?"

"One of the girls at the laundry. She can read and write, bein' younger than me. Now you watch, Anna, our fight is goin' ter git bigger. We'll git that vote one day, you'll see."

"I'm sure we will Mum and I might join you next time if I'm free."

That evening Anna told Fred about Mary's explanation of why she had walked, and Fred gave his Mum a tick of approval.

"They're calling it *The Mud March*, Anna, because of the awful weather and the state of the streets. I read all about it in the newspaper."

Anna was feeling tired and slightly nauseous since her day at the march with the children. She settled them all down after tea and put them to bed.

"I'm telling him tomorrow after church," she resolved.

News for Fred

The following evening after they'd arrived home from church, Anna decided to tell Fred before the children were in bed.

He'll be calm in front of them and won't show his feelings about it if he isn't pleased, she thought, remembering his reaction about her last pregnancy when she'd told him, and the upset that had followed. She took a deep, nervous breath and sat at the table near Fred and whispered.

"I've held off for a while Fred because I wanted to be absolutely certain …"

Fred broke in.

"We're having another one? I wondered because you looked a bit washed out the last couple of weeks," Fred whispered back, his face a blank.

"Have you got secrets? Why are you whispering?" asked a wide-eyed Freddy sitting opposite them.

"Yes, we have a secret, but we'll tell you," said Fred with a gentle smile. "One day, there's going to be a little baby come to live with us, and you'll have a new brother or sister."

"Get a boy baby, Daddy," insisted Freddy, a stern look on his face. "There's already two girls here."

"I can't guarantee it will be a boy, Freddy. We have to accept what the Lord will give us."

At this point, Freddy lost interest and went over to a cupboard and pulled out some lead toy soldiers to play with.

Later on, when they were alone and the children in bed, Anna said to Fred, "I can't understand it, Fred. You'd think I'd have fallen on

Bank Holiday last year, but on New Year's Eve, just once?"

"Well, that would be enough," answered Fred with a wry smile.

"It was that red wine, Fred. After that, we just didn't care, did we?"

"Whatever the reason, Anna. You know something? We wouldn't send one of them back, would we? So let's welcome this new one, eh? Remember what Mum says, that worrying doesn't make a damn difference? I can keep going. We've got baby things, the cot, the high chair. It'll be alright."

"We've got everything for a new baby except space Fred. I hate to say it, but I'd like you to start looking for a better place with more room as soon as possible. Please don't leave it to the last minute like the last times."

"Yes, you're right there. Now when is this baby expected?"

"Towards the end of September."

"I'll start looking straight away. One thing about this St Pancras area, people are always coming and going and changing their address. Vacancies often turn up."

"Well, Fred, every time I've been expecting, we've had to move, haven't we?"

"Yes, it's a damned nuisance. Anyway, you've never liked this place. I'll find somewhere nicer for us. Tomorrow's Monday. I'll get our names down with a few agents."

Despite Fred's diligence in finding a roomier apartment, it took four months for him to sign a lease for a suitable place. By this time, Anna was nearly six months along the way.

"It's No. 28 Howland Street, Anna, not far from here. Freddy can still walk to school."

"I'm so pleased, Fred. When do we move in?"

"In two weeks. We'll have to let Mum know. She'll have to help again."

Number Four

Mary came to the rescue and helped pack up boxes and carried bags of clothing to the new address.

She was pleased to see an alcove leading to a locked door to the outside hallway.

"This is a nice li"le space fer Freddy," she remarked, "away from the girls. Yer can fit 'is bed in 'ere an' a cupboard too."

"Yes," agreed Anna. "This place has more space but it's still a bit cramped. Luckily, the last people cleaned it for us."

Anna and Fred went through the usual routine before the birth of their third baby girl who arrived on Wednesday, the 18th of September, two weeks early.

"Wot a big girl, Anna," observed Mary. "Glad you 'ad 'er and not me. Lucky she was a bi' early or she could've killed yer. She looks a bi' like Amy. Wot yer gunna call 'er?"

"Millicent Louise, Mum," Anna announced. "I've always liked that name."

"Millicent! Well, she couldn't 'ave a be"er name," said Mary with a delighted expression, "an' I 'ope she grows up to be jus' like our Millicent Fawcett, eh? Wot a great lady."

"She'll probably get Millie, which I think is pretty," added Anna.

Fred had left to fetch Freddy, Amy and Edie and relieve old Florrie from looking after them. When they arrived home, Freddy walked over and inspected the new baby.

"I wanted a boy baby," he said, scowling.

Fred felt a bit inadequate at consoling Freddy, so he attempted to build up his role in the family.

"Freddy, you're such a wonderful big brother to your sisters. I'm sure you can handle one more."

"Well, don't get any more of them," he warned his father. "Three's enough."

"I agree with you, Freddy, and I'm sure this is the last one."

After a few days, Anna couldn't bear to stay in bed any longer. while Mary ran the household – it was wearing Mary out.

"Mum, I really do feel strong enough to get up now. This was an easy birth even though Millie was big," she argued.

"Well, I'll stay 'ere fer a bi' longer an' see 'ow yer go, anyroad," answered Mary, who was secretly longing for her own bed.

After two days, she relented, packed her bag and set off for home at Warren Street.

Mattie's Grief

Two weeks after Millie's birth, a downcast Mary called on Anna with sad news.

"Ee's gone! Yesterday mornin'. So sudden at work. Poor ol' Walter. The doctor said it was probably a 'eart attack. They took 'im away an Mattie an' young 'Ilary stayed with me last night. I squeezed 'em in some'ow. Me flatmate Audrey didn't mind. Mattie'll 'ave ter organise the funeral next week sometime. Oh! Anna, 'ow is Mattie goin' ter manage now wivout 'im? She ain't go' a job. She'll 'ave ter go out charrin' or somefin'. It's near impossible fer a woman with a child ter manage wivout a 'usband, ain't it? Wot's she goin' ter do, Anna?"

Anna felt a small stab of fear at Mattie's predicament but quickly rationalised her own situation, thinking, *Fred's not even forty yet, Walter was over sixty. We'll be alright.*

The following Sunday at Whitefields, Anna was able to find a recently donated dress in the clothing pool to wear to Walter's funeral, saying, "My wedding outfit had become so shabby, Fred."

After the funeral, Mattie and Hilary moved in permanently with Mary after Audrey found somewhere else to live.

Millie was doing well. Anna had resolved to keep feeding her for as long as possible to reduce food costs.

"It's about the only free thing we've got, Fred, but I worry I'm not getting enough meat to eat to balance out the nutrition I'm giving her."

"She looks healthy, Anna. Don't burden yourself with another worry."

Anna had become aware that Amy was due to start school after Christmas. She had turned five in June.

"I've been so busy with moving and Millie's birth and then the funeral, Fred, I'd almost forgotten that Amy will need some new clothes for school. I'll see what I can find at Whitefields next Sunday."

The only items available were a pair of girl's black stockings. Anna claimed them along with two large women's skirts.

"It's the material in them I want, Fred. I'll unpick them and start sewing two dresses for Amy. The dark serge will be good for winter, and the floral cotton will be nice for later."

Christmas Day 1907

Christmas Day arrived, and Freddy turned seven. A few days later, Fred attempted to placate Anna when she wearily complained about her workload.

"Look, Anna, Freddy's already seven now. Only two more years to go and he'll be nine. When I was that age, I had a job as a shoeshine boy outside *The Squire's Rest*. He'll be able to help out then and pay for his own shoes and other things, and …"

"Oh! shut up, Fred. He's still a little boy. Talk about it when the time comes, not now. Anyhow, two years is a long time to go with all our struggles until then. I'm sorry, but I'm tired."

Fred looked at her with a grim expression and nodded. "We'll get there, Anna. Pretty soon Amy will be at school and your day will be a bit easier."

"I don't know, Fred. Amy can be such a help during the day. She's a real little mother. She dotes on Millie and gives her her bottle now I'm not feeding her. And she loves to nurse her, which keeps her quiet and that saves my nerves. And she plays with Edie too, who's such an active child and into everything. No! I'll miss my Amy once she's at school."

Anna felt guilty that she'd complained again. Fred was looking more strained as time went by. Each night he would come home and, after he'd eaten his dinner, he'd take on the tasks of helping to clean up and attend to the children's needs. Then he'd flop down onto the bed and go to sleep immediately despite the household noise of three children and a baby.

School Days for Amy

The day arrived for Amy's first day at school. Dressed in her dark blue dress and black stockings, she hopped excitedly on the spot as she picked up her new satchel. When Freddy said, "Come on, Amy, or we'll be late," she hurried down the steps to the street with him. Anna watched her depart, a lump in her throat. This was the little girl she'd longed for all those years ago when looking after Alice at the bootmakers in Bristol. And now Amy had taken her first small step toward independence.

Anna's thoughts turned to Amy often throughout the day. Would her reaction be similar to Freddy's when he announced he would not be going back to school again after his first day? But Anna need not have worried. Amy returned tired but happy, and accepting that school was to be a regular thing from now on.

The year 1908 was passing quickly, ushering in spring. In London's parks, panoramas of springtime colour in garden beds were now fading and being replaced by summer plantings.

Amy celebrated her 6th birthday on the 6th of June. As July approached, the people of London became increasingly excited at the prospect of the fourth Olympic Games of the Modern Era, shortly to be held in their city. Fred kept up with the latest news from borrowed newspapers from Ernie and Ada at the ironmonger's shop. Each night after work, he would tell Anna, and Mary if visiting, about current preparations for the massive event.

Olympic Fever

"They've finished building the arena now at White City not far from here. The place will hold about eighty thousand people. It must be huge, Anna. All the tracks are ready, a football field, a swimming pool and everything else. And guess what? The government hasn't paid a penny. Private enterprise has paid for the lot – a credit to them all, I say."

The day dawned for the opening ceremony, and rain started to fall, to the disappointment of the population who'd been praying for sunshine.

"Bu' i' all went off quite well in spite of i' bein' wet an' all," reported Mary that evening. She'd heard about it from someone at the laundry. "English people won't let somefin' like a bi' o' rain turn us off."

"I'm interested in the marathon race," joined in Fred. "It's to start from Windsor Castle and end in the White City arena at Shepherd's Bush. It's twenty-six miles long, plus what it takes to circle the arena at the end. We've got several English chaps running in it. Surely one of them will come in first."

The Olympic events proceeded day by day during frequently wet weather until the closing ceremony took place. The winning medal tally went to Britain.

Mary was elated. "'An' I'm so proud of our English lady Sybil Queenie Somefin' gittin' a gold medal in the archery. It jus' shows yer don't i', that women can 'old their 'eads up 'igh if they be given a chance to do fings like men, eh? Bu' I'm disappointed, Fred, fer you about the Marafon. All vem English boys 'avin ter drop ou' of i' except fer one, and that Italian man comin' in first bu' I'm glad vey took the medal orf 'im. 'Ee'd been swigging Italian wine while 'ee was runnin' an' when 'ee was nearly at the finish line, 'ee took orf in the wrong direction and then collapsed. They 'ad ter pick 'im up an' 'elp 'im over the finish line. Then that American come runnin' along second and crossed the line wivvout 'elp, so 'ee was given the medal, and quite righ' I say." Everyone agreed.

Life returned to normal in London after the excitement of the Olympics.

Hard Times

"We're in the second half of the year, Fred, and Edie will be four on the 2nd of September and Millie will be one on the 18th. I'm going to ask Aunty Esther if we can have a combined birthday party for them at Whitefields. It's getting a bit crowded here now. Those two make such a mess every day. Oh! I do wish we had a bigger place. It's so hard keeping everything in order. It's wearing me out."

Fred tried hard to hide his reaction. He knew the demands made on Anna each day had been harder since Millie's birth. He'd also noticed grey hairs appearing at her temples and two worry creases forming between her brows. He strode over to Anna and put his arm around her shoulders. Anna quickly reacted to Fred's usual words of encouragement.

"I know, Fred. We're getting there," she said with a faint smile and a nod. "So far, so good, but we'll have to move out of here soon because it's too cramped with six of us now."

"You're doing fine, my love," he reassured her, "and we can't expect this place to always be spick and span with that blasted dirt and dust blowing in. But just remember this. The important thing is that the children are fed, clothed, educated and have a roof over their heads."

"And that they should feel loved," added Anna with emphasis.

"Well, they certainly are," answered Fred quietly.

The birthday party at Whitefields for Edie and Millie was a great success.

"Vem toys they give us from the pool were lovely," commented

Mary as the family made their way home, "an' I compliment yer on that cream cake, Anna. 'Ow yer found the time, I dunno. Now I must remind yer, that the women are goin' ter 'ave a surprise rush on the 'Ouse o' Commons soon, about our vote. October, actually. I 'ope you'll come along wiv me. Yer said yer would, remember?"

"I'll try, Mum," answered Anna, but she doubted whether she'd have the time these days.

One evening during October, Mary called in and asked Fred if he'd read about the news of the Suffragettes storming the House of Commons on the 13th. Her arthritis had prevented her walking to Parliament House that particular day.

"Yes, actually, Mum. You'll be pleased to know that huge crowds had gathered, including some men too but there were thirty-seven arrests and Christabel Pankhurst is to face trial for her part in it."

"Well, I ain't givin' up 'ope," said Mary determinedly.

Christmas Day 1908

Freddy turned eight and, as the family celebrated, Fred thought guiltily to himself, *only one more year and he can help somehow. He'll be old enough to be a messenger boy, maybe for the post office.* But he dared not mention his thoughts to Anna.

New Year's Eve was celebrated quietly. Anna declared with a smile, "I'm not making any New Year resolutions, Fred, because I can't keep them, you know."

Fred replied, "Well, I thought I may give up my Sunday newspaper to save a bit of money, Anna, but that's one thing I won't do. I remember Pa wouldn't do that either. It was a major thing he looked forward to each week."

"I'm glad of that, Fred. Remember how we first met? We were both going to the newsagent to get our dads' papers".

"Sooner or later, we'd have met anyway, Anna, both living in the same building. It was always meant to happen."

Fred would borrow the Dobson's daily paper to read in his lunch break. He would jot down important events to share with Anna each evening and even include Freddy now that he was eight.

"Anna, listen to this. On the 1st of January this year, the government started paying out the old age pension to people over the age of seventy. The law was apparently passed last year in August. Do you think we'll ever get it, Luv?" he asked with a laugh.

"It's ridiculous, Fred," replied Anna. "Not many working people like us reach the age of seventy. I don't think the government will go broke over that great offer."

Fred smirked and agreed.

Flying Machines and a Big Ship

"Just think of this," Fred related as January came to a close. "On the 16th of January this year, 1909, Henry Shackleton, Douglas Mawson – who is an Australian – and Lieutenant Edgeworth David arrived at the South Magnetic Pole and took possession of the place for the British Crown, giving three cheers for the King. After that, blizzards and hurricane-force winds made them turn back."

"No doubt about the British," commented Anna. "We're great explorers. Look how we've colonised nations, even Australia, so far away."

"Where's Australia?" asked Freddy.

"Too far away, Freddy," explained Fred. "It's on the other side of the world. Maybe when you've grown up, you might go there in a big ship. I read in the newspaper that a huge ocean liner called The Titanic – the biggest in the world – is going to be built in Belfast in Ireland. They're starting it soon, at the end of March. It's so big it's going to take some years to build, and they'll need three thousand men on the job."

Fred kept everyone up to date with local and overseas news as the months passed. He regarded it as important to report on progress happening in the world, particularly in the field of transport.

"Daddy, is it really true that one day people will get in big machines and fly through the sky?" asked Amy.

"It's already happening, my sweet. Listen to this …" Fred turned to a page in the Sunday paper and quoted: "On the 25th of July, a Frenchman called Louis Bleriot flew the first heavier than air aircraft from France across the English Channel and landed it in Dover. It says here the landing was very rough and the landing gear collapsed."

"There you are!" Anna stated triumphantly in a raised voice. "I've always said they're unsafe, Fred, and now you can see for yourself. The man's lucky he wasn't killed."

"These are early days, Anna, and I predict that, in the next twenty years, people will be buying tickets to travel in aircraft just like they're travelling in trains today."

"One day I want to go in one," piped up Freddy, raising Anna's eyebrows.

"I still maintain that horse-drawn vehicles and our own feet are the safest way to travel," she insisted, "… and the locomotive, of course. I was never frightened in one of those."

"You can't go backwards, Anna," Fred said firmly. "These children of ours are going to see things in their lifetime we couldn't dream of and what will their children see?"

"Oh! I don't know, Fred. Let's change the subject. As far as progress is concerned, I'm keener to see working conditions change for people like us and better wages. And when is this government going to bring in that half-day off for shop assistants they promised?"

"God only knows," Fred answered wearily. "I've almost lost hope."

Anna glanced at him and understood how he felt. The fatigue they both suffered would often cause eruptions of impatience and flare-ups of anger with each other.

At the end of September, after he'd returned home from the shop, Fred pulled out a newspaper clipping to read to the family.

"Just think of this. In Paris, they held the First Paris Air Show on the twenty-fifth of this month. Thousands flocked to the Grand Palais, and people are actually buying these planes now. Someone quoted, 'these pieces of wood and canvas with which Wright had played at being a bird' …"

"Oh, shut up, Fred! I'm sick and tired of hearing about those dangerous things. You're obsessed with them. They'll kill people. I don't want to hear about them anymore!"

Fred felt duly admonished and admitted to himself that his interest in the development of aircraft had become a diversion from the exhausting demands made upon him daily. *On the other hand*, he silently reasoned, *I need an interest apart from just the family's needs and working my fingers to the bone … but I have been flogging the topic even though Anna's not interested.*

Anna felt sorry she'd snapped at Fred. She thought, *It's irritating the way he carries on all the time about those wretched flying machines and tries to get me to enthuse about them like he does. To think that some people are spending a heap of money on them and Freddy's shoes are wearing out, and* we *can't afford to buy him a new pair.*

The subject of aeroplanes was never mentioned again.

Christmas Day 1909, and a New Schoolgirl

The rest of the year passed quickly. The family celebrated Christmas and Freddy's birthday in the usual way. He was now nine years old, but Fred never mentioned the possibility of the child getting a small paying occupation.

Not yet, he privately thought, *he's still too little, but later on, later on a bit.*

"Edie's already five. She'll be starting school soon," Anna reminded Fred after New Year's Eve. "She can wear Amy's old school clothes. They're a bit big for her, but they'll have to do."

"I can't believe it's already 1910," answered Fred, "and Edie's off to school."

He was waiting for the day, believing Anna's lot would become lighter without Edie around.

"Only Millie at home soon, my dear. It's going to be easier for you, I hope."

'Should be, Fred. Edie's such a handful. Let the teachers cope with her now, I say. She's as bright as a button and should do well."

The child happily settled in at school, and the three Nash children could be seen regularly making their way to and from school each day.

An Anniversary

In a few days, it would be the 3rd of February. Anna did not remind Fred of the date. Last year she'd wept when he'd forgotten.

Even if it goes by, she decided, *I won't make a fuss. He was more upset than I was when I reminded him.*

On Thursday, the 3rd of February, Fred took hold of Anna's hand when they awoke and gave her a long kiss on the mouth.

"Happy anniversary, my sweet Anna. Ten years, eh? Haven't the years flown by and here we are today, an old married couple with four kids."

"Cut out the 'old', Fred," said Anna as she responded with a smile which crinkled up her eyes.

"And you're still beautiful, my dear one," murmured Fred softly as he pulled a strand of grey hair away from her forehead. "Guess what? Dear old Ada! … I was telling her in the shop it was our tenth wedding anniversary and later on she slipped me an envelope and said it was a present. Just like the two of them did when we went to that moving picture show, remember? 'There's enough for dinner for two and a bunch of roses for you, Anna', she said. So, Saturday night is our night, my girl. I've already spoken to Mum and she's coming over to look after the children. You thought I'd forgotten again, didn't you?"

"Well, I wasn't quite sure," replied Anna, a little guiltily.

On Saturday night, Fred felt very tired after his week at the shop, but quickly freshened up and put on a clean shirt. Anna was ready when he arrived home. They chose a nearby pub, avoiding *The Squire's Rest* even though they hadn't been there for ages.

'Somewhere different," said Fred as they sat down at a table.

"Steak and kidney pie is always nice and how about rice pudding and peaches and a cup of coffee to follow?" suggested Anna.

"That'll be a good feed. We haven't eaten so well in ages," said Fred, looking serious.

Later, as they walked home, they paused to sit on a park bench and huddled close due to the cold February weather.

"Any regrets?" asked Fred as he put his arm around Anna.

"None!" she replied. "I won't say it hasn't been bloomin' hard for both of us, but I wouldn't change it, Fred. Our little family is worth fighting for, isn't it? One thing too is that I'm my own boss today instead of being ordered around by that la-de-dah dame in Bristol I once worked for."

"Do you still love me though, Anna? Do you remember what it was like ten years ago?"

"How could I forget those days, Fred? Of course, I love you, my dearest. But I worry about your health. You've lost weight lately. I wish I could think of some solution to make life better for us all."

"Well, we've come through ten years, Anna. We can get through the next few years. Remember our vows. For better or worse. Or through thick and thin as Mum would say."

"Why do you only say the next few years, Fred? Surely we'll have more years ahead of us than just a few."

"I don't know what made me say that," added Fred hastily. "I'm alright. I just get tired now and again."

He had never admitted to Anna that he also worried about his health. There was that all-consuming fatigue which would hit him occasionally, worse than his usual tiredness. And that night sweat about a week ago. He'd kept that to himself too. Just a cold or some infection, he'd reasoned. He'd got over it alright, and had managed to put in an honest week's work at Dobson's despite a lingering tiredness.

"Better get home, Anna, but isn't it good tomorrow's Sunday and a day off, eh?"

"I'll say!" Anna replied.

News About the King

On Saturday night, 7th of May, Fred returned home from the shop with a spare newspaper a customer had given him. The whole country was in disbelief. Mary had joined the family to discuss the recent event.

"'Ee was sixty-eight years old when 'ee went, 'an only ten years on the frone. Not like 'is old Mum Victoria, eh? I 'eard somewhere that she's been the longest king or queen on the frone, ever."

"It says here," said Fred, reading the account in the paper, "that King Edward died last night of a heart attack. He'd been sick with bronchitis for nearly a week before that. He'll be lying in his coffin in Westminster Hall before a procession through London. People are invited to file past his coffin to pay their respects. Then a train will carry him to Winsor for his funeral."

"Well, I fer one, won't be goin', even if I didn't 'ave me arfritis," said Mary firmly. "I know 'ee's been a good king 'an all that, but 'ee didn't support the vote fer women. I find that amazin' seein' 'is own muvver, a woman, was rulin' the country fer over sixty years. Funny vat, ain't it, eh?"

They all agreed with Mary. She stayed the night on the sofa, eager to meet up with Sister Esther Howell at Whitefields the next afternoon, whom she hadn't seen for some time.

A Serious Illness

On the 6th June, Amy turned eight. Anna had sewn a new pinafore for her and had found two second-hand storybooks for her to read. It happened a few days after the birthday party that Millie fell ill and Anna became very concerned. The child was tossing and turning on her bed with a burning fever.

"My throat, Mummy. My throat hurts," she wailed as Anna attempted to sponge her down to reduce the fever. But the child became hysterical. When the other children arrived home from school, Anna penned a frantic letter and gave it to Freddy to take to his father at the shop.

"Be careful on the way to Dobson's, Freddy. Daddy will be coming home to fetch a doctor for Millie. He'll probably give you a double back home on the bike."

Freddy sensed the seriousness of Millie's sickness and hurried all the way to the shop. When Fred read out the note from Anna, Ernie and Ada urged him to leave everything and go home straight away. He helped Freddy onto the bicycle seat and set off. Once home, it didn't take Fred long to realise Millie was very sick. Anna had managed to quieten the child and reduce the temperature a little by sponging her with a wet face cloth.

"I'm going to bang on the doctor's door if it's after hours," said Fred fiercely, "and make him come here at once. Our little girl is very sick."

When Fred arrived at Doctor Sommer's surgery, he was obliged to wait until his turn, cursing inwardly at the length of time a gossipy old woman took to say goodbye to the doctor.

Once inside the surgery, Fred explained Millie's symptoms and pleaded with the doctor to come and see Millie for himself. He agreed to do that but stated that he would expect his fees to be paid promptly.

"Of course, Doctor Sommers, but please don't delay. She's been thrashing about on the bed and I'm worried about her."

Fred gave the doctor his address and was assured he would call on the family in about half an hour. Fred rode back home on his bike.

"He'll be here soon," he assured a stressed and anxious Anna.

When a knock came on the door, Anna opened it to admit Doctor Sommers. He cast his eye critically around the family's living quarters to Anna's embarrassment as the place was in disarray. Fred led the doctor to the other room where Millie lay. He took her temperature, frowned and muttered something. Then he examined her chest and got her to poke out her tongue.

"There's a rash breaking out, and her tongue is quite red, and her high temperature confirms she is suffering from scarlet fever," he announced with a grim expression.

Then he added, "I'll be taking her in my car to the Hospital for Sick Children in Great Ormond Street for two reasons. She will need special care as this disease has a high mortality rate among children, and she will also have to be isolated as it's infectious. And it can lead to rheumatic fever. Also, you don't want these other children to get it, do you?"

"Oh! no!" answered Anna and Fred in unison quickly. A feeling of dread took over Anna, and she fought back tears.

"Take her quickly, Doctor, and get her better. Please."

"I'll do my best, Mrs Nash. She'll just need a nightgown and a blanket to wrap her in."

Anna was pleased the nightie she had changed Millie into was clean. The child whimpered as Fred picked her up and explained to her where she was going, and that she would soon be better. Anna followed Fred and the doctor down to the car and then spoke to her daughter.

"You'll soon be home, and Mummy and Daddy will be coming to

visit you in hospital."

"Only for an hour on Sunday afternoons in the common room, if she's well enough," the doctor cut in firmly. "Parents often upset the children. You will leave her treatment and care to us, and hopefully, she'll soon be home."

Stricken, Anna glanced at Fred then at the doctor.

"Can't we just come to the hospital and wave to her now and again through a window or something?" she pleaded.

The doctor shook his head. "Rules are rules, and they can't be broken for just one child."

Fred was invited to sit in the back seat with Millie while delivering her to the hospital. Anna waved and blew the child a kiss, but she didn't respond, her sad little face staring ahead.

Anna walked back to their apartment; sat down and cried. She'd heard from gossip in the street that a child from around the corner had recently died from scarlet fever. Freddy, Amy and Edie gathered around her, and Amy said comfortingly, "Don't cry, Mummy. Millie will be alright. Jesus will look after her, I know it."

"I'm sure He will, Amy. Daddy should be home soon. We'll have our tea, and afterwards, we'll all pray for Millie."

The hospital was in Bloomsbury, not far from where they lived and Fred arrived home in half an hour after filling in the necessary forms at the hospital.

After their meal, Fred led the family in an earnest prayer for the healing of their daughter and little sister.

"Dear Lord, in heaven above, we ask for your mighty healing hand to touch our little girl. And please give wisdom to the doctors as they treat her. Give her peace in her spirit and let her know she is not abandoned by her family. We ask that she'll be home with us soon. Amen."

"And please, Jesus, let her come home soon because I want her to play Snakes and Ladders with me," piped up Edie.

Freddy looked sternly at his sister.

"That's not the reason we want her home, Edie. We want her back because she can be well again."

Fred reacted to his son's remark.

"Freddy, that was a fine prayer of Edie's. It may sound a bit selfish, but Edie only wants her to join the family again to take up her normal life, which includes playing games."

Millie returned home after three weeks. Even though her skin was still peeling, she was regarded now as non-infectious.

"God answers prayers," announced Amy as Millie settled back home.

"Indeed, He does," affirmed Anna.

Financial Stress

The family settled down to their usual routine, but the strain on Fred and the demands on his wages were worse than ever.

"That doctor knows how to charge, Anna, even though he knows we're struggling. Now I'm having to give him the money I've saved for Freddy's shoes. Have another look for some at Whitefields next time you go there to clean. We may be lucky."

Anna held back her despair as she noticed the anguish on Fred's face, and tried hard to be positive.

"Well, Fred, at least we can be thankful the hospital hasn't charged us anything. I suppose we do get some concessions, being poor."

Then she added: "I'll go to Whitefields tomorrow. Hopefully, there'll be some shoes for Freddy. He's already through his soles, and I think the shoes have become too small. He takes them off when he gets home, and I've noticed he's got chilblains."

The next day, Anna hurried to Whitefields and searched through the Donations boxes. Unfortunately, there were no shoes for Freddy. Two weeks later, the child discarded his shoes and walked to school barefooted. Fred reminded Anna that this was probably only for a short time and that when he was as young as Freddy he'd been without shoes at times and had survived.

A few weeks later, Anna received a note from the children's school informing her that a random visit from the Medical Inspector would shortly take place.

"Oh! Fred," she anguished, "I'm worried. The Medical Inspector will be going to the school soon. Amy and Edie are looking so shabby lately, and Freddy still has no shoes on his feet. I hope that won't be held against us.”

“Don’t be silly, Anna. The man will be inspecting children’s health and how the school is being run, not how the children are dressed.”

“Please get into your funeral fund, Fred,” pleaded Anna, “I’m sick and tired of looking at Freddy with bare feet. It’s not fair to the boy.”

“I can’t do that, Anna, much as I want to. You never know when a man may need that money. I saw some figures yesterday in the newspaper which stated that working men are not living beyond the age of forty-five. That doesn’t leave much time for me, does it?”

“*FRED!*” Anna replied in a raised, shocked voice, “how can you talk like that knowing your Pa and my Dad both lived into their sixties. How would I manage on my own? Look at Mattie since Walter died. She’s had to get a job as a charwoman with her asthma and all. Please don’t talk like that.”

Fred immediately regretted his words and the effect they’d had on Anna.

“Forgive me, my darling. I’m a tough old codger. I’m good for a long time yet. Don’t worry … I was just being flippant.”

But underneath Fred had concerns. He’d recently suffered another night sweat and had made his way shakily to the shop in the morning.

It’s all the worry I’ve had lately, he’d reasoned, *with Millie’s sickness and my wages not going anywhere, and bills, school expenses and that doctor’s wretched bill still not fully paid. And I’m a week behind with the rent. I’m just a bit run-down, I suppose. Anyhow, I’ll keep quiet about everything and not worry Anna. I can keep going and catch up in time.*

A Small Break in the Park

A few days later, Anna decided to keep Edie home from school. She'd been sneezing and was developing a cold, which she'd caught from Amy who'd almost recovered and gone back to school. Edie had been whinging about being shut up in the flat and Anna had finally given in to the child's urgings to go to the park.

"Not for long though, Edie. Mummy has left the dishes in the bowl, and the place is in a mess, beds are unmade, and you haven't put away those toys and books into the box where they belong. When we come back, you'll have to do that and help me dry the dishes."

Anna wearily packed up some bread and cheese and made up some cordial, promising herself they'd be back in an hour or so, but she lingered in the park, enjoying the fresh air and the respite from her tiresome everyday tasks. On the way home, she castigated herself for leaving the flat in such a state, but then considered that she'd probably needed a break as much as Edie, that restless child of theirs always seeking new experiences and becoming bored so easily.

When they returned, Millie was put down for a sleep, and Edie started colouring in.

"Not before you've tidied up all that mess of yours," insisted Anna, but the child resisted and stamped her foot.

"I'll do it when I've finished this picture," she screamed, taking on her mother.

Anna exploded. "You're a disobedient, naughty girl and you'll do what I say straight away."

Edie continued to scream, waking up Millie who started to whimper. Exasperated, Anna strode over and gave Edie a smack on her bottom.

"Look, you've woken up your sister. Now, you'll clean up your mess, or you'll get another smack, Edie," Anna growled.

A Surprise Visit

At that moment, Anna heard a knock on the door and went to check. She opened the door to reveal a solemn-looking man with a folder under his arm.

"Are you Mrs Nash?" he asked.

"Yes, that's me," Anna said, flustered, as she shooshed the girls and asked them to be quiet.

"What do you want, sir?" she asked warily.

"I'll need to come in and interview you," the man replied. "I'm the district school inspector, and it's my job to report to the relevant authorities concerning child health and welfare in this area according to the recent Children's Act of 1908. I have recently visited your children's school."

"Not the Guardians?" questioned Anna, shocked. "What have we to do with them? They're associated with the workhouse, aren't they?"

"Yes, they are indeed, Mrs Nash. However, you have no need to worry. This is a health issue. I'll explain everything if you let me come in."

"Oh, I'm sorry, sir, please come in and sit at the table here. I'll just clear off these things first. I took the children to the park this morning before I ..."

Anna had noticed the man scrutinising her home in all of its disorder as he walked into the room, and she'd faltered as Edie interrupted with ...

"Mummy *hit* me," she announced tragically, tears still wet on her cheeks.

"You deserved it ... you were naughty," Anna said, looking sternly at Edie. Then she faced the Inspector and explained in a small voice.

"I don't normally smack my children, sir, but things got on top of me today. It's not easy living on my husband's wage as a shop assistant, in just two rooms like this. And there's six of us to fit in here."

"Well, you do have a lot of children, don't you?" said the Inspector, raising his eyebrows.

Anna detected a note of censure in the man's voice and responded, "The size of my family has nothing to do with you, sir and for your information, I wouldn't send one of them back."

"Calm down, madam, I'm not the enemy, and perhaps I can help out in some way. I'm here because it's been noticed that your eldest child, Freddy, has not been wearing shoes for quite some time at school and he appears to be underweight. Also, your daughter Amy has a cold, and lice have been seen in her hair. Firstly, Amy is not to attend school until her head has been treated. You can either shave it or soak it in kerosene to kill the infestation, and you must do this with yourself and your husband and the other children as well.

"I will contact the local Guardian about your family situation if you're having difficulties, as you say. He may agree to some assistance being granted. You may qualify for one and sixpence per week for each of your children. This would be a temporary measure of course until your situation improves, you understand. If it worsens, you might consider other measures. The local school at Leavesdon Langley under the Poor Laws Legislation doesn't charge fees. Also, some people find relief by allowing their children to have a spell in the local facility where food, education, and clothing are provided ..."

The Inspector had noticed the growing intensity of shock on Anna's face as he'd delivered his suggestions.

"*WHAT!*" Anna recoiled in disbelief. Her eyes narrowed. "I'll ignore your suggestion about a workhouse for my children, sir. That's the facility you mentioned, isn't it? In the meantime, they are happy in their present school and doing well. We will not disrupt their lives. I'm aware we're in debt of late, but that will be settled in time. Our youngest has been seriously ill with scarlet fever just recently, and the doctor's fees have almost been paid. Regarding Freddy's shoes, this has been a worry for us. I've been looking out for a pair for him at Whitefields Central Mission Church, and have asked my husband to dig into his funeral fund if no shoes are available on Sunday when we go to that church."

"I'm sorry to hear you're having so many troubles, Mrs Nash. From what you tell me though, it may be that you qualify for some assistance, but it wouldn't be much as your husband is employed unlike many others in London. I'll call again next Wednesday evening to verify your husband's financial status, any debts and other records. That will be all today, Mrs Nash."

When the Inspector left, Anna sat on the sofa and tried to hide her tears, but Edie noticed and came over to her.

"I'm sorry I was naughty, Mummy. Don't cry. I'll put my things away now and make it better for you."

"That's alright, my girl. Come and have a cuddle. We can be friends again. And later on, when we've cleaned up the place and it looks nice again, I'll get out the flour and sugar and butter and we can make some biscuits, eh?"

Peace with Edie was restored, but Anna's mind was in a whirl. Had that man assumed they were poverty-stricken because of the present squalor in the place and because Freddy needed shoes? And how to tell Fred about this visit from the Inspector? She had long decided to become Fred's protector from any worries, as best she could, knowing he'd been losing weight over the past few months. She decided not to mention the word 'workhouse' but emphasise possible out-relief for the children, measly as it might be, but underneath she was devastated. To think they were now marked people who'd been noticed by the authorities due to their neediness. The stigma! To pretend they weren't poor was deceiving themselves, but fortunately, they were still eating a reasonable diet but lacking sufficient meat. Tonight, she'd make up a hearty stew from a scrag end of beef and a few vegetables.

Good heavens! she thought, *I'm getting to cook like Mary, making out with whatever I can.*

As the school inspector made his way back to his office, he mentally prepared his report.

"Loud angry voices and screaming as I approached the front door. Woman upset and angry when I entered. Children distraught and crying. The place an absolute mess, with dirty dishes in the bowl, unmade beds and the eldest girl there confessed to me that she'd been hit. Need to establish whether they are the undeserving or deserving poor before any assistance given. Woman mentioned help from a church called Whitefields. Add to all that, an infestation of head lice in the family. No, it doesn't look good."

Fred's Response

When Fred returned home after work, Anna let him finish his dinner before she discussed the Inspector's visit. She did not mention the state of the flat, Edie's disobedience and the smack, or the tiredness she'd felt in the morning leading to her postponing the housework. She mentioned the reason for the Inspector's visit. Freddy's bare feet and his weight, Amy's cold, and the nits. She finished on a hopeful note by telling him about the Inspector's visit next Wednesday to discuss his finances and some possible out-relief for the children.

Fred replied quickly. "I'll speak to that blighter when he calls in on Wednesday night to get information about my earnings, Anna. We'll get over this hump with our money, don't worry. Now about Amy's hair. I'll bring home a bottle of kerosene from the shop and we'll fix that problem." Then, seemingly unperturbed, "Ah! I see you've made some biscuits today. I'll make a pot of tea."

Two days later, the family made their usual way to Whitefields for their evening meal and worship service. Mary was also attending church that evening, and Anna told her about the nits, but nothing else.

"People'll say our kids 'ave got dirty 'eads, yer know, an' we ain't respectable anymore. I'll come over an' 'elp yer ter ge' rid of 'em, Anna. Got some kero?"

Anna nodded.

Later on, Aunty Esther joined Anna, who was helping with cleaning up, and asked her how things were. She'd had the family on her mind of late, concerned about Freddy's bare feet and the gaunt appearance of his father.

Anna sat down on a nearby chair and collapsed in tears. It all came out.

"Of all days, Aunty Esther, that wretched Inspector from the school had to call when the place was a dreadful mess. I'd smacked Edie because she was naughty and everyone was screaming. It must have looked so bad. I haven't told Fred about everything because I don't want him to know how tired I was and that I smacked Edie. And tomorrow, we all have to soak our heads in kerosene because Amy caught the nits from school. And the Inspector insisted that Freddy was underweight. He eats more than any of us, you know."

"Freddy's always been a lean and wiry little kid, Anna. It's just his build. I know that," comforted Aunty Esther. Then she added, "I think you should tell Fred about how tired you were that day, and about the mess, and that you smacked Edie. Don't underestimate him and overprotect him. He knows how hard things can be for you. He'd understand."

"Well, I'll tell him tonight. I suppose he has a right to know the whole story. But it's shame I feel, Aunty Esther. And that man also suggested that if things got worse for us, we could put our kids into a workhouse of all places, and they could attend a Poor Laws school. I was horrified. I won't be telling him about that."

"Anna, in my capacity as a social worker within this church, I've helped a few families in my time, but I'm sure your children don't need to go into a workhouse. Now try to be positive, and hopefully the Board will grant you a bit of help. This would lessen the burden on Fred. And there's no shame to be attached to your family, understand? You are decent, hard-working people and the struggles you're having are no one else's business. Cheer up now. I'm sure things will work out for you in the long run."

"Thanks, Aunty Esther. I'll try."

Anna dried her eyes with a hankie and composed herself, not wanting Fred to find out about her distress. He'd been in another room with some menfolk. Shortly, he joined Anna and suggested they go home as tomorrow was to be the big hair wash to get rid of the nits.

Clean Heads

The next morning after he'd had his breakfast, Fred fetched the bottle of kerosene he'd brought home from the shop on Saturday evening.

"Mum should be here soon, Luv," he said to Anna as he left, giving her a peck on the cheek. "She's bringing a fine-tooth comb and some Pears soap. Good luck! I'll hear all about it tonight."

Anna and the children had their breakfast and the bigger children cleared up the dishes while Anna lit the fire to heat some water and then laid out a large bowl and some towels.

A while later there was a knock on the door and Mary entered, without waiting to be let in.

'It's a 'orrible business this, gettin' rid of 'em, but it's gotta be done," she announced as she pulled out the tooth comb and soap from her bag.

"Now you, Amy, yer not ter go and put yer 'ead near another girl's at school after the nits 'ave gone. Now the kerosene's gunna 'urt a bi' but yer Mum's already told youse all about everyfing. We'll do Amy first, then Freddy an' the girls after 'im."

Mary had taken charge of the day's procedures. She tested the heat of the water.

"It's nearly ready, Anna. Come 'ere, Amy, si' at the table and those li"le bligh'ers will soon be dead."

"Be carefu,l Mum," urged Anna. "Don't get it in her eyes."

Mary glanced impatiently at Anna. "Course I won't," she answered firmly. "I've done this before yer know."

Amy bent her head over the bowl and her hair was wetted and then towel dried. The bowl was removed, but a towel on the table remained.

A thick wad of cotton wool was soaked in the kerosene and applied liberally to the whole of Amy's head, with Mary making sure no part was left unsaturated.

"It's horrible," wailed Amy. "I can hardly breathe from the smell and it's stinging me. Oh! It's hurting, Mum. It's burning me."

"It'll stop soon, Amy. Be brave. It's got to be done. It'll soon be over, then I'll wrap your head in this tea towel. The kero must stay on your head all day. This afternoon, we'll wash it off with the soap and the nits will be dead, and we can comb them out. It's all done now, Amy. You next, Freddy."

Freddy looked apprehensive as he slowly moved to the chair.

"Are you quite sure I've got 'em, Mum?" he asked. "What if I haven't."

"You've got fair hair Freddy and I couldn't see any, but we've been told the whole family has to do it, even Dad and me who'll do it tonight. We have to obey the school Inspector."

"Alright," said Freddy resignedly. "Let's get it over with."

He winced as Mary gave him the treatment. "Crikey, it stinks and Amy's right, it burns ya. Come on, Granny, that's enough, isn't it?"

Mary gave one more swab and handed him over to Anna to wrap him up with a tea towel.

The two younger girls were cowering in a corner, terrified.

"No, Mummy, NO!" squealed the girls in unison.

"Don't let Granny do it to us," begged Edie.

"Granny's got lollies," bribed Mary. "I'll ge' 'em out when you're all done. Now, Edie, Millie, this ain't gunna kill yer, only the nits. Come on, girls, I'll be gentle with youse an' I won't use much of the kero."

Edie was finally coaxed to the chair and went through the treatment, surprisingly not objecting as much as Amy had, but the chase was on for Millie who'd crawled behind the sofa, wedging herself against the wall.

"Freddy, you'll have to help," insisted Anna. "I'll pull out the sofa and you lift her up and sit her on the chair."

With much screaming and kicking of legs, Millie was finally subdued but still tearful as Mary applied the kerosene.

"There, there, my darling," said Anna as she cradled Millie in her arms after her ordeal. Then she wrapped her head in another tea towel. "It wasn't that bad, was it? Now keep your turbans on everyone. Look, I have one Indian prince and three little princesses."

Mary brought out the sweets as promised then left to go to the laundry as she'd done her part. The day passed with frequent complaints about the lingering fumes. At about three o'clock in the afternoon, Anna washed the children's hair and got out the fine-tooth comb. No nits were found in Freddy's, Edie's or Millie's hair, but many were found in Amy's. Not only that, but angry looking blisters had formed around her hairline and parts of her scalp.

"It's because she has the fairest and finest skin that it's happened, Fred," said Anna when he came home, "and also, she was the first Mary used the kero on. She was pretty heavy-handed."

After dinner, Anna and Fred went through the kerosene process themselves, having decided they'd better do it to satisfy the authorities. It was an uncomfortable and smelly sleep through the night until they washed their heads in the morning.

Freddy and Edie went off to school with a note from Anna explaining Amy's absence due to the blisters on her head, which were still painful.

The Relieving Officer

On Wednesday evening at around eight o'clock, a relieving officer knocked on the door. Fred let him in.

"Good evening, Mr Nash. I'm Mr Olsen and have filed a report from the school Inspector who saw your wife last week. Of course, she would have explained the reason for this visit tonight, so I'll get to the point. Regarding your present circumstances, I've spoken to our district Guardian and I'm pleased to tell you that he's suggested an allocation of ninepence a week to help out with your children, pending on an inspection of your weekly payslip from your employer, of course. Furthermore, if this doesn't solve your current financial situation, you may consider moving the girls into a special school at Leavesdon Langley nearby and arrange for them to live in the facility attached to that school, if only for a short time."

Fred bristled while taking in the implications of this man's recommendations.

'Our children are happy in their present school and doing well, and you are suggesting we disrupt their lives because I'm having a temporary problem with my finances, which will be settled in due course. And that facility you mentioned is the local workhouse, isn't it? HAH! As if we'd put them in a place like that! Now, our daughter Millicent has recovered from the scarlet fever, and the doctor's fees should be settled shortly and …"

The Inspector interrupted Fred, and stated firmly, "Mr Nash, as an assistant in an Ironmonger's shop, it's quite obvious that your wage is insufficient to cover any emergencies arising which can put a strain on the household budget. Quite frankly, you haven't even been able to put a pair of shoes on your son's feet, and I've noticed he has chilblains. Now instead of complaining, you should show a bit of gratitude that you are to be given some support from the ratepayers, even though I admit it isn't much. Please remember, you are in the fortunate position of holding down a job which many heads of the household do not have in this district. And I would advise you to constrain your wife in the way she deals with your children. As I've heard, I suspect abuse here in this place. I have the forms here ready for you to sign for the assistance."

Fred and Anna gaped at the man in shock until Fred finally found his voice and spoke.

"To begin with, sir, we've never asked for any assistance, and secondly, if the Board genuinely wants to help people in needy circumstances, they should lobby the government to force landlords to lower the rents we have to pay. Almost half of my wage pays for this rundown dump where I am forced to bring up my children. And I am aware that we are not the worst in London."

Fred paused for a while and leant over in his chair; his brow furrowed. There was that two weeks unpaid rent! Then he spoke again.

"Reluctantly, I will sign a form for that assistance for my children, to tide us over, and I'll let you know when my debts have been paid. And lastly, you owe an apology to my wife for suggesting she mistreats our children based on one episode heard from outside the door which she told me about. I have full confidence that my daughter deserved the smack she got for her disobedience. Now, I'll get my current payslip and sign that form you have there, and then you can leave and not bother us anymore."

After Fred had signed the form, the man left uttering a "Hmph" as Fred opened the door.

"I'm glad you signed that form, Fred," said Anna, placing a hand on his shoulder. "I know it's been hard for you, asking for help."

"Well, I'm catching up, my dear. Freddy will soon have some shoes on his feet. Now, how about a cup of tea?"

Compromising

A week later Fred was threatened with eviction by the landlord if he didn't pay the back rent he owed. He finally opened up to Anna about the debt, and they reluctantly decided to have the children transferred to Leavesdon Langley school to cut down expenses. Amy had been distraught due to the separation from the close friend she'd made.

"Betty lives just around the corner, Amy," consoled Anna. "You can still be friends."

Mary had not given Anna the sympathy she'd expected when hearing about the children's new school and the ensuing disruption.

"Anna, ye go' a give Fred the understandin' 'ere, an' not think of yer own pride. Ee's workin' 'is fingers ter the bone for youse all."

"I know that Mum, and that's another worry," said Anna with a sigh. "Have you noticed how much weight he's lost lately?"

"I 'ave, Anna. An' that's why yer should be thankful 'ee won't 'ave school expenses anymore. Now yer can't pretend we ain't poor, Anna. That's a fact 'an we jus' 'ave ter make the best of fings."

"I know," answered Anna, subdued, "I've been doing that for a long time, Mum, but I'm upset because that school is associated with the workhouse at St Pancras. Imagine having to send the kids *there*!"

"Well, that won't 'appen because they ain't orphans or street kids and Fred 's go' a job. So stop worryin' yerself. But do you know, Anna, there's a woman at the laundry 'oose cousin 'as fallen on 'ard times. She's 'ad ter go into the poor'ouse with 'er kids because 'er 'ol man cleared ou'. She's 'avin' a rotten time 'erself, but the kids ain't doin' so badly. It ain't like it used ter be last century, in places like vat fer kids. They look after 'em today wiv food an' education an' they even train up the boys an' girls ter fi' 'em out fer jobs when they leave. The boys are taught 'ow ter become blacksmiffs and cobblers an' uvver fings an' if the girls are good at sewin' or cookin' or 'lookin' after smaller kids, they train 'em up too.

"I been talkin' ter Mattie yer know about 'Ilery because we 'aven't been 'eatin' enough lately. Not 'Ilery though, we always make sure she gits enough. But yer know I've always said worry don't change anyfin'? Well, I've 'ad ter eat me words lately. Wha' I git at the laundry and wha' Mattie gits from the charrin' work, ain't enough ter keep body an' soul togevver. So Mattie's goin' ter see the Guardians next week ter see if she can git somfin fer 'Ilery too, so we're all in the same boat."

Fred's steps were somewhat lighter after the Guardians assistance, little as it was.

"In one month," he explained to Anna, "the doctor will be paid, and shortly afterwards I can get Freddy his shoes."

"Just as well," Anna replied, relieved. Winter's on its way. I couldn't bear to think of him with no shoes on his feet through that."

It was coincidence. That Sunday afternoon at Whitefields, Anna quickly pounced on a fairly new pair of good leather shoes for Freddy, exactly his size.

"And there are some socks too, Fred, but you really should have taken some money out of your funeral savings before this," she insisted. "It hasn't been fair."

"Wouldn't have done that, Anna," Fred replied firmly.

The weather was turning cold. Anna was pleased she'd finished knitting jumpers for the children from a huge bag of assorted woollen yarns she'd found at Whitefields.

"There's enough over for a striped scarf for you, Fred. It'll keep your neck warm on the way to and from work."

Fred smiled, grateful for Anna's concern, although pink and navy blue were not his preferred colours.

Christmas Day 1910.

Mary had pooled resources with Mattie and together they had managed to cook a plum pudding.

"It wouldn' be Christmas wivvout one, would it?" she'd asked of everyone. They'd all agreed.

Later in the day, Mary looked proudly at Freddy as he ate his birthday cake after the Christmas celebrations earlier on.

"Yer gettin' big now Freddy me boy, double numbers now, already ten years old," she announced as she gave Freddy a hug and pressed a gift wrapped in brown paper into his hands. "Yer poor old granny can't afford much vese days bu' a lady from the laundry giv' me vis pork pie cap fer yer to wear, nearly new, and I go' a pack o' boiled lollies too. Give yer sisters a few and yer can keep the rest fer yerself."

"Let's hope the new year will be kinder to us," murmured Mattie. "My asthma is just as bad, and poor old Fred doesn't look too good lately, does he?"

"He's very tired, and his bronchitis isn't clearing up. I think he'll need to see a doctor for some cough syrup," Anna whispered to her sister-in-law.

Fred had made it clear that he didn't want his health discussed by anyone, insisting that his bronchitis would soon be better.

"This year, I'll have to find some sort of work to help out," Anna continued. "Fred's already agreed. It's costing more to live these days, and Fred's wage just isn't enough even with the little bit I get from cleaning at Whitefields and the kid's money we get. I'll do anything, I'm that desperate."

A New Year's Resolution

Winter had arrived in full force and Fred had been thankful for the scarf Anna had knitted. On New Year's Eve, only Freddie and Amy had been allowed to join the crowd in the street below to watch some fireworks being let off by a few local residents. Edie had insisted that her lingering cold would not get worse and Millie was still gathering strength after the scarlet fever.

"What's in store for us in 1911, Fred?" asked Anna with a wry expression. "It's got to be better than the year just gone by, eh? Hopefully, I'll get some work soon."

"We'll battle on, Luv, as we always have done," replied Fred with a faint smile. After a small pause, he added, "As you know, I've never wanted you to work before, but we do need a bit extra, and it'll help. Now here's some good news. In the Parliament, they're talking about that half day off they promised to shop workers. Should be granted sometime this year they say."

"Oh! Fred, that'll help you so much. I'm sure your chest will improve after that. You can rest up on that day, and I'll take Millie out somewhere so you can have perfect peace. And I'm going to buy a bottle of cough mixture next week for you at the chemist. That's what you need."

"Thanks, Anna. I'm sure it'll help."

Freddy and Amy returned from the fireworks below and Anna decided to make some pancakes as a treat to herald in the new year.

"I've got some strawberry jam and a jar of clotted cream and a bottle of lemonade," she announced cheerily as she got out the mixing bowl.

They ate their fill and then played Chinese Checkers until it was time for the children to go to bed.

Anna and Fred sat by the fire for a while before they decided on an early night.

"We won't wait up, Fred. It's just another night, isn't it? I think our rest is more important, don't you?"

"And tomorrow's church for us, Anna. A good way to start off the new year, eh? And Mum's coming too and hopefully, Mattie and Hilary."

"I'm thankful for church, Fred. Our faith gives us the strength to carry on, doesn't it?"

"Sure does," agreed Fred.

A Royal Announcement

Mary didn't turn up for church, but the next day after her laundry job, she called in to see Anna with some news.

"I 'eard today they've set the date for King George's coronation, Anna. It's ter be on the 22nd June. That's somefin' ter look forward to, 'ain't it? An' it's summertime then. Won't the kids love the procession, especially Freddy? 'Ee always loves the 'orses."

"It's nearly six months to go, Mum, before then. Hold *your* horses," Anna said, with a laugh. "I'll make a cuppa and we can toast in the year 1911 with tea and a crumpet, eh?"

"Freddy's ten now," said Mary as she fixed Anna with a steady gaze. "There might be a li"le job around the corner fer 'im this year sometime. 'Ee could pay fer 'is own shoes and fings an' 'elp you an' Fred a bi', eh?"

"He's still a little boy in my opinion, Mum, but perhaps towards the end of the year there may be something," answered Anna with a hint of defence in her voice.

"Well, Fred worked when 'ee was ten as a shoeshine boy at *The Squire's Rest*, yer know, Anna."

"I know that, Mum, but you always hope for something better for your children. We'll see how this year turns out before we rush at things."

Mary looked into her teacup and quietly murmured, "Mmm, I suppose so."

Breathing Exercises

Fred resumed his work at the shop after his time off after Christmas and the new year. He fancied he was feeling better as the days lengthened and spring approached.

It's that cough syrup Anna keeps getting for me, he thought. *It's quietened down the cough.*

He'd been careful to always have a handkerchief with him to cough into as he didn't want to spread his germs around.

And maybe I should start doing those breathing exercises I used to do when I was singing in the choir at Whitefields all those years ago when I was young, he thought. *But not in the fogs, only in the fresh air.*

Fred kept to his resolution and practised his exercises each day at work during his lunch break. He felt sure he was clearing up his bronchitis as the months went by.

Getting a Job

In the meantime, Anna had been looking for some part-time work. Firstly, she'd called into the Midland Grand Hotel where she'd once worked as a room servicer. She thought Mrs Reeves might still be there and understand her situation this time. But she was out of luck. Mrs Reeves had retired three years previously and had gone to live in the country, and unemployment was so high these days, so she was told, most people hung onto their jobs for ages. After that, it took six weeks of hiking around London and knocking on doors before something turned up. Footsore and weary, she'd flopped down on a chair for a rest outside a seedy-looking pub near Euston Station. A waiter approached, and Anna politely asked for a glass of water. Then, impulsively, she'd asked if any work was available. She was hired on the spot as a kitchen hand after an interview with the owner.

"I was lucky, but I hate the thought of the work," she confided to Aunty Esther at church the following Sunday, "but I suppose it's better than charring. I have to peel potatoes and vegetables, wash and dry up, wipe down dirty tables and scrub benches and make sure the tumblers and wine glasses are spotless. I'm what you'd call a 'slushie', I suppose. And then I have to go home and start all over again. Now I've got this job, Fred has to inform the Guardians, and the children's assistance will be cut out, but we should be able to manage better now."

"Would you be up to keeping your little job at Whitefields on Wednesday afternoons, Anna?" asked Auntie Esther, doubtfully.

"I can't Auntie Esther. My hours are from eleven o'clock in the morning until six in the evening each weekday. I'm starting tomorrow. But I can always come to help out on Saturday evenings if you need someone."

"Are you sure, Anna?"

"Yes! I love the concerts and the talks. I don't mind helping to clean up afterwards."

Family Squabbles

Over the next few months, Anna became increasingly tired as she coped with her extra work load at the hotel. And despite more money coming in, she wasn't sleeping well. She didn't say anything to Fred, but she was wracked by anxiety about the way he looked with his increasing weight loss and pallor. On occasions she found herself screaming at him and the children over trivial incidents. And sometimes Fred would respond and a fight would start up. On one occasion Mattie heard heated exchanges as she'd waited outside the door when visiting and before being admitted. When the fuss died down, she knocked and was let in. She accosted Anna.

"I heard all that, Anna. You should be ashamed of yourself for treating my brother like that. You know he's worn out and doing his best for you all. Do the children hear all of this too?"

Anna didn't answer immediately as she fought back tears.

"It's my nerves! And I'm worn out too. And I'm worried about what's to become of us all."

"You're lucky to have a job. You've always known that life's not easy for the likes of us. And you don't have asthma like me."

"Look," said Fred, defending Anna, "she's working her fingers to the bone. Try to understand. It's not us who are to blame but the way some people are treated in this country. Anyhow, I'm making a cup of tea, and we can all cool down."

Later on, after Mattie had left, while casting an accusing look at Anna, Fred decided on a strategy to avoid further outbursts. They'd leave the flat if tempers flared and go for a short walk to stem the intensity of their feelings.

"It's the stress of everything," they agreed. After that, things settled down somewhat, and they resolved to try harder for the sake of the children, although smaller outbreaks of irritability still happened.

The Titanic

On the 1st of June Fred returned home with a newspaper given to him by Ada and Ernie.

He greeted Anna with these words: "Listen to this, Anna, and you kids too. Remember I told you they were building that enormous ocean liner in Ireland a couple of years ago? Well, yesterday the hull was launched in Belfast. They'll have to fit it out though and that will take some time. They aim to send it on its maiden voyage next year in April sometime. The *Titanic* they call it because it's so huge, like a floating city they say."

"It must be heavy," Freddy remarked, a quizzical look on his face. "Dad, if something's so heavy in the water, how come it won't sink?"

"I can't answer you that, my lad, but that ship'll never sink. Too well built."

Getting Worried

Excitement grew in London as street decorations went up in preparation for George the Fifth's coronation. There was to be a public holiday for the occasion. Mary was particularly pleased about the coming event. She'd called in to make a time and place for the family to meet on the big day.

"It's like this, yer see," she enthused. "It's a free day out fer everybody. I'm glad you've go' a day off, Anna. We git ta see the Royals and see the marchin' 'an 'orses 'an 'ear the bands and pipers 'an everyone's smilin' at everyone else. It's a great day fer the Royals and also fer us. Only a week ter go."

During the night before the procession, Fred suffered a massive sweat.

"I can't go, Anna, I don't feel well enough today. You and Mum and Mattie take the children. I'll rest up."

"Oh! Fred, I'm disappointed for you. What's happening? Why this awful sweat last night?"

Anna moved towards Fred to give him a hug but he moved away quickly and put out his hands to dissuade her from approaching him.

"Better not touch me, Anna. I'm harbouring some sort of germs, and until I beat this thing, this 'flu or bronchitis, it's better you all keep away from me. Later on, I'll wash out the bedsheets."

Anna replied encouragingly, "Well, that sweat last night could have been the best thing to get it all out of your system, Fred. I'm sure you'll feel better tomorrow."

"I'd better feel better tomorrow. I've gotta go back to work."

During the morning, Mary, Mattie and Hilary called in to collect the others to walk to a procession viewing point, leaving Fred resting on his bed feeling happy that the family was going to have a nice time. Millie had been excited because she was going to see the King and Queen.

He sank back in bed and closed his eyes, pleased at the opportunity to have some respite. While he lay, he resolved to keep on working for as long as he could, denying the suspicion haunting his mind. Then he fell asleep but was jolted awake after a couple of hours when the family returned. Millie rushed over to him and reported on the spectacle she'd just seen.

"I saw them, Daddy. They were in a big coach and waving their hands. Mummy lifted me up high when they went by, and I waved back."

"Well, Millie got her wish then," commented Fred with a smile. He got out of bed and busied himself making cups of tea while Mary poured out lemonade for the children and made some ham sandwiches for lunch. By mid-afternoon Mary, Mattie and Hilary had said their goodbyes and left to return to Warren Street.

When Fred rode his bicycle to work the following day, he had to stop and rest against the wall of a building to gather his breath. Then he continued, arriving at the shop a few minutes late.

For the next six months, he battled on, determined to keep his job in spite of his nagging concern about his health.

Christmas Day 1911

Freddy turned eleven on Christmas Day. The whole family crowded into Mary's and Mattie's flat at Warren Street for the dual celebration.

"You can start lookin' fer a job after school now, Freddy," suggested Mary, observing Fred's pallor. "Yer old enough ter 'elp yer Mum and Dad now yer eleven years old."

"I know, Granny," Freddy agreed, drawing to his full height. "I'll be looking for something in the new year."

Mary's Suggestion

Fred had relished his time off after Christmas and the New Year celebrations and fancied he felt much better. He'd rested a lot and enjoyed simple local outings with his children. Anna had resumed her job at the hotel, but Fred was always pleased when she returned home after her shift to take charge again.

I think I'm getting over this thing, he convinced himself, as he pedalled to work after his short holiday. But over the following three months Fred knew that instead of improving, his health was deteriorating.

Anna had been worried sick and had begged Fred to take some time off work as resting at home had done him the world of good after Christmas.

"Can't afford to, Anna," he'd replied. "We have to eat."

A week passed, and Fred decided to heed Anna's advice and take a day off to rest. He'd suffered another one of those night sweats.

"Freddie, go to the shop and tell Mr Dobson I won't be in today because I'm not feeling well."

Mary had been invited to dinner that evening. When she learned that Fred had taken the day off work, she let out a deep sigh of frustration.

"Go to the *'ospital,* Fred," she urged. "It's free fer the likes of us. Git yerself checked out."

"I may have to," Fred answered quietly, a crease of anxiety lining his brow.

Have I got pneumonia? he wondered on his way to work the next day. *I haven't felt this pain in my chest before. I'll take a couple of hours off tomorrow and go to that hospital. They may have something to help get rid of this phlegm I*

Ada and Ernie willingly allowed Fred time off to seek medical advice.

"I hope he's going to be alright, Ernie," Ada remarked with a worried look after Fred left to make his way to the Poor Law Infirmary attached to the St Pancras workhouse. At least he won't have to pay anything there, which is a blessing."

"He'll be okay, Ada. He's just tired out that's all. They're bringing in that half-day off soon, and that'll make all the difference."

"I hope so," replied Ada, but her voice held a touch of doubt.

Facing the Truth

On the way to the hospital, Fred stopped off in a park and sat on a bench. Lately, he'd found riding his bike more arduous than walking, and he needed a rest. His throat felt dry, and a sudden coughing attack bent him over. He quickly pulled out his handkerchief and spat into it. What he saw shocked him. A clot of blood lay on the fabric and a further spasm produced more blood but thinner this time. He quickly dismissed the notion that he'd torn a blood vessel in his throat and acknowledged at last with a feeling of dread that it was true. That which he'd denied for so long, was true. He had all the symptoms he'd heard about. It wasn't bronchitis. It was the white plague, and it had a grip on him.

A receptionist admitted him to the waiting room when he arrived, and he sat with pounding heart, afraid of what the doctor's verdict would be.

Maybe I'm wrong, anyhow, he reasoned. *Maybe it won't be that.*

But despite it all, his thoughts ran amok. He remembered previous conversations with neighbours and customers in the shop. People with consumption were treated like lepers.

'It's catching.'

'Don't go near 'em.'

'No-one will employ 'em, ya know.'

'Pity their families. They'll end up with it too.'

'Alright if you've got plenty of money to throw around. Those people go into private sanatoriums and get the best of care, but even they don't always get better.'

Fred's turn came to see the doctor. He drew in his breath, stood up, and slowly made his way into the surgery.

"Mr Nash isn't it?" inquired the doctor. "I'm Doctor Carter. Now what can I do for you?"

He indicated a chair and Fred sat down.

"Well, I haven't felt quite well for some time, Doctor. For a couple of years, in fact. I suffer a lot of fatigue and there's been night sweats from time to time. I've had a cough, but lately it's been worse, and my chest is sore, and yesterday I coughed up some blood. I'm hoping it's just bronchitis."

The doctor looked serious. "Have you lost weight as well?"

"Yes, I have actually," answered Fred.

"I'll examine your chest then, Mr Nash," said the doctor as he approached with a stethoscope.

Fred stripped down to his waist and stood up for the examination.

"There's some crepitation there, I can hear," murmured Doctor Carter. Then, more firmly, "I'd better get an X-Ray done. Follow me to this room, Mr Nash. This is a fairly recent invention, you know. A German fellow called Roentgen in 1895 thought this thing up. Amazing, isn't it? It will give me a picture of the inside of your lungs so I can see what's going on in there."

After the image was taken by an assistant, Fred replaced his shirt and jacket and returned to the waiting room.

Doctor Carter said he'd be with Fred again in about half an hour, though he knew the verdict even before he saw the X-rays. The symptoms were classic. *I'll never get used to this part of my job*, he thought as he steeled himself after viewing the slides of Fred's chest. *Better get it over with, the poor blighter.* He slowly walked to the waiting room and invited Fred to join him in the surgery.

"Well, Mr Nash, it's not entirely without hope you know. I've known people to get over this condition with proper treatment and care."

"I think you're trying to tell me I've got tuberculosis, Doctor Carter," replied Fred with a level gaze, his voice quiet and husky. "That's what it is, isn't it?"

Working Things Out

"I'm sorry to say, Mr Nash, that is the case. Tuberculosis. However, I have some suggestions for your treatment. If you can afford it, there are excellent sanatoriums where you can stay. They will offer you complete bed rest, fresh air and exercise and nourishing food. This will give your body a good chance to overcome this illness. Some people do. Think about it and let me know what you want to do."

"I'm a working man in an ironmonger's shop, Doctor Carter, with a wife and four children to support. There's no way I could afford a private sanatorium."

"Well, then, you could set up a special isolated room in your home near an open window where you could rest. Get yourself a reclining chair. I'm sure your wife would be able to serve you up good meals, and you could go for a daily walk to get some exercise. And buy a good tonic. Be careful not to cough or sneeze anywhere near your family and use a handkerchief at all times. Also, wash them out from any sputum each day and wash your hands regularly and ..."

Fred cut short the doctor's suggestions.

"We only have two rooms between the six of us. That wouldn't work. I'll have to think about what I have to do."

Doctor Carter looked at Fred with concern. "I wasn't aware your circumstances were so bad Mr Nash, but there is a sanatorium associated with St Pancras workhouse you know. It won't cost you a penny. The National Insurance Act provides free institutional treatment for working-class men like you. I could get you in there, and I'm sure you'd improve, but you'd have to wait for a vacancy."

"Thanks, doctor," replied Fred flatly. "I have a lot of thinking to do. I'll let you know if I need your help."

"Go and see your local Guardian. If your wife can get a job somewhere, there may be a supplement available to help you out."

"My wife already has a part-time job in a hotel, but it won't be enough to support us all."

"I'm so sorry, Mr Nash," sympathised Doctor Carter, wishing he could do more to help.

Fred managed a half-smile as he took his leave.

A Secret for a While

Fred made his way back to the shop, but decided not to tell Ada and Ernie about his illness. Not yet.

"It's nothing much," he lied, replying to Ada's enquiry. "I'm just a bit run down, that's all."

On his way home from work, Fred didn't want to tell Anna the news straight away. Let her be at peace while he worked things out. It had occurred to him that his mother may be able to help. After all, she and Mattie and Hilary lived in two rooms which meant that the two families had four rooms between them. He could live in one isolated room and the others could share the other three rooms. He would approach the Board of Guardians and hopefully they would grant him some support, and Freddy was old enough now to get a little job somewhere after school. Altogether there's nine of us. The children would have to share beds. It would be cramped for a while, but he felt sure he could recover by having the rest he needed and return to work once he was better. The alternative idea that he may not recover was pushed aside. Too awful to contemplate. He managed to keep his illness to himself for a further week while he summoned up the courage to let Anna know. His coughing fits were becoming worse, and the children could not understand why he stepped back from them every time they got too close. But Anna was beginning to suspect the truth.

"What's worrying you, Fred? Something's changed you and you look preoccupied most of the time. I can see your health is getting worse and you can't hide that from me, try as you might. I think you know something I don't. But I'm beginning to suspect what it might be. We must talk about this and work out what we can do."

Fred felt a great burden lift. Anna knew. He spoke in a low voice while looking at the floor.

"I went to the hospital last week and had an x-ray, Anna. The doctor confirmed I have consumption. He gave me two options. One, to have a complete room to myself and have home care – the other, to go voluntarily to the Poor Law sanatorium attached to St Pancras workhouse. I've been breaking my head trying to work out something for the best for all of us. Maybe I could have a room here and you and the girls could share the other one and Freddy could go and live with Mum and Mattie and Hilary in Warren Street. Freddy could get a little job and I could see the local Guardian to get some assistance and …"

Anna broke in. "Be realistic, Fred. We both know we couldn't impose that arrangement on Mattie with her asthma and Mum, who is very old. And you know Mattie and I have never got on very well. I don't think she likes me much for some reason. I've always known that. And how would I manage with four of us in the kitchen room here, apart from the fact that your illness is catching. We couldn't fit in enough beds to begin with. No, Fred. The best way is for you to go into the hospital and receive the care you need. Some people do get over this and we must hope and pray you will too. I'm sure the Board of Guardians can help. I have a job, and the Guardians will help us. Freddy and Amy are big enough now to be left on their own and to look after the little ones. It'll work out."

Fred looked at Anna and nodded. She was right, then another disturbing thought occurred, *I've brought these children into the world and given them life by the grace of God. I don't want to be responsible for causing their death, so I must go to that hospital whether I want to or not.*

Resignation

The next morning Fred made his way wearily on foot to the shop to hand in a week's notice. As he walked, he experienced episodes where he felt as though he were floating in space, then jolted to the ground by his own footsteps. *Try to be strong*, he cautioned himself as he stifled a sob rising in his throat. *Men don't cry.*

When he arrived at the shop, he sat on a chair and smiled wanly at Ada as she approached.

"What's the matter, Fred Luvvie? You look awful. You don't need to work today. You're obviously not well. Go back home and spend the day in bed and come back tomorrow."

"Get Ernie here, Ada," Fred replied. "I've got something to tell you both."

Ada fetched Ernie from upstairs, and they both joined Fred with concerned expressions.

Fred stood up and drew in a deep breath. "I can only come back for a week, Ernie, then I'll have to leave. Sorry it's so sudden, but I've just found out that I've got tuberculosis. Anna and I have discussed the options for my treatment and it seems like the only choice I have is to go to hospital where hopefully, I'll recover. I'm sure you'll find a replacement for me shortly."

Ernie looked at Fred in disbelief but Ada wasn't so surprised.

"I've watched you struggle to get here for about a year now, Fred, but I never would have believed you were so unwell. You told me it was bronchitis. But you're making the right decision. Hospital is the best way for you to get well again, my dear."

"Fred," said Ernie as he moved over and placed a hand on Fred's shoulder, "I want you to know I couldn't have asked for a better employee than you've been over the years. You came here as a young lad of nineteen, and you've been thoroughly reliable and trustworthy. I will find you hard to replace, my friend."

"There are plenty of good men looking for jobs these days, Ernie," replied Fred. "Unemployment is pretty bad."

"Sit down there, and I'll get you a cup of tea and a biscuit, luvvie, before you start work and if you get tired through the day, call for me and I'll help out," said Ada in a soothing tone.

"I'll be okay. And I feel I'm going to beat this thing you know. I'm hoping that after six months of getting the rest I need I'll be fighting fit again." Fred managed a slightly confident grin.

"Bless you," murmured Ada quietly as she went upstairs to make a cup of tea.

That evening after Fred had left to go home, she shed a tear in front of Ernie. She knew the odds were stacked against Fred surviving this rotten disease.

"You hear a lot in this shop of ours, Ernie, and I've only ever heard of one person getting over it."

Telling Everyone

The week went by quickly and Fred and Anna decided they should not keep their secret any longer from Mary and Mattie. On the following Sunday morning, they left Freddie in charge of his sisters and made their way to Warren Street.

Mary in particular was shocked.

"They're makin' a mistake, Fred. I know yer ain't been well fer a coupla years, but you said it was bronchitis an' I believed yer."

"I thought it was at first, Mum, but lately I was starting to suspect I had this blasted thing, but I suppose I didn't want to admit it."

"What yer goin' ter do now? 'Ow yer gunna live, all of youse?"

Anna declared, "Well I've got that job, Mum, and Freddy should get a little something after school too, and I'm going to approach the local Guardian for assistance because Fred won't be earning. We'll manage, and when Fred's better, he can find work again."

"Well, I 'ope it works out then," Mary replied cautiously, "but Fred, don't yer get coughin' and spittin' around the kids, will ya? We don't want vem comin' down wiv it too, do we now?"

Fred reacted angrily, and his voice rose. "You should know me better, Mum. I've made sure never to cough or sneeze near anyone, and a hankie is always up to my mouth when I do, and I always wash it out anyway. And I never spit. Give me credit for protecting them."

Mary looked like she was going to cry. "Sorry, me darlin', but it's all so worryin'."

The family made their way to Whitefields in the afternoon, and Aunty Esther was told the news after the evening service.

"That explains it," she said. "I was beginning to wonder after I heard you coughing last Sunday, Fred. I hoped I was imagining things. Before that, I thought you were just worn out because of the long work hours and all the demands on you. But take heart, my dear. In the hospital, you'll be having the same care as those in private sanatoriums. And you can be sure that this church will be giving Anna and the children all the support we can. Unfortunately, not much financial support, but clothing and food parcels will be kept up. And you'll certainly have everyone's prayers."

"We've worked it out, Aunty Esther," Anna explained. "I've got my job at the hotel; Freddy can find some work after school, and Amy can look after the little ones when I'm not there. I'm going to see the Guardians for some support too. We'll keep our present flat which the health authorities are going to disinfect, they said, after the doctor informed them of Fred's condition. This is compulsory, apparently. We'll make out somehow, and Fred will be able to get the rest he's needed for so long, and get better."

Aunty Esther said nothing at first. Her eyes filled with tears as she looked at them. Then she said, "My dear ones, have you told the children yet? This is going to mean a big change for them and Freddy and Amy will have to grow up fast and take on a lot of responsibility."

"We're telling them tomorrow," replied Anna. "Fred is seeing the doctor on Tuesday to arrange for his sanatorium admission."

"The sooner, the better, I say," announced Fred, "because I don't know how long this thing has been going on. I want to be back home in six months at the most and get back to work somewhere."

When they'd collected the children and were ready to leave, Aunty Esther gave Anna and the children a hug but held back from the usual embrace for Fred. He noticed it and thought, *It's true. I'm like a leper now. Better get used to it.*

The next afternoon, when Freddy, Amy and Edie had returned home from school, Freddy asked his father a question.

"How come you're home, Dad? Why didn't you go to work today?"

"Your mother and I will tell you when she gets home from work," answered Fred.

After dinner, the children were gathered together. Fred remained silent, looking down. Anna noticed his reticence and became the spokesperson.

"We have something to tell you all. Now, Daddy hasn't been well for a long time, children, and he saw a doctor a couple of weeks ago who told him he has trouble with his lungs. This means he'll have to go into hospital so he can get well."

"How long will you be in hospital, Daddy?" asked Amy, frowning.

"I'll be there until I get well. It could be a long time Amy, about six months or so."

Anna cut in quickly. "I've got my job, Amy, and Freddy, you can start looking for something to do after school, and I'll make enquiries too. Would you like to be a shoeshine boy like dad was when he was your age, or something like that, eh?"

"Yes, Mum. I'll help out. I'll go to *The Squire's Rest* tomorrow and see if I can do something there like washing up and drying the dishes."

"Oh, Freddy, that's lovely of you!" said Anna, smiling. "But let me ask them first, eh? They'll listen to a grown-up, I'm sure."

"When are you going into hospital, Daddy?" asked Amy, still looking worried.

"Probably this week. I'm seeing the doctor tomorrow to arrange admission," answered Fred, in what he hoped was a positive tone. "Don't worry, Amy, I'm going to be alright, my sweetie."

The subject was dropped and Anna decided to see to Fred's clothes and toiletries to pack into a small suitcase in case he had to go into hospital tomorrow. The family settled down to their normal evening routine, but through the night in bed, Anna was restless and wakeful, worried about the family's future.

I'll not let him see me cry, she vowed. *That's for later.*

When Fred consulted Doctor Carter the next day, he was pleased Fred had decided to enter the St Pancras sanatorium.

"They'll do the best they can for you, Mr Nash, and I'm sure the rest will do you a world of good. I'll telephone them this afternoon. They have a vacancy, as I found out, and I'll let them know you can be admitted tomorrow."

Then the doctor patted Fred on the back and wished him good luck. "I'll be calling in at the hospital from time to time to see how you're going."

With the visit ended, Fred walked wearily back home, determined to overcome this illness. He did not allow a negative thought to enter his head.

A Difficult Walk

The next morning at nine o'clock Anna walked with Fred to the hospital, offering to carry his packed suitcase, but Fred refused her, saying in a slightly defiant way, "That's not necessary, Anna. I'm not so weak I can't carry a bloomin' bag ya know." Then he regretted his churlishness and added, "Sorry! I'm just a bit edgy, ya know."

After the admission officer at the hospital had filled out the forms, he directed Fred and Anna to the floor above, to the ward. Anna was barred from entering such an infectious area, and the two sat on a bench outside. Fred put his arm around her.

"I won't kiss you anymore, my love, but know this, I'll be out of here in under a few months. I'll be doing my level best to get better. I'll be home for next Christmas. You'll see."

"If anyone tries their best, Fred, it'll be you. I'll let the others know and Aunty Esther at church next Sunday, and we'll all be praying for you, my dearest. Goodbye for now."

Anna blew him a kiss as she departed, and Fred returned the gesture with what he hoped was a confident smile.

Fred opened the door to the ward and was met by a nurse who ushered him to his bed. He had not expected to see such a crowded place: the walls were lined with beds all fairly close to each other. The centre of the room held another row from one end to the other.

"This is your bed, Mr Nash," said the nurse cheerily as she pointed out one near the centre of the middle row.

Fred sat on the bed and glanced around the ward, taking it all in. Several of the men were lying prostrate on their beds, a few among them breathing with difficulty.

"This is not how I thought it would be," Fred muttered quietly. "If there's anywhere I can sit outside tomorrow in the fresh air, that's where I'm going."

"Did you say something?" asked the nurse standing close by.

"Well, yes," answered Fred. "I never expected this place to be so crowded and some of these fellows look like they're dying."

"Well, they are! Not many get out of here alive, but some do. I sincerely hope you're one of them, Mr Nash."

"How can people get better in such a place?" Fred asked. "… so crowded and so depressing. Are there verandas here and fresh air for people to breathe?"

"You are in a sanatorium attached to St Pancras workhouse, Mr Nash. Remember that. You'd be paying a lot for another place. But even if it's crowded here, the treatment is the same for everyone and subsidised by the government. You can go out on the balconies tomorrow to get the fresh air you want when there's no fog. Of course, that will do you good."

With those words, the nurse left to attend to another patient near the end of the room.

Fred's forehead creased as he settled back onto the bed and lay his head on the pillow.

I'm glad they didn't let Anna in to see this, he thought. *Anyhow, I'll get some sleep and tomorrow, I'll get stuck into my breathing exercises and I'll stay outside all day.*

Asking for Help

Anna walked wearily back home from the sanatorium, determined to put on a brave face in front of the children, but she was worried about Fred.

The next morning after the children had left for school, she sat on the sofa and made plans before leaving for work.

I'll have to see the relieving officer from the Board of Guardians for some help. The rent here will be the problem. We'll have enough to eat, I think. Freddy will have to get something to do to earn a bit, and Amy can supervise her sisters when I'm away.

The following Saturday Anna busied herself with thoroughly cleaning and tidying the apartment, knowing it was to be fumigated by the authorities. She did not want a bad report about her housekeeping to reach the Guardians. Surely, they would see her need for support.

She pulled out her Sunday clothes and inspected them. She'd have to work on that tomato stain on the front of her blouse or maybe hide it with a scarf. And she'd wear her hair down when she visited the Guardians. Fred always loved that look, and she fancied the years dropped off her a little too.

I'll do anything, anything at all to keep us out of the workhouse, she determined.

Mary was sympathetic. "Me and Mattie can take young Freddy to stay with us for the time bein', Anna, or until Fred gits ou' of the 'ospital. We can stretch enough ter feed 'im an' ee can sleep in 'is Dad's old bed an' if ee gits some work after school, that'd 'elp."

Anna was thankful, and Freddy moved to Warren Street.

A week later, at nine in the morning, she called on the office of the

Guardians, worried that her last encounter with the Inspector in their flat would diminish her chances of getting a fair hearing. *Calling me a bad housekeeper and child abuser, indeed,* she quietly fumed as she remembered that day when Edie had been so naughty and got a smack.

Anna was admitted into an office and sat at a desk opposite a serious-looking man. "On what grounds are you seeking relief, Mrs Nash?"

"My husband's suffering from tuberculosis and he's now in a sanatorium. I have a job as a casual kitchen hand in a hotel, sir, which doesn't bring in enough to support me and my three daughters properly. Our son, the eldest child, has gone to live with his grandmother and aunt, which is a help, and occasionally Whitefields Central Mission helps with clothing and a bit of food, but I have the cost of renting our flat. I'm asking for out-relief as I have little money behind me to keep going."

"Hmm," answered the man, looking down and stroking his chin. His job was to keep this family out of the workhouse. Being in there would cost the ratepayers of London more than giving some sort of relief to the family. He also knew the most successful Guardian of the Poor was one who had the least number of paupers in their books. But Out-Relief could only be meagre, and this woman would have to manage somehow on her own.

"You appear to have good health, Mrs Nash. I'll inspect your residence at nine o'clock tomorrow, and there may be a few suggestions I can make at this stage. Obviously, I need to thoroughly evaluate your circumstances. Now, I'll take your address down."

Anna left with a sinking feeling. She'd expected the man to grant relief immediately due to her situation, but his sceptical manner had implied she could be doing more due to her 'good health'.

During the inspection of the flat the next morning, the man formally introduced himself as Mr Porter. He sat at the table and began a barrage of questions. Were there any parents who could help? Was the eldest child, Freddy, earning anything? Would Anna be prepared to let one of these rooms here? Had she thought of taking in washing, ironing, mending? Doing things at home like assembling matchboxes, to supplement her income in her spare time?"

Anna answered each question. No, there were no relations who could help. Her husband's mother and his sister had already taken in her son. Her own mother was unwell and lived in a single room only in Clapham. There was her old Uncle John who lived in Northampton, but that was too far away. She and her daughters needed two single rooms so she wasn't able let one out. She had little spare time outside of her work hours to do anything extra, as she had to run her own home too.

"I'll consider your case and get back to you the day after tomorrow, Mrs Nash. It's reasonable to assume that you may have out-relief for your daughters of one and sixpence each. Now you mentioned yesterday that Whitefields church offers you food and clothing and that your son is being cared for by his grandmother. All that must be factored in on assessment. I'll call on you next Wednesday and let you know the Board's decision. Goodbye for now."

With these dismissive words, he doffed his hat and Anna let him out. Then she collapsed in tears on the sofa.

"Why on earth did I ever mention Aunty Esther sometimes helps us out?" she chided herself. "And that Freddy's living with Mum and Mattie." With this thought, Anna began to cry again and pleaded, "Dear God, please make Fred better and send him back to us."

On the way back to his office, Mr Porter began some preliminary calculations. "Yes, the woman needed some help, but I know she'll do anything to avoid the workhouse which would cost the government ten shillings a week per person, so we'll probably grant her one and sixpence a week for each of her girls. She's got a job, unlike a lot around here." Pleased that he would be saving the government a sum of money, and earn some kudos for that, he arrived at his office and prepared his report, ignoring the fact that the support he'd recommend was inadequate to solve Anna's problems.

A Bit of Help From Whitefields

After church on Sunday evening, Aunty Esther sat beside Anna and took her hand in hers.

"I've been to see Fred in the hospital, my dear, and he doesn't look any worse than before. They wouldn't let me into the ward though. He told me he's been getting lots of fresh air on the balcony and he sends you and the children his love. We had some prayers together. He knows you're very busy and he hopes you are not feeling too weary."

"I've seen one of the Guardians who's getting back to me on Wednesday. I feel sure I'll be offered some out-relief. Otherwise, I don't know what I'll do. That wretched man is counting up every penny I've got and even what I haven't, it seems."

"I'm packing up some leftover sandwiches and cakes for you to take home, Anna. And we'll have a rummage around and see if there's some clothing you need just now."

There was a blouse for Anna and a pair of sandals which fitted Millie. Anna was thankful. On the way home, she decided to call on Mary early the next morning to persuade Freddy to join them at church each Sunday.

Talking to Mary

She called on Mary at nine o'clock the next day, just as Freddy and Hilary were leaving for school.

Freddy flung his arms around his mother. Then he asked, "How's Dad, Mum? Is he getting better? How long before he comes home?"

"I'm seeing him soon, Freddy boy. He's no worse and I feel sure he's improving. I'll give him your love. That will cheer him up."

The children left for school, and Mary made a cup of tea.

"I'd like Freddy to come back to church, Mum. He needs to know there's Someone watching over him," said Anna, looking directly at Mary.

Mary nodded. "I ain't much of a churchgoer, Anna, but I'm a believer as yer know. 'Uman bein's don't always care fer each other as vey ought to. I've 'eard stories around 'ere which 'ud make yer cry. People bein' turfed' ou' o' their 'omes and them guardians lookin' the other way an' no' 'elpin' anyone ter live a decent life, eh?"

"I hope that doesn't happen to us, Mum," said Anna, looking stricken. "I'm expecting that fellow I saw the other day to help me."

"Sorry I talked about them poor souls I 'eard about, Luvvie. I didn't mean ter worry yer. But yer should be alright. Fred'll be gettin' be"er soon now 'ee's gettin' some rest. But about 'avin' faith in God, that's wot keeps 'im goin' yer know. 'An I'm proud of 'im that 'ee never giv' in ter the drink, bein' poor, as some do."

Anna left to go home and get ready for her lowly paid job at the hotel. She realised she'd be forced to use up the emergency fund secreted in the back of a cupboard which she and Fred had put between the pages of an old book. A whole two pounds. That would tide her over for some weeks and pay the rent. She would not be telling that wretched guardian about that money.

A Disappointment

Wednesday loomed, and Anna nervously made her way to the Guardian's Office. She was offered a seat and faced Mr Porter with a hopeful expression.

"Mrs Nash, I can help you with your daughters' expenses. Your son, I believe, is being looked after by his grandmother and aunt. The church you attend gives a helping hand. You have a position in a hotel, so in view of these circumstances, The Board of Guardians has decided to allow you one shilling and sixpence for each of your girls per week based on the costs of feeding a child on a labourer's wage. This should help out until you find added means of supporting yourself as well."

"My husband was a shop assistant, not a labourer," replied Anna hotly. "He earned enough to keep us going with some help from me. How do you think I can manage on such a paltry amount of assistance, sir?"

"I can't answer you that, Mrs Nash, but in my experience, women in your situation eventually find a solution. Something *always* turns up for them."

"Well, I can't do better than what I'm doing, Mr Porter," said Anna, choking back tears.

"Well, I wish you well then, Mrs Nash, and I'm sure your position will improve in time. Now, if you'll excuse me." He gave a fake smile and walked out of the office.

He'd been disturbed by Anna's stricken face and felt uncomfortable in her presence, all the while hoping a woman like her would be able to get by.

Anna managed to conceal her agitation from the girls when she arrived home from work. They must not be exposed to the worry she was feeling.

She took out the money from the hidden book and put it in her purse.

Good News But Too Late

Two days later, she found the courage to visit Fred. She would not under any circumstances let him know the guardians had been so mean. She would appear hopeful and bright.

In the foyer outside the ward, Fred relayed some news he'd read about in newspapers provided by the hospital.

"A bit late for me now, Anna, but the government has finally passed legislation to grant shop workers a half-day off in a week as promised all that time ago. Funny, isn't it? Now I have all the time to get some rest, I'm out of the workplace."

"Well, it's good to know that when you get back, life will be easier for you," replied Anna with a weak smile.

When she left the sanatorium, she felt troubled. She hadn't seen such dark circles under Fred's eyes before and wondered if his condition had worsened.

For the next six weeks, Anna was able to pay for rent and adequate food with the extra money from the cupboard emergency fund. But how to keep going?

An idea occurred but was accompanied with sadness. She took out the dinner set with the yellow roses and hesitated. *My beautiful wedding present from the Dobsons. I'll pack it up and take it to that pawn shop down the road.*

The owner of the pawnshop offered to hold the china at a redeemable price of fifteen shillings plus a steep interest. He knew from experience some people would never turn up again to buy things back and he could make a handsome profit on what they had left, particularly Royal Doulton like this crockery.

Anna placed the money in her handbag while determining to get her china back one day, but she finally admitted it was a vain thought. The dinner set money ran out after two weeks.

Struggling

"What's to become of us?" Anna anguished as she took down the spare tea caddy with her separate funeral fund in it. "How can I save up this again?"

It was getting harder to maintain a sense of cheerfulness each time she visited Fred. He would question her about the children. She would assure him they were healthy and doing well. She hoped he hadn't noticed her weight loss of late as she'd been skipping meals to save money.

"Freddy has settled down with Mum and Mattie for the time being, but I'm looking forward to us all being together again."

During her last time with Fred, she noticed a bloodstained area in a handkerchief poking out of his pyjama pocket. She did not react to this as the state of his health had not been discussed by either of them over the past few weeks. Anna knew, when she left this time, that Fred may not get better. Three months had passed since he'd entered the sanatorium and his condition was worse. When she arrived home, she sat on the sofa and cried.

Her funeral fund money had not lasted long. She'd had to buy shoes and clothing for the girls and Freddy from what was left. Whitefields had helped with a few small donations of cash.

"That's our secret," whispered Aunty Esther each time, knowing the Guardians would deduct those amounts if they knew; she was heartbroken over the way this family unit seemed to be falling apart. She knew there was little chance of Fred's recovery. She'd seen it all before.

"I'm going to ask the Guardians for a bigger allowance for the girls,

Aunty Esther," announced Anna. "I'm behind with the rent now. Surely, they'll help us. They know how hard I've been trying to keep going, surely."

"I hope they'll be kind, Anna," replied Aunty Esther as she tried to keep her worried expression under control. She gave Anna a tight hug and then presented her with a calico bag containing an extra helping of sandwiches and cakes.

"Eat up, my girl. You're looking thin. Must keep up your strength, you know."

Another Interview

A week went by, and the children had had enough food but Anna was suffering hunger pangs. And the landlord had sent a letter of demand for outstanding rent which she didn't have. Anna called in at the office of the Board of Guardians the next day, which was a Monday morning. She was led into a room where Mr Porter sat at a table with another member of the Board. She was offered a seat. With an effort to control her despair and her tears, she pointed out her situation.

"Have you tried everything?" asked Mr Porter, who was beginning to soften until he remembered that it was not permissible to give favour to individuals in his books. And he had a position to uphold. This woman would *have* to find a solution herself, in her predicament. Get a better-paid job!

"We can't extend any more money to you, Mrs Nash. You could sell the furniture and any other goods you have in the flat to get by."

Anna erupted. "It's all old. Who'd buy it? And what are we to sleep on, to sit on, sir? That's a ridiculous thing to expect me to do. With my hotel job, I can either pay for rent or food, not both. Should we roam the streets, or should we starve? Oh, you're a heartless lot of cruel people, sitting in your comfort here and not *really* caring about the poor like you pretend you do! And what's to become of my children? What about *them*, eh?"

Mr Porter squirmed a little in his seat, then cleared his throat and replied, "Well, I have a suggestion, Mrs Nash, which I'd like you to consider. Taking into consideration the welfare of your girls, you may like them to be cared for, temporarily mind you, in the children's section of the local facility at St Pancras. They'll be properly fed, clothed and educated. This will be for six weeks only during which time they'll be in isolation and observation as they've come from a home where a consumptive has resided. After that, if you haven't found better-paid work, the girls will become permanent residents of the facility or be sent to a cottage home nearby. Now please don't get upset, Mrs Nash. You'll always be free to take your daughters home again at *any* time when your situation improves. If you decide to take this step, I hope you will highlight the benefits for everybody and not upset the children unduly."

"Is that all you have to say?" Anna said loudly, her eyes blazing. "Not only am I losing my husband, but you're breaking up the rest of my family as well. And don't think that calling the workhouse a facility will make things sound any better. It's the workhouse you want my children in, isn't it and … …"

"Mrs Nash," interrupted Mr Porter, his face flushed, "please consider the benefits. Do you want them to starve in the streets or resort to thieving to put food into their mouths? With them being cared for, you will have far more freedom to look for better-paid work. And your girls will not be lost to you. You will be permitted to visit your daughters for two hours each Sunday afternoon."

"Two hours in a week!" exploded Anna. "That's very generous, I must say. And how do you think my daughters are going to react to this? Two hours in a week to be with their mother indeed, sir! I hope you sleep well tonight, Mr Porter."

Anna's face hardened, and she added grimly, "And have you finished with me now, gentlemen?"

"Yes, we've finished for now," replied Mr Porter's companion quietly, looking abashed.

"Well, you've finished *me!*" shouted Anna. Then, on a quieter and more level tone, "But one thing I have to tell you, is that I will never, ever, enter that workhouse myself. I know what goes on in those places. People become like zombies in the end, hardened and bitter because of the way they're treated. Just enough food, dressed like criminals, all the same, slaving in laundries, picking oakam or whatever. Seeing their children for two lousy hours in a week. I'd rather starve, and I've heard some people *do* rather than go into those places. You people and the government should be ashamed. Thanks for your help, and I hope I never have to look at your faces again."

Anna flounced out in tears, and the two men remained silent for a while. Then Mr Porter spoke.

"It's hard on them, I know, women like her, but she's got spirit, I'll say that about her. We could consider giving her a small benefit, like three shillings a week, perhaps, to help with food, but I feel she'll work something out, to support herself. She could share a single room with another woman or something."

Mr Porter was experienced in these matters. He already knew the probable outcome for the girls.

Hunger Pangs

Anna started out for the hotel, but suddenly felt dizzy; she leaned against the wall of a building, unable to take in everything that had just happened. She closed her eyes for a moment and felt a strange sensation take over, as though she were falling down a cliff and couldn't see the bottom. Then she slowly rallied and, with fresh resolve, muttered, "I will not be broken, I swear it."

"Are you alright, dearie?" asked a woman passer-by, peering into Anna's face.

"Yes, thank you," replied Anna, straightening her face. "I just have a problem to solve."

"Look after yourself then, Luvvie. You look very tired."

A week passed by, and Anna had not been eating through the day to save as much money as she could to pay some back rent. So far, they were all eating their oatmeal at breakfast and a normal meal in the evening. Anna was glad of the school lunches provided.

When she reported for work the next morning, she was given one week's notice. The old hotel had been sold to a developer and would soon be demolished.

Anna slowly walked to a nearby chair and sank into it. She'd had a sudden urge to faint at the news.

Just over one week's wage I've got, she thought, as she shakily left the hotel and made her way back to the flat. *Something will turn up; something must turn up.*

But nothing did turn up for Anna at the end of her last working week at the hotel. She struggled on for another week, feeding her girls, although scantily. Their complaints would ring in her ears.

"I'm sick of bubble and squeak and pancakes."
"We never have anything nice now."
"I'm hungry, Mummy."
The complaints got worse as money started to run out.

A Painful Decision

The girls had left for school on the day Anna made her decision. She hadn't slept well throughout the night and had woken up in a lather of sweat.

No! It wouldn't be that, she thought dismissively. *I'm so run down with all I've been through lately, it's just a bit of 'flu.* A wave of dissociation overcame her, and she knew her emotions were spent. A practical solution for her daughters became paramount in her mind. There was only one thing she could do. Not for herself. But for them. So they could *eat.*

Mary's words of some time ago invaded her mind. Practical words, bless her! Words spoken with reassurance after that first visit from the Relieving Officer after the head lice episode.

"Yer know, I've 'eard the workhouse ain't that bad fer children *these* days. It's not like fer the adults. The kids git food and clothes an' a warm bed to sleep in an' a education too."

I don't care what happens to me, but I won't let them *starve,* she vowed. *And I'll get them back. I'll get a job again as soon as possible, but today, I'll have to go back to those awful men and make arrangements straight away. There's hardly anything to eat in the place.*

Wearily, Anna traipsed to the building of the Board of Guardians and sat in the waiting room for half an hour before Mr Porter called her into his office. With eyes downcast, she pleaded her cause.

"I'm glad you've made a sensible decision, Mrs Nash, particularly as your job at that hotel is gone. I'll get the forms for admittance and you can fill them in now. I realise your case is urgent. I'll take them over straight away when you're done and you can prepare your daughters for them to be transferred tomorrow. Be assured, they'll be well fed. Please pack their underwear and school things tonight and have them ready to leave at nine-thirty tomorrow morning."

When Anna arrived back home, she sat on the sofa and stared into space, unable to take in everything that had just happened. The rest of the day was spent in a trance as she rehearsed ways to prepare the girls for the change that was about to happen in their lives.

I'll have to make sure they know it's only temporary *until I can get them out.*

Anna had saved some wheaten biscuits and a portion of milk. She set them out on the table shortly before the girls arrived home from school with their accounts of the day.

When they arrived home, they hugged their mother and hungrily ate their afternoon tea. Anna watched them eat, fighting back her tears. She retired to the other room to gain control. This was not to be a hopeless and depressing matter, but a short prospect offered to her children as a stop-gap until they were all together again. *Better get it over and done with.*

Preparing the Girls

"Well, my sweeties, now you're all sitting down, I have to tell you something. You know that I have no job now and the rent here is very much overdue. I'll try to get another job tomorrow, but until then, I hardly have any money to … …"

"We know," said Amy, interrupting, "… and that's why you've been giving us pancakes to eat for dinner so often, isn't it? And that's why we've had those sandwiches and cakes from Whitefields on other nights for tea, too. And how are we going to keep living here in this place, Mummy? I once heard you and Daddy talk about how expensive the rent is."

"Well, that's what we have to talk about, my darlings," said Anna, grateful that her beautiful Amy had been so discerning about their situation and had ushered in the subject.

"I've been to see the Board of Guardians – they are people who help those like us who've got sickness in the family and have no work. Like daddy and me, you know. And because they think I look healthy they think I should be able to get another job and do washing at home or whatever. Well, I've tried very hard to keep us all together. I thought the Guardians would give me more money, but they said they can only help you girls and not Freddy because he is with Granny now. They said you would be better off until I find work again because you'll have much more to eat than what I can give you right now. You'll still be going to Leavesdon school but it means that you'll have to live in at the home … …"

"Oh! *No!*" interrupted Amy loudly, looking aghast. "Not *Home* girls. I've seen them! They all look the same in ugly frocks, and they all look poor. And some of them look sad. *Anything* but that, Mummy!"

"I'm not going," declared Edie, defiantly. "I'm staying with you, Mummy. I'm *not* going to wear those clothes and live in a home."

For a moment, Anna was speechless as she tried to control her emotions and work out what to say. She took a deep breath, and with tears in her eyes continued to prepare the girls for the inevitable.

"My beautiful girls, there's nothing I want more than to keep living here in this place with you all, but life is not always fair, and the truth is that the rent is so behind, the landlord wants me out in a few days if I can't pay him all I owe. The Guardians have told me they want to help us. This means that, for the time being, you girls are to be cared for at the place connected to the school. You'll be fed, clothed and educated and if you get sick, you'll be looked after too. There's no need to worry. I'll call on you each week while you're there and see how you're going. It's better than starving with me or going on the streets like children I've seen in Spitalfields and having to steal your food from barrows. We have to look on the bright side for now and believe we'll soon be back together. I'll still be trying for a job, and I'll tell daddy what's going on. He'll be pleased you'll be eating better. I'll get you out of the place as soon as I can, I promise you. Now we'll have to pack up your things tonight because you're being admitted at half-past nine tomorrow morning at your new place."

The girls wailed and cried until Anna calmed them down as best she could.

She slept fitfully that night, frequently waking in panic at the thought of what could lay ahead. What was to become of them all? And could Fred possibly recover?

A Change of Home

By 9.30 the next morning, the girls were ready. A knock resounded on the door and a man and an officious-looking matron were admitted.

"I'm coming too," insisted Anna, "to see them settle in."

"We only have room for us and the girls in the automobile," said the man, "but you can visit them every Sunday afternoon."

Amy, Edie and Millie flung themselves at Anna who embraced them in turn, her face distraught.

"Mummy is coming to see you as soon as I can, in two days," she promised. "Be good girls and I'll see you soon."

The girls looked back, their eyes filled with sadness. Then they left. Anna collapsed on the bed, wondering if she'd imagined the look of accusation in Edie's eyes.

Please, dear God, look after them, she prayed. Then, looking in the almost empty larder, *I'll have potatoes and gravy tonight,* she thought wearily, *but at least the girls will be having something better. There's a bit of comfort in that.*

She would see Mary, Freddy, Mattie and Hilary tomorrow and tell them where the girls were now, and she'd ask Freddy to take a letter down to Clapham to let her mother know. On Sunday at church, after she'd seen the girls, she would tell Aunty Esther. And of course, she'd have to tell Fred. And then what? She'd find a well-paid job, she vowed.

At No.57 Warren Street

Anna felt exhausted when she arrived the next day. Mary opened the door with her usual welcome and made a pot of tea. Freddy and Hilary were at the table playing 'Ludo'. Mattie hadn't returned yet from her job. Mary got down the biscuit tin and Freddy bogged in, taking four to have with his glass of lemonade.

"Ee eats a lot," commented Mary, "but I don't begrudge it. 'E'es a growin' boy."

Anna took a deep breath and described all that had happened over the last few months, all the while fighting back tears. Then she told of the girls' removal to the Home.

"Yer talkin' about the work'ouse, ain't yer, Anna? Are yer sure yer tried 'ard enough wiv them Guardians, Anna?"

"No-one could have tried harder, Mum, and I'm so tired I often feel like fainting. And I'm not getting enough to eat. I'm sorry you may think I haven't tried."

"Well, I remember sayin' to yer earlier on, Anna, that it ain't so bad fer children bu' keep lookin' for work an' take 'em out as soon as yer can. 'Ave dinner 'ere tonight and I'll give yer some bread and cheese fer tomorrow."

Then Anna dropped the bombshell. "I have to quit the flat next week because I'm behind with rent."

"Where'll you go, Mum?" asked Freddy, looking worried. "I'll get a job after school and help out."

"That's a good idea, Freddy. You're old enough now to help Granny and Auntie Mattie, but work hard at your lessons too. Don't worry about me. Something will turn up, I'm sure."

"Stay wiv *us!*" invited Mary with a desperate look on her face.

"Some'ow we'll manage."

"You know that's not possible, Mum. Five of us in two rooms, one of them small? And if you're honest, you must admit that Mattie and I don't get along very well of late. I think it would be hell on earth for me, especially if I haven't found a job."

"It'd only be fer a short time Anna and ..."

"*No*, Mum!" Anna said emphatically. "You're already crowded in here with four."

Mattie returned from her job and heard the news. She lowered her voice as she confided in Anna, not wanting the others to hear.

"You know, it may sound awful, but I sometimes wish Hilary had a more cheerful place to live than here. Mum's always down in the mouth since Fred's been in hospital. And I must say, with Freddy here, me and Mum can barely afford to keep going these days even though we're working. Now I'm telling you a secret because Mum doesn't know yet, or even Hilary. I've been talking to the headmaster about Hilary. She's very bright, he tells me, and is good with children. I'm considering this. There's a place at Princess Alice's Orphanage in Birmingham who train up selected girls to be high-class children's nannies. Mr Morgan knows of my difficulties and has asked me to think about Hilary for a bursary. She'd have food, education and training for a very good position after leaving school. What should I do? I'd miss her. So far away. I couldn't afford to visit her and with Mum so unwell, I ..."

"Do what's best for Hilary," Anna cut in quickly, and quietly. "Think of her future. There's always letters you can write, and you'll have peace of mind about her. I wish I had that about my girls. What will their future be here in London? Look what's happened to me."

"It's your own fault," accused Mattie, turning on Anna. "You shouldn't have had so many children! One or two is enough for the likes of us."

"I wouldn't send a single one back," Anna retorted, her voice rising. Inwardly she acknowledged how Mattie had often been jealous towards her family, confessing once that she'd longed for more.

Old Uncle John

After dinner and a big cuddle with Freddy, Anna left, feeling guilty about Mattie and Mary supporting him. A faint hope stirred her heart as she walked back to the flat. Maybe Aunty Esther could help her somehow, or maybe she'd find some work next week. She had a small amount of money to tide her over for a few days. She weighed up her options of staying in London. A cheap boarding house full of drunks and no-hopers when she found work? *No!* Living with Mum and Mattie in a crowded flat despite having Freddy with her? *No!* Not with her brothers either. They were struggling too. *In the workhouse?* She'd die first. She'd heard of people starving in the streets rather than go into one of those places.

After that thought, she determined to find a way out of the mess. Then a sudden idea flicked into her mind and she pondered it. *Old Uncle John in Northampton?*

She knew he was still alive. He'd written occasionally. She came to an instant conclusion. *Yes!* She'd go up there. No time to let him know she was coming. Just somewhere to sleep and a bit of food was all she needed for a short while. Plenty of boot-making factories up there, she'd heard. She had that reference from Fergusons in Bristol. She'd do anything, even charring if uncle would give her a roof over her head for a bit. She could probably get good work up there and take the children to be with her one day. Fresh air too and cheaper rents.

But what about Fred? Should I be doing this? What will he say? Will he understand that my survival is what counts just now. He wouldn't expect me to live with Mattie, surely. He knew how churlish and quarrelsome she can be and how hard it is to resist the impulse to get angry and involved in a heated argument.

Perhaps the poor woman can't help it with her asthma, that awful job she had, and continual tiredness.

Anna firmly resolved: *I'm going up north. I've got uncle's address somewhere to give to Amy. I'll ferret it out.*

Only Two Hours

On Sunday at two o'clock, she knocked on the door of the reception room for visiting parents of children in the workhouse and was shocked to see her three girls clothed in dowdy dresses with white pinafores over them. Amy rushed over to her mother fighting back tears; the other two girls followed. A lump gathered in Anna's throat as she wondered how to conduct this reunion. What to say to make things better.

"Are you having nice dinners here?" she ventured in a shaky voice. "Better than pancakes, eh?"

"I *hate* it here," exploded Edie, glaring at Anna. "When can we go back home?"

"We need to have a little talk, my darlings. Let's go to that corner over there and sit on the sofas."

Other small groups had gathered in an adjoining room comprised mainly of mothers with their children. *A strange lack of men.* Anna and the two older girls settled down on the sofas and Millie climbed onto Anna's lap.

"We have two hours to be together, but I have to leave at four o'clock. There's a lot to talk about today but I want you to know that Mummy will be coming back as soon as I possibly can and have saved up some money. I have to go outside of London to get work because there's nothing here. There's an old uncle I have up north who I'm going to visit. Uncle John. You've heard of him. And where I'm going there's a lot of people who make boots and shoes, you know. Do you remember I told you that I used to be a maid and nanny for a bootmaker in Bristol? Well, I have the feeling that someone up there will give me a job because I was good at what I did. I saw daddy not long ago and he sends his girls lots of love and kisses and I'm seeing Aunty Esther later on at church and Freddy says he'll come and see you soon. Auntie Mattie and Granny can't come just at the moment. Now I want you to write to me and let me know how you're getting on. This is my uncle's address in Northampton, Amy. Don't lose it. Put it in a safe place. Until then, be good girls, and I'll be back as soon as I can."

Anna took a deep breath after she'd blurted out her intentions. The girls stared at her blankly until Edie quietly asked how long she'd be away.

"Until I have enough money to come back and settle us again or I might take you all up to Northampton where the air is better. Rent is cheaper there too and when I find a good job, well, wouldn't that be lovely?"

Amy looked doubtful at Anna's promises while assuring her mother that she'd put uncle's address safely in her purse and keep it there.

"When will daddy be better?" asked Edie impatiently. "Is his cough getting better?"

"Last time I saw him he didn't cough once," Anna reassured them, "and the doctor and nurses are doing all they can to make him better."

Anna had decided not to tell the girls at this stage that their father was failing. *Better to not overload them with too much heartache at this stage.*

Some attendants brought in afternoon tea and Anna felt pleased that this stopped the conversation about Fred. She had nearly faltered when answering Edie's question about her father. She had not eaten anything that day and had been feeling faint during her visit. The Eccles cakes and a cup of tea revived her and enabled her to say what she'd planned to say.

"Now I want you to know that I'm coming back as soon as I can. In the meantime, remember that I love you all very much. Be good girls and do your best at whatever you put your hands to. I'll always be watching over you even though I'm not here. Remember that!"

"Come back soon, Mummy," implored Millie, her lip trembling.

The two hours flew by quickly. A uniformed matron then approached Anna.

"Time's up, Mrs Nash. Four o'clock! All the children now have to return to their quarters – yours to isolation. Don't worry about them. They'll be alright, and you can see them again next Sunday."

Anna and the girls clung to each other and were reminded again that the visit was over.

"Remember, my darlings, I'll be coming back to London as soon as I can. That's a promise."

Amy, Edie and Millie watched their mother walk slowly to the door, pause, turn around and blow them all a kiss. Then she disappeared.

A Talk With Aunty Esther

Anna made her way to Whitefields, feeling sick at the thought that it may be a long time before she could return to London. And what about Fred? What if he died before she could come back? And how would he take the news about the girls when she told him tomorrow morning?

Wearily, she entered Whitefields Central Mission. Aunty Esther noticed a grim expression on her face as she approached.

"What's been happening, Anna?"

"Nothing and a lot," replied Anna. Then she went on to explain, her news tumbling out in a quiet sort of monotone amid efforts to control her emotions.

"My husband's sicker and may never come home. I hardly ever see my boy Freddy who lives away from me now, and I've been forced to put the girls into the workhouse so they can eat. I've just been to see them. I've got to get out of the flat in two days. I haven't got a job and I've got nowhere to live."

So shocked, Aunty Esther at first didn't know what to say.

"So, it's come to this, Anna, my dear. I was hoping you'd find a better position than in that old hotel."

"Well, even that's gone. The place has shut down. Why has God allowed all this to happen to us? He's cruel, Aunty Esther. He's cruel."

Aunty Esther levelled her gaze and spoke quietly to Anna.

"I can understand you feeling angry like that, my dear, but it's not God who is cruel. It's mankind who has done this to your family. In the beginning, God created everybody to be equal and has expected us to look after one another, but sinful human nature has taken over.

Insensitivity and greed rule the day, I'm afraid. At Whitefields here, we constantly deal with very sad cases and are stretched to the limit. Unfortunately, I'm unable to offer you any substantial help apart from a sum of money to tide you over, and some food. And I can't understand why, but widows and single women are the hardest done by from those Guardians, many of them parliamentarians, who sit in well-paid jobs and make callous decisions. Just remember though, that in adversity, Jesus loves us and gives us the strength to carry on and He will never forsake us. His heart is tender towards the poor."

Anna nodded and then said, "I've made a decision. As there is no work for me in London, I'll have to look further. I have an old uncle in Northampton. I'm sure he'll take me in for a while. I'll scout around in those parts. It'll mean I won't be able to see Fred or the children for some time but what else can I do apart from starve?"

"I promise you one thing Anna. I'll be keeping my eye on your little ones. I'll visit them often and love them. And I'll let them know how much *you* love them and miss them and how you've been driven to go somewhere out of London to find work. Amy is a mature little girl for her age and will understand I'm sure. And she's always mothered the other two. Hopefully, you'll be back soon with some money in your pocket to start afresh. And I'll visit Fred as well when I can."

At the mention of Fred, Anna started to cry.

"Oh! Aunty Esther, I'm not sure I'm ever going to see him again after tomorrow. What if he dies while I'm away? Will you visit him?"

"I certainly will, my dearest," assured Aunty Esther as she packed up a large number of sandwiches, cakes, and a packet of tea which she placed in Anna's carry bag. Then she disappeared for a while. Returning, she placed a small envelope in the bag and said, "There's a sum in the envelope to pay your train fare – it's very expensive to travel anywhere by train – and there's some left over to settle you in somewhere for a while."

"I have a little left over from my last wage, Aunty Esther. I can't thank you enough for what you're doing for me, and it's a comfort to know you'll be visiting the girls. Bless you! I'm not staying for church because I have to go and clean up the flat."

After Anna had eaten her fill at the weekly fellowship tea, the two women said their goodbyes with a long embrace. Anna left, turning to wave at the door. Aunty Esther retired to an empty adjoining room with tears in her eyes.

The next morning, Anna wrote a note to the landlord bequeathing everything in the flat for him to sell, as part contribution to the money owing for rent. She left no forwarding address.

"That's all I can do," she sighed tiredly as she placed the note in the middle of the table, knowing it would be found after she'd gone. Then she walked to the sanatorium with a heart slightly pounding and dreading the prospect of telling Fred all that had recently happened.

Fred Disagrees

He has a right to know, Anna reasoned on the way, *but I'll stress the positive aspects of the children's care where they are, and that the girls are all together and haven't been separated and young Freddy's alright with Mary and Mattie. And I'll assure him that I'll be coming back after I've saved up enough money to start over again.*

Anna arrived at the hospital, and Fred walked slowly out to the foyer to join her. He sat down and took her hand, which slightly shook. He listened carefully, nodding sadly, as Anna explained where their daughters were now living and pointed out the positive aspects. He agreed with her that she'd had no choice but to put them in that place. She let him know that she would vacate their flat in two days as the landlord had demanded. When she told him that she planned to go up north to her uncle's, he raised his eyebrows in surprise.

"Well, I think you should stay in London, Anna. It looks like you're running out on us all. Now don't get upset, it's nobody's fault," he reassured, as he noticed her face fall. "We've all done our best, but please go and stay with Mum and Mattie for the sake of the children. I'm in the place I need to be right now. They're caring well enough for me, so don't worry about me, but I must be honest. Whether I'll be leaving here or not I can't say … …" Fred's voice faltered.

"Oh! Fred, please don't leave me," cried Anna as she clung to him.

"Do you remember the first time we met?" he asked, rousing himself while attempting to bring a more cheerful note to their meeting. "On the way to the newsagents, eh? to get our dads' newspapers. I never thought a girl like you would give me a second glance."

"And all the umming and ahhing we went through before we got together, Fred," joined in Anna, smiling, "but I've never regretted it. We knew right from the beginning that for the likes of us, things may never be too easy, but I wouldn't change a thing except for you getting sick."

"That honeymoon up in 'Appy 'Ampstead, Anna. Only a couple of days, but no-one else existed then, did they, eh? Just you and me, and the whole world belonged to us."

"I'll never forget it, Fred. But what about our four beautiful children. Such a strong and earnest young man now, our Freddy, and so bright. And all the girls are different, aren't they? Amy, a blue-eyed little blondie, always so close to me. A real family girl, she is. And Edie! Oh! my goodness, with such a mind of her own, a rebel at times but she is the beauty of the family with her dark hair and those big green eyes. And our chubby-cheeked little Millie, more like Amy in her disposition, Fred."

"I agree with you," Fred replied pensively as he took her hand.

"I'm going to see Freddy this afternoon and have a talk to him when he gets home from school. And I'll say goodbye to Mum and Mattie and Hilary too."

"Surely, you'll go and live with Mattie and Mum for a while, Anna?"

"*What!*" exclaimed Anna. "That wouldn't work out and you know it, Fred. Mattie and I often clash, and there'd be hardly room to move in the place. It'd be hell for everyone. And I'm not working. I'd be a burden there and probably resented by Mattie."

Fred nodded, then added as an afterthought.

"Well, I think you should *try*, Anna. Work could turn up at any time. Think of the children. They need you here in London. I've worked my butt off over the years to keep us all together, and now it looks like you're taking off and going your own way. And Mattie's not that bad, is she?"

Anna took a deep breath and said in a quiet voice, "She's your sister. Blood's thicker than water, Fred."

"It's breaking my heart, Anna. I hate to say it, but these could be my last days. My only comfort, except for the Lord, has been to know my family is all together and happy. Please don't go now."

"I've tried everything in my power, Fred, to stop all this from happening but I have no choice if I'm not to starve. Over the last fortnight, I've had little to eat. At least the children are being fed. Aunty Esther has promised to keep an eye on them, and she always keeps her word. Your mother and Mattie are struggling and paying for Freddy. They can't support me too. I have enough money to get settled up north at my uncle's. I'm sure I'll find work there. Hopefully, I'll be back soon."

"And what if you can't get work when you come back, Anna?"

"Oh! I don't know, Fred," Anna replied with a bewildered look.

"Go and stay at Mum's and keep the family together, Anna."

Anna shook her head. "I've made up my mind, Fred. You don't see how difficult my situation is. Mattie will write to me and let me know how you're going. Please don't think I don't care or that it's easy for me to take this step. The children are alright just now, and they know I'll be coming back."

"You're making a big mistake, Anna, going up there."

"I won't discuss it anymore, Fred."

"Well, you've made up your mind, I can see that," Fred said with a deep sigh, "but keep that beautiful smile whatever you do. It's the way I'll always remember you."

Anna's mouth drooped as she knew she may not see him for some time. She dared not acknowledge that this may be their last meeting.

Fred took her in his arms, and she leant her head against his chest, fighting back tears.

"Be brave, my darling Anna. I know we'll meet again one day … sometime. Somewhere."

Anna winced at Fred's words. Finally, they drew apart, and Fred suffered an anxious moment wondering if he'd held Anna for too long knowing he could infect her. Anna made for the door, lingering there and smiling at Fred. He returned the smile. Then with a small wave, she moved out of his sight. Outside the door, she sat on a chair, bent her head and tried to conceal her tears. Shortly after, she rose and walked back to the flat where everything had been prepared for her to vacate. When she let herself in the front door, she collapsed on the double bed and immediately fell asleep. On waking, she made a cup of tea and ate a sandwich from Whitefields.

It's time to go and see Freddy and the others, she thought, wearily pulling on her shoes.

Talking to Mary

Anna set out for Warren Street, the way seeming longer than ever. She realised she was walking slowly.

It's either because I'm dog tired or I dread telling them I'm going away, she reckoned.

When she arrived, Mary insisted she stay and have dinner.

"Where's Mattie?" asked Anna. "She's usually home by now, isn't she?"

"She's gone ter the 'ospital ter visit Fred. Been gone an hour or so."

"I saw him earlier on, Mum," ventured Anna, willing herself not to cry.

"'Ow is 'ee, Anna?" Mary asked, looking downcast. "Sister 'Ester's takin' me termorrer ter see 'im."

Not wanting to paint a sad picture of Fred, nor wanting to worry her, she said, "He wasn't too bad today, Mum."

After that answer, Mary scrutinised Anna's face.

"Yer lookin' washed ou' an' y've lost weigh'. Wot yer goin' ter do?"

Anna braced herself and explained her plans briefly to Mary. The woman listened intently, occasionally shaking her head.

"Well, I don't agree wiv yer, Anna. It looks like yer runnin' ou' on us all, but I 'ope it works ou' fer yer an' yer back soon. Don't worry abou' Freddy. "Ee'll be orright 'ere."

At that moment Freddy and Hilary arrived home from school, bursting through the door. They plonked themselves at the table, waiting for their usual glass of lemonade and biscuits.

"Hello, Mummy," greeted Freddy as he bit into the first biscuit.

Strange, thought Anna. *He usually calls me Mum, but he's still my little boy, isn't he?*

They whiled away the time until Mary started preparing the evening meal.

"Sausages tonight wiv taters and peas. Goin' cheap t'day at Carrs, the butcher."

She'll never change, thought Anna. *Always pleased to be feeding her family and proud of what she cooks. God bless her!*

Mattie's Opinion

Shortly after Anna had left the hospital, Mattie called in to visit Fred. He walked slowly outside to the vestibule and sat on a chair near his sister. She noticed he looked troubled and fancied there were dried tear stains on his cheeks. Seeking Mattie's understanding of his grief over Anna's departure to Northampton, he opened up about her plans to seek work outside of London. Mattie listened intently, nodding in agreement at Fred's dismay and his disapproval of Anna's decision. Then she pounded him with her opinion.

"Good for *her*, eh? Taking off and going up north. Just like that! It sounds like desertion to me, Fred. There's no reason why she couldn't have stayed with us and continued looking for work in London. After a couple of weeks something would have turned up, I'm sure."

"Well, Mattie, she explained her situation to me," Fred offered in a weak voice, attempting to defend his wife, while deciding not to refer to the incompatible relationship of his sister and Anna, "but it's breaking my heart. The thought I may never see her again and ..."

"That *too*! I certainly hope you're getting better, Fred, but what if you go before she gets back?"

"Oh, I don't know! I don't know what to think sometimes, about all of this."

"Well, I'm telling you, Fred ... she's a *deserter*," Mattie emphasised.

Fred leaned back in his chair and suffered a violent coughing fit. A nurse nearby had been quietly listening to the exchange between Fred and Mattie and had decided it was time for this visit to end.

"You can come again another time, Mrs Harrison. Your brother needs to rest now."

Mattie fixed the nurse with a sullen look; she felt she'd been making some inroads with Fred about Anna, but complied with the nurse's request. She blew her brother a kiss as he was assisted back to the ward. With her visit over, Mattie left the hospital and started for home where she knew her mother would be getting dinner ready.

Mattie's Accusation

Mattie was surprised to see Anna when she arrived home, and Anna didn't miss the hostile glance from her; she noticed too she was strangely silent during the meal, answering her curtly and with a hardened expression.

Fred has told her about my plans to go north.

When the meal was over, Anna invited Freddy into the other room to prepare him for her absence.

"You asked me last week what I was going to do after I told you I had to get out of our place. Well, Freddy, my dearest boy, I have decided to go outside of London to find work. There's nothing here. I'm going up north to old Uncle John's place. I'm sure he'll let me stay for a while. I'll look for work up there and come back when I have enough money to start over again. In the meantime, you'll be alright with Granny and Auntie Mattie and Hilary, and your sisters are being fed and looked after where they are now. Be a brave boy and be strong. Now I want you to keep in touch with your sisters. Remember, you belong to a family. Visit them regularly. They are missing you, and I know you are missing them. Even if you can't manage to see them, write them *letters*, won't you? Promise me, Freddy, that you won't forget you have three sisters who love you. Always keep in touch. Promise!"

"As if I could forget them, Mum. I love them too, even if Edie annoys me sometimes. I promise that I'll always keep in touch with them. And come back soon, please, Mum."

"Nothing is surer, my boy. I'll be returning to London as soon as I can."

Anna and Freddy embraced before going back into the other room to join the others.

"Yer makin' a big mistake goin' up there," Mary stated firmly as Anna sat down. "Yer should be stayin' '*ere*. Git a job in London. Fred's heart is goin' ter break 'cause yer splittin' up the family. I'm not in favour of what yer doin', Anna."

"I know you're not, Mum, but it's my decision."

"You're *selfish*, Anna," accused Mattie, her eyes narrowing. "Just going off on your own and doing what you like! That's pretty easy, eh?"

"If you're honest, Mattie, you know I couldn't stay here. You'd have to support me. You wouldn't like that, would you? And neither would I."

Anna detected the note of jealousy in Mattie's accusations, as though having to move away from Fred and her children was not the hardest thing she could ever be asked to do.

"It's time I was going," she announced suddenly, after a stony silence. "I have a big journey ahead of me tomorrow."

She hugged Freddy tightly, then Mary and Hilary but she only touched Mattie on the shoulder. Then she left, feeling the familiar lump in her throat as she made her way back to the flat.

Funny! she thought, as she walked, *Mattie has accused me of splitting up my family but she's already talking about sending her daughter far away to Birmingham to an orphanage there. Doesn't she think she's splitting up* her *family if she does that?*

That night she slept fitfully and suffered the same distressing sensation of falling down a cliff which seemed to have no base.

Going

Anna awoke the next morning feeling tired and listless. Breakfast consisted of a cup of tea without milk and the cheese sandwich given to her by Mary. Her train was leaving at ten-thirty a.m.

Nothing much more to pack, she sighed as she crammed her nightgown and toiletries into the bulging suitcase.

This old sofa won't be much use to the landlord with its broken spring, she thought with a small sense of satisfaction, *and the rest of the stuff isn't much good either. The only thing worth much was my dinner set and it's gone. I'm glad that coot isn't going to get it.*

Anna knew the furniture and possessions in the flat did not relate to the value of her family or the love and unity they'd shared in the place. She sat on the sofa, resolving to somehow return to London in the shortest possible time.

Something will happen, something must happen, she thought, not daring to imagine any alternative. She glanced at her wristwatch and slowly rose; she had allowed herself three-quarters of an hour to walk to Euston Station, which would normally take fifteen minutes, knowing her heavy suitcase would slow her down.

"So, this is it!" she murmured as she gave the flat a lingering look. Then she heaved up the suitcase and with a carry bag on her other arm, walked out of the place, down the steps and into the street.

Her passage to Euston was hampered by her luggage. Every thirty yards or so, she had to stop for a while. Eventually, she arrived at the station and was directed to the correct platform after paying her fare.

I've done this before, she mused, remembering her train trip from Bristol all those years ago, *but how different is this journey. I was young then and so excited to be going to London and not know what was awaiting me. But there's no excitement this time. I hate London now! With all I've been through these last months, I'm happy to escape the place for a while. I need a break. I just wish I didn't feel so damned weak!*

The train was firing up, ready to leave in fifteen minutes. Anna entered a third-class carriage and placed her luggage in the space provided. Gratefully, she sank onto a seat, closed her eyes and fell into a light sleep. The departing whistle woke her with a start. With a resigned look on her face, she glanced out the window as the train slowly commenced its journey north.

A Cottage Home

After the six-week isolation period in the workhouse, the Nash girls were transferred to a cottage home attached to The Band of Hope organisation at Chingford, run by the Speers sisters, Mary and Helen. The girls were getting used to the idea that they may not see their mother for some time.

"I'll write to her," Amy assured her sisters, "and let her know where we are now."

"Better not do that," said a girl named Clare who'd overheard Amy's intention. "We're not allowed to get in touch with our mothers around here."

"Why on earth not?" Amy frowned.

"Well, Miss Speers reckons our mothers might lead us astray. I know mine wouldn't."

"Nor would mine," asserted Amy, shocked at the suggestion.

"She takes all the letters we write to people, and if one is to our mother, she tears it up. She looks in the envelopes before we seal them. And if our mothers write a letter to us, she rips that up too," said Clare angrily.

"That's wicked of her!" Amy answered, incensed. "Our mothers must wonder why we aren't writing to them. But thanks, Clare, for telling me."

Sure enough, Miss Helen Speers questioned Amy a few days later.

"Do you have your mother's address, Amy?"

"No!" Amy lied emphatically, "I have no idea where she is. She left London to find work in the provinces, but she needs to know where *we* are, Miss Speers.

"No, she doesn't," Helen Speers replied hastily. Then she added, "Your aunt told me she deserted you and left you all in London and if you're telling me a lie about her address, it won't help. We don't allow any girl here to contact their mother or receive letters from her. Understand?"

"She didn't desert us, Miss Speers. Our aunt is *wrong* about that," Amy objected hotly.

"Don't argue with your elders, Amy Nash, or be defiant. We know the facts here." With these words, Helen Speers turned on her heel and walked away.

Amy determined that she'd find a way to reach her mother and told her sisters that the address was safe in the bottom of her handbag and she'd also memorised it.

"Anyway, Freddy can always tell us in his letters how Mummy is doing."

"But I reckon she's going to turn up one day and surprise us," said Edie with a hopeful expression.

"Yes, she will," agreed Millie. "Mummy's coming back."

"Well, at least we've had a visit from Daddy with that nurse while we've been here, even though he's sick," added Edie.

"I'll write to Auntie Mattie tonight to see if she's heard from Mummy yet," Amy said impulsively, "and I'll say we're missing her and Freddy and Granny and Hilary, and can they come to visit us soon?"

"I'll write to her too," said Edie. "I'll be nice to her in my letter."

Letters From Auntie Mattie

Two weeks later, a letter arrived addressed to Amy. She sat on a chair to read it, jittery with excitement. Edie and Millie sat at her feet.

"It's from Auntie. I'll read it out to you. She might have some news about Mummy."

> *57 Warren Street*
> *Tottenham Ct. Rd.*
>
> *Friday 4ᵗʰ Oct. 1912*
>
> *My Dear Amy,*
>
> *We were all very pleased with your letter, also with Edie's. Freddy does not like writing or he would have sent you one before now. Your father cannot come to see you this time, his cough is very troublesome, he will try and visit you next time. We have sent you the only photograph that we have. Hilary is sitting next to Edie with her arms folded. I hope you will be pleased with it. Now dear Amy your Father sends his very best love to his three little girls and hopes you are all good children. We hope Millie's eye is better. With our best love,*
>
> *From your loving Auntie Mattie.*

A silence fell between them, eventually broken by Amy. "He's not getting better," she whispered, her mouth drooping.

"Yes, he will!" declared Millie.

"And what about Mummy? She didn't say anything about Mummy," complained Edie, looking annoyed.

"Maybe she hasn't heard from her yet," Amy placated.

Christmas Day 1912

On Christmas Day, Freddy, and a neighbour Mrs Clark and Aunty Esther, turned up at the cottage home in the afternoon to mark Christmas Day and Freddy's birthday. He was now twelve years old.

Fred did not come but sent his love and greetings to everyone.

The girls were told their father was very ill.

"Oh, no!" Edie had declared. "This is the worst Christmas! We've never had more awful news than this."

But as the weeks went by, things grew worse.

"I have a letter for you, Amy," Helen Speers declared solemnly, "and I'll stay with you and your sisters while you read it."

Amy opened the letter with trepidation, suspecting the contents which she read aloud

> *57 Warren Street,*
> *Tottenham Court Road,*
>
> *February 2nd 1913*
>
> *My dear Amy and Edie,*
>
> *I am very pleased to hear that Sister Esther has been to see you. Also Mrs Clark and Freddy. I could not come to see you myself as Gran has been ill for a month and I could not get away. I will try and come one visiting day. I hope your cold is better. Now, dear Amy, Gran and I hope you will not fret and worry about your Dad because he suffered so much during his illness that it would be wicked to wish him to live and suffer. You must*

Amy sat down on a nearby sofa and sobbed. Edie and Mille joined her and also started to cry.

"Does our mother know that Daddy's gone, Miss Speers?" asked Amy when she'd gained control.

"I don't know," came a quick answer, "but I don't think you should be focusing on her just now. She abandoned you all in London. It's your father you should be thinking of."

"Well, we *are*," Edie declared defensively, "but our mother has to know he's gone too."

"He was such a lovely father, and it wasn't *his* fault he got sick. I wonder if Mummy knows," murmured Amy softly to her sisters as she dabbed her eyes with a handkerchief.

"What was that?" asked Helen Speers sharply.

"I'm just saying, we'll never forget him as long as we live, Miss Speers," Amy replied.

During the next week, the girls resumed their lives at the cottage as best they could, but Amy became curious about their father's funeral.

"I'm writing to Auntie Mattie to ask about it," she explained to her sisters.

It was on March the thirteenth that Amy was given another letter from Auntie Mattie. Included with the letter was a card printed by the funeral director with details of the interment.

> *57 Warren Street*
> *Tottenham, Ct. Rd*
>
> *March 9ʰ 1913*
>
> *My Dear Amy,*
>
> *Thank you very much for your nice letter. Gran and I were both very pleased with it. It was very kind of Mrs Clark to go with Freddy to see you. Saturdays being the visiting days makes it very difficult for me to visit you as I am out at work every Saturday all day. Gran is much better but not quite well yet so I cannot promise you when I shall come, but as soon as Gran is better I will come and see you. Dear Amy, you asked me who went to your Daddy's funeral. Well dear, your aunt and uncle from Chislehurst, Mrs Piroth, Freddy and myself. Gran was too ill to go. I had a letter from your cousin Hilary yesterday. She is very well. Now Dear Amy, I hope you are all well. Give our love to Edie and Millie. I will now conclude with love to yourself.*
>
> *From your loving Grandmother and Auntie M. Harrison*

"Only five people went to Daddy's funeral, and they never asked us," said Edie with a look of resentment.

"You know children don't go to funerals, Edie," replied Amy. "They aren't allowed."

"Well, I think they should be. Freddy went anyway."

"He's older," answered Amy, "and a boy. He can tell us all about it when we see him."

"Show me the card from the funeral please, Amy," asked Edie. Amy handed Edie the card.

"The front page is lovely with a picture of a cross lying on a bunch of ivy and 'Peace Perfect Peace' underneath. Inside it's got Daddy's name and 'In Ever Loving Memory' and that he died on 23rd January, 1913 and he was forty-three years old. He's been buried in St Pancras Cemetery, Finchley," continued Edie.

"Read the verse on the other page," Amy said. "It's lovely."

Edie obliged.

'Gone from us, but not forgotten; Never shall thy memory fade, Loving thoughts shall ever linger, Round the spot where thou art laid.'

The girls were quiet and reflective, with Amy holding back a sob.

"Well, girls," broke in Helen Speers, "I think you should go for a walk in the garden and get your mind off all your sadness. Pick a bunch of flowers in memory of your father, and I'll put them in the common room for all to see."

While they gathered the flowers, Amy disclosed a secret to Edie.

"You know how Mummy gave me her address before she went away, Edie. Well, I'm going to write to her, even though Auntie Mattie and Miss Speers told us we should forget all about her. No-one knows I have the address except you and me. I've got it in the bottom of my purse, and I trust you not to tell anyone that I'm writing. Next time we're allowed out to go to the shops, I'm buying a stamp instead of sweets if I have enough, or I'll save up. Then I'll ask someone in a shop to post my letter for me."

"You won't get an answer. Miss Speers will rip it up," warned Edie. "But give her my love and say I hope she can come back to London soon."

"Let's write to Auntie again, Edie. Maybe she's softened and might tell us something about Mummy."

The next afternoon Freddy visited his sisters and excitedly told them he now had a job on Saturday afternoons and after school hours.

"I knew you'd get something, Freddy. Now you can pay your way and help Auntie Mattie and Granny," said Amy, looking pleased.

"But you can't come to see us anymore on Saturday afternoons," reflected Edie sadly. "Why don't they let people come here on

Sundays, Amy?"

"Because rules are more important than people in this place," Amy answered.

"Where's Hilary now?" asked Edie. "She's away somewhere. Auntie Mattie said she had a letter from her."

"Hilary was sent to Birmingham to an orphanage just before Daddy died," explained Freddy, "and one day she'll be trained up to be a children's nanny."

Still No News

Shortly before Amy's birthday, Millie came down with a serious chest infection and was moved to the Hospital for Sick Children where she'd been sent before with scarlet fever.

"I don't think she's ever got over Daddy going," Amy remarked to Edie. "She always believed he would get well and come back to us. She's too little to cope with everything, and she's still hoping Mummy will come back and we'll go back home."

"Surely, we'll hear something about her soon," replied Edie. "We've been here now for over six months."

But no information from anyone arrived.

On 6th June, Amy celebrated her eleventh birthday. Freddy took time off from his job after school, and called in to the cottage bearing a gift and a letter from Auntie Mattie.

Amy read out the letter.

57 Warren Street,
Tottenham Court Road

June 6th 1913

My dear Amy,

Thank you and Edie very much for your nice letters. I am writing to wish you Many Happy Returns of your Birthday. You are eleven years old today. You are getting a big girl. We have sent you an Album for your picture post Cards and hope you will like it. I am sorry we cannot come this visiting day. Poor Gran is not well enough to go herself, and I cannot get away from my work on the Saturday. I think Freddy told you he had a little place on Saturday afternoons and after school hours. Some of us will come as soon as we can make it convenient. Gran and I would very much like to see you, and perhaps one day we shall be able to do so. We are sorry to hear that Millie is still away. I hope she will be quite cured when she returns to you. I will bring you some cotton when I come. Now, dear Amy, I hope you are both well. Gran sends her love to you all. I must close with fondest love.

From Auntie Mattie

Two weeks later, Millie returned to the cottage completely cured from the chronic bronchitis she'd suffered.

Summer quickly passed and there was still no news about Anna.

"I hope she's alright," Edie mentioned to Amy with a frown. "I'm worried about her."

"She was pretty wrung out when she left London and didn't look at all well. Hopefully, the air in the country is doing her good," replied Amy.

A Visit From Aunty Esther

Aunty Esther had a heavy heart and was dreading her visit to the girls. A month previously she'd called on Mary at Warren Street as she lay on her sickbed. She recalled Mary's prophetic words.

"I 'ave the feelin' I won't be lastin' long, Sister 'Owell. Me darlin' boy Fred's gone ter be wiv 'is farver 'an me granddaughters are in that 'ome; Anna's gone up north 'an 'Ilary is in Birmingham and what'll 'appen ter Freddy if Mattie gets sick? Now I want yer to tell the girls 'ow *proud* of 'em I am and let 'em know 'ow much I love 'em. Tell 'em I'm goin' to a be"er place where there'll be no more cryin' 'an all our tears dried up. That's wot Jesus promised. Tell 'em ter be strong 'an keep believin' because it'll 'elp 'em along the way like nuffin' else. Tell 'em all vat, Sister 'Owell."

Esther promised while placing her arm around Mary and comforting her.

This woman, she'd thought, *who'd been the centre of joy and fun in the family, cementing them together, suddenly reduced to such a sad old lady. When will society change to care for such people and at least allow them the dignity and security of an affordable roof over their heads and enough food for their bellies?*

On the 16th of September, Aunty Esther walked up the path at the cottage home and rapped on the front door. Marion admitted her and called for Helen Speers. The two women had a quiet conversation about the matter, with Esther summing up: "I don't think she ever came to terms with her son going last January. She was always such a jolly person before and saw the best in everyone, you know. When the girls were taken to the workhouse, she tried to look on the bright side for everyone's sake, but she was devastated underneath and when her son died, the spark in her went out and she went downhill. In the end, it was pneumonia which took her and after a small funeral a few days ago she was buried next to her late husband who was the love of her life."

It was agreed that Esther should be the one to tell the girls as she was close to them and knew the family.

"Their Aunt Mattie has been most unwell since her mother went and her asthma has flared up and Freddy their brother? Well, he's very upset of course, but now he's got work after school and on Saturdays, it's harder for him to get here to see his sisters."

Aunty Esther and the girls were ushered to a quiet sitting room and they sat down on the sofas. Aunty Esther looked quite serious and the girls sensed that important news was to be revealed. She took a deep breath and got to the point.

"I know this will make you very sad. Now, you know your Granny hasn't been well for a long time and has been suffering? Well, the Lord decided that He didn't want that for her anymore so she went to be with Him a week ago."

There was a long pause while Amy took it all in. Then she said, her mouth drooping, "Not Granny too."

Aunty Esther relayed all of Mary's last words to her granddaughters as she had promised. The girls nodded their heads with weak smiles as they acknowledged Mary's affirmation of them.

"She had a small funeral and is now sleeping peacefully next to your grandpa. She loved you all dearly and wants you to remember all the fun and laughter you had when she was with you," Aunty Esther stressed. "And she hopes you will keep your faith in Jesus who will always be with you in your ups and downs, to strengthen you. Your cousin Hilary has been sent a letter and should know shortly."

Edie broke in. "Everyone's going. First it was Daddy. And Mummy's gone away. Now Granny is dead, and Hilary's gone to Birmingham to that orphanage."

"We've still got Grandma down at Clapham," reminded Amy.

"But we never get to see her," answered Edie.

"What about Freddy? He's still here. We've got *him*," stressed Millie, "and Mummy will be coming back one day. She'll be coming back *soon*," she insisted.

"I loved Granny, and I'll never forget her. She's with Jesus and Grandpa and Daddy now," said Amy tearfully.

"This is her card from her funeral," said Aunty Esther, handing it to Amy.

"She died on the 10th September 1913 and she was aged seventy-eight years," read Amy.

"She was ancient … nearly eighty," remarked Edie with a surprised look.

"For these days, that was very old indeed," affirmed Aunty Esther.

'She's been buried in St Pancras Cemetery, Finchley where daddy is," said Amy.

"That's nice … where daddy is," echoed Millie. "They're together now."

"I'll read the poem," announced Amy.

Rest, dear Mother, thy labour's o'er. Thy willing hands will toil no more; A loving Mother, true and kind. No friend on earth like thee we find. We miss thy hand clasp, miss thy loving smile. Our hearts are broken, but a little while, And we shall pass within the golden gate, God comfort, God help us while we wait.' AT REST.

Amy placed the card on her lap and the three girls looked at each other with tragic faces. Aunty Esther gave each of the girls a big hug and promised to visit them again soon. The meeting came to an end, and the girls slowly filed out of the room, dealing with their grief.

A Solution for the Girls

In the evening, Helen Speers had an idea which she discussed with her sister Mary.

"I think this may be the best thing out for them," she shared, after considering the Nash sisters' futures. "With all the upheaval in these girls' lives lately, it will give them a new perspective. A new beginning. An escape from sadness. There's nothing like new experiences to take your mind off your troubles. No need to worry about their mother. She's abandoned them, and she didn't deserve to have three such lovely little girls, did she? They're better off without her. And their brother Freddy? He could write letters to them and perhaps one day join them. Yes! Those Nash girls can be included in Mrs Warby's plan."

Mary Speers agreed. "It'll be the making of them, Helen. Lucky little girls to be chosen."

A few days later, Helen Speers answered the telephone. An expected call had been made from the Hotel Russell in London by a Mrs Eleanor Warby.

"She's *arrived!*" Helen announced joyfully to her sister. "Everything's set to go now. That woman's remarkable. To think I met her only fifteen months ago on her *first* trip to England and since then she's prepared everything. She told me she's having a short break in London before she interviews some people, and after that, she's going to Kent to visit her cousin, then she's sailing home at the end of September to put the final touches to everything."

"When will you tell the girls, Helen?" Mary asked, looking somewhat concerned.

"A few days before they leave, Mary. Better they don't have too long to brood and cause trouble. Remember that Sylvia girl last year? She went on for weeks about it. I think towards the end of October I'll tell them. They'll be leaving on the 30th."

Australia

Mrs Warby's First Trip to England

Fifteen months earlier, Eleanor Warby's holiday had lasted about eight weeks, starting from the homestead within Balangara, the cattle and sheep station she owned in the New England district of New South Wales in Australia.

This journey back to her homeland resulted from a long-held dream she'd treasured during her years of hard work running the station, while raising her children as well. She'd done it alone after her beloved husband had died in his late forties. The sheep and cattle station had finally become a successful venture in the New England district. Her eldest son Neil was now in charge and the time had arrived for Eleanor to have that trip to London and afterwards, visit her cousin Myra in Kent.

Firstly, she'd endured the bumpy ride over the rough dirt road in her son's Dodge to get to Armidale to catch the night express train to Sydney, terminating at Central Station. Then to Circular Quay to board the steamer for Southampton in England. The trip had seemed endless and tiresome on the boat despite deck games such as quoits, darts, exercising and other entertainments and impromptu concerts. When she'd arrived at Southport in England, she'd stayed for a night at a hotel to rest, then took the final leg by steam train the next day to Waterloo Station, and a cab ride from there to the Hotel Russell in west London.

For the first two weeks, she'd delighted in some of London's popular attractions. The theatre, concerts, galleries and the Changing of the Guard, to name a few of her pleasures. However, something troubled her. She'd been appalled at the number of ragged children wandering the streets, most without shoes on their feet. Young girls, some looking no older than nine, nursing babies on the doorstep of their run-down homes, looks of resignation on their tired, drawn young faces. This had shocked her.

"Why aren't you at school?" she'd asked one of the girls.

"Ma's got to work," the child had answered, "and there ain't no-one ter look after Biddy 'ere. Me farver's cleared out 'an we don't know where 'ee is. Anyroad, Ma says we're be"er off wivou' 'im, cause 'ee whacks us. She gits food from a church up the road ter 'elp out 'an 'er money pays the rent fer our room. Me bruvver goes ter school though, cause 'ee's older than me 'an can 'elp us all out one day, Ma says. That's why 'ee needs the education."

Mrs Warby had opened her handbag and drawn out a ten-shilling note which she'd slipped into the pocket of the girl's pinny.

"Keep this safe," she'd urged, "and give it to your mother when she gets home. It will help you out for a while."

A broad smile had broken out on the child's face.

"You're a kind lady, missis. Fank you very much. I'll ask Ma ter gi' us some meat. We don't 'ave vat very often."

Eleanor Warby had torn herself away, troubled by the plights of the children she'd witnessed in Spitalfields. She had wandered there by accident and got lost, finally making her way back to the Camden area.

On the following Sunday, she'd attended a church in Tottenham Court Road and spoken to a woman after the service. Sister Hester Howell was pleased to be showing hospitality to a visitor from Australia. The topic of conversation eventually led to the ragged children Eleanor had seen in the streets.

"We do the best we can, Mrs Warby. It breaks our hearts, but if we help out with any money, the Guardians cut down on poor peoples' support, little as it is. Fortunately, there are some generous folk around, who donate clothing and furniture and food parcels. But I agree, the government needs a shakeup in the social justice system here. There are inroads happening though, thank goodness."

"But those hungry-looking, ragged little souls, Miss Howell. What's to become of them? What is their future?"

"Some of them are orphans, you know, or abandoned. Their parents often cannot maintain them. Sometimes Mum or Dad have died from illnesses like consumption. Not many recover from that. I personally know of a lovely family which is being ripped apart because the father is ill from that horrible condition. Some children end up in workhouses. Others can be moved into cottage homes like those nearby, run by two sisters, Helen and Mary Speers. A nicer life there. More cheerful. The adults though in the workhouse lead a most depressing life. The women have to slave in the laundry and kitchen, pick oakum and they feel like prisoners I imagine, their identity damaged. And the men have to do backbreaking work, weak as they may be. And do you know, they are allowed to see their children for only two hours a week? How hard that must be."

"That's *terrible*," Eleanor protested, an anguished look on her face. "Oh! I wish I could do more to help. Those little waifs will haunt me when I get back home."

Taking her to leave and promising to send regular cheques to Whitefields from Australia to help the poor, Eleanor made her way back to her hotel.

For the next week, she filled in time by attending Covent Garden Opera House for a performance of La Boheme, visiting the London Portrait Gallery and other attractions, but she could not get the images of the ragged street children out of her mind despite her pleasurable diversions.

"Oh well, the money I'll send to that church I went to should help," she consoled herself, "but now, I'll have to get over to see Myra."

Eleanor's cousin lived in Kent. She'd done well for herself, having married a wealthy merchant banker. Unfortunately, he'd died when in his late fifties, but he'd left Myra well provided for. She lived in an affluent part of the county and enjoyed an indulgent life. She and her cousin Eleanor, (who lived in that 'outpost' Australia, in her opinion), were regular correspondents. When Myra had learned of Eleanor's planned holiday to England, she'd invited her to spend a few weeks with her in her home, Rosedale Grove. Eleanor had promptly replied that she'd love to come, that after all those years ago when she and Alan had left England to settle in Australia, there'd surely be a lot to talk about.

The day arrived for Eleanor to travel from St Pancras Station to West Canterbury Station on her journey to visit Myra, who would pick her up in a taxi which would then continue on to her comfortable address. The tiring walk to St Pancras Station from the Hotel Russell took nearly half an hour, and Eleanor was relieved when she'd bought her ticket for the train trip. Nearly two hours later, the steam train pulled into West Canterbury, and there was Myra, true to her word, waiting with the taxi. The driver took charge of Eleanor's luggage and settled the two women into his cab. After a short drive of a few miles, he pulled up outside Rosedale Grove. Eleanor collected her luggage, Myra paid the driver, and he pulled away, intent on picking up another fare.

"Welcome to Rosedale, my dear," smiled Myra as the two cousins embraced. They walked up a long gravel driveway to the front door with Eleanor admiring the extensive cottage garden. An elderly gardener with a long grey beard was planting out some new seedlings.

"It takes a lot of weeding and Patrick does a good job," explained Myra.

The day passed pleasantly with much catching up after decades of not having seen each other.

After dinner in the evening, Myra bundled Eleanor off to her bedroom, advising her to have a good sleep as tomorrow afternoon she'd invited a close friend over to meet her cousin from Australia.

"My girls are getting together some savouries and dainties to have with coffee or tea."

Eleanor had not expected such an imperious-looking woman to turn up the next day for afternoon tea. She was dressed in a smart navy suit over a paisley silk blouse in tones of blue, pink and navy. A fringed stole completed the outfit. Many lavish rings adorned her fingers, no doubt featuring precious gems. Eleanor felt rather homespun in her grey tweed skirt, cream cotton blouse and burgundy coloured cardigan, sensible shoes, no jewellery except for her engagement and wedding rings and a marquisate brooch pinned on the blouse.

"This is a close friend of mine, Eleanor. Please meet Lady Sybil Lloyd-Ashtonbury from Ashtonbury Manor, over the way."

"Lovely to meet you, Lady Sybil," smiled Eleanor, stifling an impulse to bob in front of her. "Kent! A beautiful part of England is Kent. How I miss England. This is the first time I've been back here since my husband and I went to Australia."

"What induced you to *go* there?" asked the Lady, studying Eleanor's face intently. "That country has little history and has grown from a convict settlement. I suppose there must be *some* people in that place who have a sense of refinement, aren't there?"

Eleanor felt offended at the lady's comment but answered her carefully while hiding her annoyance.

"My husband Alan and I were very young when we went to Australia. He had a sense of adventure and saw many possibilities in developing the country. In time, we became the owners of a large cattle and sheep property and made enough money to buy two more stations. Alan passed on in his late forties, and I had the choice of selling up everything or learning how to manage things myself. I reasoned that our holdings would become a legacy for our children, and I knew Alan would have wanted that. I'd also grown to love the way of life and the New England district with all its changing moods and seasons. It's quite high there and even sometimes snows in winter. I admit that, compared to England, it's wild and untamed, rugged and with high ridges and plunging valleys with crystal creeks, ferny and mossy. Wonderful places to swim in when the weather can be so hot. And the native animals and the bird life …! We have lyrebirds in that area, and the males have tail feathers each side of their body which reach up to form the shape of a lyre like that old musical instrument. But not only that … those birds are ventriloquists and can imitate the call of any other bird, including kookaburras."

Eleanor felt satisfied that she'd defended her adopted land, but

Lady Sybil persisted.

"It all sounds very exciting, Eleanor, and picturesque, and I'm glad you've done well, but what about the *people*? Many cultural pursuits there?"

"Of course, there are," replied Eleanor, not hiding her annoyance this time. "We have theatres, art galleries, writers and opera, universities and a lot of inventors too – some very *clever* people. If you've been to Covent Garden lately, you may have heard Nellie Melba sing. She's Australian and is regarded as the leading soprano in the world."

Lady Sybil's eyebrows rose. "Nellie Melba. That's right. A lovely voice."

At that moment, two young women entered the room with sandwiches and small fancy cakes.

"The tea's on its way, or would you prefer coffee instead, Lady Sybil?" asked Myra.

"Coffee, thank you, my dear," replied the lady with a slight nod.

Tea and coffee were duly delivered, and the two serving girls retired.

Myra turned to Lady Sybil.

"I'm really pleased, Sybil, with my two servant girls, Pamela and Margaret. You've really made something out of them. To think how you dragged them out of that cottage home near London, brought them out here to your Deportment and Domestic Arts Academy and trained them up so well, in the social graces too. They're a great help to me."

Lady Sybil acknowledged the compliment.

"There's a need for good servants lately in Kent, and it's my way of helping some girls from the working classes to find useful employment. Quite often when Reginald and I go to London to our apartment, I pop into the Speers Sisters' cottage homes to bring another girl out if there's a vacancy in the academy."

Eleanor pricked up her ears. She knew this woman was a snob, but she was apparently doing something positive to help unfortunate children. And she remembered that church worker, a Sister Esther Someone, wasn't it? … at that church in Tottenham Court Road she'd attended. She'd spoken about the street children and how some ended up in Miss Speers cottage homes. Yes! Those cottages are the places where this Sybil lady is getting the girls.

"I've heard about those cottage homes you're talking about Lady Sybil. What a coincidence! A church worker in a London church I went to mentioned them. Run by the Speers sisters?"

"Yes! That's them," beamed Lady Sybil. "They run an organisation called *The Band of Hope,* and in the cottage homes they've established there's a more humane way of caring for children. They have about ten to a cottage with a house mother or husband and wife. The homes can be somewhat regimented as in the workhouses, but it *is* a step up from those places. Some needy children, you know, get adopted by families here. Also, for many years the Child Emigration Society run by the British Government has sent orphans and abandoned boys and girls to countries like Canada, South Africa and Australia where English children are welcomed to swell the population. They're supported in whatever accommodation they end up in."

"I like that idea of sending them to other countries," chipped in Myra. "I've been through a couple of fogs in London, and I'm not surprised at the number of illnesses there. The children would be breathing fresher air overseas."

"I wish I could do more but, apart from sending money to that church I went to, I don't know what else I could do," added Eleanor with a frown.

"Time to go," announced Lady Sybil suddenly, glancing at her wristwatch. "Reginald promised he'd pick me up at four o'clock and he's never late, so I'd better be off. He's recently bought one of those new-fangled automobiles, and the thing races along at about twenty-five miles an hour. I was petrified at first but I've got used to it now. Lovely to meet you, Eleanor. Do come back to England soon. And I'll see you next week Myra at the Kent Heritage Society."

With these parting words, Lady Sybil made her way out of the house and down the driveway to meet her waiting husband parked outside the gate.

"It *is* frightening, that speed," said Myra, pulling a face of mock fear. "I get a bit nervous in taxis, you know. Anyhow for the next two weeks, we'll be walking everywhere from here. And on Sunday I thought you'd like to attend Canterbury Cathedral as you'll be going back to London the following week."

Eleanor had happily agreed and settled down to enjoy this countryside part of her trip to England. But there was something gnawing at her which gave her no peace: those poor little waifs she'd seen in London. For three nights she'd been unable to rest peacefully in bed, denying it was her business to help, praying for a change in social benefits in England until an unlikely idea occurred.

"Maybe that's a possibility," she pondered. "I think I should look into it. I wonder what Myra would think about it?"

She broached the subject with Myra the following day with growing enthusiasm.

"If you hadn't invited Lady Sybil here the other day, Myra, I wouldn't have thought of it. Apparently, it's alright to take some children out of those cottage homes she spoke about, like your Pamela and Margaret here, to give them a better future, so perhaps I could do the same. When Sybil mentioned there's a migration scheme in England that sends needy children to other countries, it suddenly hit me. I have heaps of land at Balangara and could easily get a couple of cottages built there and house some of those little ones. I'd only take girls though because they could be trained up for service in my properties."

Myra looked preoccupied for a while before she spoke.

"What a responsibility you'd be taking on, Eleanor." Then her face brightened when she considered another aspect. "Actually though, it could be good for everyone in the long run, and you wouldn't have to worry about hired help anymore from outside. You'd have servants looking after you and living in those cottages right in your own backyard."

"Exactly!" beamed Eleanor, pleased at Myra's understanding of her idea, "but the girls would be quite young at first and need nurturing and schooling. Wilma, my daughter, who is unmarried as you know, could become their teacher. She'd love that, I'm sure. Later on, when old enough, the orphans could be trained up to cook and provide domestic help. In the end, of course, they'd leave, meet nice men and become good Australian wives and mothers. Now before I get back to London, I'd like you to give me the address of those Speers sisters' cottage homes. You'd have those, wouldn't you?"

"Of course, Eleanor. Lady Sybil let me know where Pamela and Margaret came from. I'll get that address for you. I hope you'll be led in the right direction but please don't get your hopes up too high. It may not work out."

"I know," answered Eleanor, her mouth downturned a little, "but the more I think about it, Myra, the keener I am. I hope I can get approval from the authorities."

When Eleanor's visit came to an end, she and her cousin parted with promises to keep in touch by correspondence.

"Let me know if it works out with the girls. I wish you luck, Eleanor."

The journey back to the Hotel Russell in London had been without complications. Eleanor resolved to visit the cottage homes the next day.

The following morning, she hired a taxi to drive her to the Chingford address of the homes. When she arrived there, she was surprised at the standard of the two-storeyed building. She thought it looked inviting with the colourful flower garden in the front. She knocked on the door and was greeted by Marion, the housemaid who retired to let Miss Speers know there was a visitor from Australia who wanted to discuss an idea with her. Miss Speers was both surprised and puzzled.

What sort of an idea? she wondered, as her curiosity grew.

"Thank you for seeing me, Miss Speers," smiled Eleanor as the lady entered the room. "I'm Mrs Eleanor Warby from Australia, and I've been enjoying a much-needed holiday in beautiful England. I'll be returning home in ten days."

"I'm glad you're enjoying your stay, Mrs Warby, but what brings you here?"

"It's like this," answered Eleanor, "… when I was in London, I saw some ragged little children roaming the streets. They looked hungry and unkempt. I tried to get them out of my mind, but couldn't for the love of me, and when I visited a church in Tottenham Court Road, a woman there told me that some of those street children are orphans or abandoned and end up in the workhouse or cottage homes. Apparently, this church does the best it can to help the needy, but the problem in London these days is enormous. I was also told that a few lucky children are adopted or fostered in private homes. Now, this is where things become very interesting, Miss Speers. I went to stay for a while with my cousin Myra in Kent. She'd invited a friend of hers to afternoon tea. Her name is Lady Sybil Lloyd, er …."

Helen Speers interrupted with an interested expression. "Yes, I know Lady Sybil Lloyd Ashtonbury, and I've heard of Myra. Do go on."

"Well, after speaking to Lady Sybil and learning of the good work she does in helping orphaned or abandoned young girls to be trained up in her academy, I had an idea that perhaps I could do something similar in Australia to help and …"

Helen Speers interrupted.

"In Australia? Well, I know that Britain has an emigration scheme operating which sends children there to large farms run by organisations like Doctor Barnardos and other such groups. Some of those children have been recruited from our cottages here. Now how would you be able to help? Would you want to adopt a couple of orphans, or what have you in mind?"

"Let me explain, Miss Speers," answered Eleanor, feeling hopeful. "I'm interested in how you run your cottage homes here. I'm the owner of a large cattle and sheep property in Australia in wonderful, high country with plenty of fresh air. My main property, Balangara, has a lot of land around it. It would be quite easy for me to have a couple of cottages built there to house some orphan girls and train them up for useful service just like Lady Sybil does here in England. Also, my unmarried daughter is a highly skilled and talented young woman who is good with children. She'd be greatly suited to run a school on the grounds and give the girls a good education. She plays the piano too!" Eleanor added proudly.

Eleanor paused to observe how Miss Speers would react to her suggestion. She looked sceptical.

"But, Mrs Warby, why would you want to do this? These children come from varying backgrounds, some very rough indeed and difficult to manage. What advantage could they be to you?"

"Well, Miss Speers, I'd really love to help some poor little mites, and I'm willing to take a risk. Mind you, to be honest, I *would* prefer girls from a respectable background. To begin with, they'd have to earn their privilege of being brought to Australia, which would give them a far greater chance of a happier life than if they stayed in England, I'm sure. This would be pointed out to them. When old enough, they'd be trained in cooking for the station hands, household cleaning, laundry work and ironing, waiting on tables and social skills. Of course, this would benefit me, and I make no secret of it. At the moment, I have to rely on women from outlying towns like Armidale and Guyra. They never stay long, and a couple took off suddenly with station hands, leaving me stranded. With my plan, the girls would be residents of Balangara and would always be on hand to do the chores. One day, of course, they'd leave the station and go their own way, hopefully, to find good husbands. I'm sure my idea would benefit both the girls and me."

Miss Speers scrutinised Eleanor Warby and decided that her motives were sincere and her plan was feasible for the orphans, should the authorities approve. Both women agreed that recent events seemed to have lined up to confirm Eleanor's plan, what with Myra's invitation to stay with her, Lady Sybil's visit and the information about her academy and the cottage homes, where young girls could be sourced.

"I'll show you one of the cottages then, Mrs Warby, and you can see how we run it. There are ten girls to a cottage with a house mother in charge, or husband and wife in some cases. The programme is rigid as that builds character, you know. They rise at six-thirty, have ablutions first, dress and then make their beds. Then there's chapel for half an hour before breakfast. They wash the dishes afterwards and clean the kitchen before they go to the school connected to this place. They have some free time in the afternoon before revising their lessons. Or they weed the garden. Then they help in the kitchen preparing their dinner. Washing up again. Free time for reading, board games or embroidery and knitting. Prayers, then off to bed at eight-thirty, the little ones earlier. They're allowed to walk to the village nearby on Saturday afternoons for ice creams and to visit the park. By the way, we don't encourage maudlin talk about their mothers. Some have deserted their children or are a bad moral influence."

Eleanor duly inspected the girls' dormitory and bathroom facilities, recreation room, dining and kitchen areas, and assured Miss Speers that she could easily manage arrangements like that on her property in Australia.

"I'm going to make enquiries from the authorities in England and Australia to get some girls out, Miss. Speers, if I can. I'll make haste. I feel for these young children and would like to do the best I can for some of them."

Miss Speers finally applauded Eleanor's intentions and promised she would co-operate with the authorities in England. When the time was right, she would personally select some suitable girls from her place here at Chingford. The two women parted with smiles and good wishes, Eleanor assuring Miss Speers that she would be in touch again in the future, and would let her know from time to time of the progress in Australia for housing the girls, if that were to happen. Helen Speers wrote a personal recommendation for Eleanor as a future sponsor and carer for migrant children.

Eleanor made haste and applied to the British Child Emigration

Department. All of the forms were filled out and interviews conducted over the next two days and Eleanor was finally given approval to go ahead with her plans. She had three more days to spend in London before boarding the steamer back to Australia.

"I'll write a long letter to Myra tonight," resolved Eleanor, "and let her know all that's happened since I left her. She'll be amazed and can let Lady Sybil know too."

She was eager to return home to Australia and set her plans in motion. She'd obtained all the information she needed from the English end to start negotiations in Australia. The day soon arrived for her journey home. She boarded the steamer at Southampton dreading the eight-week trip to Sydney. Fortunately, the passage back was smoother than the trip over had been. When she finally arrived at Armidale after the night journey in the train from Sydney, her son Neil was waiting for her in his new automobile. She felt exhausted when she finally arrived home at Balangara.

"I'll rest up for a couple of weeks to recover," she announced to the family after telling them about her orphan rescue plan. "Then I'll get things going."

It had taken far longer than she'd wanted. There'd been letters to write, more forms to fill in, building plans for two cottages to be drawn up and passed by the local authorities, the hiring of builders and various tradesmen to fit out the cottages with furniture, beds and built-in cupboards of course.

Back to England

Fifteen months had passed before Eleanor boarded the ship in Sydney to take her second trip back to London to finalise everything. There were people to interview for the position of house parents, who'd applied by correspondence. And she'd have to see Miss Helen Speers at Chingford again even though she'd often written to her to inform her of the progress of her plan.

She was greatly relieved when her arduous journey was over and done with. As she entered her room in the Hotel Russell, she was feeling pleased that most of her preparations were complete for housing the orphan girls. Feeling tired, she'd thankfully sunk down into a comfortable chair to rest and had fallen asleep.

A knock at the door roused her from her nap. She opened the door and admitted a maid with a tray of afternoon tea, ordered from the reception desk when she'd arrived.

Refreshed after her tea, she walked down below and asked the concierge if she could use the telephone; she dialled the number of the cottage homes and was pleased at the quick reply from the other end.

"I'll rest up for a couple of days, Miss Speers, and then I'll be over to see you about things. I know you're expecting me."

"We are, indeed, Mrs Warby. Let's say, in two days at two o'clock in the afternoon?"

"I'll be there," assured Eleanor.

Two days later the cab pulled up at the exact time agreed to and Eleanor knocked on the door.

"Oh, Mrs Warby, do come in," said Helen Speers with a welcoming smile. "Lovely to see you again. I'll ask Marion to make a cup of tea and then I can tell you what's been happening here."

The women settled down to their refreshments and engaged in small talk for a while, discussing the cost of cab fares and the weather. It would soon be winter in England and summer in Australia.

"A nice time for the girls to set foot in their new land," Helen Speers exclaimed. "I've selected the seven girls you want, Mrs Warby. Jane Reynolds is just thirteen, then there's Gracie O'Neill and Doris Kirby, who are twelve, and the three Nash sisters, Amy at eleven, Edith at nine and Millicent at six. The youngest child is little Josie Haines, who is four and a half. They'll be told in a few weeks. I cannot vouch for the background of any of them you know, but the three sisters seem to be nice little girls. Even so, they may have had rough parents. You never know. Those girls were placed into the St Pancras workhouse by their mother after their father was admitted to hospital as he had consumption and couldn't work. She'd had some sort of a job for a while, but after that, she'd gone into the provinces somewhere to find work, so these children tell me. Their father died last January after a long illness. The girls have been living here for some time now, transferred from the workhouse. It's a nicer environment here for children."

Eleanor interrupted. "Are they orphans then, these three girls. What about their mother? Is she still living?"

"I was told by a relative that she's abandoned her children, Mrs Warby, or she is dead."

"Are there other family members then?" asked Eleanor.

"They have a grandmother who's recently died and another who lives in Clapham whom they never see. There's a brother and an aunt who live together in Warren Street at St Pancras and are scratching for a living. The aunt has asthma and works as a charwoman. The boy, Freddy, works after school and on Saturdays. A girl cousin, Hilary I think, has been sent to St Alice's Orphanage in Birmingham to be eventually trained as a children's nanny as her mother could not support her adequately."

"Oh! the poor things. How hard it must be," sympathised Eleanor.

"Well, at least the girls will have a decent future with you, Mrs Warby. From what you've told me, you'll be able to make something out of them. I don't doubt your kind endeavours."

Eleanor was buoyed up by this affirmation of the plans she had for her future charges.

"There are only finishing touches now for the cottages to be completed, forms to fill in here and interviews for house parents," she enthused, "and you say the children should be arriving just after Christmas. They'll have a good start to 1914 in Australia."

"They have a passage booked on *The Ballarat,* and the steamer should arrive in Sydney on Boxing Day, Mrs Warby, or thereabouts. You can arrange for transport from Sydney to your place. In the meantime, the girls will be given a pink wooden box containing all their necessities to start them off with, like bloomers, vests, petticoats, dresses, stockings, nightwear, a warm coat and toiletries."

"Well, I'll sign your forms here, Miss Speers, and I'd better get going. Tomorrow I have to interview some prospective English house parents, and I also want to spend a little time with my cousin in Kent as I did last time I was over here. My passage home on the boat is already booked and I should be back home around the start of December in time to prepare for the girls. All done then!"

"Thank you, Mrs Warby, for giving these girls a home and a future. The colonies need to be settled with good British stock you know."

"I agree, Miss Speers. I'll write to you and let you know when the girls have arrived."

Miss Speers ordered a cab and the two women parted with an affectionate handshake. Now it loomed ahead to let the girls know of the plans which had been made for them. She knew they were in for a huge shock when she'd tell them of the plans to send them away from England to another country. There was mostly strong resistance.

The House Parents

The interviews were conducted for house parents over the next two days, and Eleanor engaged a Mr and Mrs Wilcox after consideration. They had no children of their own to keep them tied to England and wanted to put down roots in Australia. Mrs Wilcox believed in strong discipline for children as 'this is what builds character'. Eleanor agreed, mentioning that the background of these girls was unknown and they may need to be knocked into shape. Alfred Wilcox had outlined his experience as a handyman and gardener in the couple's letter to Mrs Warby when applying for the position in Australia. After their successful interview, the two new house parents agreed to immediately book their passage on the same steamer as the girls.

"An excellent idea," said Eleanor smiling. "This will give you a chance to get to know them on the way out, and they'll be able to settle in better when you all get to Balangara."

Visiting Myra Again

When Eleanor arrived at her cousin's place in Kent, she was greeted with words of admiration for the time and effort she'd put into her arrangements for the migrant girls.

"I can't believe how well you've done Eleanor since you were last here. Getting everything ready in just fifteen months? It astounds me."

"It's only taken commitment and organisation," replied Eleanor modestly, pleased at Myra's compliments. Then she added, with a satisfied look. "These children will be starting a brand-new life in 1914 at Balangara with new house parents, Myra … but right now, I'm going to enjoy these few weeks with you in this lovely part of the country. My passage home is booked and I should be back at Balangara in time to welcome the girls."

Eleanor's holiday with Myra eventually came to an end and, with a fond embrace, the cousins parted. After staying just one night back at the Hotel Russell, Eleanor travelled to Southampton and boarded the ship sailing to Sydney.

After four weeks at sea, Eleanor had not suffered any seasickness, and she thanked the Lord for a calm passage. It occurred to her when she was halfway through her passage that her seven small charges would be boarding the next steamer in a few days for their journey to Sydney. She hoped all had gone smoothly in preparing the children for their big adventure. She rose from her deck chair and walked back to her cabin for an afternoon nap. In a few weeks or so she'd be in Sydney.

A Bad Reaction

On the 26th October 1913, Helen Speers squared her shoulders while preparing to tell the selected girls they would shortly be migrating to Australia. She hated this part of the business which had always been difficult during the previous overseas placements she'd arranged from the cottage.

You must be firm and not show any weakness, Helen, she told herself, knowing that a part of her felt sorry for these children. They were to be given only three days' notice of their departure, due to a history of strong resistance from many. The shorter this upsetting period, the better. For her as well.

Aware of her own heartbeat and feeling apprehensive about the approaching reaction to her news, Helen Speers took a deep breath. Then she gathered together the three Nash sisters and the four other girls. The assembled little group stood attentively while Helen Speers addressed them, smiling to mask her nervousness.

"Now, girls, I have some very exciting news for you. You seven, have been specially chosen for a great new adventure which not many children like you are privileged to experience, I must say. Now before I start to explain, do any of you know much about Australia?"

"Not much," answered Jane after a while, "… except that it's part of the British Empire and it's on the other side of the world and oh!, it's got a big hopping animal called a kangaroo that carries its baby in a pouch in its stomach. I learnt that at school," she added proudly.

"That's true, Jane, but there's much more to Australia than just kangaroos, you know. It's a place where children can have a far happier life than if they stay in London. There's sunshine and fresh air and always plenty of lovely fruit to eat like bananas and pineapples, and nothing to worry about anymore. It's a place ..."

"I'm not going *there*," shouted Edie, who'd realised they were being groomed to the idea of leaving England. "My mother is still here and my brother Freddy and Auntie Mattie and my other Grandma and Hilary too."

Miss Speers cut in sharply. "Well, your mother had the chance of staying in London with your aunt and brother, so your aunt told me, but chose to desert you all, Edith. I'm sure if she'd stayed in London things would be different. No-one knows if she's alive or dead these days, so try to be thankful that you and your sisters are being given the chance to *make* something of your lives in a wonderful new land."

Amy glared, and answered defensively. "Our mother worked harder than anyone I know to keep us together, and the worry she went through before she left London was something no-one should ever have to bear, Miss Speers. She didn't even have enough to eat. And she promised to return to us. Please don't be surprised that we don't want to go to *Australia!*"

Miss Speers felt a pang of conscience but suppressed it. This was harder than she'd expected with these Nash girls, but strangely, the other four seemed willing to go. Lord knows what they'd been through.

Edie ran sobbing into Amy's arms; Amy looked utterly shocked, while Millie stood looking confused.

"We won't be going," insisted Amy firmly. "We'll be staying here until we find out what's become of our mother."

"It says on the application form, Amy, for your migration, that your mother has forsaken you. You'll be far better off in a country where there are opportunities for a wonderful future which are not here for you."

"Who filled out that blasted form, Miss Speers?" demanded Amy, standing her ground with hostile eyes, but Miss Speers did not answer the question.

"Now you are to be sensible, Amy Nash, and appreciate the good fortune being offered to you and your sisters. I don't want to hear any more from you about this matter. A good lady from Australia has moved heaven and earth to offer you a better life and you complain. Arrangements have already been made for your passage anyhow. Just be grateful.

"I have a brother here, and what about my mother?"

"Forget about her. She has forsaken you."

"Forget about our *mother*, Miss Speers? That's something I'll never be able to do for the rest of my life. She loved us and would never wish us harm, ever! And what about Freddy, our brother?"

"He's old enough to look after himself, unlike you girls. In any case, he can write letters to you and keep in touch that way."

"You are nasty and cruel, Miss Speers, to tell us to forget about our family," shouted Edie in Helen Speer's face. "Our daddy's gone, but we still have our mother at least. And she's coming back. She *promised* us".

"Insolent girl! Calling *me* nasty and cruel. I've devoted my *life* to caring for unfortunate children. Keep your peace now. Nothing can be changed. Just get used to the idea. You and your sisters are going to Australia to a better life and that's that! And you'll be going in three days."

At this point, Miss Speers stomped out of the room, and the three sisters huddled together in a corner.

"Where's Australia, Amy?" asked Millie through sobs which had finally overtaken her.

"I'm not *going!*" insisted Edie again. "I'll run away instead."

"We are *not* orphans and we'll find a way to get the people to change their minds," said Amy comfortingly as she tried to silence Edie and Millie who were still loudly objecting.

A bell rang announcing tea. The Nash girls quietened down and walked sullenly to the dining room. Later in the evening, Amy decided to write to Aunty Esther and let her know of Miss Speer's plans to send them to Australia. She'd plead with her to prevent this from happening.

I can't write to Mummy from here, but I *can* write to Aunty Esther," she explained to Edie and Millie. "I'm sure she'll be able to help us."

The next day after school, Amy disobediently walked to the village and posted her letter to Sister Esther Howell, Care of Whitefields Central Mission Church at Tottenham Court Road, London. Two days later, the seven girls selected for emigration to Australia were told they were to start their journey to their new land at ten o'clock the following morning. A pink wooden box for each child had already been packed with their necessities.

"Let's hope Aunty Esther got the letter in time. It may not be too late," said Amy with a tear-stained face as she attempted to console her sisters. The three Nash girls cried themselves to sleep that night.

Everything is Ready at Balangara

At the end of November, Eleanor Warby arrived back at Balangara, looking forward to a time of recovery before the Wilcoxes and the girls arrived on Boxing Day. Two days later, she and her daughter walked two hundred yards down a slight slope to inspect the finished cottages and were satisfied they would provide comfortable accommodation for everyone.

"It should be lovely for them, Wilma," she commented. "Not far from a bubbling creek and they can sit on the veranda to read or embroider or learn the lessons you give them."

"And I've had some men make benches and ordered in desks and set up the school in the old traveller's hut, like you suggested, Mama. Come and have a look. Proper flooring has been laid down. All the desks and the blackboards are set out, and slates and pencils, pens and bottles of ink, rulers, and exercise books are stored in the cupboards."

"You've done a wonderful job while I've been away, Wilma, and I know you're excited to have this challenge before you. It's an outlet for all your talents, and you and the girls should do well."

After the inspections were over, the two women walked back to the homestead.

"I'll allow the children in the sitting room for Sunday School each Sunday morning, Wilma, and not in the schoolroom. That's a concession I'll make. I trust you have the material for all the grades you'll need for teaching and for their religious instruction also?"

"All organised from the Education Department, and we have our Bible here, and there's other material from the cathedral in Armidale. Anyhow, Mama, school doesn't start until January's over. That'll give the girls over four weeks to get used to everything."

"I can't believe it's nearly Christmas, Wilma. Time flies, doesn't it? I'll keep Miss Jenkins on for a while after the girls arrive, of course. She can train them and teach the older girls how to cook. A few of them are over twelve years old and big enough to start doing some cleaning work in the homestead already. The smaller ones can make their beds, wash up and help clean their cottage until they're big enough to start their training too. Anyhow the project is starting soon, and I'm so glad I'm doing this. We'll make wonderful Australian citizens out of these English girls and swell the population in Australia too."

It was hot, and they looked forward to their afternoon tea on the cool front veranda of the homestead. As they walked up the path through the garden and approached the front steps, Wilma commented on the roses.

"They're lovely, Mama, although the beds need weeding. The girls can do that too."

Leaving England

The Ballarat had been moored at the pier at Southampton for the past two weeks, being cleaned after its latest voyage, refuelled, and provisions laid in for the next passengers to Australia. Passengers already gathered on the pier were counting the hours before the gangplank would be laid down.

Earlier in the morning, Helen Speers had ordered a charabanc to take her and the girls to Waterloo Station along with their pink boxes packed with their belongings. When they arrived at the station, a middle-aged couple approached them at the arranged meeting place and introduced themselves.

"You must be Miss Speers, and these must be the girls," the woman stated in an exaggerated, friendly tone. "I'm Eileen Wilcox, and this is my husband, Alfred."

Then, addressing the girls, "We're so looking forward to getting to know you all on this big adventure, and I'm sure you're going to love it in Australia."

There was no spontaneous answer from the girls until Gracie sniggered.

"Well, I bloody well 'ope so, Missus. It ain't been so marvellous 'ere in England, yer know."

Helen Speers cleared her throat, wishing Gracie hadn't sworn. She then drew Eileen Wilcox aside, away from the group of girls. In a low, confidential tone, she wished Eileen and her husband a safe journey then smiled and warned Eileen to monitor the girls' letters to their families back in England – it was a long-standing policy that they have nothing further to do with their mothers.

"We've never allowed correspondence to and fro as the girls may fall under a bad influence. This applies to the Nash sisters too, as their mother has abandoned them."

Eileen nodded and agreed to keep her eyes open in the future.

Helen Speers then suggested they should make their way to the platform to get the train to Southampton. Porters loaded their luggage on trolleys and delivered it to the train. Before the travellers boarded their carriage, Helen spoke sternly to the girls before she left to return to Chingford.

"Girls, I want you to remember who's in charge now. Mr and Mrs Wilcox are to be treated as your new parents, and I expect absolute obedience from each of you. No playing up! Just remember how lucky you are to be going to a new country and a better life in Australia. And you must remember to be grateful to Mrs Warby, the kind lady who is taking you all in and giving you the opportunity to escape from poverty and need in England. I wish you all happiness and good health in the future."

Then Helen Speers departed.

Alfred and Eileen Wilcox smiled in pleasure at Miss Speers' address to the girls. An escape from impending poverty had applied to themselves as well, as Alfred had lost his job on the docks a few months ago due to a wrenched back. And Eileen had not fancied an arduous job as a charwoman or the like, nor relinquishing her role as wife to support her husband. *A cottage of our own in Australia with no rent to pay and a small wage provided! And I'll take no nonsense from those girls, mind you!*

The reasons she and her husband had wanted to escape London had not been mentioned during the interview with Mrs Warby. Nor had Alfred's bad back been disclosed, even though it had almost healed. Rather, Eileen had invented her partiality to children, hiding the fact that she'd had little time or patience with them in the past.

"I'm sorry, Alfie, but I never want to have children," she'd informed him firmly when he'd proposed. "I've had so much trouble in the past at home with all my brothers and sisters and with Mum being sick and all, and her drinking … I just want peace. I hope you can understand.”

“That’ll suit me to a tee,” Alfred had hastily replied, smiling. “It’ll be easier for us to live without a brood to feed.”

The journey by train to Southampton was somewhat awkward. The Wilcoxes had been mainly talking to each other. The girls had not made any friendly overtures to their new ‘parents’ except for Gracie who seemed eager to be noticed by the Wilcoxes. They finally arrived at Southampton and made it to the pier two hours early. After all the necessary forms for boarding had been filled out, deckhands helped to carry heavier luggage on to the steamer to people’s berths.

Travellers on the pier were eager to board the ship after having waited around for the last few hours while the crew made final checks to ensure all was ready to go. A siren sounded, and it was all aboard for travellers and their families and friends who’d come to farewell them. Another siren would sound an hour later to order non-passengers to vacate the ship and return to the pier.

Mr and Mrs Wilcox shepherded their seven new charges up the gangplank and finally located their berths. Gracie and Doris immediately claimed the bunks they wanted to sleep in and tried them out, bouncing on them and laughing, but Jane and the Nash girls and little Josie hung back.

“Stop doing that, you two,” demanded Eileen Wilcox. “You’ll break those wretched bunks before you even sleep on them. At your ages too! Stupid, silly girls. Behave yourselves!”

Millie looked up at Amy with a trembling lip, and Edie glared.

“Shush,” cautioned Amy as she put her arms around her sisters. This was going to be a long journey.

Later, when the Wilcoxes had gone outside to locate the toilets, Edie said to Amy just above a whisper, “Miss Speers called them our new parents. What a joke! They’ll never ever be like our Mum and Dad. I don’t want to go to Australia and live with them. What can we do, Amy?”

“Well, we’ll have to go whether we like it or not, but I’m telling you this … when we're old enough, we can get jobs and save up and come back here and find Mummy, and Freddy too."

Alfred and Eileen Wilcox returned and motioned for the children to follow. They were shown where the toilets were and taken for a tour around the deck, shown the dining room and a special playroom for children with toys and books and other activities. Then the second siren sounded and all people not travelling were ordered off the ship.

"So! this is it!" announced Eileen Wilcox with a broad smile as the steamer trumpeted and the engine revved up. "Come over to the other side of the ship, girls, and you can all wave goodbye to Merrie England."

Amy, Edie, Millie and little Josie did not wave. They stood with solemn faces as the ship slowly moved away from its mooring and started out toward the English Channel.

Back in England at Whitefields

Sister Esther Howell felt shocked and remorseful. She hadn't been to visit the Nash sisters for four weeks. And she'd just received an impassioned letter from Amy. She would most certainly intervene in this matter. Why would Helen Speers even consider sending those girls out to Australia of all places where they had no relatives, and they were vehemently against going there? And what would Anna say when she returned to London to discover her daughters were on the other side of the world? She poured out her anguish to the senior minister at Whitefields Central Mission after showing him Amy's letter.

"There's been so much to do here in the parish with all the needs lately, I've hardly had time to bless myself, let alone get out to see those children. But I must go immediately after this. Amy didn't mention the exact date they'd be leaving, except that they'd been chosen and didn't want to go. I'll put a stop to it, Ian. I promised their mother I'd watch over them until she came back to London."

"Yes, you must go, indeed," agreed Reverend Davidson. "I'll back you up. Have you heard from their mother yet, Esther?"

"Not so far. It may be the cost of postage which is quite expensive if you're on a low wage. She's written to Freddy and the girls though, their Aunt Mattie told me, but strangely the girls have never received a single letter from her. I can't understand why. She wasn't at all well when she left London, you know. I hope she's alright. After Fred died last January, Mattie wrote to her in Northampton to let her know. She would have been heartbroken. No! the girls must stay in the cottage at Chingford. They've finally settled in and are making friends. Anyhow, I'll take the day off tomorrow and go and speak to Helen Speers."

"You do that, Esther," the Reverend urged.

Angry Words

Esther ordered a cab to Chingford the next morning. A housemaid answered the cottage door and admitted Esther then went to fetch Miss Helen Speers, who appeared in a few minutes.

"Oh, Miss Speers, I'm sorry I haven't been to visit the Nash girls over the last month, but you wouldn't believe how busy I've been in the parish. How are they all? I suppose they'll be coming back from school shortly and I know how glad they'll be to see me.

"Now I've just received a letter from young Amy, who is extremely upset at the prospect of her and her sisters being sent to Australia of all places. She has pleaded with me to stop this happening. They are not suitable candidates for emigration, Miss Speers, as they have relatives here in London and they are unwilling to leave England. I'm here to intervene on their behalf and to stop any further arrangements for them to go. As a social worker, I have backing from my church, and I'll see my local politician as well. This must not happen. I'd like to speak to Amy as soon as she gets back from school, Miss Speers."

Helen Speers sat on a chair and appeared momentarily flustered. Then she took a deep breath and looked slightly defiant.

"Well, they aren't here anymore," she replied bluntly. "I was obliged to select seven girls from here to be resettled in Australia under the Child Emigration Scheme. A wealthy station owner – a very kind woman I must say – has arranged for them to be housed in a couple of cottages within her property and a married couple will be supervising them."

Esther's jaw dropped open as she took all of this in.

"Where are they *now*, Miss Speers?" she demanded hotly. "And their mother? Has she been consulted about this? And what about …"

"We're not worrying about their mother, Miss Howell, and we have encouraged the girls not to worry about her also. She has apparently forsaken them, so I've been told. Their father has died, and their grandmother passed on quite recently, as you probably know. Their brother is looking after himself I gather, and living with his aunt. The girls have been classified as orphans by now."

Esther Howell exploded in anger.

"But they are *not* orphans! And you have no idea whether their mother is alive or dead, so you've had no right to make assumptions. How *dare* you! Where are these children *now*? I will personally arrange for them to be placed elsewhere."

Miss Speers had not expected any trouble concerning the migration of her charges to a better life elsewhere, but she finally felt abashed at having to tell Sister Howell where the Nash girls were at present. In a subdued voice, she admitted, "They're already on a steamer on their way to Australia, Miss Howell. Nothing can be done now."

Then she added more strongly, "Anyhow, why would anyone want deserted little girls to stay in this country where they could be at risk of moral decay when they're older or being exploited in some other way?"

"These children come from a very nice average family, Miss Speers, and have had a good upbringing. I doubt if they would ever submit to 'moral decay' as you call it. And when their mother turns up, what are you going to say to her? How will you justify sending her daughters to the other end of the earth? You've had no right to do this without her knowledge or permission!"

Miss Speers stiffened at the rebuke. "I don't like being chastised, Miss Howell, for acting in the best interests of children who would need a better life than this country could afford them, taking in the fact they are destitute. They'll have a better future where they're going."

"But they don't *want* to go? What about their family here? What about their brother Freddy? Don't you think he'll miss his sisters?"

Miss Speers levelled her gaze and replied.

"Whether they wanted to go or not is irrelevant. They are girls at risk, in my opinion. They'll be better off where they're going, in the long run. That's what's important. And about their brother? He's been given their address in Australia. He and his aunt can write to the girls. I'm sure they'll keep in touch. And when their brother is older, he can always emigrate himself."

Esther rose to her feet. "There's no need for any further discussion about this matter, Miss Speers. I'm shocked at what has happened, and I can't think how their mother will react when she learns about this. I have been very attached to this family for many years, since Frederick Nash, their father, was a choirboy at Whitefields. He was a lovely man, I must say, and would have been incensed by all of this. Now I want the girls' address in Australia. I will keep the link to England open. And I will have nothing further to say to *you* in the future."

Miss Speers excused herself; walked to her office and fetched the address for Esther. When she returned and handed it over, the two women frostily said their goodbyes after Miss Speers had ordered a cab for Esther.

On the way back home, Esther planned to visit the remaining Nash family to see if they knew the girls were already on a ship to Australia. When she managed to see them, they had been informed. Mattie and Freddy were still seething over the sudden departure of the girls.

"I'll be writing to them, Aunty Esther," said Mattie.

"And so will I," assured Freddy. "I'll be writing *lots* of letters."

A Long Way to Go

The Ballarat had made good progress on its journey south, but many passengers had become seasick when the vessel passed the lower part of France. A fierce storm had broken out, battering the vessel and drenching the decks. Everyone was holed up in their lurching cabins, many frightened, especially the seven young girls who lay on their bunks, afraid.

"Don't worry, children, this will soon pass. Many boats have come through worse than this. We're going to be alright."

These were unusual and reassuring words from Eileen Wilcox who'd suddenly felt empathy toward her charges. She and Alfred sat on chairs in the children's cabin, holding onto bunk posts for stability. There'd been much vomiting going on, and the Wilcoxes' bucket was a quarter full.

"It's worse for Millie," observed Amy. "She's been sick from the day we set out, and she's lost weight too. Can't keep anything down and poor little Josie isn't much better."

The swaying in the cabin slowly abated after a day and the ship resumed a calmer transit. The storm had passed.

"It should be easier now," advised Alfred Wilcox, who was suddenly feeling better. "It's probably calmer from here on."

He went on to describe the entire voyage.

"We sail past the coast of Portugal, and the entrance to the Mediterranean Sea and then all the way down the west coast of Africa until we round the Cape of Good Hope, girls. Then we meet the Indian Ocean. We go all the way across it until we come to Australia and make a stop at Fremantle before we arrive at the big town of

Sydney where we get off."

"I want to get off *now*," shouted Edie. "I hate it on this ship. I wish we'd never been put on it. How much longer will it be?"

"One day you'll be grateful you were put on it, Edith Nash," Eileen retorted. Then she softened. "I know it seems a long time to a young girl, but it *will* pass, and life will be better for you in your new land."

Eileen Wilcox had mellowed a little as she'd suffered the same nausea and fears as the girls in her charge.

"How much longer will it be, Mrs Wilcox?" asked Amy seriously. "It's only been five whole days so far."

"About another seven weeks or thereabouts," replied Eileen.

"Is anyone going to die?" asked Millie in a quavering voice, "I think I will."

"No, you won't," reassured Alfred quickly. "No-one's going to die, Millie. Once you get back on land, you'll be better straightaway. And we'll be allowed off the boat in Cape Town for a break. Look, we'll all be getting our sea legs soon and won't feel sick anymore."

But for the girls that didn't happen. During patches of rough seas throughout the journey, they all became sick. The Wilcoxes, however, were lucky to suffer no further nausea.

Christmas Day 1913

The journey was almost over. It was Christmas Day and the passengers were treated to a celebratory dinner of baked ham, cooked dried peas and potatoes and slices of Christmas pudding with custard. Everyone was issued with a paper hat, and the children were given a small bag of sweets. Many adults on the ship had cobbled up a choir and Christmas carols rang out over the waters during a church service in the afternoon.

"It's Freddy's birthday today," Amy remembered. "He's now thirteen."

"When he's older he can come and join us," Edie said, smiling slightly.

"Or when we're old enough, we can go back to live with him," Amy added.

The next day was Boxing Day, and *The Ballarat* sailed through the Sydney Heads accompanied by the cheers and whistles of relieved travellers.

"I thank you, Jesus, that it's all over and we're still alive," prayed Amy.

Sydney at Last.

The steamer pulled into Circular Quay and was made fast. The gangplank was put in place and the passengers slowly made their way onto the pier. Eileen and Alfred Wilcox and their seven charges stood in a small group waiting for their heavy luggage to be unloaded by the crew.

"I told you you'd feel better, Millie, once you got onto land," Alfred said, noting the child's weight loss and pale face.

At that moment, a man of about forty years of age, with a healthy tan, scrutinised the crowd and noticed Eileen and Alfred Wilcox and the girls standing near the exit to the terminal. He ambled over.

"You must be Mr and Mrs Wilcox, as you have seven girls with you. I'm Mrs Warby's son, Neil, from Balangara Station. I know you're expecting me. We'll get a carriage to take us to Central Railway Station as we'll be catching the night train to Armidale this evening."

"Pleased to meet you, Mr Warby," Alfred greeted, extending his hand. "This is my wife, Eileen, and I'm sure we'll all be relieved to get to Balangara. Some of the crew on the ship are clearing out the luggage. Our suitcases and the girl's boxes should be here soon, and then we have to go to that immigration and customs office along there, and after that, we can get going."

The three adults engaged in small talk while waiting for the luggage to arrive. After the formalities in the customs office, they were given the all-clear to enter Australia. Later on, a horse-drawn carriage drew in outside Circular Quay and Neil engaged it to drive them to Central Railway Station. Everyone climbed in and the driver helped load the luggage.

"I can't get over it," Eileen declared as they headed to the station. "I never imagined Sydney to be so huge and busy. I expected a smaller town with bushes in between, but the buildings are so big, just like in London."

Neil laughed. "Sydney's a thriving city, Mrs Wilcox, and can only get bigger. As the population grows, so will this town, and these girls here will increase the numbers one day. Australia needs more people to expand and develop it."

"Those electric trams are a great idea for getting people around," noted Alfred, "and there's lots of modern automobiles too. I've seen those flashy Fords in London you know, but I didn't realise they were already out here."

"But there are still horse-drawn vehicles around like this one we're in," noted Eileen.

"Every year there'll be fewer," explained Neil, "and I reckon in the end most people will own their own automobile. But here we are at Central. All out, and I'll head to the booking office to pick up the train tickets. There's a big waiting room just inside the door. I'll meet you all in there."

"How long before the train goes? How long do we have to wait in here?" Edie complained. "I'm tired, and so is everyone."

"Be quiet, Edith, and mind your manners," Eileen Wilcox barked. "You'll need to learn patience in life, my girl, and be thankful you've been sent to Australia to start a new life."

Amy said nothing but moved close to Edie and put her arm around her.

"Don't give her sympathy, Amy Nash. You're just as bad. When you girls get to your new home, you're all going to have to fit in. Remember that!"

Neil returned with the tickets and suggested to Eileen and Alfred that they all go to the refreshment kiosk and have some sandwiches and cakes for their tea. Later, lemonade for the girls and coffee for the adults. Neil paid for extra sandwiches for later in the journey. He thought the girls looked washed out, particularly young Millie, one of the two youngest at six years old.

Back in the waiting room, Neil glanced at his fob watch. It was now five p.m. The steam train was scheduled to depart at seven p.m. The wait seemed endless for the girls, and they fidgeted and squirmed on the hard benches. Jane, the eldest girl at thirteen, got everyone playing *I Spy With My Little Eye*, for a while, but this distraction palled in time. Millie and Josie stretched out on spare spaces on the benches and fell asleep until they were woken up by The Wilcoxes when it was time to board the train.

"Don't dawdle, you girls. Hurry up now, or you'll have us miss the train," Eileen urged irritably as the younger ones, still drowsy from their nap on the benches, struggled to keep up.

"No need to panic, Mrs Wilcox," Neil assured, surprised at Eileen's tone. "The train won't be leaving for another fifteen minutes and the porters have to load the luggage yet. We've got plenty of time. Look, here's our carriage, second class and third from the engine. Don't be frightened by the engine, girls. It's making a big noise now. Now come on, up the steps everyone. I'll help you little ones. Find your seats and no fighting over the window seats. You can all have a turn. This should be a great new experience, eh? Riding on a steam train!"

"It's not a new experience for me, Mr Warby," piped up Amy, a little importantly. "Me and my brother Freddy, who's back in London, went down to Brighton with our church once, and we went on the pier and had a very nice time. It was there I first saw the ocean."

"So, you have a brother back in London, eh?" Neil probed, looking puzzled.

"Not only our brother Freddy, but our mother, a grandmother in Clapham, Auntie Mattie and our cousin Hilary," Amy answered, looking resentful. Then she added, "We didn't want to leave them and come to Australia, but we were told we had to."

Neil frowned. *We were told they were orphans*, but he didn't say anything more.

Amy caught a warning glare from Eileen Wilcox and decided not to pursue the subject.

On the Way to Balangara

Everyone was seated in the train and the engine was firing up.

"It's going to be a long trip up to Armidale – we should be there by seven in the morning," informed Neil. "Then we'll travel by horse and buggy to your new home."

"Do they have a lavvy on the train?" asked Josie in a small voice, but it was too late. She'd wet her bloomers and started to cry.

"You'll have to learn to control yourself, Josephine!" Eileen chided. "You went before at the station. She often did this on the boat coming out, Mr Warby, and she had to be supplied with nappies in the end and I had to wash them out. Now come with me to the lavatory, Josephine. There's a washbasin there, I presume. I'll have to clean you up and wash your bloomers. Now don't do it again!"

With her head bent in shame, Josie accompanied Eileen along the corridor to the lavatory.

With increased noise from the locomotive and a blast from the whistle, the train pulled slowly out of Central Station. The three older girls, Jane, Gracie and Doris, appeared somewhat excited but the Nash sisters' faces were resigned and impassive.

Neil gave the others a running commentary on the progress of the train as it reached important stations like Strathfield and Hornsby. By the time they had passed over The Hawkesbury River Bridge, dusk was falling. Neil distributed the sandwiches he'd bought and pointed out the water bottle and tumbler held in a bracket near a luggage rack at the end of the carriage. Everyone settled down for the long journey ahead. It had been an exhausting day for the girls. Neil found some empty double seats in their carriage and settled Josie and Millie on to them and soon the girls were asleep. The train made steady progress through the night, only stopping at some stations to drop off mailbags, and the occasional passenger. Each time, the jerking of the carriage and the loud grinding of brakes woke everyone from their light sleep. Then the whistle blew and the train started up again.

When daylight broke, sleepy eyes opened. The girls were glad the epic journey would soon be over.

"Look at those hills," Eileen pointed out to Alfred. "They're not lovely and green like in England. They're a light brown and the dirt near the railway line looks like chocolate."

"We're having a drought just now, Mrs Wilcox," Neil explained. "But rain should come soon. After that, the hills will look very much like the ones in England. Fortunately, the sheep and cattle still have plenty to eat at Balangara."

The train slowly made headway up the rise from Tamworth to the New England plateau and the high country. In another hour it pulled in at Armidale. They disembarked and a porter unloaded the luggage from the guard's van. Neil and Alfred carried it outside the station. Neil waved to a large, long buggy harnessed to two horses that was parked a little way off. A station hand was climbing down from the driver's seat.

"Glad you're not late, Doug," Neil shouted, then he added when closer, "We're all tired after the trip. It was a pretty smooth journey in the train though, but it'll be good to get home. It always is."

The Wilcox's luggage and the girls' pink boxes were heaved up onto the buggy tray, and then the girls. They were warned it would be a bumpy ride to the homestead. Edie looked at Amy and raised her eyebrows. Eileen and Alfred joined Doug on the extended driver's seat, and Neil climbed in the back with the girls. Then they were off. It was about thirty miles from Armidale but this time, the children enjoyed the trip, more so than in the train.

"We'll all 'ave sore bums when we get there," laughed Gracie, and the girls giggled. Neil was glad to see some humour finally emerging from this little troupe who'd seemed so sombre from the time he'd met them.

"Well, there'll be a lot to discover when you arrive, girls, but first you must settle in. Mrs Warby is giving you four weeks to get to know your new home, but then it'll be school time for you all."

"I didn't like my teacher back home," ventured Jane. "She was a cranky bitch!"

"You'll like Miss Wilma, your new teacher here. She's very kind and will teach you all you need to know to prepare you for your new lives in Australia. And she plays the piano too, and you'll learn to sing good old Australian songs like *Waltzing Matilda* and *Clip go the Shears*."

"Look at them bloody' 'ills way over there in the distance," pointed out Gracie as the journey proceeded. "They're a bluey sor' o' colour."

"That's because of the eucalypts, Grace. Those trees have an oil inside the leaves which makes a vapour and turns the hills that colour in the distance," explained Neil.

He'd been surprised at Gracie's vulgarity and language. His mother had told him she'd asked for girls from respectable homes to be selected by Miss Speers, but Gracie had slipped through the net somehow. He had no doubt that his sister Wilma would correct her shortcomings. Her accent would remain though, but weaken in time.

"Will we ever see a kangaroo, Mr Warby?" asked Doris. "I learnt about Australian animals at school once. They hop on two big legs, don't they?"

"You'll see plenty of them at Balangara and little joeys in their pouches too sometimes."

They were passing through open woodland with occasional patches of rainforest each side of the road. Neil went on to describe some features of the children's new environment.

"There's lots of huge granite rocks like those ones over there, big cliffs and gorges and beautiful waterfalls around here further along this road. One day you may go on a picnic to see the waterfall at Ebor. It's very grand."

"We're all a bit hungry, Mr Warby. When will we get to your place, and can we have something to eat there?" asked Jane timidly.

"We haven't far to go now and cook is already getting a nice big breakfast for everyone. And Mrs Warby is waiting to welcome you all too."

"Is she a nice lady?" asked little Josie with a quivering lip.

"Well, she's my mother, and she's always been good to me. I know she'll be good to you girls too. She wants the best for all of you, which is why she's brought you here so you can have a nicer life," answered Neil.

"But she's not our mother," whispered Edie to Amy.

"What was that?" Neil asked abruptly. He thought he'd caught the gist of the comment from the girl.

"Nothing," replied Edie, her face a blank.

The country was flattening out by now, and a large herd of sheep could be spotted in a paddock in the distance.

"This is farming country now, girls, and we'll shortly get to Balangara."

A few minutes later the buggy left the main road and turned onto a long track that led to a large gate with crossbars. Doug, the driver, hopped down from his perch, opened the gate and led the horses through. Then he closed the gate, resumed his position on the buggy and they were off again. After rounding a bend, the homestead came into view, a large sprawling house with a red roof. Attached to one side was a generously sized annex. A veranda ran along the front of the house and around the other side.

"We're here, everyone!" Neil announced loudly. He jumped down from the buggy and walked to the front to offer a hand to the Wilcoxes as they made their way down the small ladder from the driving seat. Then he and Doug helped the girls climb down over the side of the wagon.

"Look at that gorgeous garden. Lovely roses aren't they, Alfred?" gushed Eileen Wilcox.

"Mother fancies an English cottage garden, Mrs Wilcox, even though some Australian bush flowers are quite spectacular."

A Warm Welcome

Eleanor Warby had heard the arrival of her new charges and their house parents and eagerly descended the steps from the front veranda. She walked over to the Wilcoxes with an outstretched hand of greeting and a short glance over the assembly of girls.

"What a long journey you've all had. Welcome to Balangara, everyone. I know you're going to be very happy here. Now come in and have some breakfast. Cook is getting everything ready. I know you must all be hungry. Doug and Mr Warby will take the luggage down to the cottages later on."

The dining room was quite large and, when everyone was seated, they were served an egg and a lamb chop, toast, a cup of tea for the adults and a small glass of milk for the children.

"We're self-sufficient in many ways here you know," Eleanor informed the Wilcoxes. "We kill our own meat, and we have chooks and a cow to milk. Cook bakes our bread. And I make all our preserves, so we always have jam and chutney and other things, and we have fruit trees and a vegetable garden too."

"Sounds wonderful to me," beamed Eileen. "No one will ever go hungry, like some in London." She squeezed her husband's hand under the table.

Then Eleanor addressed the girls. "And you, dear girls, are going to have a lot to discover here at Balangara. I know everything's new for you but once you get used to things, I'm sure you'll grow to love it here. But you are not to wander beyond the fences around the closer paddocks near the house, or go past the willow tree near the boundary of the creek. And keep away from the cattle. Some bulls can be aggressive."

Josie started to cry, and Eleanor went to her and said in a comforting way, "Don't cry, little one, you'll be safe here. Mr and Mrs Wilcox will look after you."

Jane caught a glance from Edie, who'd raised her eyebrows, but she looked away hoping no-one had noticed Edie's implication. Better no dissension in this environment. They had to fit in.

After breakfast, Eleanor led the Wilcoxes and the girls down the gradual slope to their new homes. Neil and Doug appeared shortly after and unloaded the luggage. The girls' beds and cupboards were allocated to them while the Wilcoxes were inspecting their own quarters in the adjoining cottage.

Eleanor again spoke to the girls.

"You can all have lunch and tea at the homestead today, but afterwards your house mother will be cooking for you and supervising you. Miss Wilma, your school teacher, will be coming back here in three weeks. She left for a holiday yesterday. She's lovely, and you'll learn a lot from her. The only time you are allowed to visit the homestead will be on Sunday mornings for Sunday School in the dining room, where you were today. That is, except for you three older girls, who are all over twelve. Jane and Gracie and Doris, aren't you? You are to start coming to the homestead in four weeks each Saturday to start learning to cook, clean and do the washing. In the meantime, there are books for you to read, embroidery and cross-stitch and board games to play to pass the time. Now just settle in. I have to see how your new parents are doing next door."

"New parents, my foot!" exclaimed Jane as Eleanor passed out of earshot. "I like Mrs Warby though. She's kind and means the best for us, but I don't like that Mrs Wilcox at all. She hasn't been very nice to Josie."

"This is a blinkin' prison," exclaimed Gracie, "and there ain't no way to escape if ya don't like it 'ere."

Edie looked at Amy, stricken, and Amy looked worried.

"We're here now anyway," said Doris matter of factly, "and there's nothing we can do about it, so let's all stick together and see what happens."

All the girls nodded.

Amy, Edie and Millie, seated together on Amy's bed, felt pleased with the united front of everyone.

"But I'm getting out of here one day, as soon as I'm old enough," Edie announced determinedly.

Bushland and Creek

The next morning after breakfast, the girls gathered together and decided to explore their new surroundings. Jane, being the eldest, took authority and led the others down the veranda steps onto a stretch of newly-mown lawn. A gentle slope of gravel and dirt continued for 100 yards or so and ended where a rough track led through tall eucalypt trees and bushland. When the girls entered the track, little Josie became scared and asked Jane shakily, "Are there snakes here and will they bite me?"

"Take my hand, Josie, and I'll scare them away," Jane reassured her.

The track flattened out to an expanse of coarse grey sand leading to a bubbling, crystal creek. Close by, a large granite rock with easy footholds beckoned the girls to climb onto it. A willow tree largely overhung the rock, the long, hanging fronds creating a sheltered and peaceful environment.

"It's lovely here," Amy murmured dreamily.

Edie added, "A good place to get away from it all."

"Look at those pebbles in the water." Doris pointed them out. "All the colours they are."

The girls lingered by the creek for some time exploring their new environment, until Jane decided it was time to return to the cottage.

"We didn't tell Mrs Wilcox where we were going," she explained.

"Oh! *Her!*" muttered Edie.

During their walk back, a sudden chuckling sound started up around them then ceased. All the girls stopped and Gracie said, "Did you 'ear *that?*"

Then the chuckling started up again and exploded into noisy, ear-splitting laughter.

The girls' eyes widened as they looked at each other, puzzled. Millie pointed upward to the branches of a tree where a bird perched making the cacophony. Spontaneously the girls joined in the laughter, bending over with their infectious giggles.

"Me sides 'urt," announced Gracie, when things quietened down, "but wot sor' of a bird was *that?*"

"It must be a kookaburra, or laughing jackass," Jane offered. "I learnt about Australian animals and birds back in England."

"This is a strange bloody country!" said Gracie.

Cottage Rules

The next day, Eileen Wilcox laid down a strict routine for the girls, which eliminated many duties of her own. As well as their own clothing and underwear, they'd been told they had to wash their bed linen, towels, tablecloths and tea towels. They were to wash the dishes and keep the oven and fireplace spick and span and scrub the kitchen floor.

"All she wants to do is cook for us, and she gets us to peel the vegetables too," complained Doris, frowning.

On two occasions since the girls had arrived, Eileen Wilcox had taken the wet sheets from Josie's bed, rinsed them out in cold water and hung them out to dry.

"Don't do it again, Josephine, or I'll have to give you a smack on your bottom. Mrs Warby wouldn't like it, but I'm losing my patience with you."

"I never imagined I'd have a problem like this," Eileen complained to her husband. "Managing these kids is a heap of trouble."

"Don't be too hard on Josie, Eileen. She's only four and a half, isn't she?" Alfred had replied.

"She's not a baby anymore … should have been over this problem two years ago. I'll have to ask for a Macintosh to put under her. Drying the mattress takes too long, even in this hot sun."

On New Year's Eve, Eileen baked a special cake to welcome in the year 1914. She and Alfred retired to their cottage after dinner, leaving the girls to celebrate in their own way and to enjoy the cake. The topic of conversation soon turned to the girls' house parents.

"I don't mind him, but I can't stand *her*," Doris said, voicing everyone's thoughts.

A Letter to Anna

Mrs Warby had given Amy some postage stamps as she wanted the Nash girls to maintain contact with their relatives in England. Amy had written to her mother, but did not want Mrs Wilcox, Auntie Mattie and Miss Speers back in England to know. When she'd finished the letter, she confided to Edie and reminded her of their mother's struggles.

"I've written to Mummy. Remember how everyone said she'd forsaken us? That's not true. Remember how hard she worked and how tired she was and how she'd cry sometimes? She kept our family together with that hotel job when Daddy was sick. Then she lost her job and had to put us into the workhouse because we hardly had anything to eat. And when she couldn't find work in London, she had to go to Northampton. Why has everyone been so nasty to her? Auntie Mattie too. Now you mustn't tell anyone I've written to her, especially Mrs Wilcox. She might stop me writing to Mummy like Miss Speers did. That's our secret, Edie, and don't tell Millie either. She's too young and might blab about it."

"I won't tell Millie," Edie promised, "but I did tell Freddy before we left England that you'd be writing to her and I don't know why but he didn't seem pleased."

"Well, nobody should stop us writing to our own mother," Amy insisted.

"That's true," Edie agreed.

The letter to Anna was carefully put under Amy's mattress, away from prying eyes.

"I'm writing to Freddy as well, Edie. You can add something in it too. Mummy made him promise to write to us before she went up north and he said he would. Hopefully, a letter from him and one from Mummy are on the way."

The next morning Amy carefully carried the letters up to the homestead for posting. A housemaid answered the door and assured Amy that her letters would go out with other mail to be posted at Armidale the next day.

When she returned, Edie asked: "Do you think Mummy's got back to London yet, Amy?"

"Let's hope so but can you imagine the shock she'll get when she discovers we're out here? I told Freddy and Mummy in my letters that we're well and happy because I don't want them worrying about us. It's hard enough back there for them as it is. I also told Mummy that we were forced to come out here. I've sent kisses from all of us."

School Days and a Letter

The Nash girls were reluctantly coming to terms with their new life by the time Miss Wilma returned from holidays in mid-January.

"She's nice," said Millie after Miss Wilma had given her a hug.

School lessons soon started, and Wilma proved to be efficient and light-hearted in her manner.

The weather was hot, and the girls delighted in their swimming lessons in the creek.

"One thing I like, I must say, is when we go down to the creek," admitted Edie. "I can dog paddle right across it now to the deep water."

"But we've been told not to go anywhere close after a storm and only ever go in the water with Miss Wilma around," cautioned Amy.

Time passed without a letter from Anna or Freddy. But during mid-February, Eileen Wilcox handed an envelope to Amy after school.

"It's from Auntie Mattie," she announced to her sisters, disappointed it wasn't from her mother or Freddy. "Come over here and I'll read it to you."

The girls leant in close, and Amy commented on the date the letter had been written.

"Letters take about eight weeks to get here. She wrote it a month before Christmas."

Amy then proceeded to read the letter aloud.

57 Warren Street,
Tottenham Court Road, London.

26.11.1913

My Dearest Nieces,

"We had Christmas at sea. I must write back to her, and you too, Edie," Amy said, reflecting. "But when will we hear from Freddy? Auntie said he doesn't like writing letters. Hopefully, we'll get one soon."

One week later, Eleanor walked down to the girls' cottage and handed Amy a parcel sent from England.

"What could it be?" Amy said as she unwrapped the parcel while Edie and Millie looked on.

"They are books for us from Aunty Esther, with Christmas greetings," Amy said as she set them on the table.

"Mine is *Pride and Prejudice* by Jane Austen. Yours, Edie, is *Tanglewood Tales* by Nathaniel Hawthorne. And Millie, yours is *Bible Stories for Children*," announced Amy.

More Letters

In early April, Eileen Wilcox handed Amy two letters.

"One's from Freddy," she squealed to her sisters who'd gathered around her. "I'll read this one first, and then you can see it for yourselves."

19.02.14

57 Warren St
Tottenham Court Road
London

Dear Sisters

I was very glad to hear that you arrived in Australia safely. I have read your letter and it was very nicely put together. I was glad to hear you were well and happy, and I hope you always will be. I have left my place of work because there were two too many boys on the same kind of work so another boy and myself had to leave. I am in the seventh standard, and I can swim two hundred yards and have three swimming certificates. Dear sisters, this is all I have to say now and I will write to you again soon so Good Bye and God bless you.

I remain, your loving brother, Freddy

PS Dear Amy, have you got your album now. If so, I can send you some post cards.

"That was a short letter, and he didn't say if Mummy's got back to

London yet," Edie said, disappointed.

"She'll get back there soon. I just know she will," Amy replied, "and I have the feeling it won't be long."

"Then Mummy can come out here," said Millie hopefully.

"Or we can go back there …" Edie paused, thinking. … *when we're older.*

The other letter was from Auntie Mattie.

"It's got the same date on it as Freddy's one," observed Amy. "I bet she made him write to us."

February 19th 1914

57 Warren St
Tottenham Court Road,
London

My Dearest Amy, Edie & Millie,

I was very pleased to hear from you. I knew you had arrived safely because I watched the shipping news and saw that the boat had safely reached its destination. When you write again you will be able to tell me something about your new home. Freddy is writing a letter as well. Dear Amy, I am very sorry your mother has written to you. I cannot think where she got the address from, but I am very pleased to know that you are not allowed to write to her. You must forget all about her because you know, Dear, she behaved very bad to you Children and also to your dear Father. He was the one who loved and cared for you all, he was Father and Mother both to you and I should like you to carry out his wishes by never writing or troubling about your mother in any way. I think your Dad once told you the same in a letter. Freddy has never answered one of her letters. She sometimes writes to him but not very often. Dear Amy, did you get Sister Esther's books at Xmas. I have got all your photos that Miss Speers gave me. I had a

The girls sat on a couch on the veranda of the cottage, feeling puzzled while taking in the contents of their aunt's letter. After some time, Amy said, "So Auntie Mattie said Mummy wrote us a letter! Why haven't we received it? Has it been lost in the post? Hopefully, it'll turn up soon."

"Aunty Esther would have given her our address, I'll bet," Edie insisted importantly. "She's the only one who wasn't cross with Mummy before we left London."

"I sent her our address in my letter shortly after we got out here. And we never got a letter from Daddy when we were in England saying we shouldn't write to her. I know he was very annoyed at Mummy for going to Northampton, but he wouldn't have wanted us to forget all about her," Amy added crossly.

"And what about Auntie Mattie saying that only Daddy was the one who loved us and cared for us all? That's just so untrue," said Edie.

"She went away to find work. She had to get work," stressed Millie, looking at Amy for approval.

"And she didn't want to live with Auntie Mattie. I don't blame her," said Amy.

"She told us Mummy had run away from us all and deserted us, remember?" added Edie.

"And I think she's turned Freddy against her!" Amy snapped.

"Mummy and Daddy had some fights before Daddy went to hospital," said Millie softly.

"I know," admitted Amy, "but it was a hard time and they got cranky. Mummy told me that's what sometimes happens. Daddy was sick and couldn't work, Mummy wasn't well either. She used to say her nerves were in shreds. There was not enough money for rent, clothing or even food and everyone expecting her to solve all the problems on her own with hardly any help from the Guardians. That's why she agreed to have us put in the workhouse – so we could *eat*! But I can't understand why things changed so much after she went away and how she could have hurt Daddy so much. What could have happened? But whatever she's done, she's still our mother, and we love her."

"And she loves us too," said Millie, nodding.

"I've often wondered if she's still struggling where she is," pondered Amy. "Anyhow it's a mystery why everyone has turned against her, including Freddy, but do you know what? … I suspect Auntie Mattie. But don't worry. When we hear from Mummy, she'll explain everything. She must have let Aunty Esther know she's written to us and Aunty Esther has told Auntie Mattie."

The girls hugged each other in excitement.

"Hope we don't have too long to wait," said Edie.

"Well, after that letter from Auntie Mattie, I don't feel like writing to her anymore," Edie declared.

"I don't either," Amy agreed.

"Me too," said Millie.

Standing with Josie

Very early next morning, Eileen Wilcox smacked Josie as she'd threatened to do.

"Stop blubbering. Can't you get up and go to the lavatory like everyone else? Now I'm not washing out your sheets again, m'lady. It's time I taught you a lesson. And don't go whinging to Mrs Warby about this, will you? She doesn't realise what a heap of trouble you are."

Eileen Wilcox wrenched the wet bottom sheet from Josie's bed and draped it around the child's shoulders, which made Josie wail even louder.

"Now get to the washhouse, put that sheet in the tub and wash it out yourself."

The child clasped the sheet around her and did as she was told, tripping and stumbling, her eyes downcast as she headed to the laundry.

The other girls moved outside with her, and Jane removed Josie's obstacle. Then the girls walked alongside the child to the washhouse to help her with her task. Amy put her arms around her.

"Don't cry, Josie. If it happens again, just tell us, and we'll all help you. It's not your fault. There must be something causing this. Maybe I should tell Mrs Warby."

"No, don't do it, Amy, *please*. Mrs Wilcox will beat me if you do." Josie's eyes mirrored her fear.

"Well, you tell one of us next time. Look! Gracie's finished rinsing out the sheet. Dry your tears and we'll go back and read some stories after breakfast. You like *Grimms' Fairy Tales*, don't you?"

"I *hate* her!" Edie snarled. "She's supposed to be like a mother to us. What a joke!"

Every other girl agreed and loudly voiced their complaints. Eileen Wilcox heard the commotion across the distance and guessed they were complaining about her.

If it wasn't for the food and accommodation we have here, she murmured silently, *I'd give it all up. How can I be expected to be a mother to seven such troublesome girls with all their problems? It's asking too much. I never expected this. But I'd better ease up a bit on the four-year-old. They shouldn't have sent a child that age out here anyway.*

The girls returned to the cottage, and Jane went to the linen cupboard, pulled out a fresh sheet and made up Josie's bed. None of the girls spoke a word to Mrs Wilcox or looked in her direction. The girls set the table and prepared their breakfasts. As it was Saturday morning, four of them had free time. The three eldest walked to the homestead for a cooking class and instruction on how to set a table for a dinner party for eight. Edie and Millie busied themselves playing hopscotch on a patch of dirt outside.

Amy settled down on a sofa with Josie on the veranda. The child nestled into her embrace and asked for the story of *Rapunzel*.

"Can you be my mum?" she asked when the story ended. "My mummy died."

"I'll try, but I can never be like your real mummy, Josie. But you can tell me all your troubles, and I'll try to help."

A Sinister Assault

Stanley Otford, one of the station hands, eyed the girls from a distance as they made their way into the former traveller's shed, now converted into the girls' schoolroom. He'd been feeding his imagination shortly after the children had arrived, and never missed a chance to have another look at them. He didn't care which one it would be, but sooner or later he'd get what he wanted. He felt confident he'd get away with it. The last time in Guyra, the girl had trembled in fear and promised not to tell anyone what had gone on. The threats he'd uttered and the promise to do her harm had worked. He felt annoyed that these girls were so well supervised and always in a group with Wilma Warby shepherding them around, taking them swimming, doing exercises outside their cottage and the like. He'd almost given up the idea, but it still nagged him. He walked away and went back to his task of branding more of the sheep.

But on the following Saturday afternoon, opportunity beckoned. One was all alone, hurrying up the slope towards the schoolroom. He looked around. *No-one in sight.* He quickened his pace and followed the girl into the building.

"Oh!" said the child, apprehension clouding her face, "I left my scripture book here, and I haven't learnt my text for tomorrow when we have Sunday School. Mrs Warby won't be pleased."

This reminder of authority in this place, coupled with a vague sense of morality almost caused the man to change his mind. But the girl smiled at him as she made for the door and any censuring thoughts vanished from his head.

"Come here, little dearie," he crooned as he grabbed the child's arm; he pulled her over to a bench and put his arm around her. "Just show me," he pleaded, "I only want to have a look."

"No, stop it, stop it," the girl shrieked, as she struggled against the man, but he'd managed to get his hand into her bloomers and touch her.

"Let me go! Let me go, you horrible man! Let me *go!!*"

By now they were on the floor, the man beginning to control her. She lifted her knee up with as much force as she could muster; it connected with the man's chin, and he bit his tongue, drawing blood. Cursing loudly, he loosened his grip. The girl regained her feet and fled to the door, which the man had forgotten to lock. Shocked and sobbing, she ran down the slope to the cottage and flung herself onto her bed.

The other girls heard her crying and gathered to hear what had happened. She told them briefly, still in shock. They all agreed Mrs Wilcox must be told, but she was on her weekly Saturday afternoon visit with Mrs Warby at the homestead where they discussed the progress of the orphan girls. So they told her when she returned.

Eileen Wilcox accosted the girl after she heard the account.

"You shouldn't have gone there on your own, you *stupid* girl. Let that be a lesson to you. Now stop your crying. I know you've had a shock, but you'll get over it and forget all about it. And keep it to yourselves, all of you. No-one talks about those things. Now I don't want Mrs Warby to know about it. It'll only worry her, and she has enough on her plate with this big farm you know. Just make sure you keep away from that man, the one with the sandy hair and freckles I think you said."

And Stanley Otford kept away from the girls, fearful the child would report him to Mrs Warby. He hadn't had the chance to issue any threats to the girl to gain her silence and he didn't want to lose his job at Balangara. Strong little tyke she'd been. He reckoned he might have more luck back at Guyra or Armidale in the future, as he'd had before.

Anna's Letter

On Sunday, 5[th]June, the day before Amy's twelfth birthday, Mrs Warby handed Amy a letter from England. The children had just finished Sunday School in the dining room at the homestead and celebrated Amy's birthday with a cake and a present.

"Read it when you get back to the cottage," suggested Eleanor.

"I wonder if it's from Mummy. I think it is. Come on, Edie. Come on, Millie ... it's from *Mummy*," Amy almost screamed. "Her letter's turned up after all this time."

The girls scurried out of the homestead and hurried back to their cottage.

"I heard from over in England, Wilma, that the girls are not supposed to be speaking to their mother," Eleanor commented. "I don't know what she's done, but whatever it is, in my opinion, nothing could be bad enough to separate a child from its mother."

"I know they've been waiting to hear from her for a long time," replied Wilma.

The girls reached the cottage and sat down on a stool close to the fireplace which had been lit earlier due to unseasonable weather closing in. Eileen Wilcox was baking some biscuits for afternoon tea when she noticed the girls' excitement as Amy tore open the envelope.

"Is that from your auntie?" she inquired.

"No," squealed Edie, and Millie provided the answer. "It's from our *Mummy*."

Amy began to read,

My dearest girls, ...

Before she could get any further, Eileen Wilcox crossed the kitchen floor and snatched the letter from Amy's hands.

"You all know you're not allowed to write to her or read letters from her. You've known that from the time you were in England," she said sternly.

"Give me our mother's letter, Mrs Wilcox. You have no right to take it. It's *ours!*" shouted Amy.

Eileen Wilcox strode over to the fireplace and threw the letter into the grate where the fire started to consume it.

The three girls screamed in anguish and then began to sob.

"How *dare* you do that to us. We've been waiting for ages to hear from her. I *hate* you. You're a wicked nasty woman, and I'm going to tell Mrs Warby what you've just done," Amy exploded vehemently.

Edie rushed over to Eileen and started to punch her.

"I hate you too, and I've never liked you. You're mean and horrible, and Josie hates you too."

"And so do I," added Millie, still controlling her sobs.

Eileen extricated herself from Edie's assault and told the girls to go outside. She'd suddenly wondered if she'd gone too far in destroying the letter and hadn't expected such a violent reaction from the Nash girls.

I wouldn't have given a toss if I'd never heard from my own Ma again, she thought. *I was glad to get away from her and I'm happy she's dead, the drunken wretch.* But it occurred to her that maybe those girls' mother had been a little better than her own. *I might tell them I'm sorry later on and ask them not to say anything to Mrs Warby.*

On the veranda, Amy comforted her sisters.

"I'm writing to Mummy immediately to tell her what's happened. She'll write to us again, I know it, and Mrs Warby will not let *her* do it to us again."

The girls finally controlled their reactions and walked to the creek. They sat under the willow tree with troubled faces where they remained until Jane was sent to let them know their dinner was ready.

"I don't even want to eat what she's cooked," Edie said.

"I don't either," agreed Millie.

The Nash girls slept fitfully that night, and Amy's quiet sobs were occasionally heard. In the morning they made ready for school, ignoring Eileen Wilcox's attempts to make it up to them.

Telling Miss Wilma

At school, Wilma noticed Amy was distracted and not attentive to her lessons, and Edie spent a lot of time staring out the window. Millie was drawing a witch-like woman on her slate.

Something's happened to upset them, she thought. *I'll question Amy after school.*

At three o'clock, Wilma walked over to Amy and asked her if anything had happened to upset her and her sisters. She ordered the other girls to go back to their home and sat down with Amy on a bench.

"First of all, happy birthday, Amy dear. You've just turned twelve, and after next Christmas, you'll be joining Jane and Gracie and Doris at the homestead to learn how to run a home so when you get married one day you'll be …"

Amy started to cry so Wilma left off the topic of the future.

"What is it, Amy? You can tell me. I know you and your sisters were not yourselves today. What has happened?"

Amy blurted out the whole story about the burning of the letter then went on to tell Wilma about the way Josie had been treated, starting from the journey in the ship until the other day when she'd wet the bed again.

"We don't like Mrs Wilcox. Every one of us hates her now, even though she tried to make it up to us this morning. I feel I can never forgive her for burning my mother's letter."

"That was a dreadful thing to do, Amy, and I now understand why you've all been so upset."

"And also, Miss Wilma," continued Amy, looking embarrassed,

"one girl told us she was touched in her private place by a man with sandy hair and freckles. It happened in the schoolroom a couple of weeks ago when she'd gone to get her scripture book for Sunday School. Mrs Wilcox told her to be quiet about it."

Wilma was momentarily shocked into silence.

Then she said, "A man with sandy hair, you say? Leave it with me, Amy. Mrs Warby will be horrified at all that's been going on. I'll speak to her, and I feel sure there'll be some changes in the future for you all."

Wilma took Amy's hand and walked with her down to the cottage, urging her to have hope for the future.

"In the end, it'll all work out for the best, believe me."

Dismissal

Troubled by all she'd heard, Wilma made her way to the homestead. This was not what she and her mother had planned for the girls. These children deserved safety and security and a fresh start, away from all the trauma they'd suffered in London. Not more problems here! And that station hand … Stan Otford, it must be – he was the only man employed here with sandy hair and freckles. *He's got to go. And I'm sure mother will get rid of that awful Mrs Wilcox too.*

Mrs Warby listened, dismayed by all Wilma told her.

"I'm putting off everything and going into Armidale tomorrow to advertise for new house parents, Wilma. That woman gave me a completely different impression when I interviewed her back in London. How I've been deceived. And that Stan fellow will be leaving the place straightaway. I can't have a paedophile like him on my property. First thing in the morning he'll be out of here."

"Are you going to speak to Mrs Wilcox tomorrow, Mama? She needs to know that you've found out what's been going on."

"The day after tomorrow she and her husband can pack up their things, put them in the wagon and Neil can take them to Armidale. What they do after that is their business, not mine. Their contract will be cancelled, and I'll tell the authorities why. And Jane and Gracie and Doris can run the cottage until new people arrive. It'll be good practice for them."

True to her word, Mrs Warby left for Armidale the next day to advertise for new house parents, but not before she'd given Stan Otford the sack and demanded he leave immediately and never come near the station again. Then she'd knocked on the door of the Wilcox's cottage and spoke to Eileen Wilcox about the burning of the letter from the Nash girl's mother, her treatment of Josie and her bossy manner with everyone.

"I've been mistaken about you, Mrs Wilcox. You don't have any proper concern or understanding for these girls, or the temperament for the job, so I'm asking you and Alfred to pack your belongings. My son will deliver you into Armidale tomorrow morning."

A tirade followed from Eileen Wilcox during which Eleanor turned on her heel and walked back to the homestead.

"The cheek of her," she reported to Wilma before leaving for Armidale to advertise for new people. "She actually defended burning that letter saying it was the fault of people in London who would have approved of her doing it. No remorse or any understanding of the girls' feelings, let alone their right to hear from their own mother. Anyhow, she's happy to go, she said, and complained about the young ones in her keep, saying they were too much trouble. She also defended her treatment of the *bed-wetter* as she called her. That's poor little Josie. She's not been a suitable person for this role at all."

Two days later, the orphan girls were free of the Wilcoxes and Stan Otford. When they were told, they clapped and cheered, glad those people were gone.

"Mr Wilcox wasn't too bad, but *her!*" Doris remarked.

"Have you written to your mother yet, Amy?" Jane inquired.

"I'm writing this afternoon to let her know what happened to her letter," Amy assured everyone. "We should hear back from her in a few months, but Edie and I haven't written to our Auntie Mattie since we got her last letter in April because she said some awful things about our mother."

"What sort of things?" asked Jane.

"Just things she shouldn't have said. I'd rather not talk about it. Sorry I mentioned it," replied Amy.

Winter Days

A bitter winter had closed in. It was Sunday morning, and the girls had crunched through the frost to the homestead for the church service and Sunday School. Neil Warby bumped into them on the veranda just before they entered the double doors into the homestead.

"It's freezing!" Doris said. "I can't remember feeling so cold back in London. It's the mornings … all that mist and frost on the ground. Almost looks like snow. And so cold through the nights."

"That may be so in the New England District, Doris," Neil defended, "but after the frosts have melted and the air has cleared, you'll never get more glorious weather. Warm and sunny days, with only a slight nip in the air. Rain when it's needed and much clearer skies than you'll ever find in England in winter."

"Do yer ever get snow 'ere, Mr Warby?" Gracie asked.

"Once in a while, but not often, and I do agree with you, Doris about the mornings. We've had ice form on the roads and in horse troughs, and water freezing in the pipes but I wouldn't change it. There's an atmosphere in winter here of freshness like nowhere else. It's exhilarating! I wouldn't live anywhere else."

It was now early July and Neil called in with mail for the girls. Among the collection were two letters in one envelope for the Nash girls, but not the letter they were hoping for.

"I don't mind hearing from Freddy, but not from Auntie Mattie," commented Edie after the envelope had been torn open.

"Auntie Mattie's first," announced Amy. "Here goes."

57 Warren Street,
Tottenham Court Road,
London, England

May 28th 1914,

My Dearest Amy, I cannot think the reason I have not received another letter from you before now. Freddy and I are wondering whether the letter has been lost as you said you were allowed to write every week. I do hope you will write soon and tell us all about yourself and your Sisters. I hope you got my letter. I answered it as soon as I heard from you. I was thankful to know you had arrived safely. If I do not hear from you soon I shall write to Miss Speers because she told me I should always hear from you all and I am sure the kind lady you are with will allow you to write to Freddy and me. I shall always love you all and think about you. Now, Dear, I am not writing very much this time. Freddy is sending a little letter as well. Cousin Hilary is quite well and sends her love. Trusting, Dear Amy, you are all well. Fondest love to you all. Your loving Aunt.

"Now Freddy's," urged Millie, straightaway. "Our brother Freddy's letter please."

Dear Sisters,

I hope you are all well and happy. I and Aunt have been wondering why you have not written to us for so long a time, and Aunt is very worried about it. I have been learning Life Saving and I am going to try and get four Life-Saving Certificates before Christmas, when I leave school. I have got a place of work after school hours. Dear Sisters, I give my love to you all

"So, Freddy's got another place of work after school," remarked Amy. "That'll make it easier for Auntie Mattie, but I still don't feel like writing to her again."

"I don't either," said Edie. "I hope Mummy's answer comes soon.

War is Declared

On the 5th of August, Eleanor Warby asked Jane and Gracie to set the cane table on the veranda at the homestead for morning tea. Gladys, one of Eleanor's friends from Armidale, had been staying for the past few days and Eleanor was enjoying catching up with her friend. The two women settled into matching cane chairs and waited for the girls to appear with newly baked scones and a pot of tea.

"They're doing well here, Glad, and seem happy enough, particularly now that Wilcox woman's gone. I saw some new people last week about taking on the job. A big jolly family they are, Mr and Mrs Payne. They have two daughters, Betsy and Jean, who will attend Wilma's school here. The family's English too. Mrs Payne is very motherly and has experience in raising a family."

"Sounds ideal, Eleanor. When are they coming?"

"In two weeks. Changing the subject, Glad, what about England declaring war on Germany yesterday? Neil heard it on the wireless. Prime Minister Joseph Cook pledged full support for Britain, you know."

"It's been brewing for a while, hasn't it? It started with some Austrian duke being assassinated in Serbia and all these other countries got involved. I suppose our boys will be called up to help."

"I hope not. Let's hope this war doesn't last too long, but Germany's a strong country, isn't it?"

"No stronger than England," Gladys emphasised patriotically. "Look at the extent of our empire."

At that moment, the girls carried out the morning tea, Jane carrying a tray with teapot, milk jug and sugar bowl, Gracie bearing another tray with a plate of scones, a pot of strawberry jam and a bowl of freshly whipped cream.

"Thank you, Jane. Thank you, Gracie. The scones look lovely."

"They weren't 'ard to make, Ma'am. I 'ope you and your friend enjoy 'em."

The girls departed with a small curtsy and retired back to the kitchen.

"Wilma's doing a lovely job with them, Eleanor," observed Gladys.

"They'll make fine wives and mothers one day, I'm sure, but Gracie still drops her aitches, left over from her Cockney accent I'm afraid. I wonder a bit about her. She can swear like a wharf labourer. I specified to Miss Speers back in England that I only wanted girls from respectable families. I think Gracie might have slipped through the net somehow."

"How do they mix in with your granddaughters, Eleanor?"

"They don't. I won't allow it. They come from a different background to us."

Gladys nodded, and Eleanor continued.

"I don't know a great deal about any of them, but I wouldn't risk our children picking up bad habits. They might tell unclean jokes or something. I wouldn't consider them fit to sit at the same table as us, as I wouldn't the workmen. Mind you, if one of my granddaughters is sick and can't play shuttlecock or table tennis with her sister, then I'll get one of the orphans to partner her, but that's as far as it goes."

"Yes, I understand." Gladys nodded.

"There's another girl who turned twelve in June. Young Amy Nash. She'll be joining Jane, Gracie and Doris after Christmas to be trained up. She's a gentle little thing. Nice one that."

"How long are they in your care under this emigration scheme?"

"Until they're sixteen. They can leave then, but I'll encourage them to stay on with me. I'll be paying them a small wage then."

"I imagine it'll be cheaper than hiring help from outside, Eleanor, won't it?"

"Indeed, it will," answered Eleanor, looking down with a smile.

New House Parents

Arthur Payne and his wife Dorothy, whom he called Dottie, and their two daughters Betsy and Jean, arrived at Balangara a few months before Christmas. Dottie was a big blousy woman with a hearty laugh and a sense of fun. The girls took to her immediately after she and Arthur and their daughters had settled into their cottage next door.

Arthur was a versatile man who'd been hired as a 'jack of all trades', gardener and chauffeur for Mrs Warby.

"I won't mind all the girls around me, Dottie. I reckon I'm used to females anyhow with you lot. I'll try to be like a father to these poor kids."

The couple had only been in charge for a few days when Dottie lifted Josie onto her large lap. The child had nestled into her bosom and stayed there, enjoying the strong, comforting arms encircling her until she was released from the embrace.

Harsh rules were lifted, and the girls settled into a more relaxed way of life with fewer duties.

Awful News

Christmas was close and still no answering letter from Anna, much to the Nash girls' disappointment.

"She wrote to us before. Why doesn't she write again? What's going on?" Edie asked, scowling.

"I wish I knew, Edie. I just hope she's alright. We might get a Christmas card," Amy added hopefully.

But no card came. Instead, they received further letters from Auntie Mattie and Freddy.

57 Warren Street,

Tottenham Court Rd

November 2nd. 1914   *London W*

My Dear Amy, Edie & Millie,

This will be the third letter I have written to you and I have received no answer. I did not know until about 2 or 3 months ago that you had been writing to your mother. I suppose that is why Freddy and I have not heard from you. I must tell you, Dear Amy, that your mother is dead. She died nearly three months ago on August 30th from consumption. I did not see her, but Freddy did, and she told him that she had been hearing from you. It is just one year since you left England. I hope you are all quite well and getting on nicely with your schooling. Freddy leaves at Christmas. He will

*start work then. I expect you have all grown. Hilary
came home for her Summer Holidays. I am very proud
of her. She is growing into a nice girl. I hope you will get
this letter as I shall expect to hear from you all. Millie
would not know me now. I wonder if Edie remembers
Auntie Mattie. Freddy is 14 on Xmas Day, and you are
13 next June. Hilary is 12 on April 13th. Now, Dear Amy,
I wish you all a very Happy Xmas. I am not sure when
you will receive this, because of this dreadful war.
Please God, it will soon be over, and the country is at
peace again. Love to you all. From your loving Auntie,
M Harrison.*

The girls stared blankly at each other for a moment and then burst
into tears. Freddy's letter was laid aside while the news of their
mother's death fully impacted them.

"And we'll never ever know what was in her letter that bloody Mrs
Wilcox burnt," Edie said, sobbing.

"I think she must have been telling us she was going to die," said
Amy quietly, after a pause, "and what had been happening to her while
she was away. She would have gone shortly after we got that letter
from her, or even before."

"Well, at least Freddy went to see her and Aunty Esther would have
been there too, I'll bet," added Edie. "And Auntie Mattie didn't give
us a single word of sympathy. And she once said that Mummy had
hurt Daddy so much. I wonder how she did that?"

"Auntie Mattie and Mummy never got on very well you know,"
said Amy, reflecting. "I don't know what our mother could have done
to make Auntie Mattie hate her like that, but Auntie Mattie should
have been kinder. She was still our mother, and I know how much she
loved us all."

Edie looked thoughtful. "She probably caught the consumption
from Daddy. I remember you saying when we last saw her that you
thought she didn't look well before she went up to Northampton. I

wonder how she got on then? Was she taken in by Uncle John? And did she find work up there? Was someone else looking after her?"

"I don't know," replied Amy wearily. Then she sighed deeply. "But she did come back to London as she promised us, and how terrible it must have been for her knowing we're all out here, and she'd never see us again, and having to go into hospital to die. I want her photo. At least that."

"She had lovely blue eyes and pretty hair," Edie said wistfully.

Millie had been listening to the conversation with a sad face. Finally, she spoke. "Now Mummy's gone, we're REAL orphans, aren't we?"

Amy picked up Freddy's letter.

"Let's see what he has to say. Freddy went to see her before she died. He's lucky Auntie Mattie let him."

2.11.14   *57 Warren Street*

Dear Sisters,

I hope you are all well and happy as I am. I have not been at my little place of work very long but I hope to be working in earnest soon. I have been wondering why you have not written to Aunt or me for so long a time. Aunt has already told you mother is dead. When I went to see mother in the hospital, she told me you had been writing to her and she also had your photos. Dear Amy, Millie and Edie, I hope you have a happy Christmas. In London, nearly every man one sees is a soldier. I suppose you have seen the Australian Army. The Emden, a German cruiser, was sunk by an Australian warship. I think this is all I have to say at present.

With love to you all, I remain your affectionate brother Freddy. XXX

"He didn't say very much about Mummy," said Edie, feeling let down.

"That's boys for you," Amy replied resignedly, "and Freddy never liked discussing details."

Dottie Payne comforted the girls after she'd found out that Anna had died. When she was told about Mrs Wilcox burning the letter, tears came to her eyes.

"That was a cruel thing to do, and you must have all been so angry. But remember this, you'll carry her in your hearts forever, and no one can destroy the lovely memories you have of her."

The girls calmed down after some time.

"Christmas is in three days," Edie declared. "I wonder how they have it out here. It's hot. Do they have a Christmas pudding like Granny used to make?"

"I'm making one tomorrow," announced Dottie Payne, "and there's a fir tree arriving too for you all to decorate."

"I coloured in some angel cut-outs at Sunday School, Mrs Payne. Can I put them on the tree?" asked Millie.

"Of course, you can, sweetie," she answered.

The Nash girls wandered outside and walked to the willow tree near the creek. They sat on the rock for an hour, sharing memories of their parents and of their lives back in London.

"We'll get back there one day and put flowers on their graves," consoled Edie as Amy burst into tears.

"Yes, we will," agreed Millie.

Edie changed the subject.

"Think how awful it would be if we still had that Mrs Wilcox in our cottage. Thank goodness we've got Mrs Payne now. She's lovely, isn't she?"

"She is," Amy agreed, with a weak smile. "And I like the way she sings all those jolly songs Mummy and Daddy used to sing, like *Waiting at the Church*, and do you know, Betsy and I have become best friends. Betsy said to me, 'Amy, friends for life, you and me!'"

The three sisters returned to the cottage and spent the rest of the day on the veranda, doing the things they liked, as Dottie Payne had suggested.

The next day, Eleanor Warby called in with three parcels for the Nash sisters.

"They're from Sister Esther Howell from London. They feel like books. You are only to open them on Christmas day."

"We haven't heard from her for a long time," said Edie as she accepted the parcel addressed to her.

"She's a very busy person in that church you went to in London, Edie. In time, I'm sure you'll hear from her again. And don't forget there's a war going on over there and food is scarce now. Your friend will be more needed than ever," Eleanor advised.

"She was a big help to us, Mrs Warby," said Amy. "I don't know how we could have done without her."

"I know your story, Amy, but isn't it good you're in Australia now, and life will always be easier for you and your sisters."

"Yes," Amy nodded, somewhat reluctantly, "but I miss my Mum and Dad so much."

"And even Freddy," added Edie.

"It's been very hard for you all, but I'm sure your parents would want you to make the best of things out here, Amy, and take advantage of the opportunities you'll have."

"Yes, Mrs Warby," said Amy, slowly nodding again.

Eleanor reminded everyone in the cottage that a Christmas church service would be held in her dining room at ten o'clock on Christmas morning. A visiting minister from Armidale was attending, and there would be a large gathering of friends and relatives flowing out onto the veranda.

"I know *Away in a Manger*, Mrs Warby," said Millie proudly, with a smile.

"I'll ask Miss Wilma to include that one, especially for you, Millie," answered Eleanor.

Christmas Day 1914

On Christmas morning, the first thing Amy did was to remind her sisters that Freddy was turning fourteen.

"It's hot here and very, very cold in England," said Millie. "I hope Freddy is warm."

"They'll have a fire going, Millie," Amy assured her.

The Nash girls were allowed to open their parcels from Aunty Esther straight away.

Each of the girls received their own special Bible.

After breakfast, Dottie Payne addressed the girls.

"Now, Betty, Jean and everyone else, there are presents under the tree for you all. One at a time, please."

Skipping ropes, board games, fancywork kits, a shuttlecock set and boxes of sweets were all laid out for everyone to share and enjoy.

Dottie Payne outlined the rest of the day.

"After church, and Christmas dinner here, we all have to go back to the homestead under the peppercorn tree because Mrs Warby has got a bran tub going. It's a deep barrel, and you'll have to reach in it and dig for the buried treasures among the bran. She has a gift for each of you. Isn't that nice?"

At the end of the day, the Nash sisters reviewed their first Christmas at Balangara.

"Church was lovely, and the carols are the same we used to sing at Whitefields," said Amy.

"The pudding was soggy, not like Granny's," said Edie.

"I've got her recipe, and one day I'll make one like hers," Amy promised.

All the girls compared their gifts from the bran tub – useful things like handkerchiefs, lavender sachets, face washers and fancy soap, pastel coloured combs, hair ribbons and clips.

"It's been a lovely day," Amy concluded as the girls prepared for bed.

"An it's school 'olidays too," added Gracie as she changed into her nightie.

In the next cottage, Dottie Payne commented to Arthur, "It's been good to see the Nash girls having such fun today after all their sadness and such a hard start to their year here."

The next morning Dottie decided to teach the girls how to knit.

"In, round, through, off," she demonstrated, as the girls struggled with their new craft.

"I love it," announced Edie when she showed her finished rows to Dottie. "I'm going to knit a scarf for Freddy. It's cold over there."

"I've got a pattern for socks, Edie. I'll teach you how to turn the heel," volunteered Dottie.

The weeks passed quickly, and at the beginning of February 1915, the girls were ready to start school again.

"It's just over a year since we came out here," noted Jane, "and it hasn't been too bad since Mr and Mrs Wilcox left."

"Yes," agreed Doris, "and now we have lovely Mr and Mrs Payne looking after us and Josie doesn't wet the bed anymore."

About the War

"Lucky we ain't still in England. Mrs Warby come down 'ere yesterday and I 'eard her tell Mrs Payne some bloody bombs dropped on London a few days ago. She 'eard it on the news," Gracie announced importantly.

"Don't swear, Gracie. Mrs Warby wouldn't have said that word," cautioned Jane, "and don't drop your aitches either."

"I'll try," Gracie promised.

The Nash girls were still grieving for their mother, Amy in particular.

"I still can't believe it, Edie. I'll never stop wondering what Mummy said in her letter."

"I know. I'm still angry too at that woman. But Mummy would want us to keep on and make the best of our lives, Amy," Edie said comfortingly as Amy dabbed her eyes with her handkerchief.

"Well, I suppose we should think of what Gracie told Mrs Payne, Edie. If the Germans are starting to bomb us over there, it's better we're out here, isn't it? But what about Freddy, Auntie Mattie, Hilary, Grandma in Clapham and Aunty Esther? We must pray they'll be safe," said Amy worriedly.

One afternoon, after they'd returned to the cottage after school, Edie suggested they write a letter to Freddy and Auntie Mattie.

"Although Auntie Mattie said horrible things about Mummy, we've only got her and Freddy and Hilary, Grandma in Clapham and Aunty Esther in England who belong to us now. I want to know what's happening over there."

"Well, I suppose you're right, Edie," replied Amy slowly. "I'll get around to writing in a while."

The two girls wrote their letters at the end of March 1915 and settled down to wait for replies. No answers came, and after a few months, Amy became concerned. One evening when the Paynes, their daughters and the girls were sitting around the dinner table, Amy mentioned how worried she was about the silence from England.

"I'm writing again," she declared. "I can't help worrying about the war. Are they getting enough to eat over there? Is Freddy alright? Is he working?"

"If anything bad happened you'd be hearing about it, Amy," Arthur assured her. "Don't worry. They'll be alright."

Still no letters from England arrived. Then early in November Eleanor personally delivered one to Amy.

"I know you've been worried all the year, Amy, but this should put your mind at peace."

"Thanks, Mrs Warby," said Amy with a half-smile. She summoned Edie and Millie from the cottage lawn outside.

"There's two inside the envelope, one from Freddy and one from Auntie Pattie. Freddy's first!"

September 22nd 1915

Dear Amy, Edie and Millie.

I hope you are quite well as I am myself. Aunt has told you about the Zeppelin raid and I saw the Zeppelin, it was a pretty sight. I am getting on alright as a messenger in the Post Office. I hope you will like the ribbon. We are having grand weather for Sept. Have you still got your post card album I am saving all the post cards I get. I have got a few. Hoping to send them to you soon. This is all just now sisters. I am your loving Brother, Freddy. XXX

"What a short letter," said Edie, "but he's alright! He's alright! But what's a zeppelin?"

I'll ask Mr Payne tonight, Edie. Freddy said it was a pretty sight. Now let's read Auntie Mattie's," Amy said as she unfolded the letter.

57 Warren Street
Tottenham Ct. Rd.
London W

September 14th 1915

My Dear Amy, Edie & Millie

We were very pleased with your letter. I am sure you must wonder why we have not written before. Well Dear, there seems to have been something when we have talked of writing to put it off and so the time has gone. I am pleased that you are all so well and getting on so nicely. You write very nicely and so does Edie. I expect you have all grown very much. I should like to see you all. Freddy is getting on all right at his work. Do you hear anything about the war? The Germans were dropping bombs over London last Wednesday evening about a quarter to eleven. The people were very frightened. We were just going to bed, some people were in bed. There were many killed and wounded and a great deal of damage done to houses and property. There have been several air raids over London but none so near us as the last Wednesday. Dear Amy, I think your cousin Hilary is going to write to you. She is getting on very nicely and will be thirteen next April. You are one year older. Freddy has sent you some ribbons for your hair. You must each have a piece. I hope you will get this letter alright and then when we hear from you again I will try to answer it quicker than I have before. Now Dear, I think I must close with my best love to you all from your loving Aunt

M. Harrison

"Dropping bombs over London and one close to them," said Amy, her eyes wide in alarm. "Oh! dear God, keep them safe," she pleaded.

"Even Auntie Mattie," added Millie.

"Don't say that, Millie. She and Mummy didn't get along very well, but she loves us," Amy noted.

That evening, in answer to Edie's question about a zeppelin, Arthur Payne described one to all the girls.

"The German army is sending big airships over London called Zeppelins. These things have many bags of air or hydrogen inside them which let them float in the sky. They have engines which drive them, and they can go quite fast. They are shaped like a big fat cigar. The Germans are using them to drop bombs on England. I remember reading in the newspapers the first bombs on London dropped on the 31st of May this year, and there have been many raids since."

From then on, during every Sunday School session, Eleanor Warby and Miss Wilma would pray for the safety of any relatives of the girls living in England, particularly those in London.

A few weeks after Freddy's and Auntie Mattie's letters arrived, another one was given to Amy.

"It's from Aunty Esther," she announced to her sisters. "She must have been busy helping out during the war. That's why we haven't heard from her until now. Come close, and I'll read it to you. Oh! She's written it on a sheet of paper with a picture of Whitefields Central Mission and the address printed on it."

"Stop talking and get on with it, Amy," Edie said crossly.

Amy started to read.

My dear Friends,

We are getting so very near the Festive Season that I feel I must write and wish you all a very joyous Xmas. I should like to hear from you, how you are getting on and something about your Home and what you think you would like to be. All sorts of opportunities will be coming to you that you could not get here. Freddy is having a very busy time. He has grown very much since you saw him. I think he likes his work in the telegraph department. Delivering telegrams means much time in the open air. I trust you will find how God guides and protects those who put their trust in Him, for whoever we are and wherever, He is near to help and bless. Love and serve Him, you will then have no cause to fear either for the present or the future.

I have been in to see your Auntie today, she has not been very well and was at Bexhill for three weeks.

With much love Your sincere friend,

Sister Esther

"She didn't say much about the war," Amy noted further. "Probably doesn't want to worry us."

"I remember Aunty Esther in Sunday School," piped up Millie. "In England."

"Auntie Mattie's been in hospital," murmured Amy. "I wonder what was wrong with her? I hope she can keep working. What would happen to Freddy if she couldn't work anymore?"

"Stop worrying, Amy. He'd just have to get a better job, and they could always move into a single room together, you know." Then, after a pause, she added, "What a horrible thought."

"He could come out here," ventured Millie. "I hope he comes out here."

"Not while he has to help out Auntie Mattie, Millie. But hopefully one day he'll come," said Amy.

Then she changed the subject. "Do you know what? I'm keeping all the letters we get from everyone in England in a big biscuit tin Mrs Payne gave me. I'll never let one go. They're family, and nothing's so important as family."

"There'll be only one letter missing," Edie said seriously.

"I know," Amy said sadly, looking down.

"Hasn't this year gone quickly?" reminded Doris as she joined the Nash girls on the veranda. "Another Christmas looming up."

"Not long to go," affirmed Edie, "and our brother Freddy will be fifteen years old. And Doris, in a letter to us he said he saw a zeppelin flying over London and bombs dropping."

"Go on!" Doris replied with wide eyes, "Isn't he scared one might drop on him?"

"We pray every day that he and Auntie Mattie, Grandma in Clapham and Aunty Esther will be safe," Amy added confidently.

That evening, Doris mentioned to Arthur, who'd become the male voice of authority in the cottage, that Freddy Nash over in England, loved watching the zeppelins and bombs dropping everywhere.

"Silly young boy. He's just on fifteen you say? At that age, they have no sense of mortality and think they're indestructible. Isn't that right, Dottie?"

Dottie nodded and turned her mouth down with a fatalist look.

Amy nodded. "His birthday is on Christmas Day."

"After Christmas, Amy, you'll be going up to the homestead to start your training as you're over thirteen now and left school," Dottie Payne reminded her.

"I know, Mrs Payne, and I'm looking forward to making cakes and biscuits and other sorts of cooking."

"That's the best part," muttered Gracie darkly. "You wait till yer 'ave ter do the other parts."

Christmas Day 1915

Everyone at Balangara enjoyed a happy Christmas celebration. Amy reminded her sisters that Freddy was now fifteen years old.

January quickly arrived and the start of the year 1916.

"You can make your way up to the homestead next Saturday morning, Amy," Dottie advised. "Mrs Warby is expecting you."

Early on Saturday morning, four of the girls, now including Amy, walked up the slope to the side gate leading into the homestead and its surrounding garden profuse with English flowering annuals and perennials.

"The garden's looking beautiful now. Mr Payne is putting horse and cow manure on it," Jane explained to Amy.

"What a lovely place. This is the best I've ever seen of this part of the garden," Amy resplied.

"Up the steps to the walkway, under the grapevines, and along here to the kitchen door," Doris recited the mantra as she led the way. She opened the door and the four girls entered a very large kitchen.

A Busy Schedule

"You'll get to know where everything is," explained Jane. "These benches here we have to scrub every week, and the floor as well and we have to clean and blacken the stoves too. There's two of them. We have to make sure everything's tidy and in its place. And there's always washing up to do. We only know how to make scones and pancakes and pikelets so far, but Cook has been training us up to cook everything from breakfast to dinner for the Warbys and their workers too. Cook's leaving in two months so there'll be more and more for us to do."

"And that ain't all," joined in Gracie. "We have to do the washin' on Mondays, boilin' up a copper and even washin' some of the workmen's dirty overalls too. And they smell! The next day is ironin' day, and I've already had to heat up those heavy flat irons on the stove, and iron some big petticoats for Mrs Warby and Miss Wilma. Me arm ached for an hour after that."

"On Wednesdays," continued Jane, "we have to fold up all the linen and sort out all the ironed clothes and hang them in everyone's wardrobes and cupboards, and if anything needs mending, we have to do that too."

"What's on Thursday?" asked Amy, her eyes wide open with apprehension.

"That's cleaning day. We've got to scrub the verandas around the house and dust and sweep inside. And clean the bathroom. We've got to do things properly. Everything is inspected, and we have to do it all over again if it's not good enough," said Doris, pulling a face.

"Friday's the best day though. Baking day," said Jane, attempting to placate Amy, who was looking worried. "We're learning to cook cakes now and can have some with a cup of tea. Cream teas we've had here, but they call them Devonshire teas in Australia."

"Saturday morning … today … is kitchen cleaning and tidying and if we finish early, we can have the whole afternoon off," said Doris with an exaggerated sigh.

"The more girls who leave school and join us, the easier it'll get," explained Jane, "and Mrs Warby is going to bring out three more girls, this time from Scotland. That'll help."

At that moment, Eleanor Warby walked up a few steps from the main homestead and into the adjoining kitchen.

"Here you are, Amy dear. I'm sure you're going to prove very efficient in learning all there is to know about running a household, like your friends here. One day you'll be thankful for the training you're getting. Now the other girls know what they have to do today, but you Amy, have a special job I'm giving you. Go to that cupboard over there and pull out the top drawer. All the silver cutlery is there for you to clean and polish with Silvo and also the silver service and trays on the shelves. This shouldn't take you more than two hours. Now set to, girls and oh! Gracie, I'm delighted you don't drop your aitches now. Miss Wilma tells me your speech is improving and she hasn't heard you use bad language in three weeks. That's lovely! Keep it up."

With these words, a smiling Eleanor left the kitchen and returned to the main homestead.

"Bloody slave driver," muttered Gracie.

"Anyway, tomorrow is Sunday," ventured Amy, ignoring Gracie's language and wanting to change the subject. "The best day of the week! I'll be writing letters home after Sunday School. Edie, Millie and me are all worried about the war still going on and if silly Freddy's still standing among all the bombs."

The four girls started their work with a purpose as they wanted to get back to their cottage as soon as possible and have the afternoon free.

"I'm getting on with the cross-stitch sampler I'm doing," said Jane.

"I'm doin' a jigsaw, and I've finished the edges," said Gracie.

"I'm going down to the willow tree to paint a picture of the creek," said Doris.

Something to Look Forward to

When the girls returned to the cottage, Dottie Payne had some exciting news for them.

"I've already told the others here. Now in April we're going to the Armidale Show. Mr Tom Morley will be driving us all in the wagon, but the Warbys are going in Mr Neil's Dodge. We have to leave early in the morning, and we'll be home by six at night. There's a lot to see. There'll be a grand parade of the champion animals like horses, sheep, goats, and cattle and Balangara will have many entries in to hopefully win ribbons. There'll be chooks and ducks and other sorts of animals too. One of the dogs from here will be competing in the sheepdog trials. Good old Buster! And show jumping with the horses. There'll be boxing matches and wood chopping events for the men ..."

"What's for girls there?" interrupted Gracie. "I like dogs and cats, but I hate bulls. Will we have a picnic?"

"Yes indeed, Gracie," answered Dottie. "There'll be plenty of food stalls and ice cream too. That'll be a treat. And Mrs Warby is entering her jams and preserves in a competition. Last time she won prizes. Oh! and you can have rides on the razzle-dazzle and swings too and ponies. You all like sewing? There's an arts and crafts hall there and so much more. Now this is something to look forward to, isn't it?"

Everyone agreed.

The girls settled down to their everyday routines until the long-awaited outing arrived in April.

"Last time we went to Armidale, Mrs Warby bought us new clothes and had our teeth checked at the dentist, remember? This will be a nicer day," reminded Jane as everyone bumped along in the wagon on the way to Armidale.

"Don't talk about that time," said Doris with a shudder. "Four of us had to go back to the dentist and have the drill. It was awful."

There was a flurry of excitement among the girls after they'd entered the showground. Promising Mrs Warby they'd assemble for their picnic under a nearby gum tree at 12 o'clock, they made off to their separate pursuits. During the morning, a man announced through a loud hailer that a raffle would be held at 3 o'clock that afternoon.

"A raffle!" said Amy excitedly during the picnic lunch, when she'd heard Eleanor Warby discussing it. "I've never been in one. Please, please Mrs Warby, can Edie and I go in it?"

Amy thought she might win a box of chocolates, a painting from a local artist or cakes of fancy soap.

Eleanor looked at Amy and gave in.

She's such a sweet child, she thought, *and gone through such a lot in England. Why not let her and her sister go in the raffle if it means so much to her. They're not likely to win with hundreds buying tickets. It can do no harm.*

"Here you are, Amy," said Mrs Warby, handing Amy some money. "Go and buy a few tickets each for you and your sister, but don't get too excited. Most people don't win anything."

"I've heard the prizes are substantial and useful to the local pastoralist," mentioned Arthur Payne.

At three that afternoon, the draw took place. There were six prizes to be won. A portly local councillor stood on a roughly made dais and spun a chocolate wheel.

"Our first prize goes to ticket holder, Blue No.79, he shouted through the loud hailer. After some excitement in the crowd and a whoop of joy, a young woman emerged and made her way to the dais and collected her prize.

"It's a big money order to be spent at Henderson's produce store," she shrilled to her husband, waving the promissory note in his face. "What a help!"

Two more prizes were drawn but nothing for Amy and Edie whose eyes were filled with expectation.

"Our next prize is for ticket holder Yellow No. 57. Please come forward," shouted the councillor as a large merino sheep was led out by a man who led it to the dais.

"It's *me*," proclaimed Amy, overwhelmed by her win. Then her face fell.

"It's a sheep! What on earth can I do with it?" she asked Eleanor, bewildered.

"Well, you are lucky. Go and take your prize, Amy, and we'll talk about it later."

Amy walked over to the dais, and the man with the sheep handed it over to her. She grabbed the sheep's neck and coaxed it back to her small circle, amid congratulations from some burly men standing nearby.

The next draw was a blank for Edie, and she looked at the sheep, wishing Amy had won a box of chocolates she could share.

"This is our last draw and our biggest prize of the day. A fairly new innovation and sure to please the modern farmer. Make your work much easier, I'll be bound. You'll be able to burn up the dust on your property with this, but watch your speed, mate. Could be dangerous."

From behind a large tree, previously concealed from view, a sinewy, bronzed young man emerged steering a shiny, flashy motorbike with all the latest attachments. The onlooking men standing around slapped each other on the back and wished each other all the luck in the world, but prematurely envious of any bloke who might win this prize.

"Alright, get your tickets out, folks. This is it."

The chocolate wheel was given an extra-strong spin to emphasise the importance of this final draw and biggest prize. The crowd waited in excited anticipation.

The councillor peered at the ticket and teased the crowd while he held it up for a while.

"Go on! Let's know the verdict," screamed a middle-aged woman. "It's got to be my husband's."

"It's Green No. 41. Please come forward and claim your prize. You can ride home on it if you like."

There was a suspended hush as the crowd waited to see who had been so fortunate.

"But I don't want it, Mrs Warby," complained Edie, a disappointed look on her face. "Could I change it for a box of chocolates?"

"You'll have to go out and claim your prize, Edie," persuaded Eleanor, "and we'll talk about what to do with it later. Now go on."

A group of disgruntled farmers watched a small girl slowly walk out to the dais and hand in her ticket. Her face was trembling, and she didn't look thrilled as Neil Warby walked the motorbike back to their circle amid a few audible comments from the gathered menfolk.

"I suppose that man, Warby, who walked her back with it, will get it. Kids that age shouldn't be allowed in a raffle."

"It was a fair contest," fired back Eleanor, overhearing, "and my family will not claim the sheep or the motorbike. The prizes will be awarded to a deserving charity."

After a discussion with Amy and Edie, the girls immediately fell in with Eleanor's suggestion and walked to the Red Cross stall. Neil handed over Edie's motorbike, and Amy led over her sheep. The girls were praised for their generosity.

"I was taught at home in England, that it's better to give than receive," Amy remarked a little piously, "but I wish we could've have won some chocolates."

"I'll get a big box for you and Edie, seeing you've both been so kind," Eleanor promised.

The day came to an end, and the girls and the Paynes clambered into the buggy to go home. When they arrived, everyone pitched in and prepared ham sandwiches and bread and jam for tea.

"It's Mrs Warby's prize-winning blackberry jam. What a lovely day we've all had," said Dottie Payne.

A Piece of Shrapnel

Months passed, and Amy and Edie had written to Freddy and Auntie Mattie a few times, but no answers came. The three sisters grew increasingly worried about the fate of everyone in London as Arthur Payne would regularly report on the news in Australian newspapers.

"There's no let-up in the bombing raids, and it's already 1916. You'd think Britain would have settled the matter by now."

These remarks did not help the anxiety of the girls who had family members in England.

It was almost Christmas again when Dottie Payne handed Amy two letters in the one envelope and announced they must be from her brother and aunt.

"Auntie Mattie's first, please, Amy. We'll have Freddy's last," suggested Edie.

"I'm so glad he's alive," said Amy, looking relieved. "Listen, I'll read them out."

57 Warren Street,
Tottenham Court Rd.
London W

Nov. 8th. 1916

My Dearest Amy, Edie and Millie,

I have just received your letter and am almost ashamed to write after keeping you so long without a letter but I did not think it was twelve months, please dear forgive me. Freddy is very bad at writing as well as me. We have been very pleased with all your letters. I am quite sure you are with a good Lady who is doing a great deal for you all. I am very thankful to her for her Great Kindness as I am quite certain you would not have been so well off in England, and now dear about your letter I have just had. Fancy Edie being so lucky. I am delighted to hear such good news and you are very lucky also to win such big prizes. It was indeed very kind of Mrs Warby to put you in the raffle. I should so like to see you all and I should like to have tasted Edie's birthday cake. I thought the letter you sent us about Edie knitting the socks was very nice. Sister Esther from Whitefields thought it was splendid. Dear Amy, I have sent you three birth certificates, and then Mrs Warby will see your proper ages. I expect the mistake was made at Miss Speers' home. I have put you in a photo of your Dear Father which I am sure you will like. How pleased he would have been with you all now. Freddy said some time ago he should go to Australia after the war. I don't know whether he will or not. I shall be very sorry to lose him as it will place me very badly off as I cannot work. I have done no work for 12 months as I suffer from Asthma and my heart. All last winter I was ill, but if he wishes to go and if it is for his good I must put up with it and trust for the best. He has not been very lucky with his places. I am sorry to hear you get toothache. That is very bad. We have had some very bad air raids in London and bombs have been dropping not far from us, one in the Euston Road not far from Euston Station but it did not explode which was a good thing for us. I am very nervous. Freddy does not seem to mind them. Sometimes we have just got to bed and have to get up and go to the basement. Some of us in the house go down in the Tube Station at the corner of Warren Street. The gun firing is terrible to hear but you cannot hear anything down there. Hilary told me she had heard from you. She has two more years to stay at the orphanage and then I expect she will be sent to Service. I have not seen her for three years. I am always thinking about you all of course. Dear Amy, Freddy might write to you sometime when I don't but boys I don't think are so thoughtful as girls but I promise to send to you oftener so you must forgive us both. Now Dear, I will conclude for this time. Freddy is sending a letter. I don't know what he is going to tell you so with my fondest love to you all, I remain your loving Aunt Mattie. M. Harrison xxx

"That's a long letter," commented Edie, "and about time."

"She's sick, and don't forget what it must be like having those bombs dropping all around you. She said she was nervous, Edie. It's alright for us. We're safe out here," chastised Amy. "Now let's see what Freddy has to say."

57 Warren Street,
Tottenham Court Rd.
London NW

Dear Amy, Edie and Millie,

I have just received your letter and I am jolly pleased with it. I am very sorry I have not written to you for so long and I do hope you won't think bad of me for it. Fancy Edie winning a motor cycle, you are all beating me at saving. I and my friend Stanley Mitchell, have made up our minds to save up and come out to Australia after the war. We have plenty of excitement in London every time the Moon rises and until it sets. We have Gothas, Zeppelins and Taubes flying over London dropping bombs, and the guns go off and Star shells go up. First the policemen go round on cycles with boards on their chests and backs then all the people rush down the tube station, (the boards have "Take Cover" printed on them). After it is all over the police come round again with "All Clear" on the boards then we go to bed about 2 o'c at night. Dear Edie, thank you so much for the socks they were fine. Dear sisters will you let me have a photo of each of you the latest ones you have please. I am still at engineering and I get 24/- per week. Dear Amy I cannot send postcards this time but they will follow shortly also a piece of shell shrapnel which I found during an air raid. Dear sisters I will close now with best love and a bright and Merry Xmas and a happy New Year.

From your loving brother Freddy

XXXXXXXX for all.

Thank Mrs Warby for her kindness to you for me

PS Please excuse Writing

"Everything seems to be alright over there," said Amy, looking relieved, "except for bombs still dropping around them. Freddy seems excited about it all but why on earth would I want a piece of shell shrapnel? I wonder how they're managing with Auntie Mattie not working anymore."

"Freddy might have found better work, but it must be hard on him," said Edie thoughtfully.

"He should come out here to be with us," put in Millie. Then, hopefully, "when she dies…."

"That's not nice, Millie. Only God knows when she'll die. It could be years," Amy admonished.

The subject was dropped.

It was almost Christmas again, and all the girls were enjoying the school holidays.

"The Red Cross War Effort should have all our things by now," said Jane joyfully. "Quite a basket Mrs Warby took into Armidale yesterday. Those teapot cosies you made, Edie, should sell very quickly. They were beautiful."

"I love knitting, Jane, and I'm going to send in lots more things to the Red Cross. Socks too."

"And what about the doll's clothes you made, Amy, and the aprons?" added Doris. "I wish I could sew like you."

"We're all helping," Amy said modestly, "and the bookmarks Josie coloured in are gorgeous."

"What about my scarf?" asked Millie petulantly.

Christmas Day 1916

During Christmas dinner, Amy mentioned that Freddy was now sixteen years old.

"I can't believe 1917 is startin' soon," observed Gracie, "'an a lot of us are havin' those bloomin' awful periods. You'll be soon," she said, focusing her eyes on Edie.

"Can't wait!" replied Edie, with a grimace. "Poor Amy gets cramps."

Christmas and the New Year celebrations passed quickly. School resumed in February. Amy, now fourteen and a half, spent her days assisting Jane, Gracie and Doris at the homestead. She found the work arduous and complained to Dottie Payne about the way Mr Neil had treated her when she was scrubbing the side veranda.

"He told me to give it more elbow grease, Mrs Payne, and when I asked him where it was, he laughed and shook his head. I was doing my best."

"I'm sure you were, Amy. Mr Warby was only teasing you. Elbow grease means you should give something more energy."

"I was scrubbing as hard as I could. I was tired, and he upset me."

"Forget about it, Amy. He meant no harm. Hopefully, when Edie joins you later on, the load should become easier."

The poplar trees lining each side of the driveway to the homestead were rapidly turning gold and losing their leaves. Autumn had arrived with crisper air and a promise of colder weather to come. Cosy fires were already being lit in the fireplaces in the homestead and the two cottages.

Winter arrived, and during its course, the girls would often loll on sofas on the veranda in their spare time, to soak up some warm sunshine. One day, Dottie came out for a break and joined in the conversation.

"Spring is on its way, thank goodness," Amy said. "The time has gone so quickly since last Christmas, and I'm wondering why there are no letters from anyone. We're all writing regularly. Even you, Millie."

"Well," Dottie suggested, "you once told me Freddy doesn't like writing letters; his auntie doesn't seem well, and that other lady, Aunty Esther isn't it?, is probably run off her feet helping out because of this wretched war that doesn't want to end. Don't worry. I'm sure you're not all forgotten. You'll hear from someone soon."

"The wattles are all out in the bush down there," Doris observed, changing the subject. "Anyone want to come with me for a walk to the creek? There might be some native flowers we can pick."

"I'll come," said Amy, her answer echoed by Millie.

The three girls set out and made their way to the track which led through the bush to the creek.

"Look at them all. Aren't they beautiful?" Doris marvelled as she bent her head back to admire the blossoms on one of the taller wattle trees among the grove.

"They're fluffy, little yellow balls," Millie said as she snapped off a small sprig from a lower branch. "So pretty."

"And over there I can see that bush which has the scented pink flowers," said Amy as she walked over and picked a small bunch of boronia.

"In a couple of months, it'll be getting warmer," Doris predicted, "and we can go for a swim in the creek."

"Summer's the best time," added Millie.

"And soon, it'll be Christmas again." Doris grinned.

Christmas Day 1917 and a Letter to Follow

"I wish Freddy would send us a photo of himself," complained Edie during Christmas dinner. "He's seventeen years old today, and I probably wouldn't recognise him in the street if I saw him."

A letter arrived halfway through January. It was from Aunty Esther at Whitefields.

Amy opened the envelope, read the letter and passed it to her sisters.

Whitefield's Central Mission,
Tottenham Court Road, W
Nov 30th 1917

My dear Amy, Edie & Millie

Just a line to let you know I have been thinking about you and am always glad to hear all about you and what you are doing. Aunt has shown me some very interesting letters. I am so glad to find that you are thinking of others and trying to help and relieve suffering by your many kind acts. Was glad to know Edie has been knitting socks. That is the great secret of true happiness, thinking of and helping others. There is no other way to get the very best out of this life than just to forget ourselves. By this mail I have posted three books which I hope you may like to read but it is so difficult for me to know just what you would like now, so if you don't like them still believe I have sent them as a token of love

"It's lovely to hear from her," said Edie, "and she's sending us books again, but I wish Freddy would write to us. He's lazy. It's nearly February."

"Has he forgotten he has three sisters out here?" said Amy, looking cross. "How long does he expect us to wait for a mingy letter? He turned seventeen on Christmas day, and he didn't even send a Christmas card."

"Maybe he's working hard and if he has to look after Auntie Mattie …" Millie said sagely.

"And if there's not much money for postage stamps?" added Edie, changing her former opinion about her brother. "Anyhow, let's hope we hear from him soon."

"You girls from England have got to consider what it's like over there," Dottie thought to add on overhearing. "We have plenty to eat at Balangara, but food is not abundant now in England. You see, the ships bringing supplies to England have often been attacked by German submarines called U-boats. And Britain has to send a lot of food away to feed the soldiers. They're bringing in rationing over there now and even King George and Queen Mary have volunteered to use ration cards for things like sugar, meat, flour, butter, margarine and milk. They may bring in rationing here too. Mr Warby told Mr Payne and me about all this last week. It was in the newspaper."

"Oh!, that's awful," said Doris, her mouth opening in dismay. "I've got an aunt and uncle in Manchester."

"And I wrote to everyone again a while ago in London," said Amy, looking worried. "I wish they'd let us know how they are."

The Nash girls waited patiently over the months for letters to arrive, but none came.

A Commitment

During June, after Amy's sixteenth birthday, she reminded Edie to knuckle down and learn the Catechism. All of the orphan girls at Balangara, except Millie and Josie, who were too young, were to be confirmed in their Christian faith in the Church of England Cathedral in Armidale in August. Jean and Betsy Payne were also candidates. For several Sunday mornings at the homestead, instruction had been given and recitations from memory heard from the Catechism. The girls had been fitted out with new white frocks and short veils for the upcoming event.

"This Catechism's too long," complained Edie, "I can't learn it."

"Just do it!" chastised Amy. "A little bit each day, Edie, and you'll get there."

Edie reluctantly persevered, laying aside other reading, and two days before the event, she had the Catechism off pat.

Arthur drove Eleanor Warby, Dottie, and their daughters into Armidale in Neil Warby's Dodge on the appointed day. Neil, Miss Wilma and the other five girls travelled by wagon. Other children, including boys and girls from Armidale and surrounding farms, were to be confirmed as well. It was a long and protracted ceremony but ended at last. Trestles with food and drinks were laid out in the cathedral grounds. After the refreshments, the party from Balangara was ready to leave. On arriving home, Amy made an announcement to all in the cottage.

"I'm writing a letter to Aunty Esther about what happened today. She is a Christian and will be very pleased that I've made a commitment to follow Jesus."

"I have too," echoed the other girls.

"A good decision, girls," said Dottie, smiling.

The Eleventh of November 1918

At around three o'clock on a Monday afternoon, Neil Warby came bounding down to the girl's cottage. Arthur and Dottie had not long finished their lunch when he breathlessly announced: "My friend Norm from Armidale telephoned me a short while ago. He heard it on the wireless. Note the date today! It's the eleventh day of the eleventh month, and at the eleventh hour this morning, the Germans surrendered and signed an agreement for peace. All of the nations are to stop fighting from this day forward."

Dottie leapt from her chair and almost shouted, "I can't believe it! The war's over, the war's over!"

She rushed to Arthur and gave him a huge hug, almost knocking him over.

"They're getting a treaty going which Britain, Germany, France, Italy and Russia are to sign next year sometime to formally end the war," Neil informed them, "but the great thing is, no more guns and killing from today."

"My heart aches for all our beautiful Australian men who have given their lives. Thousands and thousands of them, even boys in their teens have died," said Dottie sadly. Tears glistened in her eyes.

"Yes," Neil nodded sombrely. "Let's hope there'll never be another like it. Surely mankind will do everything they can to prevent another horrifying war like this one."

"The girls will be so thrilled to hear this news. Particularly the Nash girls. They've had relatives in London with bombs dropping all around them, and I know they've been worried," said Dottie.

"Come up to the homestead, and we'll have a celebration with a good cup of tea and some scones one of the girls was baking," Neil suggested. "It's good to share the victory with others."

It was five o'clock before the girls heard the news. They all joined hands and danced spiritedly around the dining room table, laughing with glee.

"Now everyone will have enough to eat," Jane declared, "and the rationing will stop."

"Not so soon, Jane," Arthur reminded her sombrely. "It will take time before things get back to normal but let's give thanks that there'll be no more fighting and our brave soldiers can come back home to their loved ones."

"I'm going to bake a cake," Dottie announced as she moved to the larder to get the ingredients. "We'll celebrate here with a special cake."

"Goody! Hurrah!" the girls chorused, the younger ones jumping up and down and shouting, "The war's over!"

"It'll be a far happier Christmas this year now that wretched war's over, girls. You won't have to worry about your people in England," Dottie proclaimed with a smile.

Christmas Day 1918

On Christmas Day, Amy reminded her sisters that their brother would be turning eighteen and that they hadn't heard from him for two years.

Then halfway through January 1919 Dottie handed Amy a letter when she and Edie returned from their duties at the homestead.

"It's about time. Nearly a year since we've heard from anyone at all," muttered Edie. "Who's it from? Freddy, I hope."

"It's from Aunty Esther," Amy said, noting the Whitefields address at the top of the page. "Come over and I'll read it out to you."

Edie and Millie sat on the sofa on the veranda with Amy in the middle.

Nov. 28th 1918

My dear Friends,

I ought to have written to you all before but I want to assure you that I very much valued your letter it was so full of interest but this year I have not been well and have had to be away rather more than usual. My friends have all been rather neglected but you have been thought of very often. Now our great joyful Festival is close upon us. How glad we shall be this year that the last gun has been fired and that the message of peace and goodwill will mean much more to us this year than it has done for the last few years. I expect you did something to celebrate the great event. For my part the most fitting thing seemed to be to sing the Doxology.

"I hope Freddy will come out here now the war's over," said Edie hopefully. "Wouldn't it be lovely if we could all be together again?"

"Maybe he could get a job on the station here. He's eighteen now, and …" Amy hesitated, then added with a note of frustration, "well, maybe he can't come. Aunty Esther said Auntie Mattie's not well and never will be. I suppose he must be there to help her."

"Why can't Hilary help?" Eddie said cuttingly.

"Aunty Esther said the time would come when she could. But *when*?" asked Amy.

"If she's not well she may not last much longer," added Millie with a blank expression.

"Don't say that, Millie," Amy cautioned. "It's in God's hands when anyone goes."

A Chat With Gladys

Eleanor Warby and her friend Gladys settled themselves comfortably on the cane chairs on the front veranda and waited for the girls to serve afternoon tea.

"Can you believe it's almost April 1919, Eleanor? How quickly the time has passed since Christmas. This week has been lovely. Thank you so much for having me, but I'll have to leave before it gets dark. You know I still fail to understand how you manage all your affairs so well and make prize jams too."

"Only with the help of Neil. He's in charge now and keeps an eye on the other properties too."

Jane and Gracie soon arrived with trays and set down the refreshments on the table.

"Thank you, girls," Eleanor said a little dismissively. "The nut loaf looks very nice."

The girls left with a slight bob and Eleanor turned to her friend.

"I think the experiment's worked well. There are five of them now working here in the house and only two still at school, along with some other children from nearby farms. Wilma's done a lovely job. The girls who've left school have all attained a good standard in the subjects set out by the Education Department by leaving age."

"Those two girls who served us tea, Eleanor … they seem to have good manners and both of them are most attractive. They're going to make good wives one day and have many children. Australian children!"

"Yes, Jane is a lovely young woman, although a bit bossy with the others at times, but she is the oldest at twenty. And that Gracie! She's nineteen now and has shaped up very well over the last year. A rough diamond when she first came here, swearing and crude, but she speaks well now. I'd almost given up hope, but the perfect lady today, with only an occasional slip."

"What about the others?"

"Little Doris, short and dumpy but a sweet soul. Always eager to please, but Wilma says she can be sulky sometimes. She's nineteen too."

"And those sisters from London. What are they like?"

"Well the eldest one, Amy, is a family girl. She'll be seventeen in June. Quite gentle in fact and still very tied to her roots. Always longing to get news from England as she has a brother, an aunt, a cousin and a church worker over there and some distant relatives, I think. Always writing home she is. Her parents are gone, of course, her mother dying in 1914. I don't think she's fully recovered from the news of her death, in my opinion. It was a huge shock.

"Edith, or Edie, the middle one, is the beauty of the three. Dark hair and large bluey green eyes, unlike her sisters who are blonde and blue-eyed. I imagine the boys will swarm around that one. She can be quite wilful, almost rebellious and I have the feeling she'll be the first one to leave Balangara. She's fifteen in September.

"The youngest one, Millie, turns twelve in September. Looks a bit like Amy, but has a fuller face. She has more delicate health than her sisters and was ill with scarlet fever in London and also bronchitis. She's a good scholar like her sisters and is an obedient child and well-liked. She and Josie, the youngest, are good friends.

"And Josie?" asked Gladys.

"After a very bad start with that dreadful Wilcox woman who frightened her, she is today a happy young girl who has adjusted well. In hindsight, she was too young to send out here at aged four and a half, but Dorothy Payne has been the perfect replacement mother, and I notice Josie hangs around her a lot.

"The girls are having a social life of sorts. We have young people from outlying farms who come here and play tennis with them on

Saturday afternoons. Picnics sometimes, one to the Ebor Falls not long ago, but the older girls need more social outlets, so I'm going to talk to some people in the district and get regular bush dances going in the old woolshed in one of the paddocks."

"What a wonderful idea, Eleanor. The eldest three girls are already old enough to find husbands," Gladys noted with a knowing smile.

"Not quite yet, I hope," answered Eleanor.

"I'd better get going, Eleanor. It's been lovely seeing you again."

The two women embraced and promised to keep in touch by telephone.

Gladys left in her newly purchased little automobile to drive back to Guyra, and Eleanor walked from the veranda into the lounge room, leaving Jane and Gracie to clean up the remains of afternoon tea.

Poor Auntie Mattie

As Amy returned early from her duties at the homestead, Dottie waved a letter in Amy's face, which was eagerly snatched.

"It's from Freddy, finally, Mrs Payne," she announced happily as she opened the page.

59 Warren Street,
Tott. Ct. Rd. NW1
31.1.19

Dear Amy, Edie & Millie

I am very sorry I have not written to you before but I have to put in so many hours at work. I am very sorry to have to tell you that Aunt died on the 29th December 1918 after a few days illness, it happened quite unexpected but she was always ill more or less. We all had notice to leave 57 Warren St. as the lease had expired so I am now living with my chum's mother at 59 Warren Street. I am still at the same place of work and getting fairly good money and I am in very good health as I hope you are. Please excuse a short letter as I have not much time. I am on night work. When next you write please address envelope:-

> *F. Nash*
> *C/o Mrs Winsor*
> *59 Warren St.*
> *Tottenham Ct. Rd. NW1*

Edie returned from the homestead a while later, and Amy lifted Freddy's letter as she approached.

"Sit down, Edie. I've got some sad news," she announced seriously.

"Is Freddy alright? Is that a letter from him?"

"He's okay, but Auntie Mattie passed away just after Christmas on the 29th of December after a few days sickness. He didn't say much else."

"I'm sad to hear that, Amy. I hope she didn't suffer. She loved us, you know. We're losing everyone over there. There's only Freddy, Hilary and Aunty Esther left but she isn't a real aunty, is she?"

"As good as, Edie. She was always there for our parents and us. And even now we're out here, she still takes an interest … those lovely books she sent us at Christmas. And she prays for us too, each day. Our other relatives in England hardly ever came near us when we were back there. And I often wonder about Grandma in Clapham. I wouldn't know whether she's alive or dead today."

"She's probably gone too, Amy. She would have been very old. I wish Freddy would come out here."

"He's moved in next door to live with his best chum and his mother, a lady called Mrs Winsor. Here, read the letter yourself."

Amy gave Edie Freddy's letter.

"Millie hardly knew Auntie Mattie. We'll tell her when she gets home from school," said Edie.

When Millie returned, she expressed the appropriate words of sorrow and then quickly enquired about Freddy's news.

"He can come out here now," she said, an expectant smile on her face.

"We'll see what happens," said Amy quietly. "In his letter, he said he'd be writing again soon to explain everything."

"He's free, now poor Aunty Mattie's gone. He's got a job. I hope he's been saving up," said Edie.

A month passed, and no further letter arrived from Freddy with any plan to join his sisters.

With disappointment, the girls settled down to their usual routines.

Bush Dances

Eleanor Warby's plans were gathering momentum. She was bent on getting bush dances going for the young people in the district and the girls in her care. Neil had been instructed to renovate the old woolshed and had sent some workmen to carry out repairs to the roof. Then he'd had the shearing booths dismantled and filled in some missing floorboards. Wooden benches had been installed around two sides of the hall and a small stage at one end laid down for the musicians. Finally, the shed had been thoroughly cleaned and every stray bit of fleece removed. The floorboards on the dancing area were sanded, stained and polished.

"It's ready now, Mother," Neil announced near the end of April. "You can start organising things straight away."

"I'm getting Arthur to drive me into Armidale and Guyra tomorrow to advertise our first dance in the newspaper for June, and I'm going to the Cathedral. There'll be many from there who'll want to come. And all our workers here at Balangara have families too. We'll need a pianist, a fiddler and I'm sure old Mervyn, who dips the sheep, can play that piano accordion of his. Get a tin whistler someone said. I've got hold of some sheet music of Australian folk songs and even some Irish and American ones. You've heard some of them on our gramophone, Neil, like *The Wild Colonial Boy* and *Waltzing Matilda*."

"What about the dances, Mum? How will people know how to do them?"

"Some people would already know how, but the dances are easy to learn as they go, and a lot of oldies who know them from their younger days can walk others through them. Dances like *The Dashing White*

Sergeant and *Strip the Willow* and *The Barn Dance* are great fun and there'll be ballroom items too like *The Pride of Erin* and the *Waltz*. I'd like you to be the MC and Caller, Neil."

"Oh!" said Neil, taken aback, "I'm not sure about that."

"Neil, you'll enjoy it."

"Well, I suppose so," Neil agreed reluctantly. "You usually get what you want, Mum."

The news of the impending entertainment to be held in the old woolshed in the second paddock spread around Balangara and well beyond. Dottie Payne told the girls in their cottage.

"We'll wear our white frocks, Edie," Amy suggested. "They're our best."

"I'm not!" insisted Edie. "I'm wearing my floral blouse and my navy-blue skirt."

"I'm wearing my blue dress," stated Millie, "and blue ribbons in my hair."

The young people waited impatiently for Saturday, the 14th of June. When it arrived, straggling trails of people made their way to the shed along well-worn tracks from former shearers. By five o'clock, a large assembly had gathered and were tucking into sandwiches, cakes and drinks laid out on tables inside and outside the shed. The bush dance was scheduled to start at six, giving time for the people from Armidale, Guyra, Ebor and other towns to travel back before midnight, after the dance had ended.

Right on the dot of six o'clock Neil mounted the stage and gave his official welcome, then announced that the First Quarterly Woolshed Dance was about to start. He stepped down from the stage and the musicians stepped up.

In the packed hall, everyone waited for the music to begin. With a sudden thumping of the rhythm on the floor with their feet, the musicians began their routine. An introductory rendition of *Polly Wollie Doodle* echoed around the hall, and the elderly folk who knew the words joined in, singing.

After the first musical item, Neil shouted above the noisy

excitement, "Would you please now take your partners for the Progressive Barn Dance."

A tall, dark-haired youth walked across the floor and stood in front of Amy, extending his hand.

"Thank you," she said as she walked with him onto the floor. The dance got underway.

"I'm loving it, Edie," she proclaimed with shining eyes, when she returned to her seat after the item had finished. "It wasn't hard to learn either."

"It was great fun," agreed Edie, "but the boy who asked me wasn't as good looking as your one."

After a short interval, the *Pride of Erin* was announced. The same young man strode over and asked Amy again to partner him. She accepted and rose to her feet.

"By the way, my name's Jim. What's yours?" he asked Amy with a smile.

"I'm Amy, and I've never been to a dance before so I hope you won't find me clumsy."

"You did alright in the 'Barn Dance'," Jim answered with a twinkle in his eye. "I'll teach you how to do this one."

There'd been no shortage of young lads competing to dance with Edie as a small gathering had swarmed around her. She'd mastered the Barn Dance almost straight away, and had decided to accept the offer of a different fellow for each new number. In the meantime, she watched Amy and Jim closely. She'd previously noticed the young man staring at Amy when the introductory item was being played and had come to the conclusion that he fancied her sister. This was confirmed later on when he'd invited Amy to partner him for the third time, for the *Viennese Waltz*.

"You got the hang of it in no time, Amy," said Edie after the waltz had finished. "I was watching you now and again."

"He's a good teacher, Edie," replied Amy.

"And good looking too. Why don't you go after him, and marry him, eh? You're seventeen now. Old enough. That'd get you out of

Balangara, and you wouldn't have to work so hard anymore."

"Shut up, Edie, you're being stupid."

Edie, duly silenced, continued to enjoy the evening's program from the folk singing items to the square dancing and the traditional ballroom dancing.

At the end of the night, everyone stood and sang *God save the King*, and a short speech from Neil wished people 'God Speed' on their way back home.

The girls walked back to the cottage amid much chatter and Dottie Payne got some hot cocoa going on the stove.

"That was a nice young man who asked you to dance, Amy," she remarked. "He seemed quite taken with you."

"Oh! it's nothing," replied Amy, blushing slightly. "He's a jackeroo, and I'll probably never see him again."

Amy felt flattered after the night's events, particularly as Jim had asked *her* to dance and not Edie, who was prettier. She resolved to tell Freddy all about the dance and Jim's attention in her next letter to him, which she would write in a couple of days. He would want to know about all the exciting things happening lately at Balangara.

Over the next few months, Jim occasionally called in at the cottage, and he and Amy had sometimes walked around the property and down to the willow tree near the creek.

Reviewing the budding friendship, Amy decided not to allow things to go any further, realising that, although he was a 'nice boy', he was not 'the one' for her. And how could she leave her sisters here anyhow, particularly Millie. The time had not yet come to think of romance, so she called off the budding friendship, much to Jim's regret.

Two Lengthy Letters

There was still no letter from Freddy, and Millie was becoming impatient.

"Why won't Freddy write to us? It was last March when we got his last letter, and it's nearly October. I want to know when he's coming out."

"Well, remember Auntie Mattie once told us he was a lazy letter writer, Millie. He usually writes just before Christmas so we should hear from him before long, I hope. I wonder how he's getting on with that new family he's living with? I hope everything's alright there," Amy replied, with a frown.

"He'll be nineteen years old on Christmas Day, and I haven't seen him since I was six. Edie's just had her fifteenth birthday, and I've just turned twelve," added Millie petulantly.

"And I'm seventeen," declared Amy.

"You'll be married before he gets out here, with kids, I'll bet," said Edie, with big popping eyes.

"Shut up, Edie. That won't be for years, if it ever happens!" Amy looked annoyed.

"Only teasing," Edie replied.

True to Amy's prediction, a letter from Freddy arrived at the beginning of November. There was also another letter enclosed.

"Who's that one from?" enquired Edie.

"It's from Mrs Winsor, that lady he lives with," answered Amy.

As usual, the Nash girls sat on the cottage veranda to read their letters, starting with Freddy's.

12.9.19   *59 Warren St.*
Tottenham Ct. Rd.
London NW1

My dear Sisters,

I was so glad to get your letters and to hear you are all well and happy. Now that I have started writing I will make it a long letter. I am a very bad hand at writing as you know. I am very pleased with your fortnightly letters and I always look forward to them. I am not an Electrical Engineer any longer. The war contracts were stopped by the government in March which meant that 60 Boys and Girls were thrown out of work. I was one of them. I was 14 weeks out of work and had to spend the money I had saved for every day necessities and if it had not have been for Mrs Winsor I should have been without food. I am greatly in her debt, altogether there are a few million people out of work in England, half of them live in London. After 14 weeks I found a little job in an engineer's shop. After 8 weeks the owner who is a Belgian sold the firm and has gone back to Belgium. I tried to join the Army and Navy but I have a hammer toe and the doctors will not pass me for either branch of the services so I am still out of work. I have also tried to get work in foreign countries through agencies in England but it is no go. And if I go on like this I shall be in Australia in 1990. I never get any letters from relatives in England not even Hilary. It does not trouble them how I am getting on and I am sure I don't want them to trouble Mr and Mrs Winsor who are my greatest friends, a second mother and father. I would like you to write to them. I know you have never seen them but that does not matter. I am glad to hear you like the Australian life and the boys. You seem to have a great many pleasures which is good. I cannot dance but I can play football and cricket. I can also swim about a mile and a half. The Flu has come and gone and I only had a very slight taste of it. You are getting tall I can see by your photos. I am very tall I am 5ft 10 ½ inches. How I would like to see you again after all these years. I will send you a photo of me next time I write and as I am going to write oftener that will be soon. I should love to get a letter from dear little Millie so will you please ask her to write me one. I am glad you have a photo of Dad, I have one which is being enlarged. I have also one of Aunt but I must have that if I can and will have it reproduced so that I can send you one.

Dearest Amy, I went to Australia House which is the government house of Australia in London and asked if I could emigrate to Aussy but they said there will be no emigration for a very long time and the only way I could get to Australia would be to pay my own passage out and then I would have to be nominated by you first. But I have spent my savings so I must wait. I am sorry. I should very much like to meet Jim, perhaps I will when I get out there. I hope so. Well I think I will end now as I cannot think very well today. I am a bit worried so 'Au revoir' and don't kiss Jim too much and leave none for me when I get there. With fondest and best love to you all, not forgetting the loads of kisses.

From your ever loving brother Freddy. XXXXXX

After Freddy's letter, the three girls expressed disappointment that he was not getting ready to come to Australia.

"I can't get over those people in Australia House in England refusing to help him join us," said Amy crossly. "After all, you'd think they'd want a family to be reunited, wouldn't you, particularly as he's on his own now?"

"Especially as they were the ones to send us out here away from our family when we didn't even want to go," added Edie.

"He's having a hard time being out of work, and he seemed a bit down at the end of the letter," continued Amy, her brows creasing.

"Well at least he's got that nice lady next door looking after him, and he's not starving," said Millie reassuringly.

"You know what?" Amy decided. "Every day, we'll get together and pray for our brother and ask the Lord to help him get back on his feet and find a good job, eh?"

"Yes!" agreed Edie and Millie together.

Amy unfolded the letter from Mrs Winsor, and the others waited attentively to hear what Amy read.

59 Warren Street
Tottenham Court Road
London W
12 Sept. 1919

Dear Miss Nash,

I think it is quite time I wrote to you myself as I have asked Freddy so many times to write almost begged him to do so but of course boy-like he keeps putting it off till another time. I know he has written now but boys do not tell you all and I think you ought to know a little about him. He has got such a fine fellow 5 feet 10 ½ inches high and 10 stone six in weight, so if ever he comes to Australia you will all be very proud of him. His misfortune is his work and they are offering such low wages that if he was with strangers I do not know where he would be for I have never charged him a farthing for lodging and as little for his food as possible so that he should have a chance to get on, and whether he is in work or out of work he never goes hungry. I have 3 boys and a girl of my own and I have always done my best for Freddy and when he comes to you one day which I know he very much wants to he will tell you that I am speaking the truth. I told him the other day that you would be wondering what was the matter with him as he did not write and I said then your sisters are probably thinking all manner of things. I do not know what Freddy has written but I must tell you this Miss Nash that not one person belonging to Freddy or anybody that knows him has been here to see him or has written to him. I suppose they all think as Sister Hester said to me when I spoke up for Freddy, that he was a boy and could rough it. I told her true he was a boy and could knock about better than a girl but even so a boy wants a home and his washing and mending done. Freddy says himself I have been more than his own mother to him. I do not know whether he has told you he gave his aunt a respectable funeral. Sister Hester upset him very much when he went to her about poor Mrs Harrison's death, told him to get the cheapest funeral possible and he was not to touch a thing in the place. He had no such thought in his head I know for I have known him for 6 or 8 years, being my eldest boy's chum for years. I was with your aunt almost to the last and I believe he would have let Sister Hester carry it all through if she had not spoken so nasty to him, but of course he has a little will of his own, and he said if I would help him he would bury her himself so that it should be respectable and I can assure you it was, a few neighbours sent flowers and we all subscribed and she had 3 very nice wreaths and was laid to rest in a proper manner. She is much better off Miss Nash for she had suffered for years. I asked Freddy to come and share Sonny's room while his aunt *lay dead and when he asked me if I would let him stay altogether so I done the best I could to make room for his few things he had and I am sure he is quite happy as regards himself and me. I am hoping he will soon get some work, that is his only misfortune but still I will do the best I can for him until he does. My husband and I are only working people, so cannot do all one would like to. I must tell you also about your Aunt's cousin. She came while poor Aunt lay dead. I made her as welcome as I could and she was here for 2 or 3 hours talking to Freddy in one of my other rooms and when she went she thanked me so much for promising to look after Freddy but she has never been here since to see whether the boy is alive or dead. I do not think it very kind of her and the other relations in the country could not come so they wrote and told Freddy, so somebody had to do something for him. I hope you will not think I am writing this because I want to talk about it or want a lot of thanks, but I think it is time you knew the facts. If you should doubt my words Freddy will verify what I say. I am pleased to know you and your sisters are getting on so well and are so happy. You will be very pleased with Freddy when you do see him. I will persuade him to have his photo taken later on so you can see for yourself. I shall be pleased to hear from you if you care to write to me or you can send a message in Freddy's letter. I hope the next time you hear from him he will have good news for you. I must tell you he is also in splendid health, never has anything the matter with him, plays football and altogether is alright except misfortune in work. I expect you are tired of this letter so will now close.*

With very kind regards to your sisters and yourself.

Yours very sincerely, A. Winsor

"What a wonderful lady," said Amy after she'd placed Mrs Winsor's letter on the table. "That really eases my mind that someone has cared enough about him to take him in, especially when our relations didn't give a hoot. They never cared about Mummy either. But you know, Freddy will probably not like having to rely on someone else so we must earnestly pray that a good job turns up. One that he'll enjoy."

"Yes," Millie added, "and he gave Auntie a lovely funeral too."

"Those people, the Winsors, must have a bigger place than just two rooms," said Amy. Then she made a resolution. "I'm going to write to Mrs Winsor tomorrow and let her know how much we appreciate her kindness to our brother by taking him in."

That evening, the Nash sisters shared the news about Freddy around the dinner table.

"He'll be nineteen on Christmas Day too," announced Edie.

"Nineteen on Christmas Day?" Dottie Payne repeated, her eyebrows raised. "Good Lord! How time flies, eh? And we've had two bush dances since they started and it's already November. There's another dance coming up soon after Christmas, and it's almost upon us."

"I can't wait for Mr Warby to take us into Armidale in the buggy to do our Christmas shopping with the pocket money we've saved. I'm buying Colin a book on fishing. He loves going to Sawtell to fish off the beach," announced Gracie, who was being courted by a young man she'd met at the first bush dance.

"I'm buying Amy an autograph book. They have ones with different coloured pages. Miss Wilma asked me to write something in hers," said Edie.

"Enough chatter girls. Off to bed," Dottie insisted. "It's ten o'clock already. Tomorrow is another day."

Christmas Day 1919

"It's been a lovely Christmas Day," a smiling Amy said after the celebrations had come to an end.

"One thing I'll say about here," added Edie, "we've always had very happy Christmases and …"

"I hope Freddy's having a nice one over there," interrupted Millie, "and I hope he gets a good job in the new year. He's nineteen today, and that lady who looks after him said he's very handsome."

The festive season soon passed, and no further letters from Freddy arrived, but one turned up at the end of January 1920 from Aunty Esther. She'd written at the beginning of December shortly before Christmas. Amy opened the letter.

Dec 3 1919

My dear friends,

Although my letters to you have been so few and far between yet yours to me have been very much appreciated. I was looking at Amy's photo the other day and felt so glad you had thought of sending it to me. I am very glad to know about all your doings because from them I can learn very much about you. I had the pleasure of seeing Hilary in September. She looks well, is stout and thick set. She is passionately fond of children and is anxious to be a children's nurse as she is fond of needlework and rather clever too. I think she will be most successful. At present she is under nurse in the

"Aunty Esther had a lot to say about Hilary. I remember she loved playing with smaller kids when we were back home, and d'you know, I think the best thing for her was when she got away from 57 Warren Street and went to that orphanage in Birmingham. Auntie was so cranky at times, and Granny was unwell," said Edie.

"It must have been hard for everyone back home then, Edie. We have it easier out here than they've had, but given the choice, I would never have volunteered to leave our family. I would have stayed in England through thick and thin," Amy emphasised. "And I wonder why Aunty Esther has never said anything about Mummy," she added. "Did she see her when she came back to London to die? Did she know what happened to her after she left London to find work in Northampton?"

"We'll never know," Edie answered frankly. "I suppose it will always be a mystery."

"I'm glad we've got that photo of her. Wasn't she lovely? You know, one day I'm going to have it specially framed and hung up somewhere where we can always see her," Amy promised, looking wistful.

"That'll be nice, Amy. I miss her as much as you, you know."

Greener Pastures for Jane

The months passed quickly, and all the girls were busily occupied in their various roles. Millie and Josie were still at school while the five older girls carried out their assigned chores at the homestead. Mrs Warby was looking ahead, realising she'd be short of girls once the older ones left Balangara. She started making enquiries overseas and was keen to rescue a few Scottish girls this time, after reading about the appalling conditions of the poor in Glasgow.

Jane was the first to leave. She'd been transferred to a smaller pastoral holding of Eleanor Warby's, as housekeeper for her other son and his wife, and nursemaid for their baby. Jane hadn't been there long when a young accountant had turned up to collect some books for auditing. He'd noticed a tall, willowy young woman with curly brown hair and a ready smile. She'd been taking the baby for a walk in a stroller, and had joined her. He became a frequent visitor, and after a short while and to everyone's surprise, Jane abruptly left her job and married the young man. The newlyweds had settled in Armidale. Gracie had replaced Jane at the farm.

On a Saturday afternoon, Doris, Amy and Edie had returned to the cottage after their lunch in the kitchen at the homestead, when they heard the news.

"Good on her! She's out of here," Edie declared triumphantly. "I wish I was old enough to do the same, to leave somehow, I mean. You'll be eighteen in June, Amy. Can't you find someone? Someone at the dances like Jim. You should have got off with him."

Amy bristled. "I wish you'd mind your own business, Edie. Shut up, won't you? If I'm meant to get married, I will. Until then, I'm happy to wait for the right man to come along. I've told you before, Jim wasn't the one."

"Don't have such a thin skin, Amy. I wasn't serious. But really, wouldn't it be marvellous to escape from here. With Jane and Gracie not living in the cottage now and only you, me and Doris to do all the work in the homestead, we never get a break. I promise you, by the time I'm your age, I'll be getting out of here. The world's a bigger place than just Balangara homestead, you know."

"I know that, Edie," Amy replied wearily. "There's not much time for anything but cooking and housework, is there? But we must look ahead. Things will change for us in a few years. They'll have to. I'm almost eighteen now, and you're going on sixteen."

"And Millie's nearly thirteen. She'll be leaving school and helping us out soon. That'll make a difference, I suppose," added Edie, suddenly trying to look on the bright side to please her sister.

"Mrs Payne told me that Mrs Warby wants to bring out some Scottish girls to replace us when we leave one day. She said it would take some time for them to arrive," said Amy. "I hope it won't be too long. Jane's already gone, and Gracie's taken up *her* job."

"They don't know what they're in for, Amy, poor things," Edie said, pulling a face.

"They'll certainly have to earn their keep, Edie, but what they're leaving might be worse than what they're coming to, you know."

"Well, that might be true," Edie agreed somewhat reluctantly.

Christmas Day 1920

"He's twenty today," announced Edie at the table during Christmas dinner, "and next Christmas he'll be twenty-one. An official adult! Do you think he'll write to us more often then?"

"Hopefully," Amy replied. "In his last letter he promised to write soon, but it's been ages again. I worry about him getting work. He seemed a bit down in his last letter. We must start praying again for him, for things to change."

"Yes, we must," agreed Edie and Millie.

"I hope you hear some good news soon, girls. Something's bound to turn up, I'm sure," Dottie said encouragingly.

A few days later, Amy was handed a letter. She opened it with trepidation as it was from Freddy and she remembered the depressing contents of his last letter. She read it alone and later handed it, smiling, to her sisters.

59 Warren St.
Tottenham Court Road
London NW1

8th November 1920

Dear Amy, Edie & Millie,

At last I am writing to you, about time, Eh? I was ever so pleased to get your letter and know you are getting on so well. I'm very sorry to hear of Millie's catarrh and sincerely hope she soon gets rid of it. You all seem to have plenty of amusement, dances, concerts and goodness knows what else. I hope you will always have plenty too.

As for dancing I'm out of it. I don't even know a step of the simplest dance let alone Waltz's & One Steps but I may learn some day, one never knows. We are just starting winter here and are in the midst of Fog and Frost. I have been in employment now for a considerable time, about 10 months. Guess what I am this time? You can't? Well I am now a fireman not a household fireman but a railway fireman, of Course. I have been an Engine cleaner and have been promoted to fireman and I like the work very much indeed. It is very pleasant to be on an engine stoking and keeping a lookout for signals. I should very much like to stick to the job, don't get the wind up and think I do not mean to come to Aussi-land as we call Australia because I hope to some day. I have been on odd jobs lately because of coal strike and our train was cut out of the time-table, but the strike is over now I am glad to say. I get very good wages considering and I am going to start to save a bit now that I have pulled myself round and paid all my debts and re rigged myself out. I am very much afraid it will be a long time before I come out to you there is no emigration except to discharged or demobbed soldiers and sailors as yet but still I don't give in and hope to be out there some day. The next time I write I will send you two photos. I cannot send them now as they will not be home in time for this mail.

Well Dear Sisters by the time you receive this letter it will be Christmas so I will wish you all a very merry Christmas & a bright and Prosperous New Year. I have not heard from Hilary once. I am still living with Mrs Winsor & I am quite content. Mrs Winsor sends you her love and wishes you a very merry Christmas and says she will write to you soon. She has such a lot to do that

"That's the best Christmas present we could have," declared Amy. "He's got a job, and he loves it too. Riding on trains! I remember back in England he had a wooden toy engine which he got when he was a little boy. I think Mummy bought it for him when they went to a fair somewhere."

"And he's still with that nice lady next door and getting a good wage," Edie added, looking pleased, "and he's rigged himself out with new clothes. He'll look so handsome and …."

"Now he can save up and come out here," said Millie, interrupting and beaming.

"What else?" asked Amy with a serious expression. "What else should we be thankful for?"

"He's healthy and he's not starving," offered Edie.

"I don't know what else," puzzled Millie.

There was a pause in the conversation.

"All of those things are true," said Amy, ending the pause, "but the important thing to remember is that Jesus has answered all our prayers for Freddy and we don't have to worry about him anymore. We should give Him thanks for His faithfulness."

"That's true," Millie agreed. "He does answer prayer." Then, after another pause, she added crossly, "He's already been working for ten months. He's so naughty. He should have told us before this."

"Doesn't matter," joined in Edie. "Our prayers for him will always continue."

Six weeks after Christmas, Amy received a letter from Aunty Esther.

Whitefields
Tottenham Ct. Rd.
Dec. 15th 1920

My dear Amy,

I am again hopelessly behind with my letters. The Festive Season is close upon us. I have hoped for time but here so many other things turn up, but never the less you are very often in my thoughts. I wonder if Freddy writes to you often. I have not seen him for a very long time. The person with whom he lives told me he works hard and is very tired. Now that Hilary is at Golder's Green I am able to see her some times. I think she is very well and happy. She has grown tall and rather stout. She is very quick and observant. I have tried to picture you in your beautiful country home and rejoice to know

"She's woken up memories of our lives back then," Amy said pensively, "but I don't remember skating. We never did that."

"She didn't say much about Freddy except that she hasn't seen him for ages. And she wonders if he writes to us often," said Edie.

"Not often enough," insisted Millie, "but he's got a good job now and saving up to come out here."

"She talked about us using our abilities in her letter. Apart from learning how to scrub and scour and cook for other people, I haven't discovered what my other abilities could be," Edie said, scowling.

"We wouldn't have done much better back home, Edie. But you've become an excellent knitter and are using that talent to donate things to the Red Cross. That must give you satisfaction."

"Well, I suppose so …" Edie shrugged. "… and I have to say that your dressmaking talents are beginning to pay off. You've had two orders so far for Mrs Warby's granddaughters for frocks. How you manage that treadle machine I don't know. I couldn't."

"Just practice and determination," Amy replied with a smile.

"I'd still love to learn the piano," said Edie, quietly.

Mrs Winsor's Revealing Letter

The beginning of April was unusually hot, and the Nash girls had gone down to the creek for a swim after their work at the homestead was finished. When they returned to the cottage, Amy found a letter lying on her bed, placed there by Dottie Payne.

"It's from Mrs Winsor. She's answering my letter. I'll read it aloud."

59 Warren Street,
Tottenham Ct. Rd.
London

Feb. 12/21

My dear Amy,

I was very pleased to hear from you and you really must forgive me not writing but I have such a little time to spare. I daresay you got Freddy's letter at Xmas, he put a message in for me. No doubt you understand Amy when there is 7 of us to do for washing and everything and then I have this house to keep clean, you can guess I have not much time. However you write to me whenever you like. I shall always be pleased to hear from you. I will now answer the question in your letter first. I have asked Freddy so many times if he has written to you and he always said, no, I have not said anything to him for some time before he wrote at Xmas. I tell him it is very neglectful and thoughtless as you might think I keep him from writing. He has plenty of time also for the menfolk now only do eight hours a day. Now about him coming to Australia, he often used to speak of going to you when first he came with me and in my opinion I think it would be very nice for you all to be together Amy. What Freddy's intentions are now I do not know, but not a soul troubles about him but myself. I do not know what he told you about it when he wrote, but I do know that he has not got any money saved for it, for only today my husband and myself had to talk to him, for if he falls out of work again I do not know what will happen to him, for I shall not do as I done before. He is earning good money and has been on the Railway 16 months so I think he ought to have a little don't you, but when lads get to his age they cannot bear anyone to give them sound advice. I do not want to boast Amy, but I don't think many would have got up in all weathers at 5 o clock to call him. I have done it to help him get on. I got another room for Freddy and my Sonny so that they have got a nice room between them and Freddy has only 2 shillings a week to pay for it which is very cheap. I hope you will not think I am speaking against him Amy but I told him I should tell you the exact truth and he said he did not mind. I expect if he loses his work he will be trying to come to you then by some means. Now about Hilary, I happened to meet Sister Hester this week, the second time since poor Aunt died, and she asked me to tell Freddy that Hilary was at Hampstead not far from here. I told Freddy but what he will do I do not know. Hilary only gets out once a month and then has to be very particular where she goes on account of taking anything infectious back to the little ones. She is getting on very well so Sister Hester said. I am so pleased to think you and your sisters are so happy and comfortable. I often think it would be nice for Freddy to

Amy put the letter down firmly and looked at her sisters with an exasperated expression.

"I'm disappointed in him. To think he's been working at the Railways for sixteen months now and hasn't saved up any money to get out here. And I can sense Mrs Winsor is getting fed up. He's always been talking about coming to Australia, but he's not doing anything about it."

"Mrs Winsor is a saint, getting up at 5 o'clock to get him off to work and all that, and looking after him the way she does," said Edie, exasperated.

"And what if he loses that job on the railways like the lady said? She said she wouldn't help him again. What would happen to him then?" asked Millie, looking troubled.

"Goodness only knows," replied Amy, taking a deep breath and sighing, "but I'm going to write to Mrs Winsor tomorrow and tell her I would like her to be more strict with Freddy and let him know how he's disappointed us. We've been looking forward to seeing him for ages. And I'll write to him too and give him the rounds of the kitchen."

After Amy had written her letter to Mrs Winsor, she felt satisfied that it would placate the lady somewhat. It had been a difficult task.

On the one hand, Amy was genuinely grateful for Mrs Winsor having taken her brother in as she and her sisters were worried about him and his future. On the other hand, she was embarrassed by Freddy taking advantage of the Winsors, as it appeared, and not trying to further his cause of coming to Australia. She then wrote a stern letter to Freddy.

"The letters will be going with the post tomorrow, and I hope things will settle down now at the Winsor's place, and Freddy will be more responsible," she told her sisters. "Now I'm going to make a cup of tea."

Thinking About the Future

Two months later, on the 6th June, Dottie carried out Amy's birthday cake and summoned the other girls for the celebration.

"Nineteen tomorrow, Amy," she announced, smiling. "What plans do you have for the future, my dear? Staying on here? Mrs Warby wouldn't mind, you know."

"I'm staying on here for a while, Mrs Payne, before I leave. I know I could get a bigger wage outside, but Millie is joining us at the homestead in a few days. I want to keep an eye on her because she's not as strong as Edie and me and I'll speak up for her if she's being overtaxed."

"Good idea, Amy. You're a good sister," said Dottie, giving Amy a couple of pats on her upper arm.

"We're all she has now, Mrs Payne, except for Freddy overseas and Aunty Esther."

After the birthday celebration, the Nash girls walked out to the veranda to relax for a while with some pastimes. Amy started reading a new Jane Austen novel presented to her for her birthday, and Edie attempted to master the art of crochet. Millie wandered off somewhere with Josie.

"Amy," Edie said, interrupting her as she started the novel, "you'll never have to stay on here because of me. I'll be here for a while yet because I have to, but at the first opportunity, I'll be off."

"Well, you'll be seventeen in three months, and Millie will be fourteen. I suppose in a couple of years everything can change, can't it?" Amy noted.

"It had better," Edie replied.

"Do you realise we've been here for over seven years, Edie?"

"I wonder where we'll be in seven years from now. You and Millie will be married with kids, I'll bet."

"Why not you too, Edie? Wouldn't you like that one day?"

"One day, I suppose. But I'm tired of looking after other people. Marriage can wait as far as I'm concerned. I want to have piano lessons and go to plays. And go down to Sydney and see the sights, you know … see a bit more of life apart from around here and Armidale. But you'll get married, I'm sure, Amy. You're born to have a family, and there's nothing wrong with that. You're like granny back home. Remember her? Everyone said family was everything to her. She was lovely, wasn't she?"

"She was," Amy agreed softly, "and I take it as a compliment to be compared to her."

"Anyhow, I'm getting out of here as soon as I can," Edie vowed. "You can bet on that."

"Speaking of family, Edie, the last letter we got from Freddy was last November. He promised to write to us again shortly afterwards."

"We shouldn't have depended on that," Edie replied. "Maybe he didn't like you giving him the rounds of the kitchen in your last letter to him."

"Well, I told him if he wants to come out here he's got to be more responsible and start saving. I hope he keeps that job on the railways though. Even so, Edie, I do worry about him. In spite of everything, we really have it much better than he does, don't we?"

"We've never had bombs dropping around us, that's true, and we never go hungry, but there's times I've felt like a caged animal. At least Freddy can go where he wants."

"Edie, try to be grateful. I can remember Mummy saying you were always a restless child and on the go. Mrs Warby has done the best for us."

"She's got her money's worth. I hope we never have to work as hard in our lives as we do here. And when are those Scottish girls arriving to help out? It's been ages!"

Amy suddenly announced, "I'm going down to the creek for a walk."

"Well, Mrs Payne's lighting the fire and she's making some cocoa later on. Don't forget."

Unanswered Questions

Amy walked down the steps from the veranda and ambled slowly to the creek. A cool breeze rustled her hair and she'd wished she'd taken a cardigan.

I won't be long, she thought as she approached the familiar rock under the willow tree. She settled onto the flat area with the convenient ridge just below to rest her feet. By now, the willow fronds had grown to almost the base of the rock, creating an enclosure of cathedral-like peace and privacy. She glanced at the greyish expanse of sand leading to the shallow edge of the creek where a gentle flow over the pebbles highlighted their variety of colours in a ray of sunshine.

It's been years I know, and Edie and Millie seem to have come to terms with our mother's death, she thought. *Maybe because they're younger than me, but I'll always yearn to know what was in that letter she wrote which that blasted woman burnt. Even Mrs Payne, usually so understanding, has urged me to put the past behind me and think of the future. People seem to expect me to forget all about her.*

Amy changed position on the rock to a lower edge of it and placed her feet on the sand. The breeze became stronger and rippled the water in the creek. The fronds of the willow began to slowly sway, and one of them gently brushed her cheek. Her eyes filled with tears as she remembered a tender affirmation of her mother's love.

That felt just like her touch back then, when she'd stroke our cheeks and say 'have a happy day' before we'd leave for school, when everything was so lovely before Daddy got sick.

Another thought entered her mind.

In all the letters we've received, no-one has ever told us what happened to her.

Not Auntie Mattie, not Freddy and not Aunty Esther. Surely, Aunty Esther would have seen her when she came back to London. I'm going to write to her and ask her directly. I'll do it tomorrow afternoon.

Amy heard some footsteps crackling the dried leaves under the trees. Edie stepped onto the rock and climbed up to sit near Amy.

"Why have you been down here so long, Amy?" she questioned.

Amy didn't let on about her lingering sadness.

"Sometimes I like to get away and just be alone for a while, and it's so lovely down here," she replied.

"It sure is, Amy, but it's getting fresh. Come on up and get your cup of cocoa."

The next afternoon, Amy poured out her heart in a letter to Aunty Esther. Although her mother had been gone for years, she wanted to ask some simple questions and get some simple answers, or she would grieve forever: *Had her mother really forsaken them? What had happened to her? Why had we not been allowed to write to her? How long had she suffered from consumption?*

With the letter delivered to the homestead for posting, Amy felt relieved at having asked Aunty Esther the questions she'd always grappled with, and she looked forward to the day when a returning letter would come.

The months went by, and another Christmas arrived.

Christmas Day 1921

"I hope they're giving Freddy a party now he's twenty-one," Edie said on Christmas morning.

"I'm sure they will," Amy replied.

"He's an adult now," stated Millie. "Now he's grown up, he might change. He might start saving to come out."

"Maybe he will, Millie, but don't get your hopes up." Inwardly Amy shook her head. Then she continued, not wishing to dampen Millie's hopes. "Well, he might just surprise us one day and suddenly turn up."

"Pigs might fly too," added Edie cynically.

A Reply From Aunty Esther

New Year's Eve, 1922 was celebrated in the usual way, but no answering letter from Aunty Esther had arrived as Amy had hoped. Nor had Freddy written. Amy had almost given up hope of hearing from anyone when Dottie Payne handed her an envelope in early February. She tore it open and went down to the creek to read what Aunty Esther had written.

Whitefield's
Tottenham Court Rd.

Dec. 9th 1921

My dear Amy,

How delighted I was to receive your letter containing your photographs. I want to give you all a very hearty hug and a kiss of real affection. I will try to write to you a little more often but my time is so fully occupied that all my personal friends complain and just have to believe I would if I could. I shall look forward someday to meeting you all again and then we shall be able to talk about many things.

I could just feel the heartache you were feeling dear Amy when you wrote to me. For from my own experience I know we may have the kindest of sisters and many who love and care for you but there is something about a mother's love, her voice, her touch, which no other ever can have, for such a Christian mother is a great possession. Not even the kindest or most indulgent husband can take that place because it's a different kind of unselfish love. I therefore long for you to know that you have a very warm place in my affection and gladly comply with your modest request for my photograph.

Now with regard to your own dear mother, for whom I have a great respect, she loved you all very dearly. Your father was ill with consumption for years and was not able to work and your poor dear mother slaved to keep the home together. You were all then such tiny little children. She was always ready for work and worked here for a long time when we had a concert on a Saturday evening. She was one of those ready to come in and work from 10 to 12 on Saturday night. I firmly believe that often the knowledge that her little ones had been fed, satisfied her too. Your mother went away somewhere in the provinces but after you were in Australia came back into a London hospital to die. Somehow I heard she was there and went to see her. I was just going away for my summer holidays. She was so glad to see me. We talked and read the Scriptures together and prayed. When I came back from my holiday I went again to find that very soon after I had seen her, the call came for her to enter into her reward.

My dear ones, I hope the time will come with you as with me to know that the justice of our loving Heavenly Father is

"Oh, *NO!* The last page of this letter is *missing*," noted Amy in anguish. "What *else* could have been in it? It must have become detached or mislaid before it was posted."

Amy then gave the matter some thought and came to a conclusion.

"Aunty Esther spoke of the justice of our Heavenly Father. Somehow, I feel sure she was going to say that Mummy would receive that in heaven and not condemnation. He is a God of love."

Amy folded up Aunty Esther's incomplete letter and put it in her pocket. She'd felt a lump in her throat when she'd read of the confirmation of her mother's love for them all. But why had other members of the family been so uncaring and judgmental towards her mother? Why had she been called a deserter after she'd gone up to Northampton to find work?

Well I haven't learnt much more than what I already know, she thought, as she shed a tear, *but I'm so glad she had someone there with her at the end to comfort her and to pray with her. But why were we forbidden to write to her? Aunty Esther didn't say. Well, I suppose that will always be a mystery, but whatever the cause, she was our mother. She loved us, and we loved her.*

Feeling some small measure of comfort, she made her way back to the cottage and placed the letter with its missing page in the biscuit tin with all the others. When Edie and Millie wanted to know what Aunty Esther had written, Amy said, "I'll show it to you later on. It's to be always treasured, and you'll see why for yourselves after you read it."

As Dottie prepared tea that night, Edie and Millie read the letter.

"She went away to work and became sick," said Edie matter-of-factly. "That's what I understand. She loved us! Nothing else matters, Amy. Life has been cruel to us all, but Mummy would want us to get on with our lives, even if we're out here and not with Freddy."

Millie nodded in agreement.

"Thanks, Edie," Amy said. "You've always been the down to earth one among us, and I suppose you're right."

Then Edie remembered. "Monday tomorrow. Washing day. Those smelly men's overalls – *ugh*! Thank goodness those Scottish girls are arriving this week. It's taken Mrs Warby a jolly long time to get them out, I must say."

"Mrs Payne said they're older than we were when we came, except for one of them. Two of them'll be helping us out in the homestead once they've settled in. Poor things! It'll be a shock at first like it was for us, so we must make them welcome," Amy advised.

"I wonder what made Mrs Warby pick Scottish girls this time?" Millie said.

"Well, I hope we can understand them. That Scottish friend of Mr Warby's had such an accent I could hardly make head or tail of what he said," added Edie, grimacing.

All the Way From Scotland

The bewildered Scottish orphan girls finally arrived and settled into places vacated by Jane and Gracie, with one extra bed added. Doris, The Nash girls, and Josie went out of their way to make the new girls feel at home.

"You'll get to love it here, my Lovelies, just like the others have," assured Dottie Payne.

Edie turned her back and made a grimace which no one saw.

Laura, Morag and Eliza were given two weeks to get their bearings and adapt to their new lives before they were assigned to their occupations. Eliza joined the pupils at school while Laura and Morag joined Doris, Amy, Edie and Millie at the homestead.

"It's Harrrd worrrk herrre. Worrrse than back home," said Laura.

"Beg your pardon?" Edie said.

But Amy understood her and agreed, placating her by saying, "Saturdays we only have to cook breakfast, wash up, tidy the kitchen and the rest of the day is ours."

"But you have kirrk on Sunday morrrnings, don't you?" asked Morag.

"Yes," answered Millie, "and Miss Wilma plays the piano, and we all sing some hymns. It's lovely."

"Oh! well, this is our life now," said Eliza, resigned, "but one day I'm going back to Scotland to live with uncle again."

Summer soon faded. And autumn advanced with early morning frosts and fogs.

"It's getting cold," Eliza noted as she returned from school one afternoon. "Back in Scotland in May it would be spring, but it's autumn out herre. Is it verry cold in winterr?

"I think it's just as cold, Eliza," Amy told her, returning to the cottage to fetch a cardigan. "A bit of snow sometimes and lots of frosts."

Retrenchment

"There's two letters here for you, Amy," Dottie announced. "Probably one's from Freddy. You mentioned you hadn't heard from him for over a year."

"Thanks, Mrs Payne. I'll read it later when we're all together."

Amy returned to the homestead to her duties, and when all the girls had finished their work for the day, they returned to the cottage.

"I've got two letters," said Amy. "Come on, Edie … come on, Millie. One's from Freddy!"

The three sisters settled onto a living room sofa, excited at the prospect of Freddy's news.

59 Warren Street,
Tottenham Court Road
London NW1
March 5th, 1922

Dear Amy, Edie & Millie,

At last I am writing to you. You must think me an awful rotter for not writing before but somehow I always feel depressed lately. Thank you very much for the handkerchief and book. I am very glad to hear you are all well and happy. Once Hilary told you that I had a young lady. I certainly had a young lady friend but there was nothing serious between us and it was not very often I took her out. Hilary never calls or writes to see me and I only know that she is in some nursing home in

Golders Green. I have got the sack from the Railways. I had been expecting it for some months. During the war the Government had control of the Railways and when they released them last August the Company immediately started to cut expenses. They started by sacking hundreds of fellows and cutting out one train and making the next train longer. I hung on as long as I could but it came at last so now I have been unemployed for six weeks. Work is about as easy to find as a needle in a haystack. I have got the hump of this country and am trying for a situation abroad. I have exhausted my patience trying to get in the Merchant Service. I am writing to all foreign Railways such as Africa, India, Egypt, Borneo, well practically all countries where the people are black and have to rely on whites for master work such as Engine Driving. I have been to Australia House to try to emigrate to you repeatedly, but the officials won't look at me because I am not an ex-serviceman, so that's no good. Mrs Winsor is very good and does not say anything about being out of work and I am in her debt for Board and Lodging but I will pay her back when I get some work for what money I had did not last long. Well I must say that this is not a very bright letter rather the reverse. Dear Amy, what has become of Jim. You did not say anything about him in your last letters and I was wondering if he had joined the Navy as you said he was going to do in one of your former letters. It is getting on toward spring over here now. We have not had a very bad winter and hardly any snow so no-one can grumble about the weather. If I get another job I'll save as hard as I can to come out to you but if I take on a job abroad I daresay I shall have to sign a contract for at least three years. Please write to me as soon as you can and I promise to write a lot oftener that I have done in the past. Well Dear Sisters I think I have said my mouthful as the Yanks say so I will close wishing you the best of luck and prosperity.

I remain

Your Loving Brother   Freddy XXXXX

The three girls looked at each other in dismay, and Edie shook her head sadly.

"I'm so disappointed. He loved that job in the railways, and now he's out of work again. Talk about rotten luck."

"Will he ever get out here?" queried Millie. "It's always the same. Our hopes are built up, and then they're dashed."

"He seems to be trying hard to get other work, Millie. It's not his fault the railways over there have cut costs after that dreadful war."

"I hope Mrs Winsor won't kick him out," said Edie, staring ahead. "That would be awful."

"I don't think she will, Edie," Amy replied. "She seems to have grown fond of Freddy. You'd almost think he was her own son the way she writes about him. Let's see what she says."

Amy unfolded the letter and read it to her sisters.

> *59 Warren Street,*
> *Tottenham Ct. Rd.*
> *London W1*

Tues. March 8th

Dear Amy,

At last I am writing to you, for Freddy tells me you are going to write to me to know why he does not write to you. Well Amy the candid truth is he hates writing but of course that should not be an excuse where you are concerned for if he only wrote 2 or 3 times a year you would be pleased I know. I am always asking him to write to you so that I could send a message too but it's no good. However I think he has written you a letter now and you will see by it that he is out of work again. Well Amy I am writing on his behalf as well as my own to ask you if it would be possible for you to help him out to Australia. Freddy told me you said perhaps you could but I don't think he likes to ask you himself. He has been out of work now for a while and if I could see the slightest chance of him getting some soon I would not ask you to help him over but believe me we have got a million people unemployed here, some have been out for 18 months so it is a very poor chance for Freddy. Of course Amy he ought to have saved some money while he was in work and nobody has talked to him more than my husband and myself but there are a lot of young people who only live for the present and never think of the future. There are such a lot of pleasures to spend their money on, pictures, football matches etc that the money soon goes. It's no use talking about that now. He has written to foreign railways but there are no vacancies and I know he has been to Australia House several times to try to emigrate over but they will not entertain him at all as he is not an ex-serviceman. Only on Monday I got him to write to a gentleman who has come here from South Australia, a Mr Banwell, he wants 6000 boys between 15 and 18 to train as farmers. Freddy wrote thinking he might grant a concession regarding his age but it is of no use for in the paper today he is overwhelmed with boys so of course Freddy stands no chance there. I will do the best I can for him while he is here but my husband's wages have been reduced such a lot that of course it comes rather rough.

We have only just enough for ourselves for my husband has always earned a precarious living till a little time ago. Now if you think of sending the money or helping him I know the fare is 29 pounds, that is by your nominating him and then, of course, he wants clothes and a little money to land with I suppose. He could hardly do with less than 40 pounds. I know he will pay you back alright, Amy, if he gets to Australia and if you could find him work for he has got a good principle. I can say that for him. We see in the papers daily that there is plenty of work in Australia. It seems so silly to make such hard and fast rules when fine strong young fellows are willing to go, and Freddy is a fine chap I can tell you. You spoke about Hilary when you wrote to Freddy. She came here one Sunday some months ago. We made her welcome and asked her to stop to tea but she could not and promised to come again, but have not seen her since. She is very reserved Amy, somewhat different to you and your sisters. I do not fancy she has such a nice time as you have. You all seem so happy out there. I hope you, Edie and Millie are quite well. Freddy is in perfect health. I only hope he may get an odd job or two while he is waiting to hear from you. I hope you will not be offended at this letter but I do not see what else can be done. Well I must close now as it is time to get the tea, and you must excuse me not writing as my time is so occupied with all the family.

With very kind regards to your sisters and also to yourself.

Yours very sincerely

A Winsor

P.S. I must tell you Freddy is very like your father in

Amy wearily put the letter down and felt worried about its contents. How had Mrs Winsor got the idea that she would be able to pay the costs of Freddy's passage to Australia? There'd been some misunderstanding. Then she remembered. In one of her earlier letters to Freddy, she'd mentioned that she would see if Mrs Warby could lend Freddy the money for the passage out and she, Amy, would also contribute from her small wage, for expenses when he arrived.

"That's what's happened," Amy explained to her sisters after they'd read the letter from Mrs Winsor. "They think the money can come from here, but I hadn't even *seen* Mrs Warby yet to ask her. I was plucking up my courage to have a talk with her when we got the letter saying Freddy had a job on the railways. Then I put all that aside believing he would start saving for the fare himself."

Edie looked squarely at Amy.

"He just seems to have settled in with the Winsors, Amy, almost like he's one of *their* family instead of our brother. He has to realise he can't live with them forever."

"You're right, Edie. It sounds like he's having a good time in London even though he's out of work again. You know, as much as I'm angry with him, I have to admit that since he was just thirteen years old, life has not been very kind to him. Firstly, Mummy disappeared to get work, then Daddy died, and Granny the same year, then we were sent out here away from him and Auntie Mattie went, all in the space of six years and he suddenly found himself alone without any family. It must have felt like heaven when Mrs Winsor took him in. Remember, he said in a letter to us that they were like a second mother and father to him."

"That's true," agreed Edie, less sympathetic, "but we all had to go through what he went through. It was awful for everyone."

"But we've had a home here and security, Edie. We've had food put on the table for us."

"So has he," emphasised Edie.

"Why don't you go and see Mrs Warby, Amy, and ask for her help to get Freddy out?" Millie suggested, having listened to her sisters' conversation. "He could work here or somewhere else in Australia. There are more jobs here for him than over there."

"I'll do that," Amy decided. "I'll talk to her next Sunday afternoon."

Asking for Help

Amy felt nervous the following Sunday, and she'd been rehearsing what to say to Eleanor Warby in her plea for her brother. She walked to the homestead and after some hesitation knocked on the front door. Eleanor answered, and Amy pointed to the cane chairs on the veranda and said she'd like to have a talk. The two women sat down. It took a good five minutes for Amy to earnestly advocate for her brother with a promise to pay back any money. When the conversation ended with Eleanor's refusal to help made abundantly clear, Amy parted with a polite farewell, and made her way down the steps and back to the cottage.

"I felt so humiliated after I'd seen her, Edie. I promised to pay her back myself after I left Balangara and got a position outside, but she insisted that if she did it for Freddy then she'd have to do it for everybody else's relations."

"There's nothing we can do then," Edie summed up flatly.

"I'll write to Mrs Winsor straight away, Edie, after I get a job and clear up the misunderstanding after I gave them that false hope. With more money, I'll be able to help Freddy after all."

"Poor, Mrs Winsor! She's got such a big heart that lady. I don't think she'll be throwing Freddy out, Amy. We can only hope work turns up for him and he's learnt his lesson and will start saving."

A Sudden Decision

"I think it's about time I left here," Amy announced suddenly after the interview with Eleanor Warby. "I'll be twenty in a couple of weeks. I've only been holding off because of Millie, you know, but I think she'll be alright now. And she'll still have you here, Edie. I'm going to look for work outside of here. I'll grab hold of Mr Payne's newspapers and see what's advertised. I can cook, I can sew, and I can clean."

"If you go, I'll go," Edie added decisively. "I'll be eighteen in September. Old enough! I'll get a job too. Mrs Payne will be looking after Millie and Josie. She's always treated them like babies."

"Well, when we're working outside, I'd like to get Millie to come and live with us, somehow," Amy said determinedly. "Our mother would want us to be together."

"Have you considered that we may not have jobs where you and I are together, Amy?" Edie asked. "We'll have to go where the work is, and there aren't many towns in this area."

"Something will work out. It will have to," Amy replied dismissively, "and we'll get Millie out."

From that time on, every Saturday afternoon, Amy and Edie diligently searched the Situations Vacant column in the newspaper, but nothing was available. Amy was beginning to give up hope when a job was advertised in Guyra for an assistant cook at a large cattle station.

"I'm going for it, Edie. I have all the experience necessary now. And the weekly wage looks far better than what we get here. It's a live-in position too. I'm writing a letter to apply, and I'll post it tomorrow."

"Ask if they have anything for me if you get an interview. I'll be a cleaner. Anything! Now you're going, I don't feel like staying on here any longer."

Amy gathered all her resources together and, in her neatest handwriting, and in a courteous tone, applied for the job at Lynnewood Station.

Offensive Remarks

The next afternoon as she approached the cottage after her work at the homestead, she noticed Neil Warby talking to a visiting tradesman on the veranda. She caught the words, 'those Pommy girls', and paused just out of sight. Curious, she listened in to the conversation, drawing a little closer for clarity.

"Well, you know, my mother probably rescued them from becoming street women in London. God knows what their backgrounds were or what bad influences their families had on them, but we've been able to make something out of them."

We've been able to …

Amy turned around quietly and slowly walked down to the creek. When she sat on the familiar rock she burst into tears and sobbed for some time, glad she was alone with no-one to witness the humiliation and shame suddenly thrust upon her. Then a feeling of intense anger took over.

How dare *that man make judgements like that about us. He knows nothing, absolutely nothing about anyone's former lives back in England. My parents would be furious. We have been a respectable family. To think that's how they've been looking at us all. No wonder Mrs Warby didn't want her grandchildren to play with us or talk to us. As though we'd pollute them or something.*

Amy thought of her siblings.

I won't let Edie or Millie or even Freddy know what I've just heard. It'll only upset them, and for the time being, we are obliged to stay on here. I'll keep things to myself for now, but I just can't wait to get away from this place.

She dried her eyes and composed herself and walked back to the cottage where Edie and Millie were having a cup of tea.

"Pour me out one too, Millie. I'm writing to Aunty Esther later on."

In the letter, Amy did not identify the insult to her and the other girls that she'd overheard. In her opinion, it was too degrading a topic to be discussed, but she did refer to the imperious manner of the Warbys and the taxing amount of work expected of everyone. She mentioned that she intended to leave Balangara and had applied for a position elsewhere. She also included that she would not leave without speaking her mind to Mrs Warby because, although they had been given an opportunity here in Australia to escape the hardships they'd experienced in London, they'd been treated like second-class citizens.

The letter was duly posted the next day.

An Important Interview

In mid-July, Amy received a reply from Lynnewood Station in Guyra acknowledging receipt of her application for Assistant Cook and granting her an interview on the following Wednesday.

"I've got an interview next Wednesday," she announced excitedly when Edie joined her. "Mr Payne has offered to drive me into Guyra to Lynnewood Station in his new automobile."

"Oh! Amy, I'm so glad for you," said Edie, giving her a hug. "And do you know, I'll bet you get the job. You look so nice, and you've got such good manners and ..."

"Stop it, Edie," laughed Amy. "We'll have to wait and see."

On the appointed day, the interview went very well even though Amy felt nervous. The owners, Mr and Mrs Whitby, hired Amy on the spot, inviting her to start after she'd given her former employer a week's notice.

"I like her," commented Andrea Whitby to her husband Joseph, after Amy had taken her leave. "She's gentle yet strong at the same time. A rare combination."

When Amy returned to Balangara, she informed everyone at the cottage of her success in gaining outside employment in Guyra.

"And I'll be saving up to get my brother out here. I'm writing a letter straight away to him and Mrs Winsor to let them know. Now I'll have to tell Mrs Warby tomorrow that I'll be leaving."

Everyone crowded around, including Edie who had a woebegone expression.

'We'll have a farewell party before you go," promised Dottie Payne. "We're going to miss you, Amy."

"But you and I will always be friends, Amy," said Betsy, putting an arm around Amy's shoulder, "and Edie too. We'll always keep in touch."

"We all will," promised Josie and the Scottish girls.

"One thing I'm taking away from here are the friendships I've made," said Amy, her face dropping a little. "I'll never forget any of you."

A Confrontation

The next morning after Amy had helped to cook the breakfasts, she walked around to the front of the homestead to give her notice to Eleanor Warby. She was determined to leave in peace and debated whether she should mention the slur about her and the girls that her son had levelled at them. She drew in a deep breath as Eleanor answered the door and invited her inside.

"I'll be leaving Balangara, Ma'am, in a week, as I've secured another position in Guyra at Lynnewood Station to work for the Whitbys."

Before Amy could continue, Eleanor interrupted, her eyes widening.

"You could be giving me more than just one week's notice, Amy Nash. I consider that rather rude of you."

"Well, they want me to start next week, and I can't let this opportunity go. I'll also be getting more money than what I get here, and I want to save up to get my brother out to Australia. You wouldn't help us and …"

"Considering how much you want your family to be together, I'm surprised you'd leave your sisters and go away from them. Millie is still very young and …"

"She's nearly fifteen, Ma'am, and Edie will still be with her."

"Knowing her, she'll be off soon too. That's gratitude for you," said Eleanor sourly, turning her face away.

At this remark, Amy felt emboldened. She squared her shoulders. "I hope she *will* be leaving soon. We are both old enough to strike out on our own now. Please don't think we haven't appreciated all you've done for us by bringing us out to Australia. I know we would have been worse off back in England, but I heard some insulting remarks from your son, Neil, a short while ago. I overheard him talking to another man about us girls from England, and he implied that we would have walked the streets if your family hadn't rescued us. And he said our parents were probably a bad influence on us too. It upset me so much I couldn't stop crying. My sisters and I come from a respectable family. Our only misfortune was my father getting ill and dying, and my mother thrown out of our home because she didn't have the rent. That's the reason we had to go into care because at least we were being fed there."

Eleanor Warby looked mortified and embarrassed, and attempted to dampen down the effects of Neil's comments. "I'm sorry you heard that conversation, Amy. I can't think why he formed that opinion. He knows I only asked for girls from respectable homes, but there's no doubt that some homeless women in England do resort to that sort of thing, but he shouldn't have made comments like that about you and the girls. I'll talk to him about it."

Amy felt somewhat placated but still glad she was leaving. She decided not to mention the volume of work the girls were expected to cope with each day, but did mention that Edie was looking for work outside Balangara too and that they would try to take Millie out to live with one of them as well.

"I won't permit you to do that, Miss Nash. She is by law to stay within my jurisdiction until she is sixteen years old. And I forbid you to talk to her about my son's comments or that you consider your work assignments too harsh. I've heard from a source that this is your opinion. And you are not to visit her after you've left here. You're lucky to have been brought here with all the benefits you've had, and I suspect you are ungrateful. Now if you'll excuse me, I have a visitor calling soon, and I think we've said all that needs to be said."

With those words, Eleanor stood up and ushered Amy to the door.

She's angry, and I think it's because I told her we want Millie to come and live with us, Amy thought as she walked down the front steps and crossed the garden on the way back to the cottage. *If we all leave, there'll only be*

Amy decided to tell Edie, but not Millie, about the angry confrontation she'd had with Mrs Warby and her ban on seeing Millie. She didn't touch on Neil's defamation she'd overheard and her resultant conversation with Mrs Warby about it. Why should she burden her sisters with this rubbish when both of them were still obliged to stay on in the place? She only mentioned that Mrs Warby had considered her rude because of her short notice and that she'd banned her from seeing Millie. This only reinforced Edie's determination to leave.

"Time to go," she stated philosophically. "We don't have to take that. I'll find a job somehow, and we'll get Millie out when she turns sixteen. In the meantime, she has Mrs Payne and Josie. They've become such close friends, Amy. Don't worry. She'll be alright."

Edie accelerated her efforts to find work outside while assuring Amy that she would also save some money to help Freddy out to Australia.

Leaving Balangara

Dottie Payne had organised a farewell party for Amy on the afternoon before she left Balangara. Amy had become quite emotional. She realised she'd be missing everyone she'd been so close to in all her years at Balangara.

"We've been through a lot together, haven't we?" she said in a small stumbling speech. She dabbed her moist eyes with a handkerchief. "It's been good and bad, but mainly *good*, I suppose. The best part has been knowing all of you and having Mr and Mrs Payne as our house parents. I'll never forget any of you, and I want all your addresses before I go."

Then Amy became tongue-tied and wished she'd said a lot more. Everyone gathered around her with hugs and reciprocal compliments and good luck wishes.

"It's not goodbye, everyone. I'm sure we'll be seeing each other again in the future."

On the night before she left Balangara, Amy packed her large suitcase and her pink box that had travelled with her from London on the ship to Australia.

Early the next morning she sought out Eleanor at the homestead to say goodbye, deciding to now address her as Mrs Warby rather than Ma'am as before. Eleanor led Amy to the veranda.

"Thanks, Mrs Warby, for all you've done for me. I really *do* appreciate the chances you've given me and my sisters at Balangara, and I've made many friends here also. I'm sure we'll meet again one day. In any case, I'll be visiting Millie from time to time and Miss Wilma too."

Eleanor seemed taken aback at this promise, and her face took on hard lines.

"I won't allow Millie to see you for the time being to hear things she shouldn't. And I consider you've been rather rude which is unlike you, I must say."

Amy's eyes opened wide in disbelief. "You have no right, Mrs Warby to separate …" she objected, but Eleanor curtly said,

"Well, good luck, Amy, and all the best for your future."

With these words, she nodded and gestured toward Arthur Payne, who stood near his new Ford in the driveway, awaiting his passenger. Amy walked slowly down the steps and over to the car, resolving to write Millie a letter.

All the girls and Dottie Payne were assembled to wave Amy off, blowing kisses and promising to meet up again. Edie and Millie stood together. Millie looked downcast but Amy assured her she would get to see her again as often as she could. After hugs all round, Amy stepped into the Dodge, and it slowly pulled away.

Off to Guyra

The journey to Guyra was not so familiar as the beaten track to
Armidale. On the way, Amy shed a tear at leaving her sisters behind,
but she also felt happy at the thought of this new phase of her life. She
pondered about her new beginning in between conversation with
Arthur.

"It's the same sort of work but in a different environment, and
from now on, I'm an adult in my own right, and not under the control
of Mrs Warby anymore."

After a bumpy journey on dirt roads, the destination was reached.
There it stood: a large, sprawling homestead on the crest of a hill. All
around it, green and fertile fields and plains with occasional wooded
hills breaking the gentleness of the landscape.

"It's flatter countryside than at Balangara," Amy observed as the
Ford proceeded up the driveway and pulled up at the front door of
the homestead.

"Oh! there's rugged parts in it too," Arthur said, "but I must say,
it's magnificent country for sheep and cattle, and the Whitby's do a
great job in running this show. But it's mighty cold up here in the
highlands. Guyra is the coldest town in northern New South Wales,
and it regularly snows here in winter."

With this information, Arthur lifted out Amy's luggage and
deposited it on the driveway near the house.

"Goodbye, Amy, my girl, and good luck in your new job here," he
wished. He gave her a small hug before leaving to drive back to
Balangara.

Daisy, the maid, soon answered Amy's knock on the door and

ushered her to the sitting room. Mrs Whitby soon appeared and warmly welcomed her new employee. Daisy then escorted Amy to her quarters at the back of the house near the large kitchen. After collecting her luggage, she was taken to the kitchen to meet her fellow workmates, Gwen and Shirley, two friendly women who made her feel immediately comfortable in their presence.

"See over there," Shirley pointed out through a window, "that building about a hundred yards away? That's the quarters for the workers here. We feed them breakfast at 7 o'clock and pack them lunches. This is a large station, too far for the men to come back for lunch. They return at about 6 o'clock for their tea. They're big eaters, I can tell you," she laughed, "and big blokes too."

"We also cook for the family," added Gwen, "and for us as well of course, but we don't have to clean the house, only the kitchen. Daisy, the housemaid, does the house."

"We've got to work hard here, Amy. We're kept going all day," advised Shirley.

"I'm used to it, but I'm glad we don't have to clean. I rather like cooking though," Amy said.

The work was arduous as Amy found out during the next week, but everything was equally shared, and an atmosphere of cheerfulness and co-operation was maintained between the women.

After Amy had been working at Lynnewood Station for two months, a re-addressed letter from London arrived. She kept it in her apron pocket until after tea that night, wondering who had written. *Maybe Freddy?* she thought. When she opened it she saw it was from Mrs Winsor. She sat on her bed, opened the letter and unfolded the creased pages.

59 Warren Street
Tottenham Ct. Road
London 25/6/22

Dear Amy,

I was very pleased to hear from you and glad you are going to help Freddy to come over to you. As regards to the type of work he would like, he's willing to do anything and perhaps doing that job whatever it may be something better may turn up in the meantime. Over here there is not ever that chance for he goes after dozens of jobs and of course there are so many ex-service or others out of work they get the first choice. It is 4 months he has been out. You will have his letter a week before mine so you will see what he says. I only wish he could get one for a month or two to be able to get himself some clothes for he is looking shabby and it is impossible for us to buy him clothes, Amy. If I had had some money I would have lent him the money and he would have been in Australia by now, but I am sorry to say I haven't anything near forty pounds. However, I hope something may turn up soon. Perhaps Mrs Warby could give Freddy some work in the bush for he would like that I know. Will you thank Edie for her nice letter. I should think she is a very lovely girl and I hope you will be able to get her with you as she is in a hard place. Hilary has only been once to see Freddy. I don't know why for we both asked her to come again. I do not see Sister Hester very much, but I met her last week. I told her I was the only one who had done anything for Freddy for as I told you before not a soul belonging to him comes near. I hope your cold is much better Amy the winter time is always bad for colds. We shall be having our winter soon. I don't like the cold weather at all, it always nips me up. I expect I am getting old. I will see that Freddy has everything quite alright Amy when he gets the money and that he goes off alright. I do hope he will be able to get on in Australia, he ought to for he is a fine

Amy put the letter on her bed and felt perplexed and troubled. Not only about Freddy's unemployment but about how Mrs Winsor could have got the impression that money for Freddy's fare would soon be sent over. Maybe her letter to Mrs Winsor had been delayed. She'd explained in it that Mrs Warby would not help. She'd also promised to start saving up for Freddy's fare out, now she had a new job and was getting more money and that Edie would help too, once she got a better-paid position away from Balangara.

I'll have to write to Freddy and Mrs Winsor and clarify the situation, she thought, *and tell them it would be well over a year before Edie and I could rake up the money to help. And I'll earnestly pray that some job will turn up for him in the meantime. And where's that letter from Freddy that Mrs Winsor said would be arriving before hers? Oh! he's so unreliable!*

Amy got out her writing pad and dashed off two letters before she climbed into bed, worried not only about Freddy, but about Mrs Winsor as well.

'She's so kind to him, but she sounds desperate for him to come out here. He needs to somehow pay his own way."

Finally, after praying that some sort of job would soon turn up for Freddy, she dropped off to sleep.

Life at Lynnewood

With Amy so busy, time passed quickly. She enjoyed her life at Lynnewood Station. The working men on the station were frequent company as they called in each morning and evening for their meals. Occasionally, she, Gwen and Shirley would join them and sit on the outside benches at the tables as they all ate their dinner while sharing stories and jokes. This was eventually frowned upon by the Whitbys and stopped; the women cautioned to be more distant as flirtations in the workplace were discouraged. This by no means stopped the eye contact frequently happening between Amy and a tall, good looking ex-service man who'd fought in the Great War.

"He fancies you, Amy," Shirley noted.

Amy shrugged and replied, "Oh! he could have anyone he wants, Shirl, he's so handsome." But a fascination with Daniel lingered and Amy often found herself dreaming about him, then disciplining herself about becoming too interested in an unlikely romance.

At the beginning of December Amy received a letter from Aunty Esther. She left the kitchen to sit on a bench outside to read it.

Whitefield's Central Mission
Tottenham Court Road,
London W.1.

Oct.6th 1922

My dear Amy,

I was very glad to get your letter dear, although it has distressed me very much to know that you have taken such a serious step. I wish Amy dear you had tried to remember how much Mrs Warby has done for you three when you were quite helpless, she took you out to Australia, cared for you, educated you, given you the greatest of chances to live useful lives. In England none of you were strong. The climate where you are is the best possible to help you to grow up to be strong women under the conditions you live which have helped you to be what you are.

I know quite well you have just arrived at the age when most young folk even under ordinary circumstances are apt to find the home restraints rather irksome. You must do all you can to show Mrs Warby you are truly sorry and that you do appreciate all she has done for you. Mrs Warby has not limited you, having your bicycles learning to ride, having a banking account, are not likely to have been yours had you remained in England.

Amy dear, don't think I am cross or mean to be one sided, you did not tell me any details of what Mrs Warby desired you to do that made you so angry so I can't judge but I do know that no-one had a better mother than I had and when I was young I wanted to do things she wished me not to do and I felt rebellious, but still there was the knowledge that she must know what is best and I believe now her choice was best for me.

I do hope that Mrs Warby will feel that she can truly forgive you and receive back under her guiding care. It may not be to live with her again. Mrs Warby may not consider that to be the best for you but don't take a step without seeking her advice. I am very anxious about you and wish we could just talk it over face to face or on the telephone.

Amy folded up Aunty Esther's letter and agreed with some of it but not all of it as she processed her thoughts.

Did Aunty Esther think I took a serious step because I wanted to leave Balangara? She doesn't realise I'm no longer under Mrs Warby's control. I can't apologise for feeling so angry at Neil Warby's opinion of us and I'm still angry that I'm forbidden to see Millie, my own sister. I have actually told Mrs Warby that we appreciate all she's done for us but she must realise we are grown women now and old enough to make our own decisions, even Millie. Underneath, I know she's wanted me to keep working at Balangara. Maybe I should have told Aunty Esther about Neil's comments I overheard. Maybe she would have understood me better then. I'll just put this letter in the biscuit tin and not think about it anymore.

Amy returned to the kitchen to get some washing up done, remembering her grandmother's philosophy of long ago when Mary Nash would advise her family not to worry about things because it wouldn't change anything but only make people fret. Even so, Amy often found it hard to remove her concern about her brother in London.

Please dear God, she'd implore, *help him get a job or help Edie get a new job so we can both help him get out here.*

Christmas was approaching and the women in the kitchen were run off their feet with extra cakes and puddings to cook as gifts for some of the station hands.

Christmas Day 1922

"This is the first Christmas I've had without any family around me," Amy said sadly to Gwen and Shirley on the day. "My two sisters are stuck back there at Balangara. Things will have to change."

"I have the feeling things will be a lot better for you all in the new year," Shirley consoled.

"Let's hope for Freddy as well. He's turning twenty-two today," said Amy. "It's almost 1923 and I'll be twenty-one years old next June. How the years have flown."

New Year's Eve passed with quiet celebrations at the homestead. Then, on the 15th January, Amy received a letter. She was puzzled because the postmark was American.

"I don't know anyone there," she frowned as she opened it. She almost fell over in shock.

"It's from Freddy!" she gasped aloud, "and he's on a *boat*. He's in *America!* What's going on?"

She quickly read the letter, smiling with disbelief.

On Board
R.N.S. Majestic
Boston U.S.A.
Sunday Nov 19th 1922

Dearest Sisters,

I am writing this letter from Boston U.S.A. being on board the largest liner in the world. What do you think I am this time? You'll never guess so I'll tell you. I'm a

Fish Cook. What a change from fireman Eh? The life is simply grand. This is my third trip to America, my first two being to New York. At the present moment the ship is in dry dock having her propellers changed and being thoroughly overhauled. After Christmas I am going to try to get a berth upon a ship going to Australia just to have a look round. So far I have been to France and America but I hope to see plenty of other countries besides, with Luck I shall. When you reply to this letter, address it to the usual address 59 Warren Street, London England because I may change my boat anytime it will be alright with Mrs Winsor. I always return to Mrs Winsor after every trip so I shall be sure of getting it. I was rather disappointed when I received your last letter because I was out of work and had no idea of getting a job. I wanted so to see you and be with you in Aussie. At present Australia seems as far off as ever and as long as I can keep on travelling from one country to another I shall not trouble to come there to stop especially as there is no work to be had. At least Mrs Warby said there is none but it wants some believing. If I can get a boat to Australia I shall let you know so that you may, if you care to, come and see me, providing of course that the port of call is not far away. If I can get the time off I will come to see you. If I can get a boat that is. Dear Amy, how are you getting on now? Are you in a decent position? I hope you are and look after yourself because you are adults now and cannot go to Mrs Warby when you like for advice. I haven't your new address with me so I am addressing it to Balangara. I have just written to my girlfriend in London. She is a dear. Some months ago I was seriously thinking of becoming engaged to her but you wrote repeatedly

"Guess what, girls?" Amy laughed as she told Shirley and Gwen the news about her brother. "He's in America working on a ship and he's a fish cook. This is the third time he's been to America and he's loving it. He's hoping to get on a boat soon which will come to Australia so we may get to see him soon when it docks. What a turnabout, eh? And I was so worried about him back there in London without work."

"That's a big relief for you, Amy. That sounds like a stable job he's got now. And travelling the world too!" said Shirley, smiling.

"I'll have to let Edie know as soon as possible. This is the best Christmas present we've ever had, Shirley, and I'm sure we'll get to meet up with him soon when a ship comes to Australia. The lady he lives with in London, Mrs Winsor, says in her letters that he's tall and handsome. And he's got a girlfriend, Shirley! It's years since we've seen him. I can't wait. I remember him back in London when we were kids. Loved to tease us he did and … …"

"It'll be lovely, Amy," joined in Gwen. Then she cautioned. "Please don't burn that bread in the oven. I can smell it."

"Thanks, Gwennie. I got carried away, I know." Amy dashed to the oven and took out the loaf with an overdone crust.

"Just in time!" said Shirley.

"God answers prayers, girls. I asked God to get him a job somewhere and look what's happened. On a *ship* of all places." Amy's smile widened. "But something puzzles me. Freddy said in his letter that Mrs Warby had told him there was no work in Australia. He must have written to her and asked if she could help him, maybe work at Balangara or somewhere, and she has discouraged him. I happen to know there's a lot more work in Australia that in London just now."

"Well, the main thing is, he's got a good job now, Amy, and he'll be seeing places we can only dream about. Don't worry, you'll get to see him, and soon, I hope."

"Amy, did you hear that Daisy has put in her notice and will be leaving in ten days?" Gwen thought to advise. "Her mother isn't well and needs her at home to care for her."

Amy put down the tea towel and with eyes wide, urgently asked, "Has Mrs Whitby got anyone else to take Daisy's place, Gwen? Has she advertised yet? How long have you known about this? Do you think …?"

"Stop firing questions at me, Amy. I know what you're thinking. That's why I told you as soon as I heard. Go and see Mrs Whitby straight away. With luck, Edie will get the job. I'll finish these dishes. Go on, get a move on."

Amy took out a clean apron from a cupboard and hurried around to the front door and knocked. Daisy answered promptly and led Amy to the parlour.

"Sorry about your Mum, Daisy. I hope she's better soon."

With a stifled sob, Daisy shook her head and disappeared to let Mrs Whitby know that Amy wanted to see her. In five minutes, she appeared and ushered Amy to a seat.

A Chance for Edie

The conversation didn't last long. Andrea Whitby assured Amy that Edie could interview for the job and as she had experience in household duties, stood a fair chance of joining her sister at Lynnewood.

"Oh! thank you, thank you, Mrs Whitby. It would solve a lot of our problems just now. I'll let Edie know to ring you up and make an appointment if I may use your telephone. Straight away, please?"

After the phone call Amy bobbed a little towards Mrs Whitby and was let out the door. She gave Gwen a hopeful report when she returned to the kitchen.

That evening, Andrea Whitby told her husband about Amy's visit that afternoon.

"If Amy's sister is alright, I'll hire her. It'll save advertising and a lot of time, Joe," she advised. "Amy's already rung her up at Balangara and the girl, Edie, I think it is, should be ringing me tomorrow."

Joe nodded, knowing that this country woman, this wife of his, always made wise decisions in hiring staff.

After Edie had answered Amy's phone call she was elated. She rang Andrea Whitby the next morning for an interview which was scheduled for the Tuesday of the following week.

"She's eighteen and old enough to go her own separate way now, Arthur," Dottie Payne explained after Edie had asked him earnestly if he could drive her to Lynnewood Station at Guyra next Tuesday. "I hope she gets the job. It'll be wonderful for those two sisters to be together again."

"It will indeed," agreed Arthur, "but the little one will miss her sisters, I dare say."

"I don't know what went on, Arthur, but Mrs Warby won't let Amy see Millie, but she's fifteen now and can leave herself when she's sixteen, you know."

"Quite a while to wait," Arthur replied.

The next day Edie rehearsed what to say at the interview the following week. *I'll emphasise that I can cook as well as house clean, and can replace one of the cooks if they are sick,* she resolved to say. *That might give me the edge.*

On the day of the interview Edie hopped into Arthur Payne's automobile and started fidgeting with her fingers and taking deep breaths. Arthur attempted to quieten her nerves as he took the wheel to drive to Lynnewood Station.

"You've got the experience, Luv, and you're intelligent and a nice-looking lass. Be confident now and hold your head up high."

When they arrived at the homestead, Edie felt her heart pounding. She stood tall, composed herself and knocked on the front door. Twenty minutes later, after the interview was over, she emerged from the house with a broad smile. She almost ran to the kitchen and did a little dance through the door, interrupting the three women who were mixing batter for butter cakes. Amy had been silently praying for her sister's success.

At Edie's joyful entrance to the kitchen there was no mistaking the result. Amy dropped the spoon into the batter and rushed over to Edie where they both engaged in a triumphant hug. There were introductions to Gwen and Shirley.

"I'm starting in ten days. Oh! Amy, what luck! What a great start to 1923. And we'll be together! I'll tell Mrs Warby tonight. She won't like it because she'll be short of girls now, but that's not my worry. Mr Payne is waiting outside to drive me back. I'd better go soon because Millie will have too much to do. Oh! Amy. What about Millie? Now I'm leaving, how will she manage?"

"You'll just have to tell Mrs Warby that she should get in someone to replace you, Edie," Amy advised firmly, "and that Millie has never been strong and cannot cope with extra work in the place."

"I'd stay, Amy," said Edie, reflecting, "but I just can't let this chance go. I'm so excited at leaving Balangara and getting a bit closer to living the life I want to, you know."

"What life is that, Edie?" Shirley asked.

"Oh! I don't know. A bit more excitement. This place is closer to Guyra and Armidale and one day, when I'm older, I intend to move down to Sydney."

"Whatever will be, will be, Edie," Amy said philosophically, then added, "I'm making a cuppa for us all. Call in Mr Payne. He can have one too before he drives you back. And oh! Edie, there's another letter from Freddy? In all the excitement about you possibly coming here to work, I forgot to post it to you. It's good news, Edie."

Amy dashed to her room and fetched Freddy's letter for Edie to read. After Edie had finished reading the letter, she jumped up and down with joy and proclaimed, "This has been the best day of my life. He's got a job and in boats. He'll love that. And I've got a new job too. And you and I are together, Amy. What a day!"

There were new hugs all round and Arthur Payne smiled too. On the way back to Balangara, he congratulated Edie for getting her new job but wondered silently how the news would be received by Eleanor Warby. After they arrived, Edie made straight to the homestead and was let in by Josie who'd been dusting the living room. Mrs Warby was summoned and Edie wasted no time in telling her the news.

"You're not much better than your sister. Ten days, eh? She only gave me a week. I thought I'd instilled good manners in you while you've been here, but I've been mistaken. A month would have been more polite."

"I couldn't let the chance go by to be with Amy again, Ma'am. It's important for us."

"What about your other sister? Millie will have extra duties now," said Eleanor with raised eyebrows.

"Oh! Please, Ma'am. Don't work her too hard. She's not as strong as me and Amy," pleaded Edie.

"I'll try my best, but you've put me in a fix. I'll have to get help from outside now. And, just before I've got relations from Sydney coming to stay, *this* has to happen."

"Why haven't you let my sister see Millie?" Edie asked suddenly, feeling bold.

"We won't be going into that, if you don't mind," Eleanor replied tartly. "You can go now and I'll see you before you leave here."

"I'm sorry, Ma'am, for the inconvenience but our aim is for us all to be together again seeing my brother now has a job working on ships and … …"

"Is that so?" said Eleanor, interested. "Well I'm pleased for him because there's no work in Australia."

Edie was ushered to the door and left the homestead to join Millie and the others in the kitchen. When the girls returned to the cottage, Dottie was mixing up a sponge cake. She put her arm around Edie's shoulders.

"Wish Amy a happy new year when you see her and ask her not to forget about her old friends in the cottage here."

"As if any of us could ever forget about you and Mr Payne," Edie said sincerely. "You've been like a Mum and Dad to us since you arrived. But it's not goodbye. We'll always be in touch."

"And she's coming back here to see me," piped up Millie, "and I'm leaving when I'm sixteen too."

Edie Joins Amy

On New Year's Day, Edie packed her suitcase and her pink box from London with Millie watching and reminding her to take her embroidery from a cupboard. Edie waited impatiently for the next morning to arrive when Arthur would drive her to her new position. She slept well that night and sought out Mrs Warby in the homestead to say goodbye before she left.

"Thank you so much, Mrs Warby, for all you've done for me. Don't think I don't appreciate it because I really do. I'll be visiting Millie as often as I can and I hope her chest won't play up again in winter."

"I have cough mixture for that, Edie, as you know. I'll keep an eye on her."

Then she thought, *Funny, that girl hasn't called me Ma'am when she spoke to me this time. A bit disrespectful like her sister.*

There were hugs and promises all round at the cottage and finally Edie left for Lynnewood Station. When she arrived, she reported to Andrea Whitby and was shown to the same room her sister occupied.

"You can start work tomorrow," Andrea advised. "I'll give you your schedule then."

"Thank you so much, Mrs Whitby, for letting me work here. I'll do my best."

Andrea smiled, nodded, and then left

Edie walked around to the kitchen to give Amy, Shirley and Gwen in the kitchen a hand as they were getting ready for the influx of the workers calling around for their dinner. When the men arrived and sat down on the benches, Edie volunteered as a waitress. Amy advised Edie that they were not allowed to sit with the workers and eat their dinner among them as they had been doing. Mr and Mrs Whitby had made a new rule and wanted the women separated from the men, frowning on flirtations while working, and pairs going off together.

"That's alright by me," Edie declared. "If I ever marry it won't be to a farmhand. When the time comes, I'm moving down to the city where there's a bit more going on, not that I mind being here for the time being," she reassured Amy with a smile.

The women sat down to their meal after the men had been served, enjoying the ribald laughter and muffled bits of conversation they could pick up going on outside. After dessert and a cup of tea, the men took their leave and departed for their quarters. All except for one who lagged behind. Daniel entered the kitchen with his used plates and cutlery and made his way over to Amy.

"This might help a bit. A little less carrying, eh? I'd help with the dishes if I could but I'd better get going. Branding cattle tomorrow. Hard work. Thanks, girls, for your great cooking."

He tipped his Akubra towards Amy and, with a big grin and friendly wave to everyone, departed.

"Who was that?" Edie gushed. "He's gorgeous! I don't think I've ever seen a better-looking man."

"I think he fancies your sister," Gwen half whispered to Edie, with a conspiratorial look, but Amy cottoned on to Gwen's quiet remark and responded.

"He's a gentleman and was only helping out, bringing in his plates. Don't listen to Gwen, Edie. He could have any girl he wants, that one. Why would he look at me, for heaven's sake? I'm no oil painting."

"Well, he made a beeline straight for you, Amy," said Shirley with an impish look. "Maybe he doesn't want just looks in a woman, although there's plenty worse looking than you. Maybe he wants a quiet and steady girl. One with a big heart, like you. He's been in the war you know."

"Stop teasing me, everyone. I wouldn't even hope for anyone like him," Amy said dismissively, a look hinting at resignation on her face. "Now come on. Let's get busy. There's a lot to do."

In the coming weeks, Edie poured her heart into her work at Lynnewood Station, eager to please her new employers and enjoying the change from Balangara. With all her busyness, time passed quickly and February drew to a close. With permission from Andrea Whitby, Edie and Amy had rung up the Payne's at Balangara and spoken to Millie on a few occasions.

"She's been well so far, but very tired," Edie had commented "and she said not to worry about her."

"I'll try not to," Amy promised, "but isn't it good we don't have to worry about Freddy anymore? I wonder what he's been up to, where he's been?"

"Lucky him, seeing all those countries in the world. I wonder if we'll ever travel like that."

Amy paused and in a quiet, reflective way said, "Wouldn't it be lovely if we could go home, Edie?"

"You mean to England?" Edie mused quietly. "If ifs and ands were pots and pans, there'd be no need for tinkers."

"I suppose so," agreed Amy.

Good News from America

A month passed and a letter arrived at Lynnewood Station for Amy. It was from Freddy.

"Come on, Edie," she said excitedly, but a small doubt invaded her mind. *What if he is out of work again?*

But her fears faded as she and Edie read the letter.

59 Warren St.
Tottenham Court Rd.
London W1   *22-1-23*

Dear Amy & Edie

Thank you for your nice letter. I am glad to hear you are now both together but poor little Millie is by herself. At the time of writing I am in London after having done my sixth voyage to America but the 'Majestic' is now laid up for six weeks to be reconditioned during which time I hope to be able to sign on another ship, a ship going to Australia for preference but I shall sign on for the return journey so I shall not stop in Aussie for good, at least not yet as I want to see a lot more of the world. Travelling is fine. If I cannot get a boat to Aussie I shall take any one that goes away for some time, say, China or New Zealand or perhaps a tramp steamer that you never know the next port. Dear Amy please don't deposit any money in Sydney for my passage to Aussie, because I can work a passage quite easily now that I have my

"Let's hope he can get a boat to Australia, Amy," said Edie wistfully. "If it calls in at Sydney, we could get a night train down and see him if only for a day. We could be spared here for that."

Amy nodded at Edie's impractical plan and added, "We'll have to write to him again and let him know how pleased we are with his latest news."

Opening Up to Edie

"You know, Freddy must wonder why Millie is not allowed to speak to you. What was it you said to Mrs Warby, Amy, that made her so angry? You've never told me everything either, have you?"

"Well, I suppose I should open up to you about what happened. I didn't say anything before because I was so livid and upset. I didn't want you to go through what I did, but I overheard Neil Warby talking to a workman and he said we girls from London might have been prostitutes if they hadn't rescued us. I couldn't stop crying when I heard that. We've always been a respectable family. How would Mummy and Daddy have reacted, and Aunty Esther?"

"*What!*" Edie exploded. "How awful!" Then her eyes opened wide and an angry look crossed her face. "Do you mean to tell me the Warby's have had that opinion about us? I'd have given Ma'am the rounds of the kitchen before I left that place if I'd known about *that.*"

"I did have it out with her, Edie, and she was genuinely sorry about what Mr Neil had said. She said she'd talk to him about it. I also told her we were all overworked and I was worried about Millie doing so much. She told me I was not to talk to you or Millie about what Neil had said and that the work was not too hard. Then she told me I'd been rude to her and she didn't want me to see Millie again. I think she was frightened I'd spill the beans and upset Millie and she'd want to leave as we have."

"She should have made her son apologise for making assumptions like that about us. What a cheek! Did you ever tell Freddy about all this in a letter, Amy?"

"At first I didn't tell him. I only told him I'd had a row with Mrs

Warby and she wouldn't let me see Millie, but I told him everything in the last letter which I wrote a couple of months ago." Then Amy had an afterthought. "He should write and tell her off, as the man in the family, don't you think, Edie?"

"Yes!" Edie agreed emphatically.

"You know," Amy said after a moment of reflection, "I think it's best if we put all that stuff behind us. It doesn't help to brood on rubbish like that. We've both got new jobs and we're together. Let's just wait until Millie is sixteen and get her somewhere not far away from us, eh? Look, it's nearly April, only six months to go for her and then she can leave."

"You're right. Things are getting better for us all. We shouldn't look back."

A Man Called Daniel

Amy and Edie worked diligently at Lynnewood Station giving their best to the Whitby's. On one occasion, Daniel had lingered behind after breakfast to have a chat to Amy. She'd taken the initiative and questioned him about his service in the Great War. He'd seemed hesitant at first to talk, but after clearing his throat, he related some of his experiences.

"I lowered my age, Amy, and joined the Light Horse. After I got on the boat, *The Adelaide*, I got the measles. When I got better, I served in the desert and in France. I got rheumatic fever in the trenches and was sent home. Luckily, I missed a boat going to Gallipoli or I may not be here today. It's something I don't like to talk about," he'd replied, lowering his eyes. Then he added, "I only hope I never have to see the sights and suffering I've seen while I was over there, and that no-one has to ever go through those things again."

He looked away and something told Amy not to pursue that subject again. She squeezed his arm and changed the topic of conversation; talked about the attractions to be found in Guyra and Armidale.

"Last week we went for a picnic by the wetlands in Guyra. I had no idea there was a lake there. And once at Balangara we were taken to the Armidale Show."

"I'd like to take you there again one day, Amy," Daniel said boldly. "That is, if you'd like to go with me, I mean."

"I'd love that, Daniel." Coyly, Amy smiled.

The conversation ended when Gwen called Amy back to the kitchen to help with the dishes.

"Sorry," said Amy as she walked back, after giving Daniel a wave.

"I'm sorry I had to break it up, Love, but he'll be back again tonight. Don't worry."

Amy grinned and nursed her secret that Daniel had asked her out. She also hoped that no-one had eavesdropped on their conversation. In the next couple of weeks, there were more little trysts outside the kitchen and Amy knew that she and Daniel were drawing closer. The last time, they'd opened up about their backgrounds, Daniel explaining that he came from Scottish ancestry and his father had brought the family out to Australia when he was only a baby. Amy had felt confident in telling Daniel about her family in London, the deaths of her parents, and how she and her sisters had never really wanted to come to Australia and leave Freddy and their roots back in England. Daniel had listened intently, nodding his head in sympathy.

"You'll all have a better life here anyway, Amy," he'd said, "and won't it be good when your brother joins you?"

Sticking Up for His Sisters

The next day another letter arrived. Edie called in at the kitchen waving it to catch Amy's attention.

"Looks like it's from Freddy," she announced as the sisters went outside and sat on a bench.

"Another letter from him? So soon too," said Amy, both surprised and curious. Usually it's months before he writes to us, but I told him all about what went on back at Balangara. Our last letters must have crossed. I wonder what he has to say, Edie?"

"Quick, open it, Amy, and let's see."

Kew Gardens Inn,
Long Island
New York

February 10th 1923

Dear Amy and Edie,

> *Many thanks for your letters. I am glad to hear you're both doing well and are happy together but I am sorry Millie is not with you. I am going to write to her as soon as I finish this. I suppose Mrs Warby will let her receive a letter, anyway I'm going to see. I'd like to know by what right Mrs Warby will not let you see her and when I get out there next Nov or Dec I'll let her know just where she gets off the bus. I'm saving money in America better than I ever could in England and I shall positively be in Aussie by December barring accidents such as could make it impossible but I shall not let*

"I told him Mrs Warby had said she'd speak to Neil about his opinion of us, Edie, and I think Freddy doesn't want to go into that subject again but he sounds very angry that Mrs Warby is keeping Millie away from me. Anyhow, he says he's coming out in December and he sounds determined this time."

"Don't hold your breath. He's promised that so many times," Edie said flatly.

"He'll be coming out. I feel it in my bones. He might have some leave and can come up to Guyra. I'll suggest it next time I write. The Whitby's might let him stay for a while in one of the workmen's quarters."

"That would be lovely," Edie agreed with a yearning look.

"Back to work then," said Amy brusquely. "It won't hop away."

Edie nodded and returned to her duties in the homestead.

A Birthday Present

It happened on Wednesday, June 6th that, after the workmen's evening meal and the others had departed, Daniel approached Amy with a small packet.

"Did you have a nice birthday party today with the girls, Amy?" he asked. "Now you're twenty-one, you can do what you like, can't you?"

"Within reason, Dan," she laughed. "Yes, I got telephone messages and cards from Balangara, and Mrs Whitby came round and shared in the birthday cake, and I got a few presents too."

"Well, here's another one, Amy," said Daniel as he gave her the little packet. Then he put his arm around her shoulders and gave her a short kiss on the cheek.

Amy blushed as she accepted the gift and recoiled somewhat. Then she unwrapped the present and smiled.

"Oh! it's Eau de Cologne, Dan, my favourite. How did you know?"

"I didn't really. I asked my mother and she told me it's very popular."

"Well, thank you again, Dan. That was so nice of you, but I'll have to run inside. The girls are waiting for my help."

"So long then. I'll see you soon, Amy. Tomorrow, eh?" he asked with a grin.

"Yes," Amy said shyly, still feeling the impact of Daniel's sudden kiss on her cheek; it had taken her by surprise and left her flustered.

Daniel departed with a short wave, which Amy returned.

Getting Closer

After the work was finished in the kitchen, Amy retired to her room and filled in the time doing cross-stitch embroidery. But her mind gave her no peace, her thoughts conflicted. *Is Daniel leading me on? He's so good looking. He seems sincere. But what does he see in me? Should I encourage him?*

Despite any doubts, the next day she felt excited at meeting Daniel outside the kitchen after the men had finished their dinner. She then knew that any denial of her attraction to him would be in vain. She was falling for him, this handsome returned soldier, this steady, polite and gentle man.

"I'm going to buy myself a Douglas motor cycle, Amy," he informed her a week later. "I can't afford a motor car but I can pay off a bike. I'll get a sidecar attached and you and I can get about."

"That'll be great, Dan, but I'll be a bit nervous. My Mum back in England swore she'd never get into anything on the road driven by petrol … said those things were dangerous and could kill people. She was a horse and buggy girl."

Dan laughed. "Depends how you drive the modern automobile. If everyone obeys the road rules accidents won't happen. Anyway, you can't stop progress. There's a company in America producing millions of motor cars. Other firms are too. There's already plenty of vehicles in this country, as you've seen. My mate Pete bought a T Model Ford last year and it goes like a rocket. I've been in it a dozen times. One day I hope to have one like it."

"First the motor cycle, then the car, eh? Oh! by the way, you won't believe this but my sister Edie once owned a motor cycle for about half an hour. She won it at the Armidale show a few years ago but donated it to the Red Cross. Shame she didn't keep it, I say."

"Go on!" said Dan incredulously, his eyebrows raised. "A young girl winning a motor bike. A lot of blokes would have been jealous, I'll bet."

"I won a sheep," added Amy, giggling, "and I also gave my prize to the Red Cross."

"Well, what else would you have done with it, anyhow?" Dan laughed again.

"I could have shorn it, spun the wool and knitted a jumper," Amy quickly replied.

At this point, the two parted, laughing, and went back to their quarters.

Women's Breeches

A letter was handed to Amy in mid-October. It was addressed from America.

"It's from Freddy," she announced to Edie. "I wonder what he's up to these days?"

"The same old story. How he's planning to come out to Aussie next week or he'll write to us shortly," Edie remarked, looking resigned.

"Poor Freddy! Will he ever get out here? Will we ever get to see our brother again? It's been years, hasn't it, Edie?"

"One day he'll make it, I suppose, but what's in his letter, Amy? Open it quickly."

New York
America   *Sept. 6th 1923*

My Dear Amy,

I have suddenly taken another fit and am writing again. I am so sorry to have kept you waiting so long for a letter but I have made a new home, this time in America. I have been here nearly three months now. I have just finished a job in the Catskill Mountains here. The reason I stayed in America is that there is plenty of work here whereas there is none in England. I have already another job and I only finished my last 2 days ago. I am not sending my full address as I go from one place to another and never know where I may be from

"So he's moved to America," said Amy thoughtfully. "Well, if the work is there for him, I don't blame him. Do you, Edie?"

"No. And if he's saving more money there, then good luck to him, I say. But fancy women wearing breeches over there like men, in that photo. Do you think that fashion will ever come to Australia, Amy?"

"Probably, but it'll take time. I'd never wear them myself. Most unfeminine. Would you?"

"If they became fashionable, I certainly would. Mrs Whitby lets me read *The Ladies Home Journal* sometimes but I haven't seen any pictures of women wearing breeches in those magazines, but they're old issues."

Amy nodded and changed the subject.

"Edie, we must post Freddy's letter to Millie so she knows what's going on in his life. She's still hoping he'll be out here soon, like us, I suppose."

"She might have lost that hope, like me," Edie said with a shrug as she pulled a face.

"Don't say that, Edie. I feel he really wants to see us again but things just haven't worked out so far for him to do it. After all, a man has to go where the work is, doesn't he?"

"I'm sick of trying to work him out, Amy. I think he could have tried harder to get out here. Let's drop the subject."

With their differing opinions, Amy and Edie returned to their respective tasks.

An Invitation to a Ball

Daniel became more confident in his growing attachment to Amy. The next time they met, he took hold of her hand and led her to a gum tree a short way from the workmen's benches outside the kitchen.

"Oh! Dan," said Amy, drawing back as he put his arm around her. "You know Mrs Whitby doesn't want flirtations going on in the workplace."

"This isn't a flirtation, Amy," said Dan quickly. "Anyhow, Mrs Whitby can't stop people talking to one another and my work isn't being affected because I like a girl. Look, there's a ball in Armidale in three weeks. How about stepping out with me, eh? Have you heard of jazz music? It's the latest thing. Pete's going in his car with his girl. I'm going to ask him if he can take you and me. Pretty sure he'll say yes. Do you know a lot of the girls are wearing dresses just above the knee now. A bit cheeky, eh?"

"I'd like to go, Dan. The only music I ever got to hear was from the gramophone the Paynes had and from the bush dances we went to in the old shearing shed there. And oh! Miss Wilma playing the piano each Sunday at church."

"I want to get to know you more, Amy. Meeting outside the kitchen here doesn't give us much of a chance. If we go out together, we'll …"

"Yes, I understand, but I'll have to go now," Amy said hastily, looking a bit worried and afraid they'd be noticed by someone. "Shirley and Gwen may resent my time away."

"I'll see you tomorrow then. Same time, same place," assured Dan with a grin.

With a handclasp and a smile, the two parted and went their

separate ways.

During the time Amy and Daniel had been outside, Gwen had asked Shirley, "What does he see in her, Shirl? I know she's a lovely girl but he could have anyone, couldn't he?"

"He could, but she's steady and kind and has a loving quality about her which a lot don't have. He's been a soldier in the war, Gwen, don't forget, and God knows what he's been through. In her, he would find the calmness and serenity he needs. She's a family person too and hey! she's quite attractive and has lovely blue eyes."

The conversation abruptly ended when Amy hurried back into the kitchen. "Sorry, girls. Here, give me that tea towel, Gwen. I'll finish drying up."

"You were out there with Daniel a while, Amy. What kept you so long?" Gwen asked mischievously as she handed Amy the tea towel.

"You know what kept them, Gwen," Shirley answered with a knowing look, speaking up for Amy. "They're getting to know each other. Aren't you, Amy?"

Amy looked down a little, then felt a boldness take over, encouraged by Shirley's broaching the subject of her friendship with Daniel, and coupled with a closer connection to him after he'd put his arm around her.

"He's a very nice person and I do like him. And do you know what? He's asked me to go to Armidale in a couple of weeks to a ball and I said I'd go. Should be a lot of fun."

"Good on you, Amy! I wish some dreamboat would ask me out to somewhere like that. What are you going to wear?" Gwen asked.

"Oh! I hadn't thought of that," Amy said with a frown. "Can't wear a cotton dress there, or an old skirt and blouse, can I?"

That evening after their work was finished, Amy told Edie that Dan had asked her out to a ball in Armidale but she didn't have a suitable dress to wear.

"Oh! please, please can I come too?" begged Edie. "I get so bored here. Get Dan to ask his friend Peter if he could squeeze me in the car too, if he's driving you. Pleeease, Amy."

"I can only ask. We'll see," said Amy, trying not to show disappointment that there might be a gooseberry along with her and Dan.

Two days later, Amy told Edie that Peter had agreed to fit her in the car. Edie then decided she'd have to get into Armidale somehow to get a new outfit.

"I'll ask Mrs Whitby, Amy. She drives into town once a week in her car."

Mrs Whitby willingly agreed to drive the two girls into Armidale to buy new dresses.

"She's driving to Armidale in a week, Amy, to visit a friend and she told me that Marcus Clarks have a department with ladies' fashions. We'll go there to pick out our dresses."

Amy whooped with joy.

"Thank goodness, Edie. I was beginning to think I'd have to cancel everything because I've only got a long skirt and blouse which is old fashioned. You know that outfit."

"Yes, I'm so excited. Can't wait for next week," Edie answered.

A Shopping Spree

On the day of the shopping excursion, Andrea Whitby parked her car outside the department store and dropped off the girls.

"I'll pick you up in two hours, round about here," she promised.

Amy and Edie quickly made their way into the interior of Marcus Clark's store until they came to the Ladies' Fashion department. After rummaging through everything in the racks and on display, Amy settled for a demure, aqua-coloured, long length gown made from rayon, commonly called artificial silk. Edie was more adventurous.

"I just love this mauve velvet dress, Amy. Mauve's my favourite colour. I know it's knee length, but it has a dropped waist and a scooped out neckline and it's sleeveless. Very modern, Amy! And look at the trimmings! What do you think?"

"It's a bit daring, Edie. Try it on and I'll tell you what I think."

Edie dashed into the change room and emerged two minutes later looking pleased with herself.

"I love it! I just love it, Amy," she enthused, but Amy shook her head.

"The neckline's far too low and the skirt should be longer," she advised with a censuring frown.

"Oh! You don't know what the fashion is these days, Amy. In *McCalls* and *The Ladies' Home Journals*, the modern woman is wearing dresses just like these. I'm *having* it."

Amy tried on her dress and was also satisfied with her choice.

After they'd paid for their gowns, they moved to the shoe department.

"I'm trying on these ones," said Edie as she selected a stylish pair of Mary Jane's.

"No!" said Amy quickly. "Look at those heels. They're nearly three inches high. One inch is enough, Edie. You'll fall over in those."

"I'll practice. Other women are wearing them. If they can, I can."

"I'll wear the good ones I've got at home," Amy murmured quietly. "They'll be safer to dance in."

Edie paid for her shoes and the two women moved to the jewellery department.

"Look at these crystals!" Edie declared ecstatically as she draped them around her neck. "They'll be gorgeous with the dress."

"But Edie, look at the price of them," said Amy, her jaw dropping. "You won't have any money left."

"I'm buying them and lipstick too. Where do they sell that in here?"

"Over there, my dear," gestured a shop assistant.

Amy lamely followed Edie to the cosmetics bar and looked on as she picked out a lipstick.

"It's scarlet, Edie. Do you think that's wise? You don't want to end up looking common, do you?"

"Look, Amy! Glamour is the fashion these days and scarlet lipstick is in vogue. I'm taking it!"

"I think you've spent enough now, Edie. Those crystals are …"

"It's my business, Amy, and my money," Edie cut in crossly. "Now I've got to find a place to get my hair cut. A short bob and a fringe is the going thing now."

"But you always look lovely, Edie, after you've used the hot tongs to curl your hair."

"You use them if you to want to, Amy, but I'm getting my hair cut in the latest style. Curls are *out*!"

The girls paid for their purchases and Edie was directed to a hair salon a few doors away. The job was done after a half hour wait.

"Let's go somewhere and have a cup of tea and a piece of cake while we wait for Mrs Whitby," Amy suggested as she spotted a nearby café.

"You've only bought a dress, Amy," said Edie. "You could have bought a new necklace or something."

"I have some pearls, Edie, and I'm taking a cardigan if it gets cold."

"Well, you'll look lovely anyway. It's a lovely dress," Edie said honestly.

After their treat at the café, they made their way to the pick-up point outside Marcus Clarks Store. Andrea Whitby turned up in fifteen minutes to drive back to Lynnewood Station. She looked at Edie in surprise and remarked, "You've had your hair cut, Edie. You look like a different girl."

"It's called a bob, Mrs Whitby, and it's the latest fashion."

When they returned, Edie rushed into the bedroom and spread out her new purchases on her bed, gloating over them. "I just can't wait for the ball and to get dressed up in all of this," she said to Amy dreamily.

"Only eight days to go. I'm looking forward to it too," Amy replied, smiling.

Jazz

On the afternoon of the ball, Amy and Edie dressed carefully and waited for Pete and his girlfriend Merle and Daniel to arrive in the T Model Ford at six o'clock. Edie squashed into the back seat beside Amy and Daniel. She noticed Daniel had taken hold of Amy's hand as he murmured softly to her, "You look lovely."

It was a bumpy ride as the car would often swerve to avoid potholes caused by recent rainfall, but there was much laughter as they were often jostled during the journey. On arriving in Armidale, Pete found a convenient place to park his car not far from the Town Hall. They walked through its grand entrance and found available seating near the stage. Shortly after, the band arrived and tuned up.

"It's a real jazz band," Peter explained. "I've been to a few sessions in Sydney. Jazz is becoming very popular lately."

"What's jazz, Peter?" Edie asked.

"Well, it's a bit hard to describe. The musicians sort of create music on the spot from a certain key and work in with each other. It's usually got a good beat. Can be very loud …"

"Shush!" warned Amy, "they're starting up."

The introductory number set the dancing off for the evening. Many eager couples got on to the floor. Others started to sing *I Wish I Could Shimmy Like My Sister Kate*.

"I can do that," announced Edie as she sprang from her seat and joined the dancers on the floor. Amy watched sombrely as her sister copied the others, shaking her shoulders and then her hips, her long crystal beads swinging to the rhythm. Working her way around the room and returning to her seat laughing and panting from the exertion, she smiled at Amy and gave her a wink.

A change of mood accompanied the next item, and a waltz was announced by the bandleader who then picked up his saxophone and began to play *If You Were the Only Girl in the World.*

"Come on, Dan," Amy urged as she pulled him to his feet. This was more her style, slow and romantic, but Dan was reluctant to dance.

"I'm no good at it, Amy. I've got big feet."

"I'll teach you, Dan."

Amy was patient and managed to finally get a good enough performance from Dan even though he'd trodden on her right foot a few times and apologised.

"That band leader is very versatile because he plays an instrument as well, Amy," Edie remarked. She'd caught the conductor's eye on a few occasions when she'd sensed him looking at her during short intervals. "And I like his red, curly hair and his check suit too."

The evening passed with an assortment of old-time dances, a few barn dances. It ended with a performance from the jazz band of improvised music. People slowly started to leave when the band leader walked over to Edie and asked if she'd enjoyed the night.

"Very much. It's been great fun," she replied with a wide grin.

"My name's Cecil," said the man, "and what should I call you?"

"I'm officially Edith, but most people call me Edie," said Edie, flirting.

"Where do you live, Edie?" Cecil asked next.

"At Lynnewood Station, outside of Guyra – it's a large cattle holding."

"What do you do?"

"Oh! this and that," Edie said, hedging a little. She didn't want this modern young man to know she was only a housemaid. She quickly turned the question back on Cecil.

"And what do you do, Cecil?"

"I'm a roving jazz bandleader. I'm based in Newcastle, but we visit country towns to perform like we did tonight. Never know where we'll be from one month to another."

"What fun!" said Edie, then she became tongue-tied.

"Could I have your address? I'd like to keep in touch," said Cecil suddenly. He pulled out a notepad and short pencil from a pocket and Edie gave him her address. Then with a nod and a little wave, he departed, saying as he went, "I'll call in to see you one day."

Tired But Happy

Edie smiled at Cecil and returned his wave then hurried to catch up with the others who'd already passed through the front entrance on their way back to the car. She felt incredulous that a person like Cecil, a jazz bandleader, would have taken such notice of her. She soon caught up and scrambled into the back seat, finding herself wedged between Amy and Dan. Much talk and laughter occurred on the way back to Lynnewood, detouring firstly, to drop off Pete's girlfriend Merle, who lived closer to Guyra.

"Here at last," Pete proclaimed as they pulled up in the driveway at Lynnewood Station.

"Tired but happy," added Edie, the chief talker in the car; she professed loudly and long about what a wonderful time she'd had, and how she'd come to love jazz. She hadn't said anything about Cecil.

So Amy introduced the topic, "Edie, I saw you were talking to the band leader and …"

Edie quickly cut in, "I'm going in. I'm cold. I should have taken a shawl with me or something."

"Those bare arms," whispered Amy to Dan, "I told her to take a cardigan but she didn't want to spoil her look, she said."

Under a Peppercorn Tree

Daniel took hold of Amy's arm and led her to a large peppercorn tree not far from the driveway.

"Don't go in yet, Amy. I've got something to talk about."

By this time, Edie had disappeared through the side door of the homestead and had made her way to her and Amy's bedroom.

"I'm not going to beat about the bush, Amy. I'm a man of few words as you know. You're the girl for me. Will you marry me, dear Amy?"

Amy's eyes widened in disbelief as she took in Dan's proposal, then a broad smile broke out when she realised he was serious.

"Oh! Dan, I'd just love to. Yes! I accept your proposal my … my sweetheart."

Daniel pulled her close, and they embraced and kissed passionately. Then they both sat on the grass and started to talk about their future.

"I'm buying the motorbike after Christmas, and then I'll save up for an engagement ring," Daniel said next. "Until then, let's keep this quiet until I put that ring on your finger, eh?"

"Yes," Amy agreed excitedly. "It'll be our little secret, Dan. When do you think we should get married then? We'll have to buy a lot of things to set up home and where do you think we should live? And …"

"Hold on, Amy," Daniel laughed, pulling her close and kissing her again "You're like a waterfall. It'll all work out in time."

"Yes, I'll have to be patient, Dan, I know, and I promise I will try to be."

"I'm just as keen as you are to get hitched, you know."

The breeze that had chilled Edie earlier grew colder.

"It's getting late, Dan, and it's getting cold. I've got to be up early to help get breakfast for you lot. And what are you doing tomorrow?"

"I'm repairing some fencing in a few paddocks, and there's another field to be fenced as well. Yep! We'd better get going."

They parted with a lingering kiss and promised to be discreet until they announced their engagement.

Amy tiptoed into the bedroom determined not to awaken Edie, but her efforts were in vain.

"You were a long time out there with Dan, Amy. He likes you. Do you like him?"

"Shush! Go back to sleep. I have to be up soon to get the brekkies."

"What did you think of that band leader, Amy?" asked Edie, ignoring Amy's request to go back to sleep.

"A bit of a lair. We'll talk about *him* tomorrow, Edie," Amy insisted as she climbed into her bed.

With that, Edie also settled down and shortly afterwards both sisters were asleep.

After work the next day, when she'd heard that Edie had given Cecil her address, Amy cautioned Edie about being too friendly with someone like a roving bandleader.

"People on the stage and in bands like him, Edie, may be flighty. If he goes all around the state playing in a band, he probably flirts with all sorts of girls, you know. And you are very nice looking. Please be careful. There are many lovely men around these parts, you know."

Edie snapped at her, "You mind your own business. I don't poke my nose into your business with Dan, do I?"

"Well, you did before," Amy retorted.

"Oh, shut up," Edie replied before turning over to go back to sleep.

Amy said no more but hoped this flamboyant Cecil would lose interest in her sister and not get in touch again. Instead, she got out her pencil and pad and wrote a long letter to Aunty Esther, letting her know of her engagement to Daniel. She also informed her of her recent reaffirmation of her Christian faith and trust in Jesus as her

Saviour. She knew Aunty Esther would be pleased to hear this. The next night she wrote letters to Freddy and Mrs Winsor to wish him a happy twenty-third birthday and to tell them both of her engagement.

Christmas Day 1923

Christmas day was celebrated quietly at Lynnewood Station. Amy had taken out her grandmother Mary's recipe and four puddings were cooked.

"The best we've ever tasted," everyone agreed.

The year moved quickly into 1924 and in March, Daniel picked up Amy in his new motorcycle and drove her in the sidecar to Armidale on a Saturday morning. The local jeweller brought out his tray of diamond rings and, after a lot of deliberation, Amy and Daniel settled on a solitaire that was not too expensive for their budget. The next day, Amy proudly flashed the ring on her finger to Shirley and Gwen and Andrea and Joseph Whitby. Andrea had allowed Amy to ring Millie at Balangara to tell her the news. Daniel had announced his engagement earlier to his workmates. Edie had been secretly told a few days previously and was thrilled for her sister.

"You'll make a lovely wife and mother, Amy," she'd commented. "You're cut out for it. He's a lucky man."

A Message From Aunty Esther

In mid-May, Amy received two letters. One from Aunty Esther; the other from Mrs Winsor. She opened Aunty Esther's first, eager to read about the reaction to her engagement.

Whitefield's
Tottenham Court Rd,
March 21. 1924

My dear Amy,

Your letter gave me much pleasure and I am glad to hear you were so seriously contemplating taking such a solemn step as the open confession of love to your Lord and Master Jesus Christ. Do let it mean all that to you and not any formal thing, making the promise to be His loyal, trusty follower. I am very glad to hear too of your great possession in the love of an earthly friend and most sincerely wish you most heartily every happiness. I trust he too is striving to live near to Jesus Christ for only that can make your happiness complete. Religion is the only thing that can give us solid happiness in sickness and in health and how ever dark the day may be. It also enhances every joy. Herewith I have much pleasure in sending you on the notes as promised. I should have written immediately but I have had a great sorrow. My closest friend for nearly eleven years was suddenly called to meet her Master face to face. She was such a

She's been a bit like a mother to me, thought Amy. *I've been able to tell her everything about my life, and she's always been so encouraging. She doesn't say much about my engagement, but she was happy to hear of it.*

"And Aunty Esther, don't worry. Ours will be a Christian marriage," pledged Amy aloud, as though speaking directly to Esther.

She put the letter in the biscuit tin and opened Mrs Winsor's, curious as to what she may find out about Freddy's latest pursuits.

Where is Freddy Now?

59 Warren Street,
Tottenham Ct. Rd.
London

25/3/24

Dear Amy and Edie,

A joint letter as I know you are together. First I must thank you very much for the letters you have both written, also the photo which is very nice. Freddy's have arrived quite safe too and according to my photo you are very much like him. Now Amy I am getting rather anxious about Freddy as I have not heard from him for over 3 months. The last letter he wrote was on Nov 27th at Beunos Aires and he said he would be reaching New York about Dec. 22nd. He said he would write me a letter on the voyage to New York and post it as soon as he landed but I have not had a line. He asked me to send a letter to an address in New York. I sent about 5 I think, but have had no reply. I have written to the landlady of the house. I could not put any name so have chanced my luck whether she will answer. As soon as I hear anything I will let you know. If you hear you might let me know. I know he is a terror for writing but he has not been so long before. I shall keep the photo you sent him till I hear. I only hope he is alright. He told me some time ago he was coming to England to get some clothes and then

After Amy had shared the letters with Edie, she said "I'm puzzled as to what is going on with Freddy. Mrs Winsor doesn't know where he is or what he's doing. I was hoping he'd heard about my engagement and I'd hear from him. Where are all the letters going? I'm worried, Edie. Why doesn't he write?"

"Remember that photo he sent us a while ago, Amy? Him in the middle of all those girls in breeches? He's probably having too good a time over there to worry about his three sisters."

"Look, I know he hasn't been a great letter writer, Edie, but he always kept in touch with Mrs Winsor. I do hope we hear from him soon. Surely he'll be here for my wedding."

Marriage Plans

"Have you and Dan set a date for the wedding yet, Amy?" Shirley asked the following day.

"Hopefully, just after Christmas. We're going into Guyra next week to book the church."

Gwen counted on her fingers.

"That's roughly in seven months."

"I know it's not a long engagement, but we're saving madly and should have all we need to set up house by then. Daniel wants me to give up working. I'll love that, just keeping house. We're going to rent a place in Guyra."

Edie had called in for her afternoon tea break and joined the discussion.

"I'll help you to get some things, Amy. Next time I go to Armidale I'm going to buy you a supper cloth and embroider it."

"Thanks, Edie, that will be lovely, but you'll be twenty in September, don't forget. You should think of getting a glory box together for yourself. You never know what's around the corner. You could be getting married too in a couple of years."

"I'm not even thinking like that now, Amy. Besides, I haven't yet seen a man around these parts I could fancy. I intend to stick around here for a while, probably until you and Dan are married and then move down to Sydney. I'm saving madly too so I can have something behind me when I go."

Shirley added quickly, "Is that a wise idea, Edie. You won't have any family around you, and you don't have any connections in Sydney, do you?"

"Well, I'm going anyhow," Edie assured her. "I'll find work down there and … and I'll join things and make new friends and I can always get on a train and come and visit Millie and Amy and Dan up here."

Amy sighed. "You'll do as you want, I know, Edie, but why has the grass always been greener on the other side of the fence with you?"

"Oh! shut up, Amy. I'm old enough to know what I want. I'll be off to Sydney one day, and that's that!"

Shirley and Gwen looked at each other and pulled faces.

"You're a determined little beggar, Edie, I'll say that," said Shirley quietly.

Edie flounced out, looking cross, and Amy sighed and shrugged her shoulders, annoyed by her sister's behaviour.

Edie had been nurturing her fascination with Cecil, the band leader, and bright lights beckoned. She'd been hoping to hear from him as he'd promised, but she'd never mentioned his name again to Amy, knowing she disapproved.

An Unexpected Caller

Three months passed and Edie was beginning to lose hope that she'd ever see Cecil again. In her disappointment, she reasoned that she'd just been a passing fancy, that he'd always be meeting lots of girls during his travels with the band and, even though she knew she was pretty, she wasn't the only girl around who was nice looking.

Oh! well, she thought, dispirited, *I'll see Amy married after Christmas and then decide what to do.*

She was working her way through a pile of ironing when Mrs Whitby interrupted her; told her that a young man had knocked on the front door and had asked to see her.

Could it be Freddy? she wondered as she hurried down the hallway to the front door. Then she dismissed that idea as highly improbable. Then an image of Cecil flashed through her mind.

Don't be silly, she told herself as she neared the doorway. *He would have lost interest in me by now.*

She passed through the doorway. And there was Cecil, standing under the shade of a large oak tree near the driveway, his hand resting on the boot of a smart, green two-seater.

"Took me a while to find the place, but here I am at last. We've been in Tamworth this week, and I thought I'd pay you a call as it's not too far away. How are you doing?"

"Oh! Cecil, it's *you*," stuttered Edie, flabbergasted and abashed at appearing in an apron which she wished she could take off. "I didn't think I'd ever hear from you again."

"Well, I've tracked you down at last," said Cecil, grinning. "We've had the band in places down the south coast since I saw you last. How would you like to come for a spin in the car? Are you busy right now?"

"Yes, I am actually. I'm helping out a friend here," Edie lied, "and I'm tied up with what we're doing at the moment." Then she stuttered, "Maybe my friend can, er, spare me, er …"

"I'm sure she can for a while," urged Cecil. "Go and ask, Edie. Just for an hour or so."

Edie nodded and wandered slowly back into the house, wondering how to approach the subject of taking leave from her duties. After all, she was only a paid servant here; Mrs Whitby may not allow her to suddenly skip away for a jaunt with a man in a green car when the ironing hadn't been finished. She sought out Mrs Whitby and meekly asked for permission to be absent for an hour to catch up with an old friend whom she hadn't seen in ages. Edie was becoming proficient at lying. Mrs Whitby was touched by Edie's pleading expression.

"Of course, I'll let you go, Edie. Work never hops away, and the ironing will still be here when you get back. Off you go with your friend and enjoy the drive."

"I'll be back in an hour," Edie promised, smiling in gratitude. "Thank you so much."

I'm not telling Amy. She won't notice anything from the kitchen in the back, she thought with a small sense of satisfaction as she rushed to their bedroom; she tore off the apron and work dress and put on a floral cotton dress. Then, at the dressing table, she took out her scarlet lipstick from the top drawer and quickly applied it, making sure the cupid bows on her top lip were even. She changed into her new shoes, quickly dragged a comb through her hair, and she was ready.

"Sorry to keep you, Cecil," she called gaily as she approached him.

He opened the car's passenger door. "That's all right," he answered just as cheerily as he closed the door after Edie had slid in. With an efficient cranking, the car started up and Cecil and Edie were on their way.

"I thought I'd drive to that lake in Guyra. It's a bird sanctuary and has a nice park around it," Cecil suggested as they left the driveway.

"I've never been there. It sounds lovely," Edie agreed, still stunned by the turn of events over the last ten minutes.

On the way to the park, they remained mostly silent with only occasional bouts of small talk. Edie was working out what to say and what not to say, worried that her situation in life may be a turn-off.

Cecil eventually located the sanctuary and drove through the gate into the park where he manoeuvred the car into a place under a large jacaranda tree.

When he'd stopped the engine, he looked at Edie with amusement and suddenly questioned her.

"You're a Pom, aren't you?"

"Oh!" Edie said, taken aback and somewhat abashed. "How did you know that?"

"It's your accent, baby. Can't fool me, Edie"

"Yes, it's true. I'm English, but I thought by now I would have lost my accent," she replied, feeling pleased that Cecil had called her 'baby'.

"I like the way you talk. When did you come out to Australia?"

"We came out when I was nine, in December 1913, and settled on a farm near Armidale."

Edie changed the subject in case Cecil was to ask about her parents. "And where is your home base, Cecil, when you're not travelling with the band?"

"Newcastle. About a couple of hours drive north of Sydney. That's where my family is, and I camp down there when I'm not on the road."

"What an exciting life you have, Cecil, always travelling and performing with the band. I *love* jazz music, and I was very impressed at that ball in Armidale, watching you play."

"Well, I was rather impressed with you on the dance floor, Edie. Caught some glimpses now and again but you sure know how to shimmy."

"Oh!" Edie laughed, delighted at the compliment, "I wish I could do it more. You know, one day I intend to move down to Sydney and see what's going on down there. Personally, I know the country is very nice, but for me, it gets a bit boring."

Cecil looked at her intensely and then asked what she'd dreaded. "What about your Mum and Dad? How would they feel about you moving down to the big smoke all on your own? How old are you? I guess about twenty or thereabouts. Now let's see. If you came out here in late 1913 when you were nine, and it's now almost the end of August 1924 … …"

"I'll be twenty in a few days on the 2nd of September, Cecil. What a great guess you made. And how old are you?"

"I'm twenty-five, birthday next May. Hey! You're turning twenty in a few days. Let's celebrate. I'm driving into Guyra to a little café I know there, and I'll shout you to afternoon tea, eh?"

A sudden thought of the ironing basket back at Lynwood Station waiting to be emptied flashed into Edie's mind but she quickly dismissed the thought; resolved to make up the time when she returned.

"Well, yes Cecil, thank you," she replied, smiling. "That'll be a treat."

At the café, they sat down at a table for two and placed their order. A nearby window overlooked the street, busy with many cars.

"I call my car *the baby* because it's new and little, but it sure gets me around," said Cecil with a grin.

"It must be lovely to go wherever you want to in a car and not have to rely on trains and buses," Edie said wistfully.

At that moment a pot of tea arrived and two large slices of passionfruit cream sponge.

Impulsively and off guard, Edie said, "That's Mrs Whitby's favourite. Amy bakes it in the kitchen, and I often serve it up for afternoon tea when I've, er …"

"Sounds like you've got a job at the place I picked you up at. What do you do there?"

Edie flushed and stumbled, but found an answer. "Well, I've got to save up enough money to get me to Sydney, you know. It's only temporary."

"There's nothing wrong with having a job, and if you're that keen, I'll drive you down to Sydney one day, but it'll have to be okay with your parents."

Telling the Truth

Edie's shame welled up, and she decided then to let Cecil know the truth about her background as she couldn't suddenly manufacture a reason for explaining away her parents. After all, better to get it over and done with before anything serious happened between them. Why would Cecil want to bother with the likes of her, anyhow? He was so sophisticated, and it looked like he came from a privileged family. She looked down, embarrassed at telling him the truth – that she and her sisters were orphans from a poor family – that her parents had died from tuberculosis back in England – that she and Amy and Millie were nothing more than servant girls.

"What's the matter, Edie," Cecil asked, noting her discomfort.

"Let's have our tea, Cecil, and then go back to your car, and I'll tell you."

"Alright," said Cecil, puzzled and concerned at the change in her demeanour.

When they left the café, he steadied Edie as she tripped over a small pothole as they made their way to the car. He drove back to the park under the jacaranda tree and asked what was troubling her.

Impassively, Edie told Cecil everything, while maintaining as much dignity as possible. She knew someone like Cecil would eventually choose a fashionable girl from a well-off family, not someone like her.

"Well, you've got that off your chest, Edie. So, your parents died, and then some people split up your family and sent you and your sisters out here. That must have been tough."

"Yes, it was, because we didn't want to come anyhow and leave our mother back there. She'd gone away to find work outside of London and wouldn't have known we were being sent to Australia."

"You're kidding me, Edie. Without her permission?"

"That's what happened. Then after we'd been out here for a while, we got a letter saying she'd died. It was heartbreaking. Millie and I got over it all much better than my sister Amy. She was very close to our mother, being older, I suppose, and she still longs for her roots back in England. She's the main letter writer back home."

"Now I understand why you were like that in the café before we left. Do you believe I'd think less of you because of all the sadness and misfortune you've suffered? ... because you're an orphan?"

"Some people *do* think less of us, Cecil. Don't be mistaken. There was class distinction back in England, and many people looked down on poor people like us, although that didn't happen in the church we went to. I know my sisters and I have been lucky to have ended up where we are today in the long run. Mrs Warby at Balangara, who organised our emigration, has done her best for us. She's fed us, clothed us and educated us, with government help of course, but we were always made to feel that we were, um, how can I put it? ... less than others in some way ... that we were nothing more than servants and marriage material. I've always wanted more than that. I'd like to learn the piano one day and find out what my talents are, you know."

"Thanks for telling me all that, Edie. And you know what? You have absolutely nothing to be ashamed of. Were you responsible for your Dad having to give up his job because of illness? Were you responsible for your parents' deaths? Are you responsible for the way some people choose to look at others? As far as I can see, you should have no fear at all about your standing in society. And you're beautiful as well."

A smile broke out on Edie's face. Then she remembered she'd been far longer away from the ironing basket than just one hour as promised to Mrs Whitby.

"I'll have to get back," she said quickly, looking at her wristwatch. "I've been away for over two hours, and I promised only one. I hope she won't be angry."

"It's my fault. I took you to that tea shop for your birthday. Would you like me to talk to her?"

"Thanks, Cecil but I'll front up. I think she'll be okay."

Cecil cranked up the motor, hopped in and started the trip back to Lynnewood Station. Edie now felt relaxed as she chatted to Cecil on the way after his positive affirmation of who she is. No more pretending.

Cecil Makes a Promise

"By the way, when were you thinking of going down to Sydney, and what do you intend to do down there?"

"I want to leave as soon as I can after my sister's wedding, which is just after Christmas on the 22nd of January. I hope to get a position in a shop for ladies' fashion or some other shop work. I could manage that because I'm a quick learner. Better than being a housemaid!"

"Just after Christmas! I'm coming up to get you. You're right to break away from these parts and try new things. I'll give you my address in Newcastle. Let me know when you're ready to go."

Edie could hardly believe what had happened in the last couple of hours. Any girl worth her salt would envy all the attention a man like Cecil had just paid her. And he'd even promised to personally drive her down to Sydney one day. Her dreams were coming true.

When they pulled up outside the side entrance to the homestead, Cecil took out a notebook from his pocket and wrote down his address. He handed it to Edie.

"I'll be ready when you are, baby," he said, looking at her with a grin.

"I'll let you know in good time, Cecil," Edie stressed, looking impish and thrilled he'd called her 'baby' again.

A Surprise for Amy

Amy was making her way to the side door to enter the homestead to talk to Edie about something when she noticed a small green car proceeding up the driveway. She stopped and watched it pull up a short way off, and wondered who the visitors could be. The driver's door opened, and a young man in a smart checked suit leapt out of the car. As he walked around to the passenger's door to open it, Amy noticed the red hair. The man opened the car door, and a young woman sprang out, laughing.

Amy's jaw dropped open. *Look at her, all dressed up in her best frock and with those Mary Jane shoes and oh! she's got lipstick on too!*

Amy was astonished. Just that morning Edie had called into the kitchen to have a cup of tea and mentioned that she had a big heap of ironing to do that afternoon. *But here she is now, with that flash looking band leader.*

As Amy walked to the car, she hardly knew what to say, but words came out at last. "Oh! Edie, where have you been? I didn't know you were going out somewhere. You told me you were doing some ironing this afternoon."

"Well, I've been doing something better," Edie replied, looking proud. "This is Cecil, and he's taken me to Guyra to a café to celebrate my birthday."

Amy thought it was time to acknowledge Cecil.

"Nice to meet you, Cecil. You're the band leader at that ball we went to at Armidale, not long ago, aren't you? Thanks for looking after my little sister."

"It's been my pleasure," Cecil replied, smiling, "and nice to meet you, too." Then he added, "I'd better be off, Edie. I've got a bit of a drive ahead of me."

Edie said goodbye with a small hug, and Cecil reminded her to write and let him know when he should pick her up to take her down to Sydney.

"And hold your head up high, Edie, when you speak to Mrs Whitby."

"I will," she promised, with a wide grin and a wave.

Cecil lifted his hand in farewell and drove away. Straight away, Amy confronted Edie about what on earth was going on. And what date about Sydney was he talking about?

Oh! dear, thought Edie, *he's let the cat out of the bag.*

"I'll explain it all, Amy, after I've seen Mrs Whitby. Later on tonight."

Amy returned to the kitchen, shaking her head, and Edie made her way into the house to apologise to Mrs Whitby.

The next morning, while cooking the men's breakfasts, Amy felt resigned. Even though she'd tried to talk sense into her sister the evening before, she realised Edie would always do what she wanted and have her own way. Thinking of Edie's plan to run away with that roving band leader and going to Sydney just after the wedding filled her with dismay. The conversation had reached a stalemate.

"You don't know him. He's a lovely, understanding person," Edie had insisted firmly during their talk. "He's only giving me a lift down there, and anyhow, what if he does fancy me? I could do worse."

After hearing the story of Cecil swooping in on Edie the day before, Shirley had advised Amy to let it go. 'She's just on twenty, Amy. Old enough. And you can't control her life. She has to make her own mistakes."

After that conversation, Amy put aside her concerns about Edie and in the evening raised the subject of Freddy's silence.

"We haven't heard from him for over a year, Edie. I let him know when I got engaged, you know. Mrs Winsor said she thinks letters are being lost going to and fro to different addresses. I was hoping he'd be coming to the wedding. I do hope he's alright."

"So do I" agreed Edie, her brows creased. "It's almost like we don't have a brother anymore, just an occasional correspondent."

Chatting at a Party

"It's your birthday tomorrow," Amy declared. "I'm making the cake. Twenty, eh! Where have the years all gone? By the way, Mr and Mrs Payne are coming here and bringing Millie, Betsy, Jean and Josie with them to surprise you. A joint party it's to be for you and Millie. I can't believe she'll soon be seventeen. Oh! I shouldn't have told you about the party. Sorry about that."

"Don't worry. I'll pretend to be surprised. Gee, I'm looking forward to seeing Millie after all this time."

At noon the following day, the guests from Balangara arrived for the celebrations.

"Together again," said Amy joyfully as she embraced Millie in a close hug, "and you're to be my bridesmaid with Edie and Betsy. But we'll talk about that later. First, how are things going for you at the homestead? Actually, you're looking quite well."

Millie related the news that the three Scottish girls were now being sent out for service at Mrs Warby's other two properties as Gracie had gone off with a fisherman, and Doris had taken a job at Uralla. Two hired women had been engaged at Balangara which had made life easier, but even so, Millie looked forward to leaving the station as soon as possible. Later on, Millie whispered to Amy that Josie was only fifteen but seemed happy to remain at Balangara as she'd become like a third daughter of the Payne's.

After the birthday celebrations, Dottie took Amy aside and mentioned to her confidentially that Simon, a young man from Armidale, who was a local carrier of goods, was paying a lot of attention to Millie. "He met her a few months ago at one of the barn dances in the woolshed, and he seeks her out every week when he delivers hay and groceries. Millie's not interested in him, so she tells me, but she gives him an awful lot of time, and they laugh a lot. Mind you, he's a nice young man and very persistent, I must say. Personally, I think he's after Millie."

"Really?" Amy queried. "She's not quite seventeen. Funny! I still think of her as my baby sister, but I must admit, since I saw her last, she's grown into a lovely looking girl. Really matured. But she's too young to get involved with someone, don't you think, Mrs Payne?"

"I agree Amy and I'm keeping a watch on things, don't worry."

Before those from Balangara prepared to return home, Amy called a meeting to discuss her wedding preparations.

"I'm buying my wedding dress and veil from Marcus Clarks, but I'll be sewing the bridesmaid's dresses myself in my spare time. They'll be simple styles, and I'm buying the material and patterns next week. I'll be in white, of course, and you three girls will be in a soft shade of blue, my favourite colour."

"You're a great little dressmaker, Amy. You'll do a very good job," affirmed Dottie Payne with a nod.

Amy timidly approached Arthur Payne.

"I'd like you to give me away on my wedding day, Mr Payne, if you don't mind taking the place of my father."

"Be honoured to Amy."

An Absent Guest

During the busy time leading to Christmas, Amy became increasingly concerned about Freddy. She also felt anguished that he would not be a guest at her wedding.

It's what our parents would have wanted, she thought, sadly. *Us all being together again and I would have preferred Freddy to give me away even though Mr Payne has been like a second father to me.*

She thanked the Lord that her sewing of the frocks did much to take her mind off her worries about her brother, but a nagging doubt lingered about his welfare. She confessed her anxiety to Edie.

"Well," Edie replied with a sigh, "it's all been up to him, hasn't it? Surely after all these years, he could have got over here, but like you, I hope we hear from him soon."

A Caution for Edie

Mrs Whitby had graciously accepted notice of Amy's resignation, as Daniel had insisted he could support her. But she'd been annoyed when Edie had approached her a week later and told her that she, too, would be leaving Lynnewood Station, and it would be on the day after the wedding.

"This is sudden, Edie. I can understand your sister leaving because of her marriage, but why are you leaving and where are you going?"

"Cecil is driving me down to Sydney, and I'm going to set myself up down there. I've got enough money saved up for a room and board for a while. I'll be looking for a job in a fashion boutique or somewhere else that's a bit different to what I've been doing. Not that I haven't appreciated working for you, Mrs Whitby," she stuttered. "You've been very kind and …"

"Are you going off with that young man with the red hair who took you out in his car before?" asked Mrs Whitby, interrupting bluntly, her eyebrows raised in surprise.

"It's not what you think. He's only giving me a lift," Edie explained, slightly embarrassed. Then she added quickly, "You know I told you before that he's a professional leader of a band and he plays the latest sort of music, like jazz, and he goes all over the place doing that and …"

Mrs Whitby interrupted again as Edie enthused over Cecil.

"Please be careful, Edie. You hardly know the man. What does Amy think of him?"

"She's okay now about it all. I had a long talk to her about him. He's really nice, and she's not worried anymore."

"Well, I'll have to reluctantly let you go, I can see that. I've already found a replacement in the kitchen for Amy, thank goodness, and now I'll have to advertise for a housemaid to replace you, which is a nuisance. Anyway, I'll give you a reference as you've worked well here. This should help you get some work in Sydney. It may not be easy, you know."

"I have the feeling it's going to be fine, Mrs Whitby," Edie assured her confidently.

"I do hope so, Edie. I really do."

"I'm sorry for the trouble," said Edie softly as she took her leave.

Christmas was not far off. In the kitchen, Shirley borrowed Mary's legendary pudding recipe from Amy and cooked up two, as Amy was frantically occupied during her spare time finishing the bridesmaids' dresses.

Christmas Day 1924

"Freddy's twenty-four today," Amy reminded Edie on Christmas Day.

"All I can say is, I hope he's having a nice birthday," Edie replied, somewhat distractedly as Millie entered the kitchen. She'd been picked up at Balangara and dropped off at Lynnewood by Simon in his delivery vehicle, as prearranged. He'd then continued on to Armidale to attend his family's celebrations and was to pick Millie up at 5 o'clock to drive her back to Balangara.

After Christmas dinner, served on the outside benches, Edie asked Millie to have a look at the supper cloth she'd almost finished embroidering as a gift for Amy's glory box. The two girls scurried away.

"This young Simon doesn't seem to mind going out of his way for Millie," Gwen observed – she always wanted to know the ins and outs of everything.

"He comes from a very old established family from Armidale," said Shirley, volunteering the information. "He's a nice boy, Amy. She could do worse."

"She's too young to get serious about anyone at her age, Shirley," Amy replied firmly.

"Next year she'll be eighteen, Amy. Lots of girls in the country get married at that age."

"I don't know whether she's keen on *him*. Anyway, I'd like to see her have more experience in life than get married at such a young age," Amy stressed.

"Time will tell," ventured Shirley in a measured voice.

At Last. A Letter From Freddy

It was mid-January in the new year when Mrs Whitby approached Amy with a letter. She'd noticed the postmark from New York, and knowing Amy's concern about her brother, immediately handed over the letter with a smile.

"Good news, I hope, from your brother. You've waited long enough for it."

"Well, I've only written to him twice this year myself, even though I often think about him. There's been so many other things going on."

Amy took leave from the kitchen, went outside and sat on a bench to read it. She was surprised to notice Freddy's new address, with a printed heading on each page.

'The American Seamen's Friend Society
Sailors' Home and Institute
507 West Street, New York

November 29th 1924

Dear Amy and Edie,

It is such a long time since I heard from you or wrote to you that I hardly know how to start, and now that I have started how to keep going. How are you? Well and Happy? I hope so. It is one year since I heard word from you. No doubt you have written but I have not had a letter from England for over nine months. I can't think what I have done or what has happened that Mrs Winsor doesn't write any more. I have written four times in the

591

past 9 months without any answer. It is true two of the letters were written from foreign ports and might have been lost but the two I wrote from Long Island New York would be almost certain to reach England. The foreign ports were Colon, Panama & Bermuda. I'll write once more at Christmas and if I get no reply I'll not waste any more ink and paper. You always write so regular that Mrs Winsor must have at least three letters that you have sent for me. In Oct. last I had visions of Christmas in Aussie but that's faded. I had 300 dollars or roughly 70 pounds in English money. For two weeks I tried to get a ship to Aussie or England but shipping is terribly slack. I was unlucky. I am staying at above address until I get work or a ship. I can make either in a week or so. Pity there are not more ships on the Australian run. Dear Sisters Christmas is upon us once more. I shall be 24 Christmas day. Just think 24 years. 10 years of that 24 wasted, no trade, no prospects, just bumming around from place to place. The British Consul in Buenos Aires told me, the time I lost my ship and went to him to send me back to America or England, and after 5 days on the beach there he grudgingly gave me a job on a tramp to New York. I was a nuisance to British Authorities in Foreign Ports. Things will brighten up sometime I hope. Anyway I'm not grumbling, things could be much worse. Well Dear Sisters. Have you heard from Millie lately. How is the poor kid. I'd love to see her, I'd love to see all of you. I want to have a letter from you but I can't give you any address. When you write I may be in San Francisco or China for that matter but it's different with Mrs Winsor, she is only 6 days journey away and I always give her an address that will find me for during 2 weeks or the people will forward to me. Don't answer

*this until you hear from me again, because if Mrs Winsor
doesn't answer my next letter I'll write you and give you
an address of a friend in Brooklyn who will keep them
for me indefinitely.*

*Dear Amy and Edie, I wish you a very Merry
Christmas & a bright & Prosperous New Year. Kiss each
other for me please and if you can possibly see Millie
wish her the same and kiss her too. I really tried hard to
get out to you in October but it's a h--l of a world if luck
is against you and it certainly was against me. Well My
Darlings I think I'll close now wishing you the season's
greetings and untold Good Fortune & Good health. The
Americans don't make Christmas pudding so when you
come to the last of it please remember your Loving
Brother*

Freddy   *XXXXXXXXXXXXXXXX share 'em out.*

Amy folded up the letter and took it to her room and placed it in
the biscuit tin. She sat down on her bed and felt a lump in her throat.

Dear God, what is going on with him? she thought. *I love my brother and
long to see him again. He seems so forlorn. Why all the lost letters and non-
deliveries? I don't know. It's a worry! I'll show his letter to Edie tonight. It's
addressed to her too.*

Edie's response to Freddy's letter was down to earth and practical.
"At least he's still alive, Amy. We were worried that something could
have happened to him, weren't we? I can't answer all those questions
you've put to me just now about him. Put his letter back in the tin for
now, and you can look at it again later when you and Dan get back
from your honeymoon. At least we know he loves us all and I'm sure
any problems can be sorted out in time. I can't believe it's just over a
week before the wedding and I've got to get ready for when Cecil picks
me up too."

Wedding Day

Amy was in a state of nervous tension and spent every spare minute working on the bridesmaid's dresses right up to the evening before her wedding day. She rose early the next morning and rushed out to look at the weather.

"There's not a cloud in the sky, Edie," she reported, when she hurried back to the bedroom. "Now come on. Get out of bed and help me hem the sleeves and then the frocks will be finished. *Come on!* Do you want me to have a nervous breakdown? Two o'clock will be here before we know it. Shirley and Gwen are making us breakfast, God love 'em. Let's get dressed and get started for goodness sake."

Edie caught on to Amy's sense of panic and hopped out of bed. The two quickly dressed and walked around to the kitchen.

"Come on, Edie," Amy yelled, after their breakfast when Edie started talking to Shirley. "I've got to get those blasted sleeves hemmed if you don't mind. *Get a move on!!*"

Edie obliged and ended the conversation while raising her eyebrows. Then she obediently followed Amy, who was almost running back to their bedroom.

"Wedding day nerves, Gwennie," Shirley remarked knowingly. "I've seen it all before. She'll settle down once those dresses are finished. Everything becomes a huge drama on a day like this."

"I've never seen her like this before. She's usually so gentle and in control," added Gwen.

In their bedroom, Amy and Edie sat on their beds, quickly whipping up the hems of the sleeves with needle and thread. After half an hour, the work was finished. Amy hung up the dresses on hangers, sat down on her bed and fought back tears.

"What's the matter, Amy?" Edie asked, sitting down near her and putting her arm around her shoulders.

"I don't know, Edie. It's all been a bit much. Getting everything ready in time, and then that letter from Freddy that's worried me … and Oh! I just wish Mummy and Daddy could see us all today, don't you?"

"Maybe they can, Amy," Edie replied, looking directly at her. "I have the feeling they *are* watching, and they're feeling very proud of you."

"Thanks, Edie, and thanks for being such a beautiful sister to me," Amy replied as she dried her tears with a hankie. "And I know that even though you're going to Sydney, we'll always be close. You can come up here to Guyra whenever you want to, and the door will be open. Always."

"I know that, Amy. Now go and run your bath and have a sleep before Millie gets here with the Payne's and Betsy, Jean and Josie. I'll have my bath after you. And stop worrying! The bouquets will be at the church, and the boys have picked up their dinner suits, the minister and the organist and singer will be there. Everything's going to schedule. And those ladies from the church are arranging the wedding breakfast already. It's all going well. Now get off into the bathroom."

Edie had suddenly become the older sister and taken charge, enjoying the change of roles as she watched her sister obey her.

In two hours, Dottie and Arthur Payne arrived with their charges. A short time later, Simon in his carrier, turned up dressed in a suit; he asked apologetically if he could attend the ceremony, even though he had not been invited to the wedding. "Just the ceremony," he emphasised. "I want to see what Millie looks like, all dressed up."

"Of course, you can come, Simon, and I'm sure we can fit you in the hall too for the reception," Amy offered, glad now that she'd met Simon.

Everyone settled down to have a cup of tea and a sandwich before the girls got into their finery. Then they all assembled outside in the driveway, including Joe and Andrea Whitby, and Shirley and Gwen who'd been transformed by wearing their best outfits.

Arthur Payne squashed the bride and bridesmaids into his car and cranked up the motor.

"She looks gorgeous, Shirl," Gwen enthused, watching Amy step into the car. "And to think she made all the girls' dresses herself."

"I love that little curvette she's got on her head with the white artificial flowers and the tulle veil falling down behind it," added Shirley.

"And the hats the girls are wearing from Marcus Clarks! Those wide brims with the ribbons and flowers. What a pretty wedding party," Gwen gushed nostalgically, remembering her own wedding all those years ago. Pity her husband had left her.

Everybody climbed into the assembled cars and followed behind the Payne's vehicle. In twenty minutes or so the wedding party arrived at the Union Church, and the thirty-five guests took their place. Arthur Payne and the bride waited in the back of the church for the Bridal March to start up. Amy smiled nervously as she was slowly led down the aisle, followed by her bridesmaids. Daniel looked lovingly behind him as Amy approached. In no time it seemed, the Presbyterian wedding rites were over, and Mr and Mrs Daniel Mitcham retired to an antechamber to sign the registry. During this time, a young tenor from the church choir sang the old favourite wedding song, *Oh! Perfect Love*, a combination of a prayer and blessing for the couple.

"She looks radiant," murmured Dottie, seated next to Shirley, as two slow tears ran down her cheeks. Amy and Dan, arm in arm and smiling, walked slowly out of the church.

Photos were taken outside, with more to be taken in the hall. The women from the Auxiliary had prepared an appetising wedding breakfast with varied savoury appetisers, followed later by roast chicken and vegetables, and a dessert of trifle made with sherry. Then the speeches. One, slightly risqué from Peter, the best man. Then, from Daniel's father welcoming Amy into the family, and lastly from Daniel, who pledged eternal love for Amy. Glasses were raised to toast the newly married couple and the bridesmaids, and then the cutting of the wedding cake took place. After the bridal waltz, Amy retired to a small room and changed into her 'going away' outfit. Everyone crowded around with kisses and good luck wishes.

"Oh! Lord! that's a nice rigout," Gwen slurred too loudly on noticing Amy's colourful summer ensemble – the slur the result of too much celebratory wine, which she wasn't used to.

"Just one glass would have been enough, Gwen. Sit down over there until you feel better," Shirley remarked, embarrassed.

The wedding bouquet was fetched, and Amy threw it toward the assembled guests.

"Oh!" said Shirley to Dottie, standing near her. "Young Millie's caught it. That means she'll be the next girl to get married."

"An old wives' tale. Edie will beat her to it, Shirley. She's almost three years older," answered Dottie knowingly.

Daniel's motorbike was parked outside the church. He helped Amy into the sidecar and strapped their suitcases onto a rack behind the pillion seat. He revved up the motor, and with a big sweeping farewell wave to the gathered guests and a smaller one from Amy who was laughing, the newlyweds were on their way to Sawtell for a week's stay in a guesthouse.

Feeling Lost

Edie stood a little way off, a lump in her throat as she watched them move away. A sudden feeling of apprehension engulfed her. *My, God, I'm going to miss her*, she thought, *and am I really doing the right thing by going down to Sydney, so far away? I hope I won't be lonely, but it's too late now. Cecil will be here tomorrow. No! I'm going. And if it doesn't work out, then I can always come back up here somewhere, and be close to Amy again.*

With this resolve, she squared her shoulders and moved over to seek out Millie, who was shedding a tear.

"When will I ever see her again, Edie?" she asked, crying. "And you going down to Sydney tomorrow too. It's been bad enough being the only one of us left at Balangara. I wish I was older; I just wish I was older, then I could leave too."

"Actually, Millie, you can leave the place whenever you want now. Do what Amy and I did and start looking for a position elsewhere, close to where Amy will be living. You're over seventeen, old enough! You're old enough," Edie repeated firmly, but encouragingly.

The wedding guests said their goodbyes and climbed back into their cars to return home. When Simon firmly offered to take Millie in his vehicle and drop her off at Balangara, the Paynes agreed; it would ease the congestion in their car, what with Betsy, Jean and Josie already in the back seat.

"I'm going with Simon," Millie declared to Edie as she dried her eyes with a hankie. She gave her sister a kiss on the cheek and urged her to write and let her know how it was in Sydney. Then she climbed into the front seat of the small delivery lorry.

"She'll be safe with me. I'll look after her," Simon assured confidently as he cranked up the motor. Then he walked to the driver's door, opened it and climbed into the vehicle.

Edie's last image of Millie was of her smiling face and a blown kiss as the lorry slowly moved away. All of the guests had left except Joe and Andrea Whitby and their passengers Edie, Shirley and Gwen.

"Come on, love," said Shirley softly as she put a comforting arm around Edie. "You're feeling a bit down, eh? That's understandable. You know, I have a funny feeling that you and Amy will be living very close to one another one of these days. Can't explain it, but it's there. Anyhow, back to Lynnewood Station and out of all that finery. That young man that plays the band's picking you up tomorrow. Have you packed yet?"

"Yes, I have," Edie said listlessly. Then she brightened a little. "I'm not leaving this dress here for Amy and Dan to pick up and keep safe for me. I'm taking it with me. It'll be good to go dancing in."

"I'm sure you'll be having a lovely time down there in the big smoke. Now, here's the Whitbys with the car. You can sit between Gwen and me in the back."

"It was a beautiful wedding, Edie," said Andrea when they arrived back. "He's a lovely man your sister has married, and I'm sure they'll be very happy."

"I think they will," agreed Edie, suddenly feeling a surge of joy over Amy's happiness.

Off to Sydney

The next morning Edie killed time talking to The Whitbys and Shirley and Gwen until Cecil arrived at nine-thirty with a loud toot from his car horn. Wearing a newsboy's cap and plus fours, he looked quite dapper as he placed Edie's luggage in the boot. He then opened the passenger door and helped Edie into the front seat. Excitement took hold of her as she settled in for 'the long haul', as Cecil had described the trip to Sydney and the boarding house in Parramatta where she'd booked a room a fortnight earlier. Cecil had booked into a hotel where the band had recently played. She said her goodbyes to 'Andrea' and 'Joe' as she'd been asked to address them from now on.

"Call in and see us if you're up this way again, Edie," Andrea had invited. And Edie promised she would.

She'd already farewelled Shirley and Gwen with hugs and promises to get in touch again. The two women stood close together under the peppercorn tree near the driveway, watching as the car gradually pulled away.

"I wonder if she'll ever marry him?" Gwen mused.

"Who knows?" answered Shirley.

They both raised their hands in a large wave in response to a slender waving arm reaching out from the car and the smiling profile of a rather beautiful young woman.

Then the driver and his passenger slowly moved out of sight.

Afterword:

Many of the events in this account are factual, as are the dates of births, deaths, marriages and occupations of people in London and Australia; also, the locations where people lived. My grandfather, whom I've called Fred, was indeed an ironmonger's assistant; my grandmother, whom I've called Anna, had worked in Bristol for a boot manufacturer, as a housemaid and Nanny before she returned to London.

The contents of letters sent to the girls in Australia are real, all verbatim.

While writing this story, I chanced upon a book entitled *When Family Failed* written by Nigel Middleton in 1971. What the author has recorded has been carefully researched, and faithfully reflects the Poor Laws of the day.

I quote from Mr Middleton's book from page 59. *The most usual cause of family breakdown was the early death of the main wage earner, a third of all men dying before the age of forty-five. Such deaths were a crippling blow, not only depriving a family of its main support, but frequently following a lingering illness such as tuberculosis.*

How would this have left Anna? ? Quoting again from Middleton's book, page 52: *It was the declared policy of the Poor Law not to give help to widows, it being found that many could manage somehow with parent's help, working children, charring, letting a room, etc.'* Oral history has it that she fled London and went to 'the provinces' where rent was cheaper. It is probable that she travelled to Northampton to stay with her Uncle John. Whatever happened during her time away has remained a mystery until she returned to London to die from the same illness as her husband.

Balangara is a fictional cattle and sheep station based in the New England District in New South Wales. Many accounts of the orphan girls who lived in a similar station are real. The lady who arranged the migration of my mother and aunts from London to her property in New South Wales undoubtedly intended the best for the girls.

Mrs Wilcox's burning of Anna's letter to her daughters actually happened and was remembered. The bed-wetting episodes of Josie and the draping of soiled sheets around her shoulders were told to me by my mother (Edie). Sexual abuse on the station occurred and was told to me when I interviewed one of the orphans, by then a very elderly woman. As consequences of those offences, their first 'house parents' were dismissed as well as the sexual abuser. It was also mentioned that the girls were obliged to call 'Mrs Warby', Ma'am, and were not allowed to mingle with her grandchildren. A slur about all of the orphan girls, should they have not migrated to Australia, was once published in a booklet, along with their photos. This caused the 'Nash' girls great distress.

Amy and Edie both won prizes at the Armidale show, a sheep and a motorcycle, which were donated to the Red Cross. Edie did indeed, have a red-haired boyfriend named Cecil, who was a roving band leader.

In spite of any negativity the girls encountered in their earlier days in Australia, they ended up expressing gratitude (with a few reservations), for a more promising future they'd been afforded by Mrs Warby and her teacher daughter, Miss Wilma. Also remembered with warmth were the family who replaced the Wilcoxes, namely the Paynes who became lifelong friends.

Amy and Daniel were to settle in a neat little cottage in Guyra after their marriage. Four baby daughters were born at approximately two-year intervals. Daniel was to develop a heart condition as a result of rheumatic fever he'd suffered during The Great War. A decision was made to move to Wentworthville near Sydney, to be close to Edie and her family who were living there. Daniel was employed in light duties, and in addition, he joined the Militia. A comfortable War Service home was eventually built for the family. Amy supplemented Daniel's income with her dressmaking skills, and she had regular clients. Close family connections between Amy's and Edie's families developed and were cherished, Amy being remembered by her nieces, nephews and grandchildren for her rib crushing hugs. Daniel, who was the love of her life, passed away on 1st of December, 1976. Amy died not long afterwards on 4th of October, 1977.

When Edie moved down to Sydney, she hadn't found it as exciting as she'd thought it would be. After a while, the romance or association with Cecil fizzled out as 'she hardly ever saw him'. When her money became short, she found lodgings with an elderly woman and her husband, who lived in North Parramatta. How she'd been surviving until then is not known, but she told me once that she'd been living on bread rolls each day for a while, until 'Aunty Maud' took her in like a daughter. Edie eventually secured a job in a cotton spinning mill at Pendle Hill, not far away. She was able to afford the piano lessons she'd always wanted. In the mill, she operated a noisy winding machine close to the Despatch Department. She was to catch the eye of a shy young clerk, the eldest son of a family of eleven brothers and sisters, a lively and fun-loving bunch. Vincent had been struck by Edie's beauty and had plucked up the courage to take her home to meet his family. His sisters were to tell him later that they'd never seen a prettier girl.

Vincent and Edie became engaged on Christmas day 1930. They married on the 15th of August 1931 at St John's Church in Parramatta. The couple first settled at Westmead and later moved to Wentworthville into an old federation house. By this time, the depression had set in, but Vincent was lucky to have a well-paid and reliable job at the mill, having been promoted. A baby boy was born in 1932, a girl three years later, and another boy three years after that. Edie became a very good wife and mother and maintained a practical attitude to life, always expressing an ironic sense of humour. She died on 6th of November, 1963 at only fifty-nine years of age, taken by stomach cancer. She was greatly mourned. Vincent died on the 22nd of February, 1980.

It isn't known when Millie left Balangara, but legend has it from a granddaughter that she was relentlessly courted by Simon. They married in the Anglican Cathedral in Armidale on the 28th of August, 1926 when Millie was almost nineteen years old. The couple settled on the outskirts of Armidale and became vegetable farmers at first, later running a small dairy. A daughter was the firstborn, then a son four years later and another daughter nine years later. Amy and Edie kept in touch with Millie by letter writing and the occasional visit. The illness Millie had suffered in London when she was a small girl left its mark by weakening her heart. She died from complications on the 14th of August, 1953 when she was not quite forty-seven years old. She is buried in a local cemetery not far from the former family home. Her eldest granddaughter speaks with great affection about her grandparents, Millie and Simon.

The Nash sisters have many descendants in Australia, numbering over seventy by now.

Aunty Esther continued her letter writing and her Christian mentoring to the three Nash sisters well past their marriages, her last letter being dated November 6th 1940 and written to Edie. She mentioned that she was now seventy-four years old. Christmas gifts of books were sent to her protégé's children on many occasions over the years and to each of them, a Bible.

The Whitefields Central Mission church in Tottenham Court Road was bombed during the Second World War. What happened after this disaster in Aunty Esther's life is unknown, but she had enjoyed a well-earned holiday in Canada at some time according to oral history. Photos of her are treasured by some of the Nash girl's descendants.

Mrs Winsor, that compassionate and motherly soul who took in Freddy when he'd just turned eighteen, only a few days after his Auntie Mattie's death on the 29th of December, 1918, had kept a careful eye on Freddy. The last letter we have of hers was written to Amy and

Edie on the 25th of March, 1924. She'd become a rich source of information to the sisters about their brother and what was going on in his life. Her letters remain as a testimony of true Christianity in caring for the forlorn, as Freddy became after the death of key members of his family and the separation from his sisters.

There may have been further letters from Mrs Winsor to the Nash girls, but they are not in our possession. Mrs Winsor would have been remembered with gratitude from my mother and aunts for having helped out their brother in London.

I'm sure it would be the desire of most storytellers to end their tale on a happy note. For Amy, Edie and Millie this was the case, but for Freddy, it turned out differently. The question remained. Should I print Freddy's last letter to Amy or not? She and her sisters would have been deeply concerned by it and even more so later on, as time went by. But I came to reason that the reader has a right to know about the fate of Freddy seeing they have followed the events in his life from the moment of his birth in London.

This is his last letter to Amy, now Mrs Mitcham.

May 1st 1927   *265 West 2nd Street*

New York City, America

Dear Mrs Mitcham,

Congratulations are Year Old. Am glad you are Happily Married and proud to be able to say I have a niece. I never wrote because I could not make promises any longer and anyway I had nothing to write about. I am no shining light in the world and Amy, I'm a pretty poor specimen of Manhood. It comes. It goes. This year I really thought I would go home to England at least but I was sick and doctors here charge heavy. Tomorrow I am going to the Hospital to have my tonsils removed. Please forgive pencil because I am not steady with pen.

I can bear on pencil. Please send Via Mrs Winsor a photo of the happy family. Want to know somehow and that's the only way my Relations at least could say How do to my Brother in Law and little Adele. Say Amy You sure are a Dear Old Scout writing to me, getting no answer but still kept on writing in Hopes. Now you know that I can only get out there when the wind changes. The Lord knows when that will be. I'll write oftener from now on. See Millie is Married. Please send the address and Edie too if you know them. I'll have to write to them. So Daniel's going to build you a house. Great Power to his Elbow. I am nearly or getting on for 27 and haven't the ambition to build a fire let alone houses. Well Amy there is no more news now. Mrs Winsor is going to write to you and I guess she will tell you more about myself in that you'll understand when you get her letter. I hope to write to you in two weeks from now and write a cheery letter not Moth Bitten like this one. Well Dear Amy please do me two favours. Shake hands with Daniel for me and kiss little Adele. The Best of health, Strength and Prosperity follow you always.

This is the Sincere Wish of Your Loving Brother

Freddy.

There were never any further letters from Freddy to his sisters. And no letters from Mrs Winsor in the family's possession explaining his absence. Had my mother and aunts been informed of his fate? If not, over the years, they must have wondered whatever could have happened to him. In time they would have surmised he was no longer living. It is obvious that Freddy had been suffering from depression in his last letter and he'd mentioned he'd been sick in New York over the year and was facing a tonsillectomy. He may have left Mrs

Winsor's forwarding address with hospital staff for notification to relatives if anything were to go wrong. Did his last letter suggest he was expecting to die?

His sisters were to get on with their lives nurturing their own families, but Freddy was never forgotten. Amy, Edie and Millie were to one day face their own mortality with many unanswered questions, not only about their mother but also about their brother.

Amy's granddaughter Allyson, who has a talent for digging out obscure facts when researching family history, was to solve the mystery about Freddy. Around the year 2013, and after so many decades, Freddy's surviving nieces and great-nieces found the answer.

Allyson posted an enquiry on the internet about Freddy, and surprisingly, a reply came a few days later. Allyson received a death certificate from New York. Freddy died on the 12th of May, 1927 in the Bellevue Hospital, Borough of Manhattan. Included with this information was a list describing seven of his journeys and occupations as assistant cook, on the Star Line merchant ships. Also, his description, six feet in height, his weight, and colour eyes (blue).

To everyone's surprise, he had passed away from tuberculosis as had his parents. This happened eleven days after he'd written that last letter to Amy, on the 1st of May 1927. Had he known his death was imminent? Had he concealed his illness from his sisters, not wanting them to know that this wretched disease was to also take their brother's life as well as their parent's lives? Mrs Winsor had described Freddy in her letters as a very healthy and handsome young man while he was in England and under her care. Had he contracted T.B. during his service in The Merchant Navy?

Quoting again from *When Family Failed* by Nigel Middleton, the author refers to life in the Merchant Navy for some of the crew, *There were other hazards to life, chief among them being tuberculosis, which in the cramped crew quarters which the boys shared with the men was dangerously prevalent.* Had Freddy been unaware of his condition? Was the tonsillectomy operation a cover-up? We'll never know. All we know is that the events in the closing chapters of

Freddy's life were extremely sad.

Our dearest Freddy is buried in the Woodlawn Cemetery, New York, in an unmarked grave, very close to the YMCA building. May he rest in peace and be eventually reunited in a happier place with the family he loved.

David and Mary
aka Daniel and Amy

Winnie
aka Edie

Lily aka Millie

Frank aka Freddy

Aunty Esther

About the Author

Judith Frenda was born in Westmead just west of Parramatta, New South Wales.

Her early exposure to classical music and reading led to an interest in all the arts. In later life, she joined a creative writing course and specialised in stories and articles featuring humorous and historical content. Taking on family history revealed much of her mother's English background.

Freddy's Letters, comprising both fact and fiction, is her first novel, resulting from a batch of letters handed to her from a cousin. The letters were written from London to her mother and aunts, then girls in Australia, who'd migrated under the British Child Emigration Scheme. The letters provided many answers to questions about life in London for her English grandparents and their four children during the Edwardian and Georgian periods. Life in Australia for the girls continued as the second part of the story.

Judith firmly believes that nurturing family relationships is the basis for a healthy and strong nation.